LAST CHRISTMAS

CLARE SWATMAN

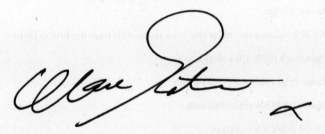

B
Boldwood

First published in Great Britain in 2024 by Boldwood Books Ltd.

Copyright © Clare Swatman, 2024

Cover Design by Leah Jacobs-Gordon

Cover Photography: Shutterstock

The moral right of Clare Swatman to be identified as the author of this work has been asserted in accordance with the Copyright, Designs and Patents Act 1988.

All rights reserved. No part of this book may be reproduced in any form or by any electronic or mechanical means, including information storage and retrieval systems, without written permission from the author, except for the use of brief quotations in a book review.

This book is a work of fiction and, except in the case of historical fact, any resemblance to actual persons, living or dead, is purely coincidental.

Every effort has been made to obtain the necessary permissions with reference to copyright material, both illustrative and quoted. We apologise for any omissions in this respect and will be pleased to make the appropriate acknowledgements in any future edition.

A CIP catalogue record for this book is available from the British Library.

Paperback ISBN 978-1-78513-072-4

Large Print ISBN 978-1-78513-070-0

Hardback ISBN 978-1-78513-068-7

Ebook ISBN 978-1-78513-071-7

Kindle ISBN 978-1-78513-069-4

Audio CD ISBN 978-1-78513-063-2

MP3 CD ISBN 978-1-78513-064-9

Digital audio download ISBN 978-1-78513-065-6

Boldwood Books Ltd
23 Bowerdean Street
London SW6 3TN
www.boldwoodbooks.com

For Leia and Violet, with love.

PROLOGUE

IN THE BEGINNING: 22 DECEMBER 2002

Bea was always early for everything. Even, it turned out, when she was running away from her life.

Right now, she was standing in the middle of a busy departure lounge at Heathrow Airport, her body being buffeted from side to side like a pebble caught in a stormy sea, staring blindly at the departure board in the hope that it might give her a sign: should she stay, or should she go?

She squinted, trying to make out the words. As they swam into focus, her heart lurched.

JFK: 16.15.

It was too early for any check-in information yet, so she gripped the handle of her suitcase until her knuckles turned white. Four hours was a long time to change her mind. But then again, she seemed to change it every four minutes at the moment so perhaps it made no difference that she was early. She breathed in deeply and tried to relax, but her shoulders remained stubbornly by her ears.

She should eat. Her stomach was in knots, but she headed towards Pret a Manger and picked up a sandwich at random, paid and took a seat at a grimy table. She tucked her suitcase under her legs, swiped away the crumbs with the back of her hand and rubbed pointlessly at a patch of grease with her napkin. A roar of voices bounced off the cavernous roof of the departure lounge, and she closed her eyes and tried to picture herself somewhere else entirely: on a beach, in the middle of the ocean; at Mia's house, drinking cider and putting the world to rights.

At the thought of her best friend, her stomach tightened again. Mia was one of the few people who knew where Bea was heading right now, and she had done everything in her power to convince her not to go.

'Not yet. Not like this,' Mia had begged, in one last-ditch attempt to change Bea's mind two nights ago.

'I have to,' Bea had insisted, even while her head was screaming at her to admit that Mia might just have a point.

'Come and spend Christmas here, with me and Deacon, and then decide,' she'd wheedled.

Bea had cast a glance at Mia's ridiculous fluffball of a cat who was curled on the best chair in the room licking his front paw with a look of disdain and shook her head. 'Tempting as it is, I have to do this.' She wasn't sure she believed the words even as they left her mouth.

Mia had fixed her with *that look* – the one she'd always given her ever since they were little girls and Mia had been trying to convince Bea to play the game she wanted to play – but Bea had looked away, refusing to give in the way she usually did.

'Fine,' Mia had said eventually. 'But this isn't you, Bea. This isn't what you do: run away from things. You're making a big mistake.'

Mia's words churned through Bea's mind now as she sat with her head turned deliberately away from the departures board, as though by not looking at it, the flight she was currently booked onto might magically disappear.

This isn't you, Bea.

Mia was right, of course. This wasn't the way Bea behaved. Bea was good. Reliable. Quiet.

A bit of a pushover? Some might say so, but Bea preferred to think of herself as flexible. Easy to please.

Something she most definitely *wasn't* was a spur-of-the-moment girl. The kind of girl who left her partner of five years to run off to New York three days before Christmas with absolutely no idea of what she was going to do when she got there.

She ripped the plastic from her sandwich and pulled a corner of it away, crumbs of grated cheese scattering across the table, then popped it in her mouth and chewed, the bread like a lump of clay in her dry mouth.

Until last year, when someone had decided to fly a plane into the Twin Towers, killing thousands of people and changing the world forever, New York had seemed like a fairy-tale to her. Growing up, she'd loved watching films set in New York – *When Harry Met Sally*, *Breakfast at Tiffany's*, *West Side Story* – and had devoured *Friends* and *Sex and the City* in her twenties, which meant this city that she'd never actually visited had always felt totally familiar to her. She'd long held what she thought of as an impossible dream that she might live there one day: renting a lofty Manhattan apartment, sipping a coffee as she wafted down Broadway on her way to work at a fancy magazine – a far cry from her drab job in the marketing department of a pharmaceutical company where the most exciting thing she was ever given to write was a press release on pile cream. At weekends she'd take the railroad out east to Long Island, ride the Ferris wheel at Coney Island, spend Saturday nights sipping Cosmopolitans at the Soho Grande, followed by lazy Sunday afternoons brunching in Katz's diner.

In every single one of these fantasies she'd imagined doing

these things with other people: a husband, a partner, girlfriends. She was never alone.

Yet now she was. Completely. Utterly.

She shook the thought away and glanced up at the departures board again, trying to ignore the lump in her throat.

Three and a half hours to go. Still no check-in desk.

From the depths of her bag she heard the tinny sound of her ringtone, and her whole body tensed as she dug it out. It was silent now, but the words on the screen glowed at her accusingly. One missed call: Dom.

She stared at it for a few moments, imagining what Dom might be doing right now – apart from ringing her, of course. Usually at this time on a Sunday morning he'd be kicking off his running trainers, stretching his hamstrings, then standing at the sink, downing a glass of water, rehydrating after a long run. After that he'd make buttery scrambled eggs with crispy bacon and fried bread which they'd eat together in front of the tiny coal fire in their living room. Bea couldn't see out of the window from where she was sitting, but she already knew how cold it was, having arrived at the airport just as it was starting to get light, the hazy peach sky peeling off its night-time coat to reveal a chink of light at the end of the runway. It had been absolutely Baltic then, the sort of cold that felt like it might rip the skin from the back of your throat and seep into your bones, but she knew, under normal circumstances, that Dom would still have gone for his run no matter what. The roads could be sheer ice, the pipes frozen solid, and Dom would simply add more clothes and off he'd go. She wondered whether he'd been today, and if he'd remembered to get the fire going before he'd gone out – that was usually her job. She pictured him on the sofa in their freezing living room, fingers of ice creeping through gaps in the ancient sash windows, the walls failing to cling onto any remnant of warmth whatsoever, and her stomach lurched.

How could she be doing this to him? He hadn't done anything to deserve this.

She jumped as her phone beeped loudly and the screen lit up with a ghostly green light. 'One new text message.'

Her thumb hovered over the green accept button. Should she read it?

Before she could over-think it, she clicked through to the message.

> I know you're probably not going to change your mind but I just want you to know you're being ridiculous. Also, get a flat sorted soon so I can come and stay. M x

She smiled. Not Dom after all, but Mia, making her smile even now. God, she loved the bones of that girl. It was as much of a wrench to leave her behind as it was Dom. And yet here she was, regardless.

Bea stood, threw the rest of her sandwich in the bin, and marched towards the British Airways check-in desks. A few people were hovering, looking lost. A lone woman in the blue, white and red of BA loitered behind a counter, trying not to catch anyone's eye. Bea swooped towards her before anyone else spotted her.

'Hi,' she said, trying out her friendliest smile.

'Good morning madam, how may I help you?'

'I—' Bea stopped, the words caught in her throat. Something about the kindness in this woman's eyes had undone her and she knew if she tried to say another word she might cry. She swallowed. 'Sorry, I... can you tell me which desk I need for the flight to New York please?' The words felt scratchy in her throat.

'It will be desks fourteen to eighteen,' she said, pointing over Bea's left shoulder. 'They should open in about' – she checked her watch – 'twenty minutes.'

'Great, thank you.'

Bea turned to walk away when the woman's voice stopped her in her tracks again. She swivelled round.

'Sorry?'

'I was just letting you know that the flight has been delayed.'

'Oh. How long?'

'About an hour I'm afraid. Sorry.'

Bea nodded, tears pricking her eyes. 'Okay, thanks.'

As Bea walked away she felt as if she'd been punctured, all the excitement and decisiveness of a moment ago seeping away, leaving her deflated. Was this the sign she'd been looking for? The sign telling her she shouldn't go?

'You do know the universe isn't going round giving out signs to Bea Preston every five minutes, don't you?' She could hear Mia's laughter now as she stood in the middle of the departure hall. Mia was always telling her she was daft for believing in fate and signs. But how were you supposed to know whether something was a good idea or not if you didn't listen to what the universe was trying to tell you? In Bea's opinion, if something kept going wrong, then *surely* it must be the universe telling you not to do it?

She shook the thought from her head. She was just looking for excuses now, for a get-out clause. She dragged her case across the tiled floor, one of the wheels squealing in protest, and followed the barriers marking the as-yet non-existent queue for check-in until she reached the front. Despite the early hour, there were already a couple of people in front of her: one a woman in her fifties or thereabouts, whip-thin, not a perfectly highlighted hair out of place, tapping away on her mobile phone; the other a younger man in dark jeans and a battered leather jacket, his short dark hair spiked on top. He turned and gave Bea a smile, then turned away again before she could smile back. She sighed, propped her carry-on bag on top of her suitcase, and pulled out a copy of *Red* magazine.

Even though she loved these magazines – devoured them every single month as if by reading about all these amazing places, beauty tricks and fashion tips, she could turn herself into the perfect woman – she knew it wasn't healthy. She didn't like to dwell too much on why she was so desperate to work for a publication like this – but at least for now, the features were helping to take her mind off everything else.

By the time the queue began to move, there was a line snaking behind Bea and she was glad she'd had the foresight to get near the front. The longer the wait to get rid of her suitcase, the more likely she was to change her mind. Once that was gone, she had to get on that plane no matter what. She hauled her case onto the scales and handed over her passport.

This was it.

* * *

Since 9/11, airport security had been a nightmare and it was another hour before Bea emerged through the other side into the duty-free shop, buckling her belt back up, putting her watch back on and re-attaching her necklace. Lighter now without her suitcase, she hitched her holdall onto her shoulder and meandered around the perfume section. The air was thick with a mixture of heady scents and Bea felt the beginnings of a sneeze. She picked up a bottle, sniffed it, put it back down. She spritzed herself with Clarins Eau Dynamisante, which always reminded her of Mia, who seemed to douse herself in the stuff daily, and took a deep breath in.

She trailed her fingers over the giant Toblerones, her mind wandering. Her mum loved these, especially the dark chocolate ones. It never ceased to amaze Bea how her mum stayed so slim when she could mainline chocolate like it was going out of fashion.

But that was what happened when you couldn't sit still, when your life revolved around looking after everyone else's needs before your own.

Her heart contracted now as she thought about her mum, about how confused and hurt she'd been when Bea had told her she was going to New York.

'But that's a long way to go for a couple of days, isn't it?' Ange had said.

'I'm not going for a couple of days, Mum. I'm going to stay.'

'*Stay?* What do you mean? For *Christmas?* But you're always here for Christmas.'

Bea had held her breath as she said the next words, ready for the onslaught of indignation when realisation dawned.

'Yes, for Christmas. And for a while after that.'

The silence that followed had been worse than any angry words Ange might have thrown at her. The only time her mum kept quiet was when she was so furious she couldn't form the words to express it.

So Bea had gabbled, had told her it wouldn't be forever, that she might not even like it, that she just needed to get some distance from everything, to try something new, to work out what she wanted to do with the rest of her life.

The one thing she didn't tell her was the truth, but she didn't *ever* plan to do that.

'Oh Bea,' her mum had said eventually. 'You've always had your head in the clouds, but life isn't a fairy-tale you know, no matter how much you want it to be.'

Bea knew that only too well, but didn't say so. Instead she just whispered, 'I'm sorry,' and hung up before her mum could ask her anything else.

But her mum was right, wasn't she? Life wasn't a fairy-tale. You only had to look at her to see that. This time last week Bea had been holding down a steady job – okay, she wasn't exactly respected, and a promotion seemed to be getting further out of reach rather than closer, but she could be patient – as well as a lovely flat and a kind, loving partner.

But now? Now she was running away from something that she could barely even admit to herself in some sort of hair-brained scheme to – what? Start again? Reinvent herself? *Find* herself? She felt embarrassed even thinking those words. The truth was, she was terrified she was about to make the biggest mistake of her life.

* * *

Less than an hour to go and already a final call had gone out for all passengers on BA flight 0468 to please make their way to gate number sixty-three. Bea's heart was hammering so fast she felt as though she might pass out. Her hands shook so much she could barely keep hold of the passport and boarding pass she was clinging on to for dear life. Her knuckles were white, her face ashen.

This isn't you, Bea.

Mia's words were imprinted on her brain. But Mia was wrong. Bea *could* do this. She *was* doing it.

She stood, brushed imaginary crumbs from her jeans, hooked her jacket over her arm and picked up her cabin holdall. It weighed a tonne and her shoulder ached. She peered inside. Phone, book, notebook, bottle of water, packet of mint humbugs, alongside details of how to get to the hotel she'd booked. Finding accommodation in New York a few days before Christmas was harder than she'd imagined and this had been the best of what was left: a single bed in a three-star hotel in Hell's Kitchen. 'A short walk from the iconic Times Square,' the advert said. It would be fine. It was only for a couple of weeks. She was trying not to think too much about what she was going to do after that. Her savings wouldn't last for long if she didn't find somewhere more permanent pretty quickly.

She swallowed, then glanced at the departure board one last time. Her flight was flashing amber now, 'Last call for all passengers to JFK' scrolling across the screen like tickertape. Her stomached tightened.

It was time.

She took a few steps away from the bank of chairs and began to stride in the direction of the gate, keeping her pace steady, her breathing regular. She didn't want to be the last person to board, everyone staring at her as she bumbled down the aisle.

She stepped onto the travelator, then off the other end. The gate was closer now, she could see it in the distance, above the heads of all the other passengers off to celebrate the festive season with loved ones. Was she the only person travelling to spend Christmas Day alone? Her mouth felt dry and she tried to lick her lips.

And that was when it happened.

BAM!

It felt as though a fissure had ripped through the ground beneath her feet, and she crashed onto the tiled floor. At first, the pain in her left thigh was all she could think about. Then her left wrist began to throb. She lifted her head, her vision blurred. Where was her bag? She twisted round, saw it skittering across the floor, its contents spilling as it went.

'Oh my God, I am *so* sorry.' Bea twisted her head towards the source of the voice. A figure hovered beside her, silhouetted against the glass ceiling. The person was holding out a hand. 'I'm so sorry, I wasn't looking where I was going. I'm such a moron.'

Bea still didn't reply but took the hand. It felt warm as it gently tugged her to her feet. The ground tipped for a moment, and a hand rested on her elbow. Finally, she looked at the person who had sent her flying. The first thing she noticed was his deep blue eyes watching her, a deep groove between his eyebrows.

'Did you hit your head?'

She lifted her hand up to her head and patted it. She shook her head. The man's hand was still on her elbow and he steered her slowly towards a nearby bank of chairs where someone scooched up to let her sit.

'My bag,' she managed to croak, and pointed towards where it lay in the middle of the concourse, its contents spread out like a mini obstacle course.

'Wait there,' he said. She watched as he gathered her belongings and scooped them up. She hoped her brand-new MP3 player wasn't broken.

'Here, I think that's everything,' the man said, returning and handing her bag over.

'Thanks.'

He crouched down beside her again and she looked at him, surprised.

'Are you sure you're okay?' His voice was laced with real concern and she nodded again. 'I'm fine.'

'Do you mind if... it's just I'm...' He gestured helplessly towards the mass of people crushing forwards. 'I'm really late.'

'Oh right. Yes. Don't miss your flight. Go.' She waved her hand in the direction of the gates.

'Are you sure?'

'Yes!' She just wanted him to leave now, couldn't stand the fussing, so when he finally stood and hitched his rucksack onto his shoulder, she felt relieved.

'Well, okay. I—' He glanced towards the gate again. 'Look, have a safe flight. And sorry. Again.' He hovered a moment longer, then he was gone, and she watched his ancient leather jacket and dark head until he melted away into the crowd.

She sat for a moment longer. She still felt a little dazed and let her vision blur as she watched people hurrying for planes, holding hands, buying coffee, reading books. This wasn't a sign not to go. It absolutely wasn't. It was only some clumsy man not looking where he was going. She needed to stop looking for signs and get on that bloody plane. She just needed a moment of calm before—

Her phone was ringing. Or maybe it was someone else's. She strained to hear it properly. Nope, it was definitely hers, she could feel the vibrations through her thighs from the bag on her lap.

She should ignore it. Her plane was boarding right now. It was due to leave in twenty minutes. She was going to miss it. But still something kept her there, glued to the seat. What if it was important? It could be Mum, ringing to tell her Dad had finally got a date for his knee replacement. Or her sister, Alice, telling her that her niece Lara had fallen from a horse and broken her arm. What if it was Mia? She'd give anything to hear her voice right now, telling one of her ridiculous jokes, or even telling her how stupid she was being again.

Except it could be Dom, of course. And she knew that, if she heard his voice begging her to come home, she might not be strong enough to put up a fight.

The phone stopped ringing. That was that then.

She stood and began to move towards the gate again. She had to hurry. She was almost there now and the crowd had thinned ahead of her. She was the last one. She picked up her pace, striding as fast as she could.

Her bloody phone was ringing again. She slowed, then came to a stop.

She should definitely ignore it. But what if it was an emergency? She should at least check before she got on the plane and switched her phone off for eight hours, right?

Cross with herself for being weak, she dug her hand in her bag and rooted around for her phone and pulled out her tiny Nokia.

Fuck. It *was* Dom.

She couldn't ignore him again. She pressed the green answer button and held the phone to her ear.

'Hi Dom.'

'Oh thank God.' She flinched at the relief in his voice. 'You're still here? In London?'

'I am, I—'

'Does this mean you've changed your mind? That you're coming home?' His voice sounded reedy, full of hope.

She didn't reply straight away and the silence stretched and warped.

'Bea? Are you still there?'

'I'm still here, Dom.'

'In Heathrow?'

'In Heathrow.'

'So does—'

'It doesn't mean anything.'

They spoke at the same time and both stopped. Bea spoke next.

'The plane is just delayed,' she said, as gently as she could.

'So you haven't—' He stopped. 'You haven't changed your mind then?' His voice sounded small, hurt, and she felt herself soften a little. She should throw him a rope here. Anything to stop him sounding so utterly bereft. Before she could say anything else, Dom spoke again.

'Please come home. I'll change. Things will change. I'll do whatever you want.'

His words sliced through her heart, cleaving it in two.

But she had to stay strong. Because this wasn't about Dom. It was about her, and trying to work out why she was so desperately unhappy. And although she had no intention of telling Dom what had made her finally snap – she couldn't, she never would – she did know that, at some point – next week, next month, next year – she would probably have broken Dom's heart anyway. Because she wanted more. She wanted the fairy-tale, or at least a chance of it.

But now here he was, pleading with her to change her mind, to stay. And after five years together, didn't he deserve better than this?

The truth was, if she got on that plane, she'd break Dom's heart.

But if she stayed, she'd break her own.

Everything rested on her next words...

Should she go... or should she stay?

1

GO

December 2002

Bea bundled up the aisle, her armpits damp, her face flushed. She steadfastly refused to meet the eyes of the other passengers as the air steward, with his bleach-blond hair and clean-shaven jawbone, showed her to her seat towards the back of the plane. He was trying to be polite but it was clear she was persona non-grata given that she'd almost held up an entire 747 full of passengers by being so disgustingly, inexplicably late.

'I'm so sorry, I had to take an important call,' she'd offered inadequately, as she'd almost skidded to a halt at the boarding gate just as the British Airways staff were pulling the barrier across.

'We've closed the gate madam,' the woman had said, smiling politely.

'I know, I'm so sorry,' Bea said. 'Please, you have to let me on the plane.'

They'd stood for a split-second, a mini stand-off, before the air stewardess had let out a long puff of air and opened the barrier and ushered her through.

Bea had handed over her passport gratefully, and now here she was, facing the wrath of several hundred people as they waited for her to sit down so they could finally take off. She was almost tempted to get off and book a seat on another flight just so she didn't have to face everyone for the next eight hours. Almost.

'Here you are madam,' the air steward said, gripping her elbow and pointing at the only empty seat in the whole plane.

'Thank you,' she said. To her absolute horror, her seat was in the middle of a row of three, which meant the person seated in the aisle had to stand up to let her in. And he certainly made a good show of it, huffing and puffing and heaving himself around while Bea slipped in beside him, mortified.

Finally, she was settled. There was no going back now. As the man beside her sat, pulling his table down and re-clipping his seat-belt noisily, she dug her iPod out of her bag, shoved her bag under her seat – there was no way she was asking aisle man to stand again so she could put it in the overhead luggage compartment – and kept her gaze firmly on the back of the seat in front of her. This was going to be a long flight.

She could feel her breath slowing and she tipped her head back, closed her eyes and sucked in some long, slow lungfuls of air. Thank God. Now was not the time for a panic attack. She let her shoulders relax and—

'Well, this is awkward.' A deep voice made her eyes snap open and she whipped her head round to see where it was coming from. It took her a moment to focus on the face of the man in the window seat who was studying her with a lopsided grin. But then she felt her face redden in recognition.

'Oh. It's you.'

'It is,' said the man who'd sent her sprawling across the busy airport concourse just a short while ago. Her heart sank. She turned away from him and started to untangle her headphones, hoping he'd get the message and leave her alone.

'Listen, I really am sorry about before, I was running really late.' He gave a sheepish grin. 'Although it looks as though there wasn't any need for me to be in such a hurry, given I was nowhere near the last person on the plane.' His voice was rich and deep with a broad Irish twang.

She rolled her eyes. 'Very funny.'

'Ah come on, I was just kidding, so. How's the wrist?'

She *really* didn't want to engage in conversation with anyone, she had too much on her mind. But it was also deeply ingrained in her not to be rude. She rotated her wrist a few times and winced. 'I think I'll live.'

'Well that's a relief. Any other injuries?'

'Only my ego.'

'Ah you're fine. It's me that should be embarrassed, barrelling around like a feckin' eejit not looking where I was going.'

'That's true.'

He was silent for a moment and she hoped he'd got the message that she didn't want to talk. But then: 'Shall we try that again then?'

She stared at his hand which he held between them, tempted to leave him hanging. Because this was her problem, wasn't it, that she always worried what other people thought: worried that if she said no to someone, they wouldn't like her? And even though it didn't make any difference to her life whether or not this man thought well of her, old habits die hard, so she reluctantly took his hand and gave it a brief shake. 'Sure. I'm Bea.'

'Like the insect?'

She frowned. 'Like the princess.' He looked puzzled and she rolled her eyes. 'It's what I always got called at school. You know, after Princess Beatrice was born?' When he still looked none the wiser, she added: 'The Royal Family?'

'Oh,' he said eventually, clearly disinterested. 'I can't be arsed with that entitled lot.' His face broke into a grin again; a grin, Bea couldn't help noticing, that lit up his whole face. 'Anyway Bea, it's very nice to meet you properly, when you're not sprawled across the floor.'

She was about to reply something about that being entirely his fault when the plane began to move backwards, and the safety announcement crackled into life. Bea turned to face the front, watching blankly as the familiar words about airbags and emergency exits and inflatable life jackets washed over her.

Then they were taxiing along the runway, and speeding up, her head pressed back into the headrest, her hands gripping the armrests until her knuckles turned white, and she was doing this, she was really doing this. She was leaving behind everything she knew, everyone she loved, and she was flying to New York by herself. For a fresh start, right?

Oh God, what was she doing?

Her heart thumped loudly and her mouth was dry. She thought she might faint and she took deep breaths in through her mouth and out through her nose. To one side of her, aisle man was already sound asleep and she envied him, being able to relax like that. She'd never loved flying, but as she'd got older she'd begun to dread it – take-off at least. It was as though she finally realised how delicate the line was between life and death.

Heart in her throat, she strained to listen to the sounds the engine was making – as if she would recognise a problem if there were one – and studied the reactions of the cabin crew carefully. If seasoned flyers were worried, she would be too, otherwise she could usually talk herself down from her panic. They seemed perfectly relaxed and she tried to do the same.

Finally, as the plane levelled out and the seatbelt signs went off, Bea felt her breath begin to even out, her heartrate begin to slow. They were cruising now; maybe she could sleep for a bit, give her brain a rest after the last few days.

'So, how come you're off to New York all on your lonesome?' Her heart sank as she turned to face her companion in the window seat.

'It's a long story,' she said, hoping he'd leave it at that.

No such luck.

'We've got eight hours.'

She shook her head and turned away.

'Come on now, throw me a scrap here. It's bloody boring flying; we might as well pass the time.'

'I thought I might watch a film,' she said, plucking the in-flight magazine from the back of the seat in front of her.

'Ah sure, but you can do that later. Come on, humour me. Please?'

She sighed and twisted round to face him as much as the cramped space would allow – which wasn't a lot, as she discovered when her leg brushed against his. She pulled it away.

'You haven't even told me your name,' she said.

He grinned. 'Nope.'

She frowned. 'What do you mean, nope?'

'I mean nope, you're right, I haven't told you my name. And I'm not going to either.'

'But I've told you mine!'

'I know. Still not telling you though. Not yet, at least.'

'But...' She didn't really know what to say to that. She squinted at him, trying to read his face. 'Why, are you some sort of spy?'

'Yep. A top-secret spy, which means that if I told you my name, I'd have to kill you.'

She rolled her eyes again.

'Come on, tell me. Unless you're on the run or something? Wanted by Interpol.' She didn't even really care what his name was to be honest, but now she was determined to make him spill the beans, intrigued as to what the big mystery might be.

But he still shook his head. 'Can't.'

'Why not?'

'Because it's rubbish and you'll judge me.'

'I would never do that!' She felt indignation rising in her chest.

But he just laughed. 'Believe me, you would. I'd judge me if I met me. People always do. And it always feels unfair to have people deciding I'm a prick when they've only just met me because of something my parents did to me.' He smirked. 'I'm quite capable of making them think that by myself.'

'It can't be *that* bad.'

'Believe me, I've had enough women ghost me after a first date to know it is.'

'That might just be your terrible personality.'

He let out a bark of laughter. 'Oof, touché.'

They both paused. Then, even though Bea really wanted to stop talking to this man and lose herself in her own thoughts about what a mess she'd made of everything, she couldn't help herself.

'Can I guess?'

He shrugged. 'If you like. But I'm confident you'll never get it.'

'I might.'

'Go on then.'

'Trevor.'

'Nope. Trevor's a perfectly nice name.'

'Boris?'

'Nope.'

'Elvis?'

'No! That would be cool.'

She frowned. 'Ebenezer.'

He shook his head, grinning. 'Told you you'd never get it.'

She scratched her head, then her eyes widened as something occurred to her. 'Oh my God, it's not something awful like Adolf is it?'

'No! Now that *would* be worse.'

'Okay, so come on then. If it's not as bad as Adolf it can't be *that* terrible.'

He shook his head. 'Nope, you're not getting me that easily.'

'Fine. Don't then.' She turned away and folded her arms across her chest. This conversation was clearly finished, which meant she could finally wallow in peace.

And to her amazement, mystery man seemed to get the message. Relieved to have some quiet at last, Bea stuck her headphones over her ears, closed her eyes, and let her mind wander to the sound of Kula Shaker's 'Hush'.

She must have drifted off because the next thing she knew someone was tugging at her sleeve and she snapped her eyes open to find a plate of cheese and biscuits hovering in front of her face.

'Oh, thanks,' she mumbled, taking it from the smiling cabin crew, along with a cup of tea.

She pulled her table down and balanced the plate and drink on it, then checked her watch. She'd been asleep for almost an hour, which felt like a miracle after the last few nights of snatched hours here and there. Somehow though it had made her feel worse, and a band of pressure now stretched across her neck and head. She rubbed at it.

'Headache?' Mystery man was watching her with concern. His face was sleep-crumpled and he had a small bottle of red wine on his pull-down table.

'A bit, yeah.'

'It wasn't me, was it?'

She frowned. What was he on about now? She rubbed her eyes. 'Was what you?'

'Your head.' He gestured vaguely in the direction of where she was rubbing. 'When you fell.'

'Oh, no.' She shook her head and winced. 'No, don't worry about that. I'm just exhausted. It's been a bit of a shit week.' That was the understatement of the decade.

'Oh. Good. Well, not good but... you know what I mean.'

She nodded and unwrapped her packet of crackers.

'You can talk about it if you like.'

She sighed and turned to face him again. 'Talk about what?'

'Your shit week. The state of British politics. Planes. My disastrous fashion sense.' He shrugged. 'Anything you like.'

Wow, this guy really wanted to talk. And now she thought about it, perhaps having a meaningless chat with a stranger might actually be a good thing, especially if the alternative involved her wallowing in her misery alone.

'Are you sure you want to hear it?'

'I'm all ears.' He took a swig of his wine.

She turned to look at him, properly this time. She hadn't noticed before how handsome he was. Not in the traditional sense – he was no Brad Pitt – but in a quirky, slightly scruffy way. His dark hair was tousled and spiked – deliberately or not she had no idea – and his arms, exposed now he'd taken his jacket off, were covered in tattoos, dark and swirling. She found herself staring at them for longer than was strictly polite.

'Nice tattoos,' she said.

'Thanks. Me mam hates them, but most of them have got a meaning.' He glanced at her, gave a quick grin. 'Don't worry, I'll wait until we run out of interesting conversation before I bore you with that.'

'Thanks.' She smiled back.

Mystery man – it felt weird that she was about to start telling him all her problems when she didn't even know his name – twisted in his seat so that they were half-facing each other, and folded his arms over his chest. 'So, what brings you to New York all alone two days before Christmas?'

'It's three days.'

'Fine. But it will be almost two by the time we get there and anyway, that's just semantics. What gives?'

She looked at her hands, wondering how much she should confide in this complete stranger. Perhaps it would be good for her to get it out there, hear the words. Perhaps it would jolt her out of herself, make her realise how ridiculous she was being. Perhaps.

'I'm running away.' Best to keep it simple after all.

He gave a slow nod. 'Right. What from?'

She let out a long sigh. 'Life. Stuff. Arseholes.'

He studied her. 'Now I'm intrigued by the plural of arseholes. More than one of them is bad luck.'

'Yeah. Except, well, actually, my boyfriend wasn't – *isn't* – an arsehole. Not at all really. He's... he's pretty decent actually.' She felt a tear leak from the corner of her eye and track down her cheek. She brushed it away.

'I see. So it's not an evil ex then, as I'd suspected.'

'No. It's not.' She felt more tears building and she swallowed and took a sip of tea until she felt them subside. 'Sorry. I just – it's been a tricky week.'

'It's fine. You don't have to explain anything to me. I'm just a pair of ears.' He flicked his ears with his fingertips and grinned. 'Seriously though, I'm not judging. I'm hardly in a position to even if I wanted to.'

She smiled gratefully, surprised at how much she wanted to open up to this man she'd only just met and tell him all her secrets. But she wouldn't. Not all of them.

'Dom – my boyfriend. Ex-boyfriend now, I guess.' The realisation hit her like a kick to the stomach. 'He's the reason I was so late onto the plane because he rang and begged me to change my mind and go home.' She thought about his voice now, how he'd sounded so hurt and confused. She'd been so close to turning round and walking out of that airport, getting into a taxi and going home and telling him she was sorry and she was home and she'd never leave him again.

But then she'd thought about how stuck she felt in her life. How she could never talk to him about her hopes and dreams without him somehow making her feel she was being silly, over-reaching, *unrealistic*.

And she also thought about how she would feel if she told him the truth about what had happened to make her finally walk out of her seemingly happy life and he down-played it or, worse, simply didn't believe her. And in the end that was what had carried her feet towards the plane, towards New York instead; towards this man.

She looked up at him now, at his warm, expectant face.

'Actually do you mind if we talk about something else? This is too hard. It's just – it's not me at all.'

'Sure.' He had such an easy way about him. So different to Dom, who over-analysed everything, who needed to get to the nitty-gritty of something every time. It could be exhausting, and something about this man was refreshing.

'So, if we're going to chat all the way across the Atlantic and you're not going to tell me your name, I'm going to have to make one up,' she said.

'Make one up?'

'Yeah.'

His lips curled into a lopsided smile again. 'Right, what did you have in mind?'

She thought for a minute. 'Paddy.'

'Nice cliché.'

'Sorry.' She grinned back at him. 'Well come on, you must have a nickname at least?'

'I do.'

'And?'

'I'm not telling you that either.'

'Right then, Paddy it is.'

'Fine.' He drained his glass. 'Drink?'

'Why not?'

He reached up and flicked on his light to get the attention of the air steward and Bea tried not to notice the strip of tanned skin that was exposed above his waistband as he did. She did *not* need to be thinking about another man right now.

An air steward was by their side within seconds.

'What can I get you, sir?'

Paddy looked at Bea, eyebrows raised in a question. 'Gin?'

'Sure.'

'We'll have a couple of doubles each please,' he said. 'Oh and a bottle of' – he looked at her – 'red? White?'

'Really? Wine too?'

He shrugged. 'It is Christmas.'

'Okay, red then.'

As the air steward passed them their drinks, Paddy leaned over her and she could smell his unfamiliar scent – was it his usual one or something he'd spritzed on himself in the duty-free shop, the way she had? She breathed it in deeply, a mixture of lemon and thyme and something else, a deeper, thicker smell.

'You okay?'

She snapped her eyes open, her face flaming. 'What? Yes, sorry. I was just closing my eyes for a second.' God how *mortifying*. Thank

God he couldn't read her mind. She took the proffered bottle of red and tried not to meet Paddy's eye.

'Wine or gin first?'

'Gin.'

'Atta girl.'

Paddy poured their gins and added the smallest splash of tonic water, and she took the opportunity to compose herself. When he held up his plastic cup and tapped it soundlessly against hers, she smiled at him. She hadn't planned on getting drunk on the first day of her new life but perhaps it would help her forget her worries, just for a little bit. She took a sip and let the icy liquid settle and relax her limbs.

She turned her head. 'So, I've told you my sorry little tale of why I'm flying to New York all by myself. Why are you going?'

'I live there.'

'Oh? You don't sound like a native New Yorker.'

'No. But I've lived there a few years.'

'With someone?'

A look flitted across his face that she couldn't read, but then he straightened his features so quickly she wondered whether she'd imagined it. 'Not any more, no.' It was clear from his tone that particular avenue of conversation was closed so she didn't push it.

'What do you do over there then?' she said, deftly changing the subject.

He took a gulp of his gin, knocking almost half of it back in one go and wiping his hand across his mouth before answering. 'I'm in advertising,' he said.

'Fancy.'

'Yeah it's all right.' He downed the rest of his gin. 'Pays the bills.' He glanced down at her half-full drink. 'Come on, you're falling behind.'

'Sorry.' She dutifully took a delicate sip of gin and tonic.

'So, have you sorted somewhere to stay?'

She quickly finished her drink and waited for him to pour the next one. It felt like she was going to need it. 'Kind of.'

'So?'

She squirmed. 'I've booked a couple of weeks at a hotel near Times Square. But I can't afford to stay for long.'

'And after that?'

She shook her head. 'I don't know yet.'

A silence fell and Bea didn't know what to say. Eventually she asked: 'Where do you live?'

'I'm in West Village.' When she looked puzzled, he explained, 'It's downtown. About twenty minutes from Brooklyn Bridge.'

West Village. Downtown. Brooklyn Bridge. She rolled the names over in her mouth. They felt as familiar to her as yellow taxicabs and the Empire State Building, even though they were places she'd only seen and heard about from the comfort of her home in London. The idea that she was about to see these places in real life – maybe even to *live* in them – filled her with a fresh wave of excitement that spread from the tips of her toes to the top of her head and made her shudder.

'...if you like?'

She realised Paddy had been saying something. 'Sorry, what was that?' Her vision was already a bit blurry from too much gin, and her face tingled.

'Are you pissed?' He was studying her face rather too closely.

'No!' She grinned. 'Maybe a little. But in my defence I haven't had much to eat apart from these crackers all day.'

'God you are a lightweight, aren't you?'

'I think it's the stress of everything...' She trailed off, aware that was somewhere she didn't want to go. She reached for the wine bottle. 'Shall we start this?'

'Are you sure you should drink any more just yet?'

She shrugged. 'In for a penny, eh? Besides, we wouldn't want to waste it.'

She splashed wine into both their glasses then took a sip. The wine felt rich and fruity in her mouth, and as she swallowed, it warmed her from the inside.

'So, what were you saying?' Her mouth felt woolly. It wasn't unpleasant.

'I was just saying if you need any recommendations, or someone to show you around, I'd be happy to.'

She froze. As tempting as it would be to let this handsome man show her the sights of New York, she also knew it would be a mistake. She was here to find herself. Clear her head, work out what she wanted from her life. Not to throw herself straight into another relationship – or something more complicated – with someone else. No, she had to be firm here.

'Thanks,' she muttered vaguely. 'I'll see how I get on.'

Really firm Bea.

They fell into a silence for a while and Bea took the opportunity to watch a movie – she chose Two Weeks' Notice, simply because it was set in New York. Beside her, Paddy did the same.

Film finished, Bea was beginning to need the loo but the man beside her was sound asleep. She unclipped her seatbelt and carefully shimmied into position, before sliding her body over his sleeping form. Halfway across, she thought she should probably just have woken him and that if he opened his eyes right at this moment to find her straddling him she'd have to throw herself out of the plane with shame. But she was committed to this stupid idea now, so she kept moving, inch by agonising inch, closer to freedom. And then she was there! She was free and in the aisle and as she wobbled towards the loo – it was *definitely* just the plane making her stumble, not the gin – she felt a sense of relief to be away from Paddy for a few moments. What was it about him that was making her feel so unbalanced, so unlike herself? Was it just that someone was showing an interest in talking to her about things she wasn't keen to shine a light on just yet?

Yes, that was it. It must be.

The toilet was free and she slid the lock shut behind her and almost fell onto the loo seat. The mirror above the sink reflected her image back at her and she peered at it more closely. Why was she so blurry? She rubbed the mirror with her sleeve. Oh. It wasn't the mirror that was blurry, it was her. She grinned. Her teeth were slightly purple. Her cheeks were flushed and she had a manic glow in her eyes. Christ, she looked insane.

She splashed her face with water and took a couple of deep breaths. Okay, she could do this. She could get through the rest of this flight without fucking up, without saying anything she shouldn't, and without throwing herself at a random man. Yes, she could.

Hands washed, she unlocked the door and walked as straight as she could manage back to her seat. The man in the aisle was awake now and when she stood beside him waiting for him to move, he paused a few seconds before hauling himself to his feet. *God, if you don't want to move, don't choose an aisle seat,* she thought, but didn't say. He wouldn't look her in the eye and as she slid in she could see Paddy grinning at her.

'What's so funny?' she said, more irritably than she intended.

He studied her for a moment and her cheeks began to flush. Did she have something on her face? Oh *God*, were her flies undone? She glanced down, but all seemed fine. By the time she looked back up, Paddy was looking away, drinking his almost-finished glass of wine.

'So, what were we talking about?' he said.

She shrugged. 'Not much I don't think.'

'Well then, why don't you tell me a bit more about yourself? Not the complicated stuff' – he waved his hands in the air like he was getting rid of an unsavoury smell – 'but just general stuff. You know, like what your parents are like, who your friends are, what you like doing.'

'Really? You want to know all this stuff?'

He shrugged. 'There's feck all else to do for the next' – he checked his watch – 'two and a half hours.'

Her heart sank. God, two and a half hours and she'd be in New York. Alone. At Christmas. She swallowed.

'There's not much to tell you. I grew up in north London with my mum and dad, Ange and Pete. Mum has spent her entire life trying to look after everyone else, while Dad always worked nights so we hardly ever saw him. He's obsessed with Arsenal and used to take us to watch matches on the weekends he had off.' She gulped some more wine. 'I've got an older sister, Alice, who is like a carbon copy of Mum except with more money, and has two kids and a husband and still lives about five minutes away from our parents which is why she's always going to be the favourite. My twin brothers Charlie and Rob are six years older than me so we're not very close.'

'Wow, you're one of four?'

'Yeah.'

'And I'm the Irish one.'

She turned her head to face him. 'How many siblings do you have then?'

He looked sheepish for a moment. 'Well, five. But in my defence, most English people I know only ever seem to have one sibling. It's weird.'

Bea smiled. 'We're a weird family. My gran only lives a couple of doors down too. She's who I was named after.'

'Oh, not the princess then?'

'No, she wasn't born 'til I was thirteen. It was at school people used to call me that.'

'Annoying.'

'It was all right.' She paused. 'So five siblings, hey?'

'Yeah.'

'Do they all still live in Ireland?'

'Yeah, every single one of them. It's only me who's disgraced the family by moving to America.'

'And you don't plan to move back?'

Bea felt Paddy stiffen beside her. His shoulders hunched and he stared at the back of the seat in front like it was the most interesting thing in the world. 'No. I'm tied to the US for a while longer.'

She nodded. She longed to ask more, but she also knew what it was like when people pried into things you didn't want to talk about.

'This is a big thing for me, too,' she said instead. 'None of my family has ever moved abroad. I can't quite believe it's me doing it, to be honest.'

'Why's that?'

'I'm not brave. Never have been. I almost changed my mind about coming five minutes before I got on the plane for God's sake. But... well' – she held her hands out, palms up – 'here I am.'

'Here you are. And here I am.' He held his cup up and she tapped hers against it again.

'You are brave, though.'

She snapped her head round. 'Sorry?'

He turned to look at her. His eyes were warm and she felt a shiver run down her spine.

'You are brave.'

She shook her head. 'I'm really not. I've always been a coward. In secondary school I was the only one who didn't dare climb up the climbing wall on a school trip, and everyone laughed at me, but as I stood at the bottom and looked up, all I could think about was what would happen if I fell. I just couldn't make my feet move any closer.' She shrugged. 'It sort of set the tone for my life.'

He was still staring at her. Why was he still staring at her? 'You're braver than you think you are,' he said, his voice low.

'What makes you say that?'

'You're starting again. Pressing the reset button. That's not cowardly. It takes a lot of balls.'

She looked down at the plastic cup in her hands. *Was* she braver than she gave herself credit for? From the moment she decided to book this flight, she'd thought of it as running away. But maybe Paddy was right. Maybe she *was* brave. Maybe, instead of running away from her life, she was giving herself the chance to make a new one.

Maybe, this was the bravest choice of all.

* * *

Bea's face felt cold. Why was her face cold? She prised one eye open and could only make out the back of the seat in front. Her neck ached and when she put her hand to her cheek, it was wet.

Oh God, she'd been dribbling! She swiped the dampness away and hoped nobody had noticed. But when she finally opened her eyes fully, she saw Paddy watching her and smiling.

'Hello sleepy head,' he said.

'Hi.' She sat up properly. 'What time is it?' Her voice was croaky and she cleared her throat.

'We'll be landing in about twenty minutes.'

She was fully alert now. 'Twenty minutes?'

'Yep. Almost in the Big Apple. Excited?'

'I—' She stopped. How *did* she feel? Excited, sure. But what else? Her stomach churned and she had a slight headache, but that was probably a hangover. She held her hands out in front of her. They shook slightly. 'I think I'm fucking petrified.'

Before she knew what had happened, Paddy had threaded his fingers through hers. His palm felt warm and she watched as if from a distance as he rested their entwined hands on the armrest between them.

She wanted to ask him what he was doing; she should probably pull her hand away. But she didn't do either of those things and instead they sat in silence as the plane lowered slowly towards JFK airport. Bea didn't move a muscle until the wheels touched the tarmac, and then she felt the tension slide from her just at the moment Paddy took his hand away.

As they taxied towards the airport, the lights came on full. She was glad to see that aisle man had also dribbled a bit, and as they came to a halt, he stood and she realised how close she'd been shoved towards Paddy.

The next few minutes were spent retrieving bags from overhead lockers and under seats, pulling on coats and trudging in single file towards the open doors. Bea's back ached and her legs were stiff, and she felt vaguely self-conscious as she made her way through the doors and along the air bridge towards the terminal, unsure whether Paddy was still following her. She glanced behind. There were a few people between her and Paddy. She was surprised to feel disappointed.

Passport control was hell. Paddy was quite far behind her by now and she kept passing him as the queue snaked round the temporary barriers. They smiled at each other every time they passed but said nothing. Bea could still feel the memory of his palm against hers and wondered what it had meant. Had he just been comforting her as they landed?

Bea still hadn't switched on her phone, not yet ready to hear the slew of messages that had no doubt been left while she'd been in the air.

Finally, she reached the front of the queue and handed over her passport. As the humourless guard behind the plexiglass studied her face she tried to wipe what she felt was a guilty expression off it. Authority always made her feel as though she were doing something wrong, even though she'd never done anything wrong in her life. At least not in a legal sense. The seconds stretched on and for a moment she had a horrible vision of being dragged away to be strip-searched, sniffer dogs finding drugs stashed in her bag, being thrown in jail surrounded by murderers and rapists and—

'Thank you ma'am, have a good day.' The guard was holding out her passport and she snatched it from him and hurried towards the baggage reclaim.

The carousel was at a standstill, the crowd surrounding it growing fidgety and agitated. Bea spotted the man from the aisle seat and made a beeline for the opposite side where she waited nervously for her bag. This was it. She was here.

'Well that was as welcoming as usual.' A familiar voice made her jump and she turned to find Paddy standing beside her, looking tired in the harsh strip lighting.

'Is it always like that?' she said.

He shrugged. 'Worse, sometimes. They like to make you feel like you're about to be thrown out of the country before you've even arrived, even though I've never known anyone to be refused entry before. It's some sort of game they like to play.'

'I'm glad it wasn't just me.'

There was a loud beeping sound, and the luggage carousel began to chug into life. A titter of excitement rippled round the crowd. Paddy rubbed his hands together and Bea felt a shudder of disappointment that soon she'd be leaving this airport and she'd probably never see this man again.

Maybe she should ask him what his real name was. Just so, you know, she had at least one person she knew in this city of strangers. That wouldn't be so unusual, would it? She was about to open her mouth to ask him when he said, 'Here they come.' She glanced in the direction he was indicating to see the first of the suitcases being spewed out, and the moment was gone.

A few minutes passed and finally her little red suitcase emerged and made its grinding way towards her. She hauled it off just at the same moment that Paddy pulled his case from the carousel too. He grinned at her. 'Looks like we're destined to be together,' he said.

'Wha – oh! The cases!' She forced a laugh. 'Yes, it does...' She trailed off, hoping her face didn't show how embarrassed she was that, for just a split-second, she'd thought he was talking about something else entirely.

They made their way out of the luggage hall and through arrivals, past lines of people holding up signs and searching expectantly for loved ones, then out through the sliding doors. The air outside was so cold it felt like a slap and for a moment Bea couldn't catch her breath.

'I guess this is where we finally say goodbye,' Paddy said, turning to face her.

'I guess so. Thanks for keeping me company.'

'The pleasure was all mine.'

They stood still, neither of them speaking. Bea wondered whether she should ask for his phone number. But before she could summon the courage, Paddy said, 'Right, well. The cabs are there if you need one.'

She glanced towards the line of yellow cabs that snaked along the road and a shiver of excitement ran down her spine despite herself.

'Are you not getting one?'

He shook his head. 'I've got a lift. Sorry. I would offer but...' He trailed off awkwardly.

'Oh, no, it's fine,' she blustered, forcing a smile. 'Well, thanks again then. It was nice to meet you.' She stuck out her hand and as Paddy took it and gave it a shake she tried not to think too much about how nice his hand felt, wrapped around her own.

'You too. See you around, Princess Beatrice,' he said, then he turned and walked away, leaving her standing there all alone in a sea of people.

* * *

Bea opened her eyes. The room was pitch black and for a moment she wondered whether she was dead. She sat up and the blood rushed from her head, leaving her light-headed.

Where the fuck was she?

She squinted into the darkness, trying to make out the familiar shape of her wardrobe, the chest of drawers with the mirror balanced precariously on top, a chink of light filtering under the door. But there was nothing.

Heart pounding, she reached out her hands and fumbled around for a light switch – there had to be one here somewhere. When her hands finally fell on one, relief flooded her. Flicking the light on, she blinked like a deer in headlights as her eyes began to adjust. This wasn't her room... Shit, where *was* she? Had she been kidnapped?

Just as she was about to start screaming for help, it all came rushing back in like a dam that had been released, the realisation of where she was and why she was here racing towards her like a tsunami.

She was in New York.

She'd left Dom.

She was in *New York*.

And then she remembered something else too – the handsome man she'd spent most of the flight over here chatting and drinking with – and she groaned. No wonder she had a headache, all that booze they'd downed. And lord only knows what she told him.

Pushing back the bedspread, she padded over to the window. She hesitated for a moment; the minute she yanked back this curtain to reveal the outside world, her new life and everything it entailed would be real.

She took a deep breath and pulled. And as she did, she wanted to scream all over again – but this time, a good scream. Because there, in front of her, was the view she'd always dreamed of. Her room was a few floors up – twelve, if she remembered correctly – and from here she could see the grey stone of the building opposite, a flashing neon light turning it alternately blue then pink then back to blue again. But beside that was the view that really took her breath away: a chunk of pale blue sky, sliced through by the jagged skyline and towering skyscrapers that winked like giant Hollywood teeth in the weak summer sun. Tiny windows watched her like eyes while buildings jostled and clamoured for prominence and, when she rested her head on the glass and peered down, she could make out tiny cars beetling along a spiderweb of streets.

She stood motionless, drinking it in.

She'd done it. She'd actually gone and done it.

Her body trembled with a mixture of excitement and fear. Her future was a blank canvas onto which she needed to start painting.

Tearing herself away, she took in the room where she was going to be spending Christmas. Plain wooden wardrobe, flowered bedspread, walls painted a mid-blue and adorned with a selection of Manhattan skyline photos. Slightly down-at-heel but given she'd paid for two weeks upfront she didn't think she'd done too badly on her limited budget.

She made her way back to the bed, climbed under the bedspread and picked her phone off the bedside table where she'd had the wherewithal to plug it in last night.

There were nine messages. Two were from Dom, and her heart sank. Two were from her mum, another three from Mia, and one each from her friend Michael and her sister Alice. She suspected she knew what most of them would say – something along the lines of her having made a huge mistake and begging her to reconsider and come home for Christmas. Assuming that Mia would be the least irritating, she clicked open one of hers first.

> Oh my God, you haven't been answering your phone for hours now – does this mean you actually went? I can't believe it. I'm so fucking proud of you. Can I come and stay? Love you. M x

Tears pricked the backs of her eyes. Good old Mia. She missed her terribly and she knew her friend probably felt the same way, but she hadn't made her feel bad. The other two were similar, with the third one signing off with:

> You'd better ring me the SECOND you wake up to tell me how amazing it is or I'll never speak to you again.

She smiled, then steeled herself to read the others.

She opened Michael's next, certain she would be getting a bollocking of some kind. She was right.

> I can't believe you actually went. What an absolute shit show. Ring me when you can, you lunatic.
> Michael. x

Michael wasn't afraid to mince his words and he'd made it quite clear he thought she was being a complete idiot since she'd told him her plans a few days before. He'd come round eventually. She hoped.

Her mum, predictably, had left a couple of messages telling her she'd bought a turkey big enough for everyone and that it still wasn't too late to change her mind.

> Oh, and I've invited Dom round because I didn't want him to feel lonely. I hope you don't mind.

Oof. Mum certainly knew how to tighten the guilt screws. She took a deep breath.

It would be easier to simply ignore the three messages from Dom. But it would also be cruel, and anyway, she couldn't ignore him forever. She opened the first of the three messages.

> I guess you got on the plane then?

That was it. Opening the next one, her hand began to tremble.

> Your mum has invited me for Christmas dinner because she doesn't want me to be alone. I've accepted. I hope you change your mind and come too.

He rarely left kisses or signed his name so that wasn't unusual but the terse tone was new, if understandable. She clicked open the third and final one and her heart sank.

> Please ring me. I need to hear your voice. I love you.

She dropped her phone on the bed and tipped her head back to look at the ceiling. All her fizzing excitement from just a moment before had evaporated, leaving in its place a vast, empty space inside her which she had no idea how to fill. She was an idiot, coming here on her own without any kind of plan of what she was going to do when she got here.

And yet, if she'd have stayed, would she have been unhappy forever?

The loud shrill of her phone snapped her out of her reverie and she picked it up with shaking hands. Dom.

Her thumb hovered over the answer button. She should speak to him. And yet she didn't know if she could face it. What if he begged her to go home? She felt so vulnerable right now, there was a strong chance she would go.

She stood, crossed the few feet to the window on wobbly legs and took in the view, the magical skyline of the city she'd always dreamed about. As she stood there, a few flakes of snow began to fall from the sky, floating gently to earth and vanishing into the cold concrete below. Snow in New York. Perhaps *this* was the sign she'd been waiting for; the sign that this was just where she was meant to be after all.

Taking a deep breath she pressed 'answer' and held the phone to her ear.

'Hi Dom.'

* * *

An hour later Bea was showered and dressed and ready to face the world. The conversation with Dom had gone largely as expected. He was still unable to understand why she'd left, and she was still unable to fully explain her drastic action. He begged her to go home, she said she needed some time.

He'd sounded utterly miserable, and Bea felt terrible by the time they said their goodbyes.

She needed to get out of this room.

The air was take-your-breath-away cold as she stepped out of the hotel, and she tugged her hat down tighter. The wind was strong and the snow, which was heavier now, was falling diagonally, ice crystals covering her wool coat and melting into the fabric. She'd taken a quick glance at the map she'd brought before she'd left, and she knew she needed to head right to get to Times Square, so she set off, head down, into the blizzard.

It was two days before Christmas so even a snowstorm couldn't stop New Yorkers from venturing out, and as she walked, Bea marvelled at all these people going about their daily lives as if it was perfectly normal to be working, dating, shopping, eating in this movie-backdrop of a city. Which, she supposed, it was, to them. But to her it was like living in a dream, with every corner she turned and every road intersection she crossed revealing yet more views to marvel over: the neon lights and enormous sparkling Christmas tree of Times Square, where bodies queued four deep to cross the road, then down Broadway – *actual Broadway!* – past pizza stalls and hotdog stands, sports shops, drug stores, shuttered office blocks and bustling restaurants, her eyes widening and heart quickening with every step. All of which meant that, by the time she arrived outside the revolving doors of Macy's on the corner of 34th Street her mood had begun to lift, and the guilt that had settled like a stone in her belly since her conversation with Dom had dissipated a little.

She stepped through the doors of the world-famous department store she'd only ever seen in pictures or on screen, and wandered round like a kid in a sweet shop, open-mouthed. She strolled through the perfumed-scented beauty hall, the floors filled with funky clothes she could never imagine wearing, and the colourful rows of beautifully wrapped treats in the food hall, before finally heading towards the enormous Christmas section, where the combination of tinsel, lights, music and over-excited children felt a little overwhelming. She battled her way towards the exit and was spat back out onto Broadway again, where she turned left, heading north until she once again hit Times Square. This time she paused for breath, standing motionless and taking it all in as people flowed past her like water.

It felt like a dream.

The snow was lighter now and the streets were even more packed as she picked her way carefully through the crowds until she reached Seventh Avenue. Trying to remember the layout of the city, she took a right, past the ice rink outside the Rockefeller Center and onto traffic-choked and sprawling Fifth Avenue.

The pavements – she should probably call them sidewalks now – were full of puddles of melted snow, and her feet felt damp in her leaky boots. She moved closer to the brightly lit storefronts, Saks and Armani and Longchamp, where lights twinkled and music played, trying to entice people in before the shutters came down for two whole days.

The further north she walked the grander the buildings grew, red carpets and gold lettering picking out the names of private apartments on canopies that over-hung the street, straight-faced doormen standing guard. She passed the gaudy bling of Trump Tower, then the road began to open up and there it was like an oasis in the desert: Central Park. Bea's heart hammered as she hurried across the road, past the yellow cabs and lines of horse-drawn carriages where couples waited to take romantic rides through the park.

The park was full of joggers and skate-boarders, families swinging young children by the arms, couples strolling hand in hand, people on benches eating solo lunches. After spending a few minutes watching ice-skaters glide round the rink with varying degrees of skill, the cold began to seep into Bea's bones, so she found a stand selling hot chocolate and pretzels, bought one of each and found a bench to perch on. She brushed the snow from it and sat down, determined to soak it all in.

After finishing the last mouthful of pretzel – which in all honesty was disappointingly dry – Bea felt her spirits start to drop again. She'd been buoyed along this morning by the excitement of arriving. But now, it was lunchtime on 23 December, and the sight of everyone taking strolls as families or couples, or out getting last-minute gifts for loved ones, made her feel more alone than she'd ever felt in her life.

Even the fairy lights in the trees opposite did nothing to lift her mood. She stood, brushed a few stray crumbs from her trousers and began the long trudge back to her hotel, this time much more slowly. She couldn't worry about being alone at Christmas. After all, she'd had the chance to be with her family. This had been her choice, her decision. It was down to her to make the most of it.

It took longer than she expected to get back. She'd stopped for a few supplies on the way, including a bottle of wine, a huge bag of Cheetos, a packet of chocolate chip cookies and some Reese's Pieces as well as some eye-wateringly expensive teabags from the food hall in Bloomingdale's – and by the time she trudged up the few steps into her hotel lobby, the bag was slicing into her ice-cold fingers and her whole body ached. The lift squealed in protest as it arrived at the ground floor and continued to squeal all the way up to the twelfth. She wondered, as she staggered past the closed doors of the other rooms, who else was staying here over Christmas. Were they alone too, or with loved ones? Was anyone else here running away from their lives? More to the point, was anyone else feeling a sense of dread at being completely alone for the next few days?

She pressed her key card against the door and let herself in when the green light flashed. Housekeeping had been in and straightened her bed and left her more toiletries. It was only early afternoon but it was already beginning to get dark outside, and the room felt gloomy and unloved. She flicked on the bedside lights and walked over to the window. From here she could see the streets beginning to empty and lights coming on across the city as people drifted home.

A wave of loneliness washed over her and she tugged the curtains closed firmly, then turned to tip the contents of her carrier bags out onto the bed. She'd bought some tinsel in one shop with the thought that it might cheer her up. But as she strung it up above her bed now it just made the room look sadder, sagging unhappily across the middle of the headboard. She picked up a mini Christmas tree and flicked on the battery-operated lights, then stood it on the desk beside the window. It cheered her a little, and she opened the bottle of Chardonnay and poured some into one of the tumblers on the coffee tray. It was a bit warm, but she grimaced and swallowed it down anyway.

Settling in the fabric-covered chair by the desk, she fought the overwhelming urge to ring home. She knew it would only make her feel worse to hear the guilt she felt articulated by the people she loved most in the world. Instead she took another gulp of wine, the vinegary taste burning her tongue and curdling in her belly, closed her eyes and let her mind settle, allowed her thoughts to intrude, at last.

Coming to New York had always been a dream of hers, but one Dom had never shared and as a result had never taken seriously. She thought back to when they'd first met, at an eighties night in a pub in Highgate, north London. Michael had dragged them all there against their will because he'd heard a rumour that Boy George was going to make an appearance. Boy George hadn't made an appearance of course, so by ten o'clock everyone except for Michael was keen to call it a night.

'Ah come on, the night's still young,' Michael had said, glancing over at the door hopefully. 'What if he turns up the second we leave? I'd never forgive myself. And I'd never forgive you lot either.' He jabbed his finger at the group one by one.

Michael had always been hard to say no to, so they'd stayed. And that was when Bea had bumped into Dom – literally, in fact, as she smacked into him as he came out of the loo and spilt her glass of wine all down his jeans.

'Oh fuck!' she said, swiping ineffectually at his denim-clad leg. When she finally looked up and realised he was smiling at her rather than giving her the stern look she'd been expecting, she found herself smiling back, partly in relief. They'd chatted for the rest of the evening, and by the time Michael finally admitted defeat and announced he wanted to go home – 'Yes, I know it was unlikely, but you can't risk these things can you?' he said, as he stared miserably into the bottom of his whisky glass – Bea and Dom had swapped numbers and shared a sneaky kiss out the back of the pub.

Their romance was speedy, in the end, and by the time they moved in together six months later, Bea was smitten. Unfortunately that was when she began to notice that perhaps Dom wasn't as happy and optimistic as he'd first seemed. By the time he fell deep into a bout of depression and admitted it was something he'd suffered from on and off his entire life, she was in too deep to get out. She loved him.

At least, she had, for five years. He was a lovable man, most of the time. She loved the way he always included everyone in a conversation, keen for nobody to feel left out; she loved how intense he was about the things that mattered to him – running, good food, eighties music. And she really loved how much he adored her family; having grown up with a mother who didn't have a maternal bone in her body and a father who didn't understand mental health problems, a big, rowdy, loving family was exactly what Dom had always dreamed of, and he embraced them all completely.

But the things she didn't love about him had, over time, begun to bother her more. The way he could never understand anyone else's point of view – if he didn't think something was worthwhile, how could it be; the way he put her down without realising he was doing it, making her feel as though her ambitions, dreams and desires were nothing more than childish fantasies. She never told him this was how he made her feel because he'd be heartbroken. But, combined with his increasingly regular bouts of depression, she'd begun to wonder whether this was her life from now on and, if so, whether it was really what she wanted.

Then The Thing That She Would Never Talk About happened, and it was the final straw.

She wondered now, why hadn't she felt she could tell Dom about it? Because she thought he'd judge her? Disbelieve her? Make it seem smaller than it was? And why hadn't she told her mum, or Mia, Michael or Harry?

She shook her head. She knew exactly why.

Because she felt ashamed.

Because these sorts of things didn't happen to strong people. To good people. To people who didn't deserve it.

And even though she was fully aware that running away had never solved any problem, ever, she hadn't been able to see any other way out.

Her heart felt heavy in her chest, as though it was being weighted down by a tonne of rocks. The wine bottle was already half empty and she knew if she didn't pull herself out of this funk, she'd finish it and then open another and that, in anyone's book, was a fucking depressing way to spend an evening alone in New York.

She needed to speak to someone who loved her, no matter what she'd done, so she reached for her phone from the bed, found the number she was looking for, and dialled.

It took fewer than three rings for a voice to come on the line.

'Thank *fuck*. I was about to call Interpol.' The sound of her best friend's husky, swearing voice soothed her instantly, and she sank onto the edge of the bed and tipped backwards, staring straight up at the ceiling.

'Hi Mia,' she said, her voice meek.

'Hey,' Mia said, her voice softer now. 'You sound terrible. What's wrong?'

For a moment Bea found she couldn't say anything; all the words stuck in her throat. Because the second she'd heard her best friend's voice, all the emotions that had built up, all the doubts, the worries, came flooding to the surface, and she realised something. 'I—' she started.

'Bea?'

'I'm fine,' she finally managed. 'Really. I...' She trailed off again, the lights from the Christmas tree on the desk making her eyes water. 'I think I might have made a terrible mistake, Mee.'

2

STAY

December 2002

Bea climbed out of the taxi, thanked the driver and stood on the pavement, watching the car retreat until the lights disappeared round the corner and out of sight. Only then did she turn to face the building that was so familiar to her she could have described it with her eyes closed. She looked up at the Edwardian house, which had been divided into flats decades ago. The front door was a glossy black, painted by the freeholder last year, while the tiny patch of ground in front – it wasn't big enough to call a garden – was home to a couple of pots holding flowers that had been killed off by the cold. She raised her eyes up to the first floor and tried to see through the blank face of the living room window that looked out onto the street. Was Dom in there right now waiting for her, or was he in the kitchen at the back, sitting at the small dining table, hands wrapped round a cup of coffee as he listened for the sound of her key in the lock?

The rain that had started as a light drizzle on the way back from Heathrow Airport had quickly accelerated to downpour status, leaving her hair plastered against her cheeks and rivers of water running down the inside of her coat. She gave her red suitcase a tug and bumped it up the steps to the front door, slipped the key in the lock and pushed it open. Closing the door behind her quietly, she wondered whether she was trying to stay quiet because she wanted to surprise Dom, or whether she was still unsure if she was going to change her mind again. She breathed in deeply, the familiar smell of the musty hallway filling her nostrils, then headed up the scruffy staircase to their first-floor flat.

She stopped outside again, listening. Could she hear Dom moving around? Was that a tapping noise, the sound of a tap dripping? On high alert to everything, she pushed the key in the lock, opened the door and stepped inside.

'Hello?' She hadn't intended to say the word like a question, but it had come out that way. She was ashamed to admit she'd half-expected Dom to be standing right there in the hallway, holding a bunch of flowers, and crying with happiness that she'd decided to come home.

She really needed to stop watching so many romcoms.

But, now she came to think of it, where *was* Dom, and why hadn't he answered her?

Leaving her suitcase in the hallway, she took the three or four steps into the living room. The light was dim in here, the curtains half-drawn against the gloomy afternoon. It was also immediately clear that the room was empty. Bea stepped back out and popped her head round their bedroom door, then into the spare bedroom, the bathroom. Nope. She carried on into the kitchen, certain that was where Dom had to be. But when she got there, she stopped dead. He wasn't here either.

Frowning, she turned and looked back in the direction from which she'd come, then back at the kitchen. She stepped fully inside and approached the table. No note to say he'd popped out for milk.

A text! Of course, this was 2002, not 1992, he'd send a text, not leave a note. She pulled her phone out of her bag and clicked on it. It lit up, but there were no missed calls, no texts waiting for her to read.

'Dom? Dominic?' Her voice got louder with each repetition, bouncing off the walls and back at her.

Not quite sure what she was looking for, she walked up to the kettle and pressed her hand against it. There was a hint of warmth so he hadn't been gone long. She walked out of the kitchen and back to the bedroom, searching for a clue as to his whereabouts, although she had no idea what that clue might be. Dust hung forlornly in the grey air, a head-shaped dent marked the pillow on her side – Dom's, she noticed, had been plumped up. There was no sign of his phone, his watch, or his travel card. She thought of her dad, repeating his checklist out loud every time he left the house: *Testicles, spectacles, wallet and watch*, and smiled. She ran her hand over the duvet, which was slightly rumpled at the corners, and knew how much it would have irritated Dom that it wasn't perfectly smooth. She stuck her head in the living room again. Unlit fairy lights were strung along the bookshelf where her bodice rippers and Dom's autobiographies jostled for space; the Christmas tree they'd put up two weeks before was already beginning to shed its needles, and a piece of tinsel hung forlornly from the bottom branch. A couple of presents sat beneath the tree, wrapped neatly in silver paper and she knew they were for her, from Dom, because he always put presents under the tree before Christmas Eve. It had annoyed her every Christmas since they'd been together.

'You have to wait until Christmas Eve,' she'd insisted.

'But we're not five,' Dom had said.

In the end it hadn't been worth the fight, so she'd stopped mentioning it. But she still refused to put hers there early.

Closing the door, she hurried back to the kitchen again and picked her phone off the table where she'd discarded it, and dialled Dom's number. Maybe he'd gone for his run later than usual, not expecting her to be back so quickly. Her taxi driver *had* driven pretty fast. She listened to the hum as the phone tried to connect, then a click, and Dom's voicemail message played into her ear.

Sorry I can't take your call right now, please leave me a message.

She ended the call, irritation rising in her throat now. She didn't need a welcoming committee, but was it really too much to expect Dom to actually be here when she got home from changing her entire life plans for him?

She threw the phone on the table with a clatter. She flicked the kettle on and stuck a teabag in a mug, then sat at the table while it brewed, drumming her fingernails on the wooden table and trying to dampen down her rising annoyance. If Dom came home now it would be better if she wasn't in a foul temper.

But where the hell *was* he?

She tried his number again, but it went straight through to voicemail again. This time she didn't hang up, but waited for the beep.

'Dom it's me. I've just got home. Where are you? Hopefully you'll be back before you even hear this message.' She hesitated, then: 'Love you.'

She ended the call and stood again, not quite sure what to do next. She wandered over to the fridge. A couple of photos were stuck to the front with an 'I Love Brighton' magnet, and she pulled them off and studied them. One was of her and Dom back when they'd first met. They were standing on Brighton pier, the sky behind them a dark, angry grey, and the wind had whipped Bea's hair up so it surrounded her head like Medusa. Dom was laughing as he pushed it away from his lips with his fingers. They both looked so young, so happy. She studied Dom's face to see if there was any sign in his eyes, in the set of his mouth, that he could ever be anything but this happy; that he would ever give them anything but joy.

But there was nothing. And it would be several months after this picture was taken before she discovered that the man she'd fallen in love with because of his youthful, fizzing energy, because of his ability to talk to anyone, to be the life and soul of any party, suffered from bouts of almost crippling depression.

Over the five years they'd been together, and the three since they'd bought this place, Bea had helped Dom through three separate, distinct episodes. The first was almost a year after they'd met – about nine months after this photo was taken – when he'd asked if they could leave a party early. Bea had noticed he'd been quiet all night, that he hadn't been laughing and joking with his usual gusto. She'd assumed he was just coming down with something – a winter cold or a sick bug. But by the time the taxi had pulled up outside their flat and they'd climbed the stairs and let themselves in the front door, it was already clear it was more than that.

'What's going on?' Bea asked, as Dom hovered on the edge of the sofa staring blank-faced into the unlit fireplace, his damp coat still hanging from his shoulders.

Dom hadn't replied and Bea sat down next to him, put her hand on his arm. He didn't move it away but she felt him tense beneath her touch. 'Are you ill?'

He gave a tiny shake of his head and continued staring into the fireplace. Something about the emptiness in his eyes made her shiver, and she knelt on the floor in front of him and pressed her palms either side of his face.

'Dom, sweetheart. Talk to me.'

Finally, he dragged his eyes away from the spot in the distance and focused on her. His dark eyes were glassy, scared, and he gave another tiny shake of his head, as if he was trying to bat away a fly without anyone noticing.

'I can't.' The words were flat, emotionless. 'I'm sorry.'

She was scared, her mouth dry. She didn't understand what was going on. With no idea what to say, action took over. She eased his coat off his shoulders and tugged it out from under him, then she watched him for a moment as he brought his feet up onto the sofa and curled into a foetal position, hugging his knees to his chest. She draped a blanket over him then dug her phone from her pocket and left the room, closing the door gently behind her.

At first she thought the call was going to ring out, but, just as she was about to give up, a breathless voice answered.

'Beatrice. Is everything all right?'

'No,' she said. 'No, everything is not all right.'

She wasn't close to Dom's dad Richard, but apart from her, he was the only person who knew Dom well. His mum barely knew him at all, having spent most of Dom's childhood swanning round having affairs and trying to make it in the West End. Richard was far from being dad of the year, but at least he cared. He was Bea's only hope.

'Ah, yes,' Richard said, when Bea finished describing Dom's behaviour. 'Well, it says a lot about you that you've never experienced it before. You must make him happy.'

'What do you mean?' Bea said. The phone felt hot against her ear and she was gripping it too tightly.

'Dominic suffers from depression, Beatrice. Had it since he was a child.' He coughed, as Bea's blood turned to ice in her veins. 'I'm amazed he's never told you.'

A year. A year they'd been together, and he'd never told her he had depression. There had been brief moments when Dom seemed less happy and relaxed than usual, when his eyes briefly glazed over or he seemed less chatty, but she'd always put it down to tiredness, nothing more. There had certainly never been anything that had set alarm bells ringing. Bea felt as though she'd been hit in the stomach by a cricket ball, leaving her doubled up and winded.

When it became clear she wasn't going to speak, Richard carried on. 'The best thing is to check he's taking his medication and get him to bed. A bit of rest and it might pass more quickly.' He sounded so matter-of-fact, and Bea tried to picture him, leading his son gently to bed, tucking him in, giving him a kiss on the forehead as he said goodnight, but she couldn't do it.

'How...' She cleared her throat. 'How long will it last?'

'Depends,' Richard said. 'Sometimes it's gone in a few days, others, it can be a few weeks. There's never any telling. But you can't force it.'

She didn't listen to much more, the words 'a few weeks' running around her brain. The image of Dom's vacant, numb stare was imprinted on her retinas, and she had no idea how she was going to help him through this. But she was going to try.

Over the next few days, Dom barely responded to the help Bea offered, spending most of his days staring blankly at the TV, or sleeping. The doctor wouldn't tell her anything, but she did get Dom to admit that he'd stopped taking his medication shortly after they'd met because he'd felt happier. He'd believed Bea was his cure.

He'd been wrong.

Slowly, as the dark cloud had started to lift, Dom had begun to talk. He told her about his 'episodes' as he called them, how his dad had been practical and efficient when he was like this, as though showing any affection might have made him worse. 'At least he was there though,' he said. 'Mum stayed well away. I think she was scared it might rub off on her.'

'Why didn't you tell me?'

This was the question Bea had been wanting to ask since that first night, but hadn't dared. But finally she was confronting it head on. Why had the man she thought she knew inside out kept such an important piece of information from her?

'I thought I was better,' he said. 'I didn't want to be *Dom who you loved despite his depression*. I just wanted to be Dom, who you loved.' His eyes filled with tears and she brushed them away softly.

'You need to start taking your medication again, you know that, don't you?'

He nodded. 'I will. Just...' He looked up at her, his eyes wide.

'What, love?'

'You won't leave me, will you? Because of this?'

She shook her head. 'I'd only leave you if you started wearing chinos and slip-ons and listening to jazz,' she said, and he smiled as she kissed him.

Since then it had happened twice more, the first time after he tried to reduce his dosage, and the second time seemingly from nowhere. Each time it had lingered a little longer.

But in between these episodes, Dom was so different it was almost impossible to imagine he'd ever been that sad, that empty; his sense of humour returned and his eyes lit up once more, until the memory of how bad it had been began to fade and they both began to believe that it would never happen again.

Until it did.

Bea had accepted a long time ago that this was who Dom was and that, if she wanted to be with him, it was something she had to live with.

Except that now, of course, his depression had been one of the main reasons that she had walked away from the airport – away from her dreams – and back to this flat instead of getting on the plane to New York. Because she was so frightened that, by leaving him, she would trigger the depression again – and this time who would be there to look after him?

She smacked the flat of her hand against the fridge door, causing the rest of the pieces of paper – a photo, a couple of take-away leaflets, the phone number of a plumber they'd used to fix the boiler a few months ago – to flutter to the floor. How *dare* he guilt-trip her into coming home and then not even be here when she arrived?

She hadn't expected a red carpet, but it would have been nice if he could at least have stayed to welcome her home, to tell her he was happy she'd chosen to come back. But of *course* he'd gone out. Once he'd known she was on her way home, that everything had gone back to normal, he'd had no reason to change his plans. Why would he?

Her anger boiled and she checked her watch to distract herself. She should have been landing in New York in a couple of hours. She wondered what she'd be doing right now if she'd got on that plane. Would she be drinking her way through the flight, becoming more and more morose as she watched endless sad films? Would she be regretting her decision, or would she have felt a sense of excitement, a thrill that she'd actually done it?

She bent down and picked the leaflets off the floor and stuck them back onto the fridge with the Brighton magnet, as well as the photo of them both.

Then she picked up her phone, went through to the bedroom, climbed into bed, and rang her best friend.

* * *

'For fuck's sake, how am I meant to meet a sexy American and fall in love and go ice skating in Central Park now?' Mia's throaty voice never failed to cheer her up, and right now her best friend was exactly what she needed.

'Sorry,' she said, a smile playing on her lips.

Mia didn't say anything for a moment and Bea pictured her on her sofa, lying flat-out, Deacon curled up on her belly.

'You're not surprised he's gone out, are you?'

'I guess not.'

'But you wish he hadn't.'

Bea shrugged, then realised Mia couldn't see that. 'To be honest I was terrified of seeing him before I'd had a chance to get used to the idea of being back, so I guess it's a good thing.' Her inflection went up at the end of the sentence so that it sounded like a question.

'So, we should go out.'

'Out?' The last thing Bea felt like doing was going out in public. She needed to sit at home and lick her wounds, try and mend her relationship.

'Yeah. You know, drinks, dancing, laughing. Ashton will be up for it and we can convince Michael and Harry it's worth leaving their flat for a night out to celebrate you being home.'

'I didn't even leave London,' Bea said.

'Ah, but we thought you were leaving, and that counts in my book.'

Bea let out a long sigh. 'I'm not sure. It can't be tonight. I've got to sort things out with Dom.' She gave a bitter laugh. 'If he ever decides to come home.'

'Sure, course. Although...' She stopped, and Bea waited for her to continue. When she didn't, Bea said, 'What?'

'I just... you never told me exactly why you were running away.'

'No.'

'Right. So, are you gonna?'

Bea felt her shoulders tense, her teeth grind. She hadn't told anyone the real reason she'd decided to leave. Mia knew New York was always somewhere Bea had dreamed of going – everyone knew that. But to run away there with no explanation?

'I will tell you one day. I just – I needed a change.'

'From Dom?'

'From everything.'

Mia was silent for a moment but Bea knew she wouldn't ask her anything more. That was one of the things she loved about Mia. She always knew how far to push things, and when to hold back.

'Well, tomorrow night then. It'll be almost Christmas.' She was back on safe ground now, and Bea found herself agreeing.

'Okay, but don't expect me to be happy about it,' she said.

'God no. You must be an absolute misery guts, and I don't want to see a hint of a smile on that face. Got it?'

'Got it.'

Bea heard a clatter and a bang, then Mia said, 'Listen, I'd better go, that's the door. But thank fuck you didn't get on that plane. I'm not sure I could have carried on without you. Love you.' Then the line went dead.

Bea threw her phone on the bed and tipped her head back on the pillow. The flat was so quiet, and she tuned her ears to every tiny sound, every movement; the creak of floorboards from the flat upstairs, the hiss of cars passing distantly in the street outside, the in and out of her breath, tight through her nostrils. She stared at a patch on the ceiling where the paint had begun to peel and wondered whether Dom had noticed it. Perhaps they should get the bedroom decorated. Perhaps they should get the whole flat renovated, gut it and start again, make it all fresh and shiny and new, as though nothing had ever been wrong.

More than likely they'd just patch it up, stop noticing it, and pretend it had never been there in the first place.

She pushed the duvet back and swung her legs out. The flat was chilly, and she walked back to the living room. If she got a fire going, made something nice for dinner, opened a bottle of wine, perhaps by the time Dom got home she could almost pretend that nothing had ever happened. That she'd just been here all day, waiting for him to get home. That nothing had ever gone wrong.

* * *

It was almost dark by the time Bea heard Dom's key in the lock, and the tread of his footsteps in the hallway. She heard the clatter of keys against the table, the shuffle of clothing as he removed his coat and hung it on the hook by the door.

Come on, she thought, *why don't you just come and sweep me up in your arms and tell me you love me, and forget the coat, the shoes, the routine. This is not just any other day.*

When he finally appeared in the doorway of the living room, Bea was in the middle of the room waiting for him. Neither of them moved for a moment, unsure. Then Dom took a couple of steps towards her and she moved towards him at the same time until they met, a carefully choreographed dance that looked for all the world as if they'd practised it. But neither of them knew what came next, and, for a few seconds they stood in front of each other, awkward.

'You're back.'

'I'm back.'

Dom swallowed and glanced at his feet. 'I wasn't sure if you'd change your mind again.'

'I wasn't sure if you were coming home.'

'Of course I was.' He looked up at her, his eyes filled with pain. 'I just needed to clear my head. Work out what to say to you.'

Bea nodded. She'd hurt him so badly and he didn't deserve any of this. She held out her arms, closed the gap between them and rested her cheek on his chest. He felt warm, and she breathed in his familiar smell and moulded herself into the familiar shape of his body as he wrapped his arms around her.

'I'm sorry,' she whispered. His heart thumped against her cheek.

'Me too,' he whispered back.

Bea pulled away and looked up at him. The fire had turned his face golden, and she wondered what had made her want to walk out of the life she'd built with this man. He was so kind, so loving. How could she ever have wanted anything else?

Later, over dinner, as they chewed their way through the over-cooked pasta and chicken dish Bea had made – one of three things she knew how to cook, and even they were usually pretty terrible – Dom finally asked her.

'Why did you leave?'

He wasn't looking at her, but concentrating on twirling the tagliatelle round his fork as though it was the most difficult task in the world. She clutched her wine glass tightly in her left hand, her right hand holding the fork in the space between her plate and her mouth.

She should tell him. This was the moment she could finally explain what had happened, why she'd been so scared to tell him before; why everything had become so muddled in her brain that she hadn't been able to think straight, so that running away from everything had seemed like the only option.

Except when she opened her mouth to say the words, none of them came out.

'I needed...' she started, lowering her fork with a clatter. Her hand shook. Dom noticed and slid his hand across the table and pressed it into hers. She took a ragged breath in and shook her head. 'I needed some space.'

'From me?'

She shook her head again. 'No. Yes. Partly. I...' She stopped, swallowed. 'I needed space from everything. At least I thought I did. But I was wrong.' She couldn't look Dom in the eye, terrified of what she might see there. His grip tightened on her hand and she finally looked up.

'Talk to me, Bea. Please.'

'I—'

'I know you think you have to treat me with kid gloves in case something tips me over the edge again, but I'm stronger than you think. I just... if there's something going on that's so bad it made you want to leave, you have to talk to me.'

Bea nodded. He was right, of course.

'So?' He closed his eyes for the briefest of moments and swallowed. 'Have you stopped loving me, Bea?'

'No!' The word burst out of her and she squeezed his fingers. 'Of course I still love you.'

Dom tipped his head to one side. 'So what is it then?' he said, gently.

She smiled sadly, all the words dammed up inside her throat, ready to pour out. But instead she just shook her head. 'It's nothing, Dom, I promise. I'm fine now. I'm home. It's over.'

He studied her for a moment longer and she waited for him to challenge her but, to her relief, he simply said, 'For good?'

She looked at him, his eyes warm in the treacly light. 'For good.'

3

GO

23 December 2003

The hammering on the door was so loud, Bea was convinced a fist was about to come bursting through the flimsy plywood. 'Come *on!*' the voice shouted. 'You've been in there for fucking *hours!*'

'Give me a minute,' Bea yelled back, struggling to make herself heard over the thump of 'Seven Nation Army' by The White Stripes blasting from the CD player. She'd told everyone to keep it down, but the second she'd left the room to come for a shower they'd cranked it up to full volume again, and she was fully expecting her downstairs neighbour to come thumping on her door any minute.

She leaned into the mirror and carefully applied her second set of fake eyelashes, her hand shaking slightly and leaving it a little bit wonky. She moved back, blinked a couple of times and studied her face. It didn't look too bad. Perhaps nobody would notice.

She took a couple of deep breaths, then turned and pulled the door open, and almost screamed. Mia was right in front of her, almost nose-to-nose, a bottle of fizz clutched in her left hand.

'At fucking last,' she said, handing Bea the bottle. 'You're miles behind.'

Bea put the bottle to her lips and tipped it back, the acidic wine fizzing in her mouth and down to her belly. 'Your eyelashes are on the wonk by the way,' Mia said, turning away with a grin. Ignoring her, Bea followed her into the living room.

'Here she is!' Mia yelled, and everyone in the tiny space cheered. Bea held the bottle in the air and someone clinked another one against it. It was hot in here, the windows steamed up so that the view beyond was obscured. Bea took a couple of steps across the room to the stereo and turned it down a few notches.

'Oi!' someone said, and Bea flashed an apologetic smile.

The conversation resumed almost immediately, and Bea took a moment to herself. She'd been feeling out of sorts all day, and she knew it was because today marked the anniversary of her move to New York. And while she appreciated just how far she'd come since those dark early days, she couldn't seem to shake the sense of emptiness that had dogged her since she woke up this morning.

She'd been so lonely back then. So lonely and scared and worried that she'd made the biggest mistake of her life. It didn't help that everyone – except for her friend Ashton who was just excited about coming out to visit her so he could sow his seed round New York the way he had round London – had agreed with her. Christmas Day 2002 had been one of the lowest points of her life.

In fact, she'd nearly gone to the airport and booked a return flight before she saw the new year in. The thought of going home with her tail between her legs and admitting she'd fucked up had been the only thing that had stopped her.

Fortunately, 2003 quickly began to look a whole lot better than the previous year. It had taken a month or so, but by the time February was almost over and Mia had announced she was flying out to visit, life was finally beginning to look up. Not only had Bea been offered her dream job as features assistant at *Glamour* magazine which had come with the promise of a work visa – she still had to pinch herself about that one – but she'd also made some friends and found herself somewhere to live.

It really was the beginning of a brand-new Bea, and she'd embraced it.

The only dark cloud on the horizon had been the guilt she felt about Dom. Far from moving on the way she'd hoped he would and getting on with life without her, he'd seemingly spent the last year wallowing. For the first few months of her time in New York, her family – mainly her mum and her sister Alice – had given her regular updates on Dom's state of mind, making it clear he was struggling. Regular calls from Dom himself had confirmed that, with almost every conversation ending with him crying and telling her he missed her and wanted her back.

After several months of this she'd felt wretched. She still cared deeply about Dom and hated the thought of him so unhappy. But it had been her friend Ashton who had made her realise that he was no longer her responsibility.

'You've got a new life now, Bea. You need to live it and stop worrying about the past.'

This had been surprisingly meaningful for Ashton, who spent most of his life thinking with something other than his brain, and it had been the catalyst that had made her finally break ties with Dom once and for all – firstly by asking her family to stop talking about him, and then by asking Dom to stop ringing her. It had been hard but it had definitely been the right thing to do. It was just a shame that it wasn't so easy to stop worrying about him.

For tonight, though, she was determined to push all thoughts of Dom and her past life out of her mind. Tonight was a time for celebration. Her first *proper* Christmas in New York, and she was damn well going to enjoy it.

She took another long swig of slightly warm wine and let her gaze wander across the faces of some of the people who had already come to mean so much to her.

First, of course, there was Mia. This was already Mia's third visit to New York this year and although at first she'd been convinced Bea had been making a mistake by running away from her problems, she'd never made her feel guilty about it. She'd been a (long-distance) shoulder to cry on – even though Bea still hadn't admitted what had happened to make her leave – and had never once complained about it, even when Bea rang her late at night because she'd felt sad and forgotten the time difference. Now, Mia was happy to admit she'd been wrong and that, in fact, she wished she had the guts to do exactly the same as Bea had done. Perhaps one day, when Mia's beloved granny no longer needed her in London, she would.

Then there was Ashton. Bea had known Ashton since he'd briefly dated Mia back in 1996. The pair had quickly realised they were better as friends, and Mia, Bea and Ashton along with Bea and Mia's childhood friend Michael and his long-term partner Harry had become thick as thieves. This was Ashton's first visit to New York, and Bea couldn't help smiling as she watched him flirt outrageously with anyone who would let him. He couldn't help himself, it seemed to be wired into his DNA. Right now, he was chatting up Maggie. Tall, leggy Maggie who, with her long chestnut hair and drain-like laugh, had no idea just how beautiful she was, was Bea's flatmate. The pair had been living together in this tiny but perfectly formed apartment between Little Italy and the Lower East Side for nine months now. Maggie was the perfect flatmate – she let Bea borrow her clothes (not that many fit her, what with Maggie being at least a size smaller than her and about four inches taller, but at least shoes and bags worked), she was a great cook, and she was funny, self-deprecating and kind.

'Steady on, she'll be taking over my role soon,' Mia had said, disgruntled, when Bea had sung her new friend's praises shortly after they'd met.

'Nobody will ever replace you,' Bea had reassured her. 'But she is a great stand-in when you're thousands of miles away in London.'

Bea had ignored the noise Mia made at those words, and luckily Mia and Maggie had got on like a house on fire from the moment they met a few weeks later.

The other two bodies in the tightly packed room were Lori and Nancy, Bea's new friends from the magazine who were also, respectively, feature writer and assistant editor. They'd bonded over bagels and coffee (*so* New York!) in the publisher's canteen one lunchtime after Lori had helped Bea decipher what cilantro was, and they'd been friends ever since. In fact, it was thanks to Nancy that Bea had found a flat so quickly – Nancy and Maggie were friends from college and Maggie had been looking to replace her ex-flatmate. It felt serendipitous.

'You're going to tell me it's a sign again, aren't you?' Mia had laughed when Bea had told her exactly this.

'Well, it does feel like it,' Bea had defended herself. 'I mean, a job and a flat with a ready-made flatmate all within a month – the universe is definitely trying to tell me I've made the right decision coming here.'

'As long as there's space for me in this swanky new flat then I'm sold,' Mia had said.

'Bea!'

A voice from across the other side of the room snapped Bea out of her reverie, and she looked up to see Maggie beckoning her over. She took the few steps across the room and hooked her arm through Maggie's.

'I see you've been Ashton-ed,' Bea said.

'Hey!' Ashton objected, but his face showed he wasn't cross. 'We were just talking, weren't we Mags?'

Maggie looked down at him – at almost six foot she was a good three inches taller than Ashton and he lifted his chin to meet her gaze – and said, 'Well, *you* were. I didn't get much of a chance.'

Ashton's face turned pink and Maggie laughed. 'Ah, I'm only kidding.' She turned to Bea. 'You have very lovely friends,' she said. 'I approve.' She leaned across Bea and plucked the bottle from her other hand and took a long gulp. A dribble escaped her mouth and ran down her chin and she swiped it away. Ashton gazed up at her like a dog on heat and Bea smiled. She didn't think she'd ever seen Ashton so smitten.

'Are we nearly ready to go?'

Maggie surveyed the room. 'I believe we are.' She unhooked her arm from Bea's, handed Ashton the half-empty bottle, and clapped her hands together. Everyone looked round. 'Let's party!' she yelled, and a whoop of excitement went up.

There followed a few moments of coat-gathering – this was still winter in New York after all, and nobody was prepared to risk frost-bite for the sake of coolness – before the apartment door was shut behind them. As they trooped down the stairs – they were on the fifth floor and the lift was cranky at the best of times – Bea tried not to make eye contact with her downstairs neighbour who was standing with her door open and watching them pass with open disdain.

'Merry Christmas Mrs Delaney,' Ashton said, and her forehead folded into a frown before she shut the door with a tut.

Moments later they emerged onto the street, popping out one by one like bingo balls. There were no cabs in sight so they began to wind their way haphazardly towards the intersection with

Delancey Street, linking arms so they were six-wide across the sidewalk.

'There's one!' Maggie unhooked her arm from Bea's and stuck it out coolly as a minicab slid smoothly into the space beside them.

'Right, Bea, Mia and Ashton, you take this one, and us three will wait for the next one,' Maggie said, ushering them towards the already open door.

'Are you sure?' Bea said.

'Totally,' Maggie said with a grin. 'Now get in and we'll see you in a sec.'

The three of them climbed in obediently and Bea leaned forward to speak to the driver. 'Bungalow 8 please,' she said, then settled back into the seat with a shiver of excitement. She was the local now, the one who knew her way around.

'I can't believe you let Maggie get in the other cab,' Ashton said.

Bea rolled her eyes. 'Can't you think about anything else even for a second?'

Ashton grinned and waggled his eyebrows. 'Not really.'

'Anyway, I won't allow you to sleep with my flatmate and break her heart.'

'Who said anything about breaking her heart?' he said in false indignation.

'Ashton,' Mia warned.

'Whevs.' He held his hands up in mock surrender. 'You two are such bloody spoilsports.'

The cab was stuck in traffic and, after the wine and the excitement, the hum of the engine was making Bea feel sleepy.

'I wish we didn't have to fly home tomorrow,' Mia said, face pressed against the window, her breath creating a patch of steam on the glass. 'I bloody love this place.'

'I know. And I can't believe you're abandoning me to have Christmas all by myself again,' Bea said.

Mia whipped her head round, her eyes wide.

'You've got Maggie!' she cried.

Beside her, Ashton made a groaning sound. 'Ahh, Maggie.'

'Oh shut up Ash,' Bea said, digging him in the ribs.

'Ow!' he cried, but they both ignored him.

'I know, and I'm lucky. But it doesn't mean I won't miss you both,' Bea said. 'Well, you anyway, Mee.'

Ashton gave a hurt look and Bea grinned at him.

'What did your mum say when you told her you're not coming home for Christmas again this year?' Mia said.

'She wasn't happy,' Bea admitted. That was an understatement. Ange had clearly been under the impression that either Bea would have given up and come home for good by now, or would at least be flying home to spend Christmas with her family this year. When Bea had finally admitted last month that she was planning to stay in New York to spend Christmas with Maggie, who had also decided not to go home to her family in Texas, Ange had been apoplectic.

'But you haven't been home for more than a year! And it's Christmas, we always spend Christmas together,' she'd said.

Her mum was right. Even when she'd been with Dom, Bea had always seen her parents on Christmas Day, even if they'd seen Dom's dad too. It was tradition.

'I know Mum, I really am sorry, but flights are just so expensive at this time of year.'

'But I thought you had an amazing job now?' Ange had retaliated.

Bea sighed. 'I do. It's great. But it doesn't pay brilliantly.' She'd already told her mum how expensive it was to live in Manhattan – and given that Ange lived in London, she was sure she understood better than she was letting on. But her mum wasn't about to let her off that easily.

'Do you want me to pop round and see them?' Mia asked now.

'Would you?' Ange loved Mia, and although Bea knew it wouldn't get her off the hook completely, it might appease her mum a little if Mia went round with tales of how well Bea was doing. At the very least it might put Ange's mind at rest.

'Course, you know I love your parents,' Mia said. 'And if I get some of Ange's Christmas pudding, even better.'

'Thanks Mee, you're the best.'

'I know.'

The cab came to a stop again, and this time a glance out of the window told Bea they'd arrived at their destination. She handed the cab driver a twenty-dollar bill, and they piled onto the pavement just as another cab pulled up behind them and Maggie, Lori and Nancy climbed out, a tangle of legs and cleavage and big hair.

An icy gust of wind blasted down the street and Bea shivered, pulling her coat tighter round herself.

'Come on, let's get inside before we die of hypothermia,' Nancy said, leading them all towards the door of the club. Nancy was born and bred in New York and seemingly knew everyone, and as such had bagged them VIP passes for tonight. As they were waved past the queue and straight inside by the two burly doormen, Bea felt a thrill of excitement. She'd made it!

They deposited their coats and picked their way through the throngs of people. Pink's 'Lady Marmalade' blasted through the speakers and the place was packed to the rafters with all the beautiful people of New York City.

Ashton's eyes were like saucers.

'This is amazing!' he said, as they stepped into a sectioned-off area surrounded by palm trees and settled into the plush striped couches.

'Behave yourself,' Bea warned.

'I always do,' Ashton said, flashing her the smile that turned most women to jelly. Bea had always been immune to it though and she planted a kiss on his cheek and grinned. 'Course you do darling.'

A tray carrying half a dozen glasses of champagne cocktails appeared from nowhere, and Bea took one gratefully.

'Let's dance,' Lori said, grabbing Bea by the hand.

'Not yet!' Bea said, tugging her hand gently away from her friend's grip. She loved a dance but wanted a drink first, to settle into the night. Lori stuck her tongue out at her and swiped a drink from the tray too. 'Fine, I'll give you ten minutes,' she said, knocking back her drink in one go.

The club was packed but the VIP section was a little less over-crowded, and Bea felt herself relax quickly, helped in no small part by the drinks that seemed to keep arriving. Bea idly plucked a menu from the low table beside her and almost fell off her chair when she saw the prices. How the hell was she going to pay for this?

'Where have all these cocktails come from?' Bea said, turning to Nancy as she slipped in beside her.

'My friend works here and let us have us a few for free,' Nancy said, her face lit up by the flashing lights. 'It's a bit pretentious this place, but you can't turn down free drinks and she promised to let me know when we have to start paying so don't worry.'

'That's amazing. You have some very helpful friends!'

'I know, right? Growing up in New York has a few advantages.'

Bea didn't like to say she thought it must have had more than a few – I mean, imagine growing up in a place like this. But she also knew that Nancy felt she'd missed out on lots of things that other kids took for granted, that she'd had to grow up too quickly because her parents worked long hours to afford her expensive private school.

'I'd much rather have had a mom and dad who actually wanted

to spend time with me,' she'd told Bea once shortly after they'd first met. But still, it felt like another world to Bea and her upbringing in their small terrace in north London where she'd shared a room with her big sister until her brothers had moved out, and where you never got a moment's privacy. 'Sounds like bliss,' Nancy had said when Bea had tried to explain what it had been like, and Bea had stopped trying to argue.

After a couple more drinks, Lori persuaded them all to head onto the dancefloor. There was barely any space to breathe, but Bea made an effort to move anyway, throwing her arms in the air at the chorus, and trying not to bump into anyone.

Mia leaned towards her to shout something in her ear.

'What?' Bea said.

Mia leaned right in so Bea could feel her breath tickling her ear.

'I said, Michael and H would love this place!'

Bea smiled and nodded. 'They really would.'

'I wish they were here.'

She nodded. 'Me too,' she mouthed. Back in London, Bea had spent most weekends with Michael and his partner Harry – Mia still did. At first it had been clubbing every weekend, then when Michael and Harry moved in together and Bea and Dom had done the same, it had become all about dinner parties and nights in. But she knew Michael and Harry still loved a crazy club night – and she felt a pang of sadness that they were missing out.

'Sorry treasure, I promised Harry we'd spend Christmas with his parents and New Year with mine,' Michael had said apologetically. 'But I'll be there in spirit.'

Bea danced to a couple more songs, until finally, hot and sweaty, she beat a retreat from the dancefloor. She was light-headed after no food and too much to drink in a short space of time, so she made a beeline for the loo, hoping the queue wouldn't be too long.

To her relief there were only half a dozen people waiting in line, so she tucked herself in at the back and waited, tapping her foot to the beat that pounded through the floor and up through her body.

Closing the cubicle behind herself a few minutes later, she sat down with relief on the seat. Her feet were sore in her too-high shoes, and she slipped them off and gave her toes a rub. There was a small blister forming on her heel. Great. Hopefully more booze would stop her feeling it until the morning.

Pulling herself off the loo and stepping back into her uncomfortable heels, she opened the door and washed her hands. She caught a glimpse of herself in the mirror and stopped for a moment to take in her appearance. She looked different, she knew, and the thought popped into her head that Dom wouldn't like the new her. When they'd been together, she'd always kept her look safe; while she always admired – and, yes, envied – others being able to pull off more outrageous, individual looks, she'd told herself they weren't for her. So she'd kept her hair shoulder-length and brown, and her clothes fashionable but safe. Now, though, the person looking back at her was a woman slowly emerging from her shell; her hair was cut into a sleek bob and dyed a few shades darker than her natural dark blonde, her eyes were ringed with heavy make-up, and her dress was tighter and shorter than anything she would ever have dreamed of wearing before. She looked good. But did she feel like her?

Turning away from the mirror, she headed out of the loos and back towards the VIP area, hoping her friends might be having a rest from dancing. But as she reached the end of the corridor, she felt her ankle buckle and then, as if in slow motion, she tipped forwards, the ground coming up to meet her. Instinctively, she put her hands out to break her fall... but then, as quickly as it had happened, the ground began to recede again, and before she knew it she was upright once more.

It took a few seconds to work out where she was, and when she did she realised someone had her upper arm in a vice-like grip. She pulled it away and looked up to see...

'Oh!' she said, at the same time as the person who'd stopped her from falling said, 'It's you!'

For a moment all the other people in the club disappeared; the music faded away and it was just the two of them facing each other in a perfect little bubble.

Then a drunk woman bashed into the back of Bea, dripping liquid down her legs and making her lurch forward, and the bubble was broken.

'You're going to have to stop throwing yourself at me like this,' Paddy said, his face splitting into a grin as she righted herself once more, apologising profusely.

Bea stood for a moment, open-mouthed. 'Paddy,' she said, uselessly.

'Princess Beatrice,' Paddy said, taking a small bow.

Her legs felt weak and her head spun.

'You stayed in New York then?' Paddy said.

She nodded, momentarily unable to form words. Why was she so flustered?

'So, do you come here often?' Paddy's line broke the tension and she let out a bark of laughter.

'Does that line ever work?'

'Not for me, but I'm sure it must have done once,' he said, and Bea was reminded once more of his soft Irish lilt. She shivered, aware suddenly of his proximity, their bodies almost pressed together in the narrow corridor.

'I'm just...' She gestured over to where her friends were now pouring more champagne. Paddy glanced over and raised his eyebrows. 'Champers, eh?' he said.

'Yeah, it's – my friend bought it...' She felt the beat of her heart beneath her ribcage and the thump of the bassline rising through her feet. Paddy's body was inches from her and she could feel the puff of his breath on her face as he spoke.

'I'm here with a couple of friends too.' He glanced over his shoulder and the space between them opened up. Bea felt herself breathe again. 'Although God knows where they've gone.' He paused, then, 'Listen, I was just on the way to the bar, would you like a drink?'

Bea hesitated. Part of her was desperate to get away from this man who reminded her of a time in her life she'd spent the last year trying to forget. But there was also something about him, something drawing her to him. After all, one drink couldn't do any harm, could it?

She nodded, aware her voice probably wouldn't be heard above the roar of the music, which seemed to have been ramped up a notch. Before she knew what had happened, Paddy grabbed her hand and led her through the crowds of people towards a small bar at the back of the club, one she hadn't seen when she came in. It was quieter here, away from the speakers, and when they reached the bar where there was just a handful of people waiting, Paddy let go of her hand. She didn't dare look at him, but she could see his reflection in the mirror behind the bar and she allowed herself fleeting glances. He was still as handsome as she remembered.

They stood side by side, not speaking, until the barman came. 'A bottle of champagne please,' Paddy yelled. He turned to her. 'I hope that's okay?'

She nodded. She'd seen the prices in this place and hoped he wasn't expecting her to pay half.

Drinks paid for – by Paddy, to Bea's relief – Paddy grabbed the silver ice bucket in one hand and scooped the glasses into the other, then turned to look for somewhere to sit.

'Over there?' Bea said, spotting a couple of seats tucked away in a corner. Paddy nodded and they hurried over before someone else nabbed them.

'Okay, let's have a toast,' Paddy said, once they were settled and he was ripping the foil from the top of the bottle.

'What to?'

Paddy looked thoughtful for a minute. 'To fate, for bringing us together again?' He was smiling but she felt her belly flip-flop.

'How about we toast to Christmas for now?' she said, picking up her glass and holding it in the air.

'That seems fair,' Paddy said, chinking his glass against hers.

'So. Tell me about the last year.'

Bea took a long sip of her drink, trying to gather her thoughts. So much had happened in the last twelve months, and she'd spent most of the last few days – weeks, really – trying not to think too much about her life before. Did she really want to relive it all over again?

Placing her drink on the table, she leaned forward to make herself heard. 'I fell in love with New York,' she said, simply.

Paddy studied her for a moment, their eyes locked. 'Just New York?'

'I—' A loud cheer went up beside them and she stopped to let the noise die down. She felt the intensity of his gaze, his pupils wide, and she wondered whether he was more drunk than she'd realised. 'Just New York,' she said, eventually, and looked away on the pretence of watching the people nearby dancing.

A thought occurred to her then and she turned back to face him. He was still watching her. 'You never did tell me your real name.'

He looked surprised. 'No, and I'm not about to now either.'

'What? I can't keep calling you Paddy!'

He shook his head, a look of mischief on his face. 'Nope, absolutely not.'

'But why?'

'Same reason as always. You'll laugh, then you'll make an excuse to leave and I'll never see you again.'

'Don't be ridiculous. No name can possibly be that bad.'

He laughed. 'You may think that, but I've been burned before.' He looked at her, suddenly serious. 'And I don't want to risk messing this up a second time, before it's even had a chance to get started.'

Bea's insides were burning. Was he saying what she thought he was saying?

'I...' she started, but then stopped when Paddy's hand closed round hers. It felt like a jolt of electricity had passed through her.

'I've thought about you a lot in the last year,' he said, watching her intently. This time there was no trace of a joke in his voice. She didn't know what to say. The truth was she'd thought about him too, on and off. But there hadn't been much point thinking about him too much, because – well, she hadn't even known his name. But now he was here in front of her, she felt like she'd never really got him out of her mind at all.

'Have you?' she said, her voice too quiet to be heard. Their gazes were locked, their hands joined, and for the first time in years, Bea felt the stirrings of something deep in her soul.

'Hello, what's going on here then?' Mia's voice jolted them both out of the moment as surely as if she'd thrown a bucket of cold water over their heads. Bea snatched her hands away to find her friend looking from her to Paddy and back again, hands on hips. 'Who's this handsome young man?' Mia slurred.

'This is...' Bea hesitated, and when she looked at Paddy he was grinning goofily at her. 'This is Paddy,' she said, giving him a look. 'Sort of.'

Mia wobbled slightly then stuck out her hand. 'Hello sort of Paddy, s'very nice to meet you. I'm Mia. Bea's best friend.'

'Lovely to meet you,' Paddy said, shaking her hand.

'Why are you both sitting here all on your own?' Mia waved her hand vaguely in the direction of the VIP area. 'Come and join us. Bea's friends will all want to meet you.' She waggled her eyebrows at Bea and Bea rolled her eyes and stood up.

'Sorry, I don't think she's going to let us get away with staying here,' Bea said.

Paddy stood too. 'Absolutely. We don't want to go upsetting best friends,' he said, grabbing the ice bucket in one hand and taking Bea's hand in the other. Mia hooked her arm through his arm that held the champagne, then dragged them both across the dancefloor. When they arrived at the roped-off section, Mia threw her hands in the air and shouted, 'Everyone, look who I found!'

Bea's friends looked round and a loud cheer went up. Bea was aware that Paddy was still holding her hand, and as he placed the ice bucket on a nearby table she felt his fingers tighten round hers. She squeezed back.

For the next ten minutes she introduced Paddy to her friends who, she realised, had quickly become much more inebriated than her.

'He's gorgeous,' a voice said hotly in her ear while Paddy was ensconced in a conversation with Ashton and Maggie, and she turned to find Lori with her mouth pressed against her cheek. 'And that *accent*. Where did you find him?'

Bea smiled. 'We met last year on the plane,' she said.

Lori's eyes widened like a little girl who had just been given the keys to her mum's dressing-up box. 'You've known him all this time and kept it a secret?'

Bea shook her head, laughing. 'No, we haven't seen each other since then. I just bumped into him over there.'

Lori's gaze slid over to where Paddy was standing, a lopsided smile on her face. 'Well whaddya know,' she said. She tapped Bea's nose with her finger. 'Someone's a lucky girl, eh?'

Before Bea could protest about there being nothing going on between her and Paddy, Lori had moved away to top up her glass, and Bea took the opportunity to stop for a minute and take everything in.

Of course Lori was right, Paddy *was* gorgeous. Last year she'd only noticed it in passing because, let's face it, she'd been in too much of a state to notice anything. But now she could appreciate the dark hair – longer now, than before – that fell across his face, the dimple that appeared when he smiled, his sharp jawbone.

But it was more than his good looks making her feel intoxicated. The words he had said just before Mia had made an appearance were what she couldn't get out of her mind. *I've thought about you a lot in the last year.*

Had he really? And if so, what did that mean?

She didn't have time to dwell on it though, because Mia's arm was round her shoulder and she was being dragged back onto the dancefloor to the opening bars of 'Murder on the Dancefloor' – hers and Mia's latest favourite song – and all she could see was Paddy, watching her from the sidelines, a smile on his face.

Later, when midnight had come and gone and night had slid into early morning, and Bea was feeling hot and sweaty and drunk, her feet screaming in pain, she realised she hadn't seen Paddy for a while. She squinted across the sea of people on the dancefloor, searching for his dark head. Then she spotted him, standing to one side with a group of men and women. One of the women had her arm curled around his waist, and she was laughing at something Paddy had said. He didn't seem to be pushing her away either and oh *God*, was she jealous? She had no right to be of course. And yet she felt the familiar lurch of something in her belly.

She turned away just as Maggie stumbled up to her.

'Wanna go home?'

Her words were slurred and Bea smiled. She rarely saw Maggie lose control, but when she did it was in a spectacular fashion. She glanced towards where Paddy was still talking, and nodded.

'Yeah, I do.'

'Is your man coming?'

'My man?'

'Your sexy Irish man' – she nodded her head – 'over there.' Her eyes widened. 'Oh God, you have to go and rescue him. Get him away from that woman!'

'I'm not rescuing anyone,' Bea said, but before she could stop her Maggie was striding across the dancefloor, the crowd parting as she weaved her unsteady way through. Bea watched in horror as Maggie approached the group and tapped Paddy on the shoulder. He whipped round, looking surprised. When the woman beside him saw Maggie, she pulled Paddy closer, and Bea let out a groan.

'We going home?' Ashton's voice was loud in Bea's ear and she jumped.

'Yeah.' She tipped the dregs of her drink down her throat, and turned away from Maggie and Paddy, unable to watch any longer.

'Lesss go then.' Ashton hooked his arm through Bea's, beckoned to Lori, Mia and Nancy, and the five of them began marching towards the exit.

'Coats,' Ashton said, tugging her towards the cloakroom. Bea's heart sank when she saw the queue. She just wanted to get out of there, get home and put this evening behind her.

'Where's Maggie?'

'I'm here,' a voice said, and Bea turned to give her friend a piece of her mind – but stopped dead. Because Paddy was beside her.

'Bea, I'm so sorry about that,' he said, stepping towards her.

'S'fine.' She was more drunk than she'd realised. She turned back to face the front, hoping he'd just go.

'Bea.' His voice was right by her ear and she could feel his breath on her skin. She shivered but didn't turn round. 'Bea!'

Relenting, she turned her head slightly and he pressed his fingertips against her chin and slowly pulled her face towards his. They were so close now there was barely an inch between them. Bea felt her breath catch in her throat. 'I was just saying goodbye to my friends. I couldn't leave without telling them, they'd worry.' Paddy's voice was low.

'It's fine,' Bea repeated, enunciating as clearly as she could. Her heart thumped low against her ribcage.

The lights were brighter out here and she noticed for the first time how blue Paddy's eyes were. Like cornflowers.

'What?' Paddy looked confused and Bea realised to her horror that she must have said that out loud. Oh God she was drunk. She shook her head, the moment broken.

'Nothing.'

Her coat was shoved roughly into her hands, and Bea noticed her friends all waiting for her by the exit over Paddy's shoulder.

'I'd better—'

'Can I come?'

Bea stopped. 'Oh, I...' She glanced round. She wanted nothing more than for Paddy to come home with her. She didn't want to walk away from him and risk never bumping into him again. And yet...

'Come on you two lovebirds, let's go!' Mia yelled, and Bea wanted the ground to swallow her up.

'Your flatmate – Maggie is it?' – Bea nodded – 'asked me if I wanted to come back and have some drinks with you all.' He shrugged. 'So I wondered if it would be all right?'

Bea gave a small nod, hardly daring to speak. 'Yes, course,' she squeaked.

Without saying another word, Paddy took her hand and turned

to face her friends. 'We're coming!' he said, and Mia cheered. 'At bloody last.'

Outside, a few flakes of snow had started to fall and Bea shivered, even her winter coat no match for the bitter New York wind. She was already sobering up, and as she climbed into a cab she felt self-conscious. What was she doing, bringing a strange man home with her? She didn't behave like this.

As Paddy settled into the seat beside her, Mia on the other side, her leg felt like it was on fire where his thigh pressed into hers. He threaded his fingers through hers and she couldn't focus on anything else. The rest of the world seemed to recede – Mia, chattering away about the night, the lights of Manhattan flashing by outside the cab window. She felt like she was floating above her own body.

Then they were pulling up outside her and Maggie's apartment, and clattering up the stairs and tumbling through the door, and all she could think about was how relieved she was to be inside in the warm. Mia headed to the stereo and started the music, and Bea shushed her. 'The neighbours already want to kill us,' she said, turning it right down.

As Mia danced around her own little dancefloor in the middle of the room, arms thrown in the air, Bea felt suddenly shy. Paddy was watching her, and she didn't know where to look. She was saved from having to think of something to say by the sound of singing coming up the stairs, and seconds later the front door flew open again and Ashton, Maggie, Lori and Nancy came crashing into the apartment.

'Oh God, I'm going to vomit,' Lori said, racing straight to the bathroom while Maggie headed to the tiny kitchen. 'I'm making more drinks,' she announced, and Nancy went to help her as Ashton threw himself onto the sofa.

'So, this is my bed. Mia's in there with Bea,' he said, turning to

Paddy. 'So where are you sleeping tonight?' He waggled his eyebrows and Bea wanted to chuck something at him.

From the corner of her eye she saw Paddy looking at her, a question on his face, but before she could get any words out, Nancy said, 'Mia's staying at mine, aren't you Mia?'

'Are you?' Bea said, turning to her best friend in surprise.

'Oh yes, we arranged it in the taxi when we realised your bed might not be... er, free tonight.' She gave a grin and Bea felt her whole body burning with embarrassment.

'But what about tomorrow? Your flight?' she said, weakly.

'I'll take my stuff with me later.' She waved her arm around. 'Don't worry about me. I don't want to be the one to stand in the way of love.'

Bea didn't know where to look, but when she did finally glance at Paddy she saw him grinning at her and she couldn't help grinning back. This was completely absurd, but thankfully he didn't look mortified at the thought of staying here. With her.

Oh God. He was staying with her.

She'd had a couple of dates since she'd arrived in New York, but none of them had gone any further than a snog and a fumble in the back of a taxi. She hadn't had a man in her bed since she'd left Dom – and they had been together for five years, since she was twenty-one. She'd never done anything like this before.

But fuck it, this was the new Bea.

She sidled over to Paddy and slid her arm round his waist. They hadn't even kissed yet and it was all she could think about as her friends danced around them, laughing and drinking and getting more and more drunk.

Finally, one by one, they began to drift off. First Ash fell asleep on the sofa, fully dressed. Then Nancy announced she should be going home. As Lori and now Mia were staying with her, they waited while Mia shoved her belongings haphazardly into her case.

'Got your passport?' Maggie said, as Mia trundled her case towards the front door.

'Yeah, yeah, got everything,' Mia said. 'Bye darling Bea.' She pulled her into a hug. 'Have fun,' she whispered and her breath was hot against Bea's ear.

And then they were gone. By the time Bea came back into the room, Maggie had gone to bed too, leaving Bea and Paddy alone – if you didn't count Ashton, passed out on the sofa – for the first time.

'So,' Paddy said, taking a step towards her.

Bea didn't speak. She wasn't sure whether she could. Paddy took another step closer, and then another and then he was right in front of her, their bodies barely touching. She tipped her head back so she could look at him properly and was struck once more by the intensity of his gaze. His fingers brushed against hers and she gripped them. The air seemed to have been sucked from the room and she could barely breathe... and then Paddy leaned towards her, and their lips touched, and Bea felt as though she'd been struck by lightning. Every nerve ending sizzled, and she pressed herself against him, wanting to get closer, to feel him. His hands were in her hair now, and her arms slipped round his shoulders, sinking into him. And then he pulled away.

'Shall we go to your room?' His voice was low.

Bea had never slept with anyone this quickly before.

And yet she knew with every fibre of her being that it was what she wanted more than anything else in the world. She gave a tiny nod, then followed Paddy into her room, a tangle of limbs by the time they hit the bed...

* * *

Bea lay, eyes wide open, staring at the ceiling. She'd been awake for what felt like hours, going over the events of the previous evening in her head. The room was cold and she tugged the covers higher up over her shoulders. Beside her, Paddy stirred.

She turned to face him, and his eyes peeled open. As he saw her, his lips curled into a smile.

'Hello you.' His voice was rough, smoky.

'Hi.'

Despite how close they'd been last night she felt shy now, aware of her nakedness beneath the blankets.

'You're a sight for sore eyes.'

She grimaced. 'I'm sure I'm not.'

'Well, if you're into wild hair and Alice Cooper make-up, then you definitely are.'

Despite herself, she laughed. 'You don't look too hot yourself.' It was a lie. He looked hotter than ever but she wasn't about to let him know that. He cocked an eyebrow at her then hauled himself up onto his elbow so he was hovering above her, looking down. She held her breath, simultaneously waiting to see what he was going to do, and hoping he couldn't smell her breath. Then he leaned down and planted a gentle kiss on her lips and her insides were on fire again. She melted into the kiss; nothing else mattered but this man, this—

She pulled away abruptly.

'What—' Paddy started.

'You're in my bed and you still haven't told me your real name,' she said, before he could say any more.

Paddy's eyes widened and his face split into a huge grin.

'Oh my God, I haven't, have I?' He rubbed his face with his hands. She could feel the warmth from his body and tried to stay focused. She moved away, and he looked at her with puppy dog eyes. 'What if I tell you, and you throw me out?'

She shrugged. 'Given where we are I think you've left it a bit late to be worrying about that.'

He groaned, and buried his face in her belly, then looked up again. 'Right, okay. But you've got to promise not to laugh.'

'I promise.'

'Brace yourself.'

She nodded.

'It's Alvin.'

She stared at him for so long he began to squirm. 'Well, aren't you going to say anything?' It was the first time she'd seen him look unsure of himself.

'Oh my God,' she whispered. 'It doesn't suit you at all!'

'I know!' He moved closer again, his lips hovering near hers. 'As you can imagine it went down really well in rural Ireland in the eighties.'

She grinned. 'Alvin what?'

He closed his eyes as though in pain and said, 'Flynn.'

'Alvin Flynn.' She rolled the name over on her tongue. 'Is it really?'

'Yup. So now can you see why I don't tell anyone my name when I first meet them?'

'I think I can.'

'So are you going to ask me to leave?' He grazed her lip with his. 'Or can I stay?' He ran his tongue over her mouth at the same time as his fingertips ran up her side, and she arched her back in pleasure.

'You can stay.' She kissed him deeply. When they finally pulled away he sat up and pushed the blanket away. 'Anyway, my middle name is James, and everyone just calls me AJ.'

'So why didn't you just tell me that in the first place?'

He shrugged. 'Everyone always asks what it stands for, and then it starts all over again.' He grinned and stood up, and she took a moment to savour his naked body, letting her eyes run over his toned torso, down across the tattoos that covered his arms and shoulders, and then across at—

'I'm just nipping to the loo, don't miss me too much.' She tore her eyes away as he wrapped her dressing gown around himself, her face burning. Paddy – *AJ* – closed the bedroom door and she rolled onto her back with a groan.

Oh God. This was bad.

She liked this man.

She wasn't looking for a man.

But she *really* liked him.

Her phone beeped with a message. She stretched out to reach for it and smiled. It was a text from Mia.

> Off to catch my flight. Hope last night went well.
> RING ME WHEN HE'S GONE – I WANT ALL THE
> GOSSIP! M x

She was about to put the phone down when she saw there was a missed call from her sister Alice. Her stomach dropped. She'd just decided to ignore her for now when it started vibrating in her hand and she nearly dropped it on her face.

'Shit,' she said, pulling herself up to sitting. The change of position revealed how full her bladder was, but AJ was in the apartment's only bathroom so she'd have to wait. She might as well get this over and done with.

'Hi!' she said, trying to sound pleased to hear from her big sister.

'Oh, you are alive then?' Bea rolled her eyes but was determined not to let Alice's surliness puncture her happiness.

'Alive and very well thanks, big sis. How are you?'

She heard an intake of breath and braced herself.

'I'm okay. It's Mum I'm worried about.'

Bea's heart stopped momentarily. 'Mum? Has something happened?'

'Nothing new, no,' Alice said, and Bea took a couple of deep breaths and let her panic subside. 'But she's beside herself about you being away for a second Christmas in a row.'

Bea's heart sank. She'd already had this conversation endless times with both Alice and her mum. Funny how the men of the family – her dad, her two brothers Charlie and Rob – didn't seem to give two hoots what she did, nor did they get the same shit for spending Christmas however and wherever they chose. Normally she would have said something to that effect. But today she refused to take the bait.

'I know, and I'm sorry,' she said, which seemed to take the wind out of Alice's sails. 'I'd love to be there with you all, but it's just so expensive to get home at this time of the year.'

Alice made a sort of harrumphing sound and Bea smiled to herself. It was rare that her sister didn't know how to respond, and she savoured having surprised her. She might have known it wouldn't last.

'I suppose you know she's taken it upon herself to invite Dom round for Christmas dinner again, don't you?'

Bea froze. 'Dom? Why?'

Alice let out a loud sigh which, Bea assumed, was meant to indicate that she should know this, and said, '*Because*, Bea, he's still desperately unhappy and Mum's worried about him.'

Bea didn't reply. What could she say? Her mum had mentioned Dom a few times recently but she'd had no idea she still had regular contact with him after Bea had asked her not to.

'It's not my fault he can't move on,' Bea muttered, hating herself for sounding so belligerent. Why did this always happen when she spoke to Alice?

'Well, I think he would beg to differ,' she said sniffily.

Bea didn't dignify that with a response, so Alice plunged on. 'You know full well the problems Dom has had over the years with his depression.' She said 'depression' in a half-whisper, as though to say it out loud would make it contagious. 'And when Mum popped round to see him the other day' *(her mum had been round there?!)* 'he hadn't shaved for a few days and the house stank. He hadn't been to work for a week.'

Bea didn't know what to say. She knew she wasn't faultless. She'd known that by upping and leaving him there was a high chance of triggering another bout of depression. But she also knew that, despite what everyone else seemed to think, this wasn't her fault, and that staying with someone just so they didn't get ill was no reason at all to stay.

None of this seemed the right thing to say right now though. Instead, Bea just said: 'Tell Mum I'll ring her later.' Then she hung up before Alice could say anything further and switched her phone to silent.

She was still thinking about Dom, and how bad he must be for Mum to have taken him under her wing, when her bedroom door opened. She looked up to find Maggie grinning at her from the doorway.

'I knew the coast was clear because he asked me if it was okay to have a quick shower so he's still in the bathroom,' she hissed, stepping across the piles of last night's clothing littering the floor and perching on the end of the bed. 'So, what's the goss?'

'I don't know,' Bea whispered back, and wondered why they were whispering if AJ was in the bathroom.

'You're a dark horse,' Maggie said. She glanced over her shoulder. 'Is he... you know. Staying?'

'Staying?'

'For the next few days? For Christmas?'

'Christmas? God, no, I don't think—' She stopped as the

bedroom door opened and AJ walked back in again, topless, a towel wrapped round his waist, her dressing gown slung over his arm. He stopped in the doorway as Maggie sprang up from the bed.

'Sorry, I was just...' She grinned. 'Well, I was obviously just grilling Bea about you, but let's pretend I'm not here.' And with that she slipped out of the door and closed it firmly behind her. AJ grinned.

'Talking about me?' he said, sitting down in the space Maggie had just vacated. Bea couldn't help noticing the droplets of water glistening on his chest and she desperately wanted to lean over and lick them off.

'Bea?'

She snapped her head up. 'Sorry, what?'

'I said, I hope you told her nice things.' He stopped and frowned. 'Are you all right? You look...' He shrugged. 'Perturbed.'

'I'm fine. Just, my sister rang and she's...' She trailed off.

'Say no more,' he said, holding up his hands. 'I know families, and they're nothing but trouble, especially at Christmas. Getting shit for not being there to carve the turkey?'

'Something like that.'

AJ pulled himself up on the bed so his face was right by hers. He inched closer so his lips were touching her cheek, and ran them slowly, slowly down to her neck, onto her shoulder and she shivered. He took her breast in his mouth and tipped her slowly back, and as he continued down she forgot the conversation with Alice, her worries about Dom, she forgot everything apart from the feeling of his mouth on her skin...

* * *

Bea ran her fingers down AJ's arms, tracing the shape of a snake down his bicep. 'Tell me about these tattoos,' she said.

He peered down at his arm which was slung across Bea's waist.

'What do you want to know?'

'How long you've had them. What do they mean? Anything.'

'Well this one here,' he said, outlining a jagged line that snaked from the inner crease of his elbow down his forearm, 'represents New York.' He ran his fingers along it. 'See, it's the New York skyline.' He moved his finger up. 'This here is a Celtic design which, obviously, is about my roots.'

Bea pointed at a design that looked like the intertwined branches of a tree. 'And this one? A past girlfriend?'

AJ frowned as though he was trying to remember, then shrugged. 'No. I just liked the look of that one.' He grinned. 'Me mam hates them of course. Says it's a sin to "mutilate the body God gave you". Or something like that.'

'Well I love them.' Bea traced her finger over his arm again.

'I'm glad.'

'Tell me about your parents.' She glanced up at him.

'You really want to know?'

'Why not?'

He shrugged. 'There's not much to tell. Mam and dad, five siblings. Idyllic if hectic childhood in rural Ireland and misspent youth smoking weed and drinking too much, then escaped as soon as I could. It was so smothering and I needed something more exciting.' He ran his fingers round her belly button and she shivered.

'Is that why you ended up living here?' His finger stopped tracing circles on her skin.

'Yeah, I guess so.' His voice sounded suddenly stiff, forced. She was desperate to pump him for information but it was clear he didn't want to talk about it. It didn't matter, there was plenty of time. Hopefully.

'What about you?' he said. 'You told me your ex wasn't horrible when I saw you on the plane, but you didn't say what had actually made you run away.'

Now it was her turn to freeze. In the year since she'd arrived in New York, she'd avoided talking about this at all. She'd managed not to think about it most of the time.

'I just needed excitement too,' she said.

He looked down at her, eyebrows raised. 'I guess we're both allowed our secrets, eh?'

She didn't reply, but looked out of the small window where she could see the windows of the apartment block opposite and a tiny slice of sky. It was gun metal grey and looked like it was about to snow again. 'I guess so.'

A tinny ringing sound interrupted her thoughts. AJ pushed the covers back and rolled out of bed, picked up his jeans and pulled his phone out of the pocket. He glanced at it and his shoulders tensed.

'Sorry, I just need to take this,' he said, stepping into his jeans and slipping out of the bedroom. Bea lay there, wondering what had just happened to sour the atmosphere so quickly. She pulled herself up to sitting and tugged the bedspread up. It was chilly in here now, the clunky radiator too temperamental to heat the room properly. She climbed out of bed and pulled on a pair of trousers hanging over the back of a chair. She picked up her clothes that had been discarded last night and threw them in the laundry basket in the corner. AJ still wasn't back, so she wandered over to the window. The rooftops were still clinging onto the snow that had fallen overnight, but otherwise the only trace that remained were the piles of grey sludge lining the kerbs.

Behind her the door opened and she turned to find AJ looking apologetic.

'Sorry. My friends I'm spending Christmas with, just checking I'm still coming.' He bent down and picked his T-shirt from the floor and tugged it on. Bea averted her gaze. 'I'd better get going, I've got to get a few things before I get to theirs.'

'Course,' Bea said, trying to hide the disappointment in her voice. Of course he had somewhere to be; it was Christmas Eve.

He pulled his jumper over his head, tugged on his socks, and stuffed his phone in his back pocket, looking round, confused.

'Your coat's in the lounge,' Bea said.

'Ah right. Thanks.'

They both stood for a moment, awkward now after the intimacy of earlier.

'Right, well. It was – well, it was amazing,' AJ said. He closed the gap between them and pressed his lips against her cheek. His fingers grazed hers, and he held them there and met her eyes with his electric blue gaze.

'Can I ring you, after Christmas? I'd love to see you again.'

'Of course.'

'Great.' He planted a gentle, lingering kiss on her lips. 'Merry Christmas, Princess Beatrice.'

Then he was gone.

4

STAY

23 December 2003

Bea watched the minute hand of the clock tick... tick... tick, and it felt like time had almost stood still. Four more hours and she would be out of here, having drinks with her friends and letting her hair down. Three more hours and she'd be out of here. Two more hours...

It wasn't Christmas she was looking forward to the most. It was getting out of this office and not having to look at her boss Jonathon's smug face for the next ten days.

'Can you just make sure you finish that press release before you leave this evening?' he said, standing slightly too close behind her. She flinched and moved away so she could no longer feel his thigh pressing into her arm, and nodded without looking up.

'Nearly done,' she said, pretending to study her screen intently in the hope he'd leave her alone. It worked, eventually, and as she heard his footsteps retreating she let out a long exhale, feeling her shoulders relax.

'He's such a twat.' Bea looked up, startled. Her colleague Robin was applying bright red lip gloss in a compact mirror cupped in her hand. She flicked her gazed towards Bea so she knew she'd been talking to her.

'Yeah, he is,' Bea agreed.

Robin clicked the lip gloss shut and leaned closer. 'You shouldn't let him bully you like that. Tell him to fuck off; he doesn't need that press release before Christmas.'

Bea felt a prickle of tears behind her eyes and she blinked rapidly and forced a smile. 'I know. It's a power trip,' she said.

'Exactly,' Robin said.

Bea looked away before Robin noticed her tears. It wasn't Robin's fault, she didn't know the history between Bea and this company, or between Bea and Jonathon – she'd only started here six months ago. How was she to know that this was the second time Bea had worked here, and that she'd had to come crawling back after walking out a few weeks before?

Bea cringed when she thought back to the conversation between her and Dom about it. It had been his idea for her to ask for her old job back rather than going through the whole job-hunting process again.

'Jonathon won't have had time to replace you yet,' he'd said. 'And you need somewhere to work. So it suits both of you.'

It had seemed so reasonable when he said it, and she hadn't been able to conjure up a counter-argument that made sense.

In the end she'd emailed Jonathon to keep Dom happy, certain – and hopeful – he'd tell her where to stick it.

But instead he'd said it was hers if she wanted it. *Although given the circumstances, your job title will be editorial assistant, promotion pending,* he'd written. A searing rage had ripped through her at the obvious demotion and she'd wanted nothing more than to punch him in his smug face. Instead, desperate to make things up to Dom, she'd accepted it.

She'd regretted it from the moment she pressed send.

'I'm going to look for a new job next year anyway,' she whispered to Robin, who looked over, her immaculately plucked eyebrows raised.

'Can I come with you?'

Bea smiled. 'Yeah, let's both get out of here.'

Robin held her hand up above the divide and Bea high fived her.

An hour later the press release was finished, emailed to Jonathon, and Bea and Robin were pulling their coats on, ready to leave.

'Doing anything exciting over Christmas?' Robin said.

'I'm at my parents' house with my boyfriend,' Bea said. 'Same as every year.'

'Ah that sounds lovely.'

'It's great, but chaotic. My sister, her husband and kids and my brothers and their families all descend too, so it's never quiet.'

'It sounds like bliss to me. I've got a choice between spending the day with my parents in the Cotswolds but they both hate Christmas and don't particularly like each other, or spending it on my own.' She grimaced. 'Actually now I've said it out loud I don't know why I'm even considering going anywhere.'

'I wish I could invite you to come to mine, but we're already almost out in the street. Although I don't suppose one more would matter.'

Robin waved her hand at Bea. 'It's fine. I'm just going to watch crap telly and eat Dairy Milk until I feel sick. What's not to love about that?'

They walked out of the office. Most people had already left, but Bea still didn't relax until the door had closed behind her in case Jonathon decided to call her back for 'one last job'. She shuddered, then pulled her coat tightly round herself at the icy blast of London air.

As Robin and Bea went their separate ways, Bea thought about Robin all alone on Christmas Day, and realised how lucky she was. Sure, she might have a boss she hated and a job she tolerated, and she might not be living the New York dream, but she was lucky. She had everyone she loved right here, in one place. And how many people could say that?

* * *

The pub was packed as Bea walked in, the air steamy with breath and sweat, a low bassline losing its battle with the roar of voices. Bea's feet were already killing her in her too-high heels, and she wished she'd listened to Dom when he'd suggested she wear something more comfortable.

'If you can't wear ridiculous heels at Christmas, when can you?' she'd said, and tried to ignore the disapproving purse of his lips. She would see hell freeze over before she admitted he'd been right.

She felt a pang as she thought about Dom. She wished he'd felt up to coming, because she always felt guilty coming out on her own. But he'd insisted, telling her he just needed to rest to feel better for Christmas Day, and that she'd have a nicer time without him.

She wound her way towards the back of the pub where she knew Michael and Harry had reserved a table. Harry noticed her first, and threw his hands in the air, a bottle of champagne in one hand, a half-empty glass in the other.

'You're here!' he said, walking towards her and wrapping her in a tight embrace. 'Thank God we reserved, it's bloody carnage in here.' He smelt divine, of expensive aftershave and washing powder.

Everyone else was already here, and she hugged Michael, Ashton and Mia, and a couple of Ashton's female colleagues he'd brought with him.

'Thinks he's bloody Peter Stringfellow,' Mia said, rolling her eyes.

'Do I detect a hint of jealousy?' Bea said.

'Me? Jealous of him?' Mia screeched. 'Are you fucking *kidding* me? They're welcome to him.' She crossed her eyes and stuck her tongue out the side of her mouth. But Bea wasn't convinced. Mia and Ashton were better as friends than they'd ever been when they were going out, but that didn't mean Mia wanted him to be with anyone else.

'So, what are we drinking?' Bea said.

'Anything wet,' Mia said.

'Helpful,' she said, laughing. 'I'll get some more fizz.' It took Bea ages to elbow her way through the throngs of people, some in party gear, the rest still in their office clothes; most of them already half-cut. It was so close to Christmas the atmosphere was full-on party and by the time Bea got back to the table she felt like she'd gone three rounds with Mike Tyson. She filled everyone's glasses and knocked hers back.

'Dom not coming?' Michael said.

Bea shook her head.

'Oh love. I'm sorry.'

'Thanks. Me too.' Bea was eager to change the subject because she didn't want to cry and ruin everyone's night. Tonight, she needed fun. And after the last few months, she felt she deserved it.

Looking back, Dom's decline had started at the end of the summer, but it had taken Bea a few weeks to realise what was happening. She always assumed, having been through 'episodes' with Dom before, that she'd recognise one when it started. But she never seemed to, and by the time she realised the dark cloud had descended again it was too late to stop it. All she could do – all anyone could do – was to be there, and wait for it to lift.

By the end of September, Dom was signed off work. He spent his days in bed, sleeping, or blindly watching reruns of *The Sopranos* and *Frasier*, or, on really bad days, ringing Bea at work and begging her to come home. In the end, she'd been forced to ask her mum for help, and Ange had been round for a couple of hours every day to check up on him.

'I don't need a babysitter, Bea,' Dom said. 'I'm fine on my own.'

'I beg to differ,' Bea replied, and, clearly defeated, Dom didn't put up any further argument.

Now, things were finally getting better. The gentle, kind and funny Dom that Bea loved was beginning to re-emerge. He'd even gone back to work last month, just a couple of days a week at first, building up until he was almost full-time again by the end of last week. Bea was hopeful and relieved that was the end of this episode, that she'd have Dom back completely for Christmas – and tonight was supposed to have been their first night out together for months.

But when Bea arrived home from work, Dom was on the sofa, wrapped in his duvet, staring at the news on TV.

'I'm so sorry Bea, I just don't think I can do it tonight.' He said it as soon as she walked into the room, still in the act of taking her coat off. She perched beside him.

'Oh love. Are you sure? It might perk you up a bit.'

Dom shook his head miserably. 'I'm not the best company.'

She looked at him, studied his face. 'Has something happened? I thought you were feeling better.'

'I was. I am.' He looked at her, his eyes full of sorrow. 'Please don't worry love, this isn't a relapse. I think it's just taking some time to adjust, you know, to being at work again.' He pulled his hand out from beneath the duvet and placed it on Bea's arm. 'I'll be fine tomorrow after a good sleep.'

'Are you sure?'

'I promise.'

Bea pulled her legs up and huddled into him. 'I'll stay with you then.'

'No!' The word came out of Dom like a cannonball.

'But I can't leave you on your own. I'll stay here, we can watch *Die Hard* together, argue about whether it's a Christmas film or not.'

'It's not.' He gave a small smile. 'But seriously, please go. I feel bad enough anyway, I know how much you've been looking forward to tonight. Please go and have fun with your friends. And tell them I'm sorry.'

She paused for a moment, uncertain. If she went, she'd spend the evening worrying about Dom. If she stayed, she'd feel resentful that she'd missed out on seeing her friends. Again.

She stood. 'Okay, I'll go. But I'll be home early.'

'No, just go and have fun. Please.'

He'd been asleep by the time she left so she'd planted a gentle kiss on his forehead and crept out. Now, she was determined to make the most of it.

'Right you lot, drink up. Just for tonight I need to forget about Dom's mental health, about my shitty job and my shittier boss and just get pissed. Who's with me?' she said, proffering the bottle of prosecco and topping everyone's glasses up whether they needed it or not. Fizzy wine ran down her arm and dripped onto the floor.

'Always darling,' Michael said, slipping his arm round her shoulder. 'Just make sure you take it easy though, right?'

'I can't promise anything,' she said.

A couple of hours later they were all outrageously drunk, and when Ashton suggested karaoke, a cheer went up.

'Oh God,' Harry groaned. 'The indignity of it.'

'Ah come on H, it'll be fun,' Ashton said, slinging his arm around Harry's shoulders. Harry peered at him disbelievingly. 'Anyway, nobody can have a worse singing voice than Bea.'

'Hey!'

Ashton grinned at Bea, his eyes shining, and shrugged. 'Sorry Bea, but can I help it if you sound like a cat being strangled when you sing Madonna?'

Bea looked for the nearest thing to hand and, unable to find anything better, picked up a cardboard beer mat and chucked it at him. Aggrieved, Ashton covered the sticky floor between them, scooped her up and carried her out of the pub over his shoulder, with Bea kicking and screaming and only half-laughing at the same time. By the time he deposited her on the pavement with a thump, everyone else had joined them, pulling on coats and jumping from foot to foot in an effort to stay warm.

'Right, follow me,' Ashton said, marching along Wardour Street, holding his arm in the air like a school teacher herding a Year 4 class. The streets of Soho were empty of the usual lingerers and crowds that hung around drinking during the balmy evenings of summer. Now, in the depths of winter, they navigated the narrow pavements quickly and easily, the only people they needed to dodge were those hurrying, heads down against the cold, towards their next indoor destination.

Bea felt her breath labour in her chest, as though an icy hand had reached down and squeezed her windpipe. When Michael took hold of her arm, she leaned into him gratefully, trying to absorb some of the warmth from his body. She rested her cheek on his shoulder, her face bouncing up and down rhythmically as they walked.

'You all right my Bea?' he said. His voice was soft. She nodded, the bone of his shoulder grinding against her cheekbone.

'Do you ever wonder what you'd be doing right now if you'd gone to New York?'

She tried not to think about New York as a rule, and was surprised anyone else did. She lifted her head and looked at him, quizzically. He turned to meet her gaze, and something she saw in his eyes made her tell the truth.

'Sometimes, yeah.'

He nodded and faced the front again. 'For what it's worth I think you should have gone.'

'Do you?' Nobody had ever really said much about Bea's 'return'. Probably, she supposed at the time, because it wasn't so much as a return as simply a 'not going'. And so, while leaving her life behind and going to the airport to board a flight to New York had been a major incident in her life, in everyone else's – with the exception of Dom's of course – it had barely created a ripple. She'd got up one morning, and by that afternoon, she was back home.

She realised now, though, that Michael at least had understood how much it had meant to her. And what it had cost her to come home.

'I try not to think about it too often,' she said, but the moment the words were out of her mouth she knew they were a lie. She thought about it most days, comparing what she was doing right now with what her life might have been had she made a different decision that day. When she was at work, hating her job, she wondered. When she was with her parents, she wondered. Even when she was with Dom... sometimes she wondered.

But that was all it was. Because this was her life, and she was happy. And as Michael's grip tightened on her arm, she realised once more how lucky she was. How lucky she'd always been, to have such amazing people in her life. She wouldn't swap it for the world.

5

GO

December 2004

'Fuck!' Bea snatched her hand away from the searing hot baking tray, which clattered across the floor, scattering uncooked potatoes in its wake. She ran to the sink and held her hand under the cold tap.

As the pain eased, arms slipped around her waist and lips pressed against her neck, and she turned her head for a kiss.

'You okay?'

She nodded, holding her scorched fingers up, and he pressed his lips against them then spun her round and kissed her deeply. When he pulled away he searched her face.

'Happy?'

'Happy,' she murmured.

He took a step back to survey the damage. 'Reckon we can save them?'

'We might be able to save the potatoes, but I think it's too late for my shredded nerves.' Her voice wobbled and AJ looked at her again, this time with concern on his face.

'You know they're not judging you on your ability to cook pota-toes, don't you?'

She shrugged, and sniffed. 'No, I know. But – I just want them to see that I'm happy. That they were wrong, that I didn't make a mistake, coming here.'

He reached for her hand and cupped his fingers round it. 'Your parents are just excited about seeing you, they don't care about bloody potatoes. Come on, they're not Irish.' A smile flickered across her lips as AJ continued. 'And anyway, you know your mum loves me, even though she really didn't want to.'

'That's true.' She smiled.

AJ hesitated a moment longer, then swiped his keys from the counter. 'Right, if I don't want to be in your mother's bad books, I'd better get going. They'll be landing in about' – he checked his watch – 'fifteen minutes. The traffic will be horrific at this time of day.' He kissed her knuckles. 'Are you sure you're okay?'

She nodded. 'I'm grand. Get out of here and go and get my parents.'

As soon as the door to the apartment slammed shut, Bea dropped to her knees and began to gather up the spilt potatoes. She was cross with herself. She was spending Christmas with her parents for the first time in three years and rather than looking forward to it she'd got herself in a complete tizz.

Mind you, it was hardly a surprise, given everything that had happened this year.

After AJ had left her apartment last Christmas, she'd felt sure she was never going to see him again. So she'd been surprised and delighted when he'd texted her just after Christmas and asked if she wanted to go ice skating.

They'd spent a magical day together. Then another day, and another until, by the middle of January, Bea was completely and utterly smitten. She felt certain AJ felt the same. At least, she'd hoped he did. They certainly spent enough time together, hanging out with Maggie at their apartment, or going out for dinner, or drinks.

There was just one thing bothering Bea.

'As much as I love you being here, are you ever going to invite me to your place?' she asked one evening as they watched TV together. AJ didn't reply immediately, and she peered up at him quizzically.

'AJ? Have I said something wrong?'

'What? No, course not. Sorry.' He rubbed his hand over his face and whatever unreadable expression she'd seen there before vanished.

'Right. So...?'

He sat up a little, pushed her hair back from her face and pecked her on the nose. 'Of course you can come to mine. Sorry, I didn't even think.'

A couple of weeks later, she finally did stay at AJ's place. It was a gorgeous old brownstone building in the West Village, and as Bea climbed the steps up to the front door she felt a shiver of excitement. From the outside it looked just like the apartment where Carrie lived in *Sex and the City*, and even after more than a year here she still got excited about things like that.

Inside, AJ's apartment was stunning – it stretched across the entire top floor of the building, with floor-to-ceiling picture windows and stunning views across the city.

'This place is amazing,' she said, as she walked round, trying not to let her mouth drop open. She'd had no idea AJ was this wealthy.

'Thanks,' he said, slipping his arms around her waist and kissing her.

From then on they split their time between Bea's tiny bedroom in her just-as-tiny apartment and AJ's palatial place with its four-poster bed and roll-top bath. And although Bea felt as though she was getting to know AJ more and more as the weeks passed, there was still something mysterious about him. Something she couldn't quite put her finger on.

She never met any of his friends.

Sometimes he disappeared to take a phone call.

Other times whole weekends would pass when he seemed to disappear off the face of the earth and return on a Monday morning with no explanation. Not that he had any obligation to tell her what he was doing every second of his life, but it weighed on Bea's mind all the same.

Because the truth was, Bea was completely and utterly besotted with this man. Sure, she'd loved Dom. But this truly felt like something else, like another level. As though her mind had been taken over by him.

When she wasn't with AJ, she thought about him, and when she *was* with him she felt a constant need to be touching him, or to have him looking at her with those piercing blue eyes. If he didn't reply to a text immediately she imagined the worst, and the relief she felt when he did reply was shameful even to her. When had she become so needy, so desperate?

AJ had become everything to her, but she worried constantly that she didn't mean quite as much to him, despite his constant reassurances.

'I adore you, Princess Beatrice,' he told her, almost every day they were together. 'I can't imagine my life without you in it.'

And yet, she still couldn't shake the feeling that he was holding her at arm's length, at times.

'You're being paranoid,' Harry reassured her when he and Michael came to visit earlier that year.

'Do you think?' Bea had said, hopefully.

'Absolutely. That man adores the bones of you,' he said.

Michael hadn't said anything to back him up, and Bea hadn't pushed, because they both seemed to like AJ and that was enough for her.

But then there had been that incident a few weeks ago. The strange woman who'd turned up at AJ's apartment unannounced. Bea had been on her own, AJ working later than expected. Bea had been watching mindless TV with a glass of wine when the buzzer had gone. It still made her jump, and she'd splashed wine down her top as she'd stood to answer the intercom.

'Hello?' she said, still swiping ineffectually at the wine stain on her jumper.

'Who is this?' The voice was crackly, but she could hear the accusation in the strong New York accent. The woman sounded older than her.

'It's Bea. Who's this?'

There was a silence and Bea wondered whether the woman had gone. But then she spoke again.

'Is Alvin in please?'

It had taken Bea a moment to realise who she meant because she never thought of AJ as Alvin. 'I'm afraid he's not here at the moment.'

'I see.' A beat. 'Do you know when he'll be back?'

'He shouldn't be long. Would you...' She'd stopped. 'Do you want to come up and wait for him?'

'No. Thank you.'

Then she'd gone. When AJ had returned a couple of hours later, bleary-eyed, she'd asked him who the woman could have been.

'I have absolutely no idea,' he'd said, wiping his hand across his face. He looked exhausted and she felt guilty for pushing it, but couldn't help it.

'But she seemed to know you. She called you Alvin.'

Did she imagine it or did he flinch at the name? He'd sighed, poured himself a beer from the fridge and finally turned round to face her. 'Honestly, Bea, I have literally no idea who it could have been. And if you didn't see her, it's impossible to work it out.' He'd shrugged, and taken a long swig of beer. He had dark circles under his eyes and the stubble that usually sprinkled his chin was longer, straggly. She stepped towards him and he wrapped his arms around her, leaned his chin on her head. 'But I can't imagine she's anyone you need to worry about.' She tilted her head up to look at him.

'Are you sure?'

He kissed her softly and whispered, 'I'm sure.'

Since then she'd tried to parcel the incident away in the back of her mind. Perhaps it had been a work colleague, or an old friend of his parents, or someone he used to know and simply wasn't interested in seeing any more. Whoever it was he clearly didn't want to discuss it, and she decided to wait until after Christmas to bring it up again. Or not.

She stood, the potatoes now returned to the baking tray. Some had specks of fluff stuck to them, and she wiped them over with a cloth and hoped nobody would notice. The chicken was ready to go in the oven. Checking her watch, she opened the oven door and placed everything carefully inside.

She couldn't work out why she was so nervous about seeing her parents. They'd already met AJ, back in early summer when they'd paid a flying visit home for her gran's eightieth birthday (a visit that Mia, Ashton, Michael and Harry still hadn't forgiven her for because she didn't have time to see any of them for more than a quick coffee).

'I need to go and see her or I'll never hear the end of it,' Bea had said when she'd told AJ she was going home.

'Can I come?'

'What?' She hadn't meant it to sound rude, but after only six months together she didn't think he'd be interested in meeting her family – especially as he seemed to avoid seeing his own at all costs.

'I just thought it would be nice to meet them. And the famous Beatrice that you're named after.'

Despite her misgivings – she knew her mum still hadn't really forgiven her for what she did to Dom, and harboured hopes that they might get back together one day – Bea had agreed. And AJ had been a bigger hit than she'd ever have imagined. Even Alice had managed to get through the entire long weekend without mentioning Dom's name once when AJ was around.

'He's lovely Bea,' she'd conceded, as they said goodbye. 'Just be careful he doesn't break your heart.'

She hadn't asked Alice what she'd meant because she'd known, really. There was something about AJ that was hidden away; a part of him that she didn't know if she would ever access, unless he really wanted her to. So she'd just hugged Alice and said, 'I will.'

Now her parents were coming to spend Christmas with them, and she couldn't help the anxiety returning. She just wanted everything to be perfect, to show them that she really had made it on her own.

That she was happy.

Her phone beeped and she picked it up and read the message.

Just got them. Heading home now. AJ x

She dropped the phone back on the table and stood in the middle of the kitchen, taking a few long, deep breaths. Tonight was going to be fine.

While the food cooked, Bea had a shower. Maggie had gone out tonight. 'I'll give you space,' she'd said, even though Bea had insisted she should join them, although she had at least accepted Bea's invitation to spend Christmas Day with them. 'If you're sure; I'd much prefer to spend it with your family than mine,' she'd said, and Bea had hugged her hard.

She was just dressed when she heard footsteps outside the front door, and seconds later AJ entered, followed closely by her mum and, at the back looking sheepish, her dad.

'Hello sweetheart,' her mum said, running towards her and throwing her arms around her. Bea felt the press of her mum's delicate frame against her and breathed in her familiar smell of laundry detergent and Rive Gauche and realised she'd never been so happy to see her. She pulled away and gave her dad a squeeze too.

'How was the flight? Did you have any delays? Do you need a drink? Shall I make you a cup of tea?' Bea buzzed round the kitchen like a wasp trapped between double glazing.

'Don't fuss love.' Pete's voice was quiet, but authoritative.

'Sorry Dad. I'm just excited you're here.' Beside him, Ange was gazing round at her flat, taking it all in.

'So, what do you think?' Bea said.

'It's lovely,' Ange said, running her hands over the back of a chair, still peering round like a wide-eyed child. 'It's very small though isn't it?'

'Yes, well that's Manhattan prices for you,' AJ said, and Ange giggled.

'Bit like London I suppose, for youngsters these days,' Pete said.

'Exactly.'

'I've made dinner,' Bea said, bending to peer into the oven. 'It'll be about twenty minutes. Would you like a drink?'

'Yes please,' Ange said.

'I'll sort the drinks. You all sit and relax.' AJ stepped in and guided them towards the sofas.

'Don't be daft, I've been sitting down for hours,' Ange said. Bea shrugged and let her mum do what she always did – help – while she led her dad into the living room.

'So, did you see much of New York on the way in?' she said.

'Some of it. It was very busy,' Pete said, settling onto the sofa.

'Yes, it always is.'

'Very kind of Dom to come and pick us up though.'

Bea froze for a minute, unsure whether her dad had realised his mistake. 'AJ doesn't mind at all,' she said, pointedly, and frowned when Pete said nothing more.

They sat in silence until Ange and AJ entered, the latter carrying a tray laden with glasses, a bottle of fizz and a couple of cans of lager. He laid them on the small table and handed them out as Ange headed straight for the window.

'We're quite high up, aren't we?'

'Fifth floor.'

Ange sighed. 'Gosh, the whole city is like a film set.'

Bea had grown used to the view from her window which was mainly windows and the odd rooftop. But she still remembered the sheer excitement she'd felt at being in New York when she'd first arrived, so humoured her mum as she chattered excitedly about all the things she'd seen on the journey here. Pete sat quietly sipping his beer.

'I can't believe you live here Bea. You always said you wanted to one day and now here you are.' Before Bea could reply, Ange turned and pressed her palms against Bea's cheeks. 'I'm so proud of you darling. We both are, aren't we Pete?'

Her dad held his beer up in acknowledgement.

'Thanks.' She turned back to face the room. 'It's not all excitement though. I mean, I miss you. And I miss my friends.'

'Hey!' AJ said.

'You know what I mean.' She looked at her mum and then her dad. 'I do love it here, but London will always be my home.'

There was a beat of silence, then Ange smiled. 'Well that's good to know.'

'Right, I think dinner might be just about ready,' AJ said from across the room.

'Great, I'm starving,' Pete said, hauling himself out of his chair. 'Those plane meals are only just big enough to feed a small child.' Bea smiled to herself. Her dad loved his food, while her mum seemed to spend most of her life feeding everyone else rather than herself.

They filed through to the kitchen where there was a tiny table laid with cutlery and napkins.

'Sorry, it's a bit of a squeeze,' Bea said as they bashed elbows and scraped chairs.

'It's perfect love,' Ange said. 'We're just happy to be here.'

Bea served up dinner, and for a few moments they all ate in silence. Bea had been so nervous about their arrival she hadn't realised how tense she was, and she drank wine faster than she intended.

'The boys are furious you know,' Ange said, spearing a potato with her fork. 'Think you should have just come home for Christmas.'

Bea rolled her eyes. Even though they were both well into their thirties and had families of their own, Bea knew her mother was referring to her brothers, Charlie and Rob.

'Only because it means they have to cook Christmas dinner themselves,' Pete muttered through a mouthful of chicken.

'I know. But I do feel guilty. We always see them at Christmas and now we've abandoned them. Alice too, although they're going to Andrew's parents this year so she's not as cross.'

'I'm sure they'll cope,' Bea said. 'Anyway, I'm glad you're here.'

'I know, and we're glad to be here too.' She put her fork down, a light shining in her eyes. 'Can we go to Bloomingdale's tomorrow? And Central Park? And that diner from *When Harry Met Sally*?'

Bea grinned. It had always been her and Ange's favourite film, and she'd already planned to take her there.

'Katz's Diner – it's not far from here,' she said. 'We can go wherever you want.'

'Oh, that reminds me,' AJ said. He looked at Ange and Pete imploringly. 'I hope you don't think I'm being rude but I'll have to join you later tomorrow.' He didn't meet Bea's eye.

'I thought you said you said you'd finished work now,' she said.

'I have. Officially.' He speared a piece of broccoli and chewed. 'I've just got a couple of things to sort out. Sorry.'

Bea didn't want to cause a row in front of her parents so she didn't say anything else. But she suspected that was exactly AJ's plan – mention it front of them so she couldn't get cross. 'Never mind, I'm sure we can amuse ourselves,' she said, coolly.

For the rest of the meal Ange regaled them with stories of friends and neighbours that Bea could barely remember. In turn Bea told them all about her job and how much she loved it – she'd recently been promoted to feature writer and loved the challenge, the interesting people she got to speak to every day. AJ was quieter than usual as he told them all about his job and his upbringing in rural Ireland. Bea couldn't help noticing that when they pumped him for information about his past, he was vague, and moved the conversation on quickly.

To her relief Ange didn't mention Dom at all – and Pete didn't slip up again either – although she was sure Ange would tell Bea all about him tomorrow. But she already knew from Alice's regular updates that he wasn't doing well and she could do without the guilt-trip.

By eight o'clock, Ange and Pete seemed to have run out of energy.

'Why don't we take you to your hotel, and you can get some sleep and be refreshed for sight-seeing tomorrow?' Bea said, when her dad looked as though he was about to fall asleep in his chair.

'Are you sure love?'

'Absolutely. We've got the next few days to see each other, but this is almost 1 a.m. for you.'

'Thanks love,' Ange said, standing and starting to move the plates to the sink. Bea swooped in and took them from her. 'And that's enough of that,' she said. 'Let me look after you for once.'

Ange looked sheepish but was clearly so exhausted she didn't argue.

'Do you want me to come with you?' AJ said, as they were ready to leave.

'Why don't you stay here and clear up, I won't be long,' Bea said. After his announcement, she felt like a bit of time away from him.

'Okay if you're sure. Night Ange, night Pete, see you tomorrow.'

* * *

After dropping her parents off and making sure they were safely settled in their hotel room, as well as agreeing to come and meet them at 10 a.m. the following morning, Bea decided to take a slightly longer route home, to clear her head.

She took a left turn out of the hotel and marched up Second Avenue. The air was frigid and she stuck her hands in her pockets and pulled her hood further onto her head. Her breath formed clouds around her as she walked, and she tried to figure out what was bothering her the most. Was it the fact that AJ often did this – disappeared without telling her where he was going, sometimes for days at a time, and refused to answer any questions about where he'd been? Or was she more annoyed at the fact that she let it bother her so much? After all, he was allowed to do whatever he wanted. They'd only been together a year and didn't live together. He wasn't answerable to her.

But she did hate it, there was no denying it. Because it was clear there was something going on that he didn't want her to know about. She wished she could talk to Mia about it, but she didn't feel like discussing it on the phone, and with Mia's new job she'd only managed to visit once this year, all the way back in April. As much as she loved her friends in New York, she longed for the easy intimacy of the people she'd known for more than half her life. People who had seen her at her worst, had picked her up when times were bad, and celebrated with her when things were good. Sometimes, without them there, she felt as if she were missing a limb.

Her feet were cold and she turned in the direction of her flat. AJ would be wondering where she'd got to and however cross she was with him she didn't want to make him worry. But she did need to ask him what he was doing tomorrow morning that he couldn't change. She suspected he wouldn't answer.

By the time she arrived home her fingers and toes were numb and her nose was beginning to tingle. She removed her boots and coat and hung them on the hook and stepped into the living room, ready to confront AJ.

'Heeeey!' Maggie threw her arms out as Bea walked in. She had the glazed look of someone who had been drinking all day, and the remains of the bottle of fizz they'd started over dinner swung precariously in her left hand.

'Hey you,' Bea said, stepping into her friend's embrace. Pulling away, she glanced round the living room. 'Where's AJ?'

'He went out,' she said, her words slightly slurry.

'Out? Did he say where?'

'Nope.'

'Oh.' Bea tried to ignore the tug of anxiety pulling at her insides. It was probably nothing, he'd probably just gone for some fresh air.

She painted a smile on her face. 'So, how's your night been? You're back early.'

'Oh God, it was a disaster.' Maggie threw herself on the sofa dramatically, her long limbs bending like Bambi. Bea perched beside her as she told her the events of the evening. They seemed to involve a terrible date with a man she'd hoped was going to be The One (Bea didn't hold much store in Maggie telling her that as almost every date was meant to be The One), but who spent the evening talking about himself and disappearing to the toilet every five minutes.

'Maybe he just drank too much,' Bea said. But she was only half-listening, focused as she was on where AJ might have gone, and half-listening for his key in the lock.

'Well, whatever. I won't be seeing him again,' Maggie said, her head tipped back on the sofa. The bottle in her hand was in danger of spilling over so Bea slid it carefully from her grasp. Maggie looked up suddenly, her eyes wide. 'Oh, how were your parents?' She looked round as if they might be hiding somewhere in the tiny living room.

'Fine,' Bea said. 'They went back to their hotel.'

'Oh. I was looking forward to meeting them.'

'You'll meet them tomorrow.'

'Good.' Maggie tilted her head back again and closed her eyes, a wonky smile on her lips. Bea stood, put the bottle on the table and went into her bedroom. It was only small – like all the rooms in this apartment – but it was hers. Her duvet was neatly tucked in, and she'd hung framed book covers above her bed. There were fairy lights strung over the full-length mirror and the doors to her small closet hung open. There were hardly any signs that AJ had even been here, and she wondered whether she would ever feel completely secure with him.

She took the few steps towards the window and peered into the night, clearing the mist her breath had made with her sleeve. They were five floors up, but she could still make out people in the street, and as she watched she spotted a familiar figure striding towards the house, hat pulled down over his head. She watched as he paused outside her building, checked his phone, typed something, then stuck it in his back pocket. Then he disappeared into the building.

A few minutes passed before she heard a key in the lock and the sound of the door opening and closing. She held her breath.

'You're back.'

Bea turned round to find AJ standing in the doorway.

'Yeah.'

He stepped towards her and pulled her into his arms and despite herself she felt her body melt into his, the way it always did. She felt drawn to him, always, and she let him kiss her deeply. He pulled away, a frown creasing his forehead, and tipped her chin up with his finger so she was forced to look him in the eye.

'What's wrong Princess Bea?' he said.

She shrugged. She really wanted to ask him where he'd been, who he'd been messaging, where he was going tomorrow, who the mystery woman was who'd come to the flat asking for him and where he went on those days when he just seemed to vanish into thin air. She could feel the questions gathering at the base of her throat, but she just couldn't make herself say any of them. Dom had always said she worried too much, that she fussed. She didn't want AJ to feel the same. So she decided, there and then, that she wasn't going to say any of those things. At least not before Christmas. It could wait.

She smiled and kissed the tip of his nose. 'I'm fine, honestly. I'm just really tired; it's been a long day.'

He studied her a moment longer, as though trying to work out whether she was telling the truth. Finally, seemingly satisfied, he threaded his fingers into her hair and pulled her to him. 'In that case, let's go to bed,' he said, his lips grazing her mouth.

'What about Maggie?' she whispered breathily.

'She's out for the count,' he said, and as he pushed her gently back onto the bed she forgot all about her worries and let herself sink into the moment.

6

STAY

December 2004

'It's ridiculous that you have to go and do this a week before Christmas,' Dom said, his arms folded angrily over his chest.

'I know. But Julia said it's for the first issue of the new year so it can't wait.'

Dom rolled his eyes. 'Like it would matter if it went in a couple of weeks later.'

Bea felt a spark of anger flare in her chest. 'I know it's not life or death, Dom, but it's scheduled, so someone needs to do it.' The truth was that Bea was thrilled to have been asked to take on this assignment for a special feature in the newspaper early in the new year. It was a big deal. At least, it was for her.

She loved her new job working for a lifestyle supplement of a broadsheet newspaper. It was a dream come true to finally be where she wanted to be. But it had come at a cost.

Because Bea had finally had to confront the elephant that had been in the room ever since she'd walked out on Dom and admit what had driven her away.

Jonathon, her smarmy, lecherous boss at the marketing company she'd previously worked for, had made a pass at her after a meeting late one evening. He'd pressed himself against her and rested his hand against her breast, and made it clear that if she refused him, there would be consequences for her career.

It was almost a mirror image of what had happened eighteen months before. But this Bea wasn't the same woman she used to be. This Bea was stronger, older and wiser. And she wasn't going through that again.

This time, instead of pretending it hadn't happened, telling herself it must have been her fault, that it was something she'd done, she went home and told Dom about it straight away. He had, of course, been furious, had threatened to go to the office and smack Jonathon and tried to get Bea to ring the police. Bea had managed to calm him down, in the end. But the next day she'd reported Jonathon to senior management, and said she wanted to take him to tribunal.

She'd also handed her notice in with immediate effect.

At first she wondered whether she'd made a mistake. She had no job and wasn't sure what she wanted to do next. On top of that, she'd finally told Dom that this wasn't the first time Jonathon had done this; that he had been the reason she'd been about to run away to New York.

'But... why didn't you tell me? Back then?'

'I just...' Bea started, but stopped when she saw realisation dawn in Dom's eyes.

'You're only telling me now because he's done it again, aren't you? You would never have told me otherwise... would you?'

She shook her head. 'I always wanted to tell you. But...' She took a shaky breath in. 'I was going to. A couple of nights later.' Beside her, Dom was rigid, waiting. 'But then... we were watching something on TV. I can't remember what it was. Some drama on ITV, it doesn't matter. There was a woman on it. She'd been—' The words caught in her throat like razorblades. 'She was attacked. By a man.' She looked at Dom and saw nothing but confusion in his eyes.

'Afterwards, when the programme finished, I mentioned the attack. I was – I was trying to find a way in, to start the conversation.' She shook her head. 'I don't know why I couldn't just say it, but I was so ashamed, I...' She stopped again, lifted her chin. 'Anyway you said something that night, something that made me realise I couldn't tell you. I just couldn't.'

Dom didn't move beside her and she wondered what he was thinking. She looked at him again and his face was pale in the lamplight.

'What did I say, Bea?' His voice cracked as he said her name. She looked back down at her hands.

'You said she was stupid to have gone down that alley on her own at night.'

The words hung in the air, looking for somewhere to land. Bea held her breath.

'You thought I would blame you.' It wasn't a question, but Bea nodded anyway.

In an instant Dom was right next to her, one of his hands cupped round her clasped ones, the other on her cheek, trying to get her to look at him. She did, and saw nothing but sadness in his eyes.

'I'm sorry,' she said.

He shook his head. 'I can't believe you thought that of me.'

'I know. I just – I was struggling. I thought it was my fault that this had happened to me, that I must have done something to encourage him. I thought—'

'None of this is your fault Bea. None of it. It's Jonathon's, no one else's. I'm just so, so sorry that I made you feel that way.' His eyes widened. 'Oh, God, and I made you go back there, to work for that... that...'

'It's not your fault,' she said, gently. 'I knew it wasn't what you meant, not really. I guess I just needed someone to blame, for the way I felt.'

'But I still made you go back to work there.'

She shook her head again. 'You didn't make me. I just didn't know what else to do.'

'God I'm so sorry, Bea,' he said. He buried his face in his hands. 'And to think I nearly lost you, because of a stupid, meaningless comment.'

'You would never lose me,' she said. 'I would never really have gone.'

Did she mean that? She thought back to that moment in the airport more than two years before, when she still had the choice of whether to go or whether to stay. That moment when she'd stood, right by the departure gate and hovered between doing what she desperately wanted to do, and what she felt she ought to do. *Had* there been no way she would have ever got on that plane? It had been a split-second decision, after all. It could, realistically, have gone either way.

She didn't say that to Dom.

A couple of months later, after applying for all kinds of jobs, from shop assistant to junior reporter on the local paper, Bea received an email from a woman called Misty, who was the editorial assistant for one of the lifestyle supplements of a Sunday newspaper, saying her editor would like Bea to come for an interview for the position of feature writer. Bea felt like the breath had left her body as she read those words, and her hands shook uncontrollably. She read and re-read the email over and over again until the words became meaningless, wondering whether she'd misunderstood. But no. There they were, in black and white. The job that Bea had applied for on the spur of the moment even though she didn't think she had a hope in hell of getting, had just got one step closer.

The interview itself and the two agonising weeks of waiting afterwards, during which time Bea had convinced herself there was no way she would ever get that job, had blurred in Bea's mind and now all she could remember was that first day, during a heatwave in the second week in June, when she had walked through the front door of the publishing company, taken the lift to the second floor, and walked into her new job as feature writer.

A completely new beginning.

She hadn't been given anything to do for quite some time. Nothing significant, at least, and for a while she wondered whether they realised they'd made a mistake, giving her the job. Whether they'd imagined they'd given the job to someone else, someone better, and were trying to work out what to do with this impostor. This young girl who had no idea what she was doing.

But then, slowly, she started to be given stories to write. Short, pithy pieces on TV programmes; interviews with chefs and business people, and interesting, non-famous people who had fascinating stories to tell. Bea loved it. She loved speaking to these people who had so much to say, who wanted to tell their stories. She loved everything about it.

Then she'd been asked to fly to New York a week before Christmas and interview someone for the lead story in the first issue of the new year, and there was no way she was ever going to say no.

Perhaps this was the way she was meant to go to New York, after all.

'Sorry Bea,' Dom said now, wrapping his arms around her and pulling her in for a hug. She let herself be held by him, her body relaxing as he pressed his lips into her hair. 'I know how much this means to you. I'm being a dick.'

She pulled away slightly and looked up at him. 'You're not being a dick. You're never a dick.'

'I'm not sure your friends would always agree with that.'

She frowned at him. 'Of course they would, why would you say that?'

Dom shrugged. 'I dunno. I just sometimes feel they think you'd be better off without me.'

She watched him for a moment, his face a mask, then she shook her head. 'Don't be daft. Everyone loves you. How could they not?' She buried her cheek against his chest. 'And anyway they're not *my* friends, they're *our* friends.'

He held her for a minute and she felt safe, comforted. Then she stepped out of his embrace and hooked her finger under his chin. 'Listen, I know this is annoying timing, but I'll be back in two days' time, and then we can put our feet up and relax and enjoy ourselves.'

'And cook dinner for your entire family,' Dom said, a grin creeping across his face.

'And that,' she said, grimacing as she glanced round the living room. 'Although I might have to leave you to work out where exactly we're going to put everyone.'

'Yeah, thanks for that.'

'You're welcome.' She bent down and picked up the small case she'd just pulled out from under their bed, then pecked Dom gently on the lips. 'Now I'd better go and pack or I'll never get there.'

* * *

Two hours later Bea was on the way to Heathrow, her black cab stop-starting at seemingly endless sets of traffic lights and making her feel car sick. She stared out of the window, even though she couldn't see much through the fat drops of rain that coated the glass apart from the blurry outlines of cars passing slowly on the other side of the road.

She thought about the last time she'd taken this journey, two years previously, and how different everything felt now. The last couple of years might not have been easy, but Dom was so much better now; for the first time in years he seemed truly happy, as though the dark cloud that had followed him round for so long had finally lifted. She hoped it had. Because Dom had been talking about getting married, and she was on the verge of saying yes.

She was ridiculously early to the airport, of course, because she always was. She browsed Duty Free, spraying perfumes on herself until she couldn't distinguish one scent from another. She bought herself a coffee and a sandwich and scrolled through her phone while she sat in Pret, trying not to get too excited at the thought that she was about to see New York at last. She knew there wouldn't be much time to sightsee in the two days she would be there, but she still couldn't wait to see the city she'd always dreamed of visiting.

On the flight she read through her notes for the interview, she watched a film, she ate her meal and drank a couple of glasses of wine. The man beside her in the aisle seat snoozed throughout the entire flight and she wondered whether she should wake him so she could go to the loo. The woman on the other side of her, by the window, spent the whole flight with her headphones in. Bea wished she had someone to talk to.

Finally, eight hours later, the flight landed in JFK, and when Bea came out of the airport dragging her small case behind her, she was hit first by the icy air which smacked her in the face like she'd walked into a wall of snow, and then by the sounds, smells and sights of New York. Yellow cabs idled, waiting for passengers, people smoked outside the automatic doors, and car horns honked on the nearby freeway. This was New York.

Her hotel was only a couple of blocks from Times Square, and when she stepped out of the cab she stood for a moment, in wonder, letting the crowds of Christmas shoppers flow past her. She was here. She was finally here.

It was every bit as magical as she'd always imagined it would be.

She dragged her case up the steps to the hotel entrance and made her way to the reception desk. She refused help from a bell-hop, and minutes later she was in her room, staring out of the window at the scene below. She felt as though she was living in a fairy-tale. Her room was a few floors up – twelve, if she remembered correctly – and from here she could see the grey stone of the building opposite, a flashing neon light turning it alternately blue then pink then back to blue again. But beside that was the view that really took her breath away: a chunk of pale blue sky, sliced through by the jagged skyline and towering skyscrapers that winked like giant Hollywood teeth in the weak summer sun. Tiny windows watched her like eyes while buildings jostled and clamoured for prominence and, when she rested her head on the glass and peered down, she could make out tiny cars beetling along a spiderweb of streets.

New. Fucking. York.

She was here, at last.

She turned back to the room and quickly changed. She only had a few hours spare today before the interview tomorrow, and she needed to make the most of her time. Moments later she was out on the street outside the hotel again. She should have felt exhausted but instead she felt excited, energised. Giddy.

It was bitterly cold and she tugged her hat down over her head. The sky was a bright, brilliant blue, although the weak winter sun seemed to be doing nothing to warm the air. She headed off in the direction of Times Square, and as she rounded the corner, it opened up onto the slice of New York she had seen hundreds of times on TV: the neon tower with its flashing adverts, the soaring, glittering Christmas tree, people wrapped up against the cold, as if it were perfectly normal to be in this city that was the backdrop to all the best films ever made: *When Harry Met Sally*, *West Side Story*, *Breakfast at Tiffany's*, *The Godfather*. Which, she supposed, it was, to them. But to her it felt like she was in a dream, with every corner and every road intersection revealing yet more views to marvel over.

She was here, at long last.

She longed to go to Macy's but she wanted to see Central Park first, so she cut through the crowds of people and headed north, past 42nd Street, then across to Fifth Avenue.

The pavements – she should probably call them sidewalks now – were full of puddles and her feet felt damp in her leaky boots. She moved closer to the brightly lit storefronts, Saks and Armani and Longchamp, where lights twinkled and music played, trying to entice people in before the shutters came down for two whole days.

The further north she walked the grander the buildings grew, red carpets and gold lettering picking out the names of the private apartments on canopies that over-hung the street, straight-faced doormen standing guard. She passed the gaudy bling of Trump Tower, then the road began to open up and there it was like an oasis in the desert: Central Park.

She hurried across the road, past the endless stream of yellow cabs and the lines of horse-drawn carriages where couples waited to take a romantic ride through the park. Inside, the park was still full of joggers and skate-boarders, as well as families swinging young children by the arms, couples strolling hand in hand, people sitting on benches to eat their lunch alone.

After watching the ice-skaters glide round the ice with varying degrees of skill, she found a stand selling hot chocolate and pretzels, bought one of each and found herself a bench to perch on. She brushed the snow from it and sat down, ignoring the chill that seeped through her coat into her skin, determined to just sit and soak it all in. She watched the lights twinkling in the trees, the couples strolling arm-in-arm, the harried workers still not quite finished for Christmas, and she felt her spirits soar. She wished Dom could have been there with her, or Mia, who would love it just as much as she did. But she was just happy to be here, in this city she'd always dreamed about.

She finished the last mouthful of pretzel, which was much drier than she'd expected, and stood, brushing the crumbs from her coat onto the icy ground. A frost lingered on the grass, making the park feel like a winter wonderland, and she set off, her spirits buoyed, determined to see as much of the city as possible before nightfall.

She headed down south again, past the town houses overlooking Central Park, down past Tiffany's and The Rockefeller Center, past Times Square, and finally, forty minutes later, she was whirling through the swing doors of Macy's and walking round, open-mouthed, like a child in a sweet shop. She strolled through the perfumed-scented beauty hall, the floors filled with funky clothes she could never imagine wearing, and the colourful rows of beautifully wrapped treats in the food hall, before finally heading towards the enormous Christmas section, where the tinsel and lights and tinkly music assaulted her senses.

By the time she re-emerged onto Broadway – actual Broadway! – the day was beginning to darken. She tipped her head back and looked up at the navy blue of the sky peeking above the towering buildings, and wondered whether it was going to snow. It certainly felt cold enough. That would be utterly magical.

Stomping her feet, she marched back towards her hotel. Suddenly ravenous, she stopped at a busy diner where she was served the most enormous burger she'd ever seen in her life, then bought a bottle of wine to take back to her hotel. She wasn't sure she was brave enough to sit in the bar by herself tonight. Besides, she needed to be fresh for her interview early in the morning.

As she climbed into bed a couple of hours later, her body finally succumbing to exhaustion, she felt utterly elated. She was here, at last, in the city of her dreams.

* * *

The next morning there was a light scattering of snow and frost on the rooftops, but the pavements and roads were clear. Bea gathered her notebook, pens, Dictaphone and notes together, double-checked where she was going, and set off. The hotel bar where she had arranged to meet her interviewee was a good twenty-five-minute walk away and she felt her cheeks reddening and her heart pumping as she marched, her mind full of the questions she'd prepared. This was a big deal for her, and she had to get it right. She needed to prove to her editor that she'd made the right choice, giving her a chance.

She ran up the steps of the hotel. She was ten minutes early, and she let her eyes wander round the bar. There were a few people dotted around but no one who looked like the man she'd arranged to meet, so she ordered herself a coffee and settled at a seat overlooking the street. She still felt the same excitement this morning as she'd felt yesterday on arrival, except this morning it was tinged with nerves and her hands felt jittery as she sipped her latte. She checked her notes, checked the Dictaphone was working, checked her pens.

'Are you Beatrice?' said a voice next to her and Bea jumped up, wiped her damp palms on her trousers before finally looking at the man who the voice belonged to. Her stomach flipped. She'd known he was attractive from the photos she'd been given by the charity who'd arranged the interview, but he was much more attractive in the flesh and she felt her face flush. Dark hair, leather jacket, tattoos peeking out from beneath his sweatshirt.

'Hi, yes, I am,' she stammered, holding out her hand. He took it in his own warm hand and gave it a brief shake.

'God it's feckin' cold out there,' he said, as he peeled off his coat and took a seat opposite her.

'Oh, you're Irish,' she said then flushed again.

He smiled warmly. 'Sure am. And you're English. I assumed you'd be American.'

'No, they flew me over for the interview,' Bea said.

He gave a low whistle. 'Woah, who knew I was interesting enough for that.'

Bea smiled. 'Anyway, thank you for meeting me Mr Flynn.'

'Oh God please don't call me that, you make me sound like my father. Not that he's not a lovely man but Jesus. I'm AJ.'

'AJ,' she repeated. 'Just the letters?'

'Just the letters,' he confirmed, and she wrote it carefully at the top of the page.

'What do they stand for?'

'Ah no way, you're not getting me that easily,' he said, with a flash of white teeth. He leaned forward. 'Nobody gets to know my first name if I can really help it.'

'Why not?'

'Believe me, if you knew what it was, you'd understand. As it is, you'll just have to trust me. Can I call you Beatrice? Is that what most people call you?'

'Actually most people call me Bea.'

'Like the insect?'

She shook her head. 'Like the princess.' He looked puzzled. 'It's what I always got when I was at school. You know, after Princess Beatrice was born?' When he still looked none the wiser, she added, 'The Royal Family?'

'Ah right,' he said. 'I'm not really a fan of that lot. But it is a lovely name.'

'Thank you.'

He stood suddenly. 'How rude of me, I haven't offered you a drink.'

Bea gasped. 'Oh no, I'm meant to be getting you a drink, sorry.' She stood too, knocking the table with her knees and spilling coffee onto the tabletop. 'Shit.'

AJ waved his arms at her. 'Honestly, please sit. I'll get the drinks – and some napkins to mop that up,' he said. 'What was it, a latte?'

'Yes please,' she said, sitting down, mortified. 'Thank you.'

He walked towards the bar and she took a moment to compose herself. This had not been the best start to the interview. She felt unexpectedly thrown by how good looking this man was, and her mind was all over the place. She just needed to take a few deep breaths, calm herself down, and switch to serious journalist mode.

By the time AJ returned to the table she felt calmer, and she smiled as he sat back down. He wasn't carrying any drinks.

'She said she'd bring them over,' he said. 'So. You want to hear about Cassandra then.' His face was unreadable.

'Yes,' Bea said. 'We're going to run it in our first issue of the new year.'

AJ steepled his fingers beneath his chin. 'I'm guessing you know the basics. That Cassie is essentially brain dead, and that she has no quality of life?'

Bea nodded. 'I do, yes.'

'Right, so. Do you want to just fire away with the questions, like?'

'Yes. Yes sure.' She fumbled with her notes, typed up neatly on several sheets of paper. She peered at the first one. 'Do you mind if I just set this to record, so I don't forget anything?' She held the small tape recorder up.

'Sure, whatever you need,' he said.

'Thanks.' She pressed 'record', then looked up at him. 'So, I understand Cassandra was...' She stopped, coughed, and looked back up at him. 'That she was caught up in the events of 9/11, and that she was left in a coma,' she said. 'But would you mind if we went back to the beginning? Back to when you first met her? It would be good to get some background, build up a picture of your relationship.' She felt herself blushing at the mention of the word relationship.

AJ studied her for a moment, although Bea wasn't quite sure whether he was looking at her or staring into space, lost in his memories. Then a look passed across his face that she couldn't read, and he was back in the room.

'Sure. Cassie and I met when she was in London on a work trip in 1996. She came into the office where I was working and *boom!* – I couldn't take my eyes off her.' His eyes shone. 'She was incredible. This amazing, Amazonian woman, beautiful dark hair tumbling down her back. But it was about more than how she looked. She had this presence, you know. She commanded a room when she walked in. She was fierce and clever, but she still made you feel like the most important person in the world when she spoke to you.' He cleared his throat. 'Is this the sort of thing you want to know?'

'Yes, absolutely,' Bea said, her pen hovering above her notepad.

'Okay good.' AJ smiled and something about the angle of his chin startled her. He looked familiar, and she had the sudden overwhelming feeling that they'd met somewhere before, although she had no idea where.

'Anyway, I never thought someone like Cassie would look twice at me,' AJ continued. 'You know, some Irish eejit with no clue what was going on, who lived in band T-shirts, spent his weekends going to the pub or to gigs. But by some miracle, she did, and within a week we were dating, and within two months we'd agreed I was going to move to New York with her.'

'So she was from New York?' Bea asked.

AJ nodded. 'Born and bred. Wealthy parents, live out towards Long Island. Me and Cassie lived in the apartment her father bought for her – I still live there now – and she was already quite senior at a New York law firm whereas my career could only have got better by coming to the States.' He shrugged. 'It seemed like a win-win situation. We were happy, most of the time. I mean, we didn't see each other enough, and we often went out separately with our friends because she thought mine were childish and I thought hers were snobs, but when we were together, we were great.

'We got married in 1998, a huge do out at her parents' house. My mum and dad came over, my siblings all did too with their other halves and kids. It was a big deal. A proper, wealthy New York affair.' He smiled. 'It wasn't for me of course. Or for Cassie, really. Her father paid for it and he wanted to make sure everyone knew he could afford it. But Cassie was happy and so I didn't care. I just wanted to be her husband.' He paused and rubbed his hand over his face.

'And so then 9/11 happened?' Bea said gently.

AJ nodded, his eyes fixed on a point on the table. 'She was running away from the World Trade Center when a piece of debris hit her in the head and she was knocked unconscious. By the time she got to hospital she was in a coma.' He looked up at her and the pain in his eyes was almost unreadable. 'Four years, and nothing has changed and nothing ever will.' He let out a long breath and his body sagged as though air had been let out of a balloon.

'Could you tell me about her? About what happened afterwards.'

AJ picked up his coffee and took a sip and grimaced. 'Ugh, that's gone cold.'

'Shall I get you another one?'

'No, you're good.' He changed position and started again. 'God, what happened after the accident,' he said, as though he was trying to arrange the order of events in his head. 'Well, she was in a coma for three months. It was awful. She just lay in this hospital bed day after day, night after night. It was the worst feeling in the world, seeing her there, not knowing whether she was ever going to get better. Whether she was ever going to be Cassie again. It felt like we were living in some sort of terrible limbo.

'When doctors told us she was beginning to respond to things around her, we were all so excited. She could open her eyes, and smile. She could cry, laugh – but that was it. There was nothing else there. Doctors explained that she was in what's called a permanent vegetative state which means... it means she can't feed herself, she doesn't know where she is, who we are. She... she...' He stopped and put his head in his hands. Bea didn't say anything, and after a few seconds, AJ looked up at her.

'Sorry. It's just... We used to have these conversations, me and Cass. Mostly when we were drunk, about what we'd do if we were paralysed, or if we left unable to do anything for ourselves. What we'd want to happen. And I remember very clearly Cassie telling me there was no way she'd want to live like that. "I'd want you to turn off the life support or whatever was keeping me awake, and let me die with some dignity," she told me. She got quite agitated about it, made me promise that I wouldn't let her go on like that. I agreed, of course, never thinking for one minute that I'd ever actually have to make that decision.'

He looked up at Bea, and the look in his eyes cut right through her so that she could almost feel his pain.

'Another three months passed and doctors told us there was almost zero chance of Cassie ever getting better, and suggested we might want to start thinking about letting her go. They explained that, although she could breathe for herself, she had no quality of life, and that to peacefully end her life, we would need to agree to withdraw nutrition. Basically, to stop feeding her, under the guidance of doctors. They explained it all, and how it was for the best.

'I told her parents I thought it was what we should do. But they had other ideas. Sandra, Cassie's mum, in particular, couldn't let go.' He shook his head. 'Of course she couldn't, how could anyone? I tried to explain how this was the kindest thing to do. That it's what Cassie would want. And then we agreed that, if there was no change by September, a year after her accident, then we would let her go.'

'But Sandra changed her mind?' Bea asked.

AJ gave a curt nod. 'She refused to let us end Cassie's life. Even Cassie's dad, Anthony, thought it was for the best by then but Sandra she just... she couldn't do it.'

A silence hummed in the room, filling all the spaces.

'So do you...' She stopped, unsure what to ask. 'Do you help look after her?'

'No. Not any more. I did at first, I was there every day. But now... I can't. I can't be complicit in letting this continue. Now I visit once a week. Sometimes less. But that's all I can give.'

Bea didn't speak for a while, letting the words settle. She couldn't begin to imagine how hard this was for AJ. He was married, and yet he'd lost his wife a long time ago. He knew this wasn't what Cassie would want, yet he had no power to do anything about it.

She could see why her editor had wanted this story so much. It was utterly heart-breaking.

'And now, what's the situation?' Bea asked gently.

'Now?' AJ shrugged. 'Now all I can do is get on with my life and hope that they see sense, sooner or later. But I can't just sit around and wait for that to happen. Cassie has gone, and that's all there is to it.'

'So can you—' Bea stopped, suddenly shy about asking her next question. She swallowed. 'Can you picture yourself moving on?'

'Finding someone else you mean? Getting married again?'

Bea nodded, and AJ fixed her with a look that made her stomach flutter.

'Yes. If I met the right woman. I said goodbye to Cassie a long time ago, and I know she wouldn't want me to put my life on hold for her.' His gaze intensified and Bea felt mesmerised, drawn in by his intense look. She forced herself to look away, down at her notebook. Her shorthand was a scrawl on the page, and she hoped she'd be able to read it later. She didn't think she was likely to forget any of it though. It was seared on her memory.

'Is that any good?'

Bea snapped her head up. 'Sorry?'

'For your article? Was that what you needed?'

'Oh yes. Perfect. Thank you.' She felt flustered and reached for her coffee for something to do. It was totally cold and she put it straight back down again.

'Thank you for—' she started.

'Do you want—' AJ said at the same time, then laughed. 'Sorry, you go ahead.'

'Oh, right. Yes. I was just going to say thank you for taking the time to talk to me today. I mean, this close to Christmas...' She trailed off.

'It's fine,' he said. 'In fact, I've enjoyed. it. Meeting you.'

'Yes. Yes me too.' Bea wasn't sure where to look so she looked back down at the notebook in her lap. 'What was it you were going to say?'

'I was going to ask if you fancied something stronger. To drink.'

'Oh right.' She'd been about to leave, to let him get on with his day. But now she could think of nothing she'd like to do more than stay here and have a drink with this man.

'You don't have to, I won't force you against your will if you've got somewhere else you need to be,' he said, a smile playing on his lips.

'Oh no! I'd love to!' Bea said, cursing herself for saying it in her children's TV presenter voice.

'Great.' He stood. 'What can I get you?'

'A gin and tonic please,' she said.

'Coming up.'

* * *

'Can I ask you something?' Bea could feel the gin loosening her tongue.

'Shoot.'

'I feel like I've met you before.'

'That's not a question.'

'No.' Bea grinned, and rephrased. 'Have I met you before?'

'I don't think so. I think I'd have remembered,' AJ said, draining his third whisky and slamming the glass down on the table. 'What makes you think you have?'

Bea shrugged. 'I don't know. You just seem familiar.'

'Must just be my devastating good looks,' he said.

'That'll be it.'

Bea felt emboldened by the three gins she'd already had. This was not how she'd expected the evening to turn out – having drinks with the man she'd been sent to interview. But here they were. She tried not to think about Dom back home getting everything ready for Christmas Day. This was just a couple of drinks, nothing more. It wasn't harming anyone.

So why did she feel giddy at the thought of spending the rest of the evening with this man?

7

GO

December 2005

Bea lay in bed listening to the clatter of pots and pans downstairs and felt a pang of guilt that she wasn't down there helping. She stared at the ceiling, the familiar Artex, the paint peeling in one corner. Something was digging into her back and she shuffled away, the ruck of sheet crumpling underneath her. There was a bang, and the rumble of the TV drifted under her door, the ever-present sounds of her childhood.

She sat up and took in the room. The only light was filtering round the edges of the curtains, but she could make out the immaculate desk in the corner, an ergonomic chair tucked underneath; a pine wardrobe was squeezed into the corner, and a small bookshelf ran along the wall beside the desk. Apart from that the only piece of furniture in the room was this slightly lumpy sofa-bed she was sleeping on.

She turned to face the wall and ran her fingertips over the faded outline of the Corey Haim and Brad Pitt posters that had once hung here. But other than the grease left behind from the Blu

Tack, there was no sign whatsoever that this used to be her child-hood bedroom.

A gentle knocking on the door made her start.

'Bea?' A whispered voice.

Bea lay completely still in the hope she would be left alone.

'Bea love, it's Mum. Are you awake?'

She knew she should reply but she just needed a few more minutes to wallow, so she waited, rigid, until her mum's footsteps shuffled across the carpet and down the stairs, then she pulled the duvet over her head.

Two weeks she'd been back. Two weeks of feeling miserable and having everyone – well, mainly Mum – fussing round her, making sure she was okay.

She wondered what AJ was doing right now, then immediately tried to push the thought from her mind. But it was no good. It was persistent, and she'd learned it was better to give in to it, let the thought take form.

It had been almost nine months since she'd last seen AJ and she still missed him like she would miss a limb. She tortured herself daily, imagining him with other women, and at least once a week had to be stopped by one of her friends from ringing him or sending him a text to see how he was.

A tear tracked down her cheek and dripped onto the sheet. She breathed in, a muffled breath full of duvet, then blew out again, hard, feeling her lungs empty.

This time last year, she'd been so happy. Most of the time at least. After AJ's mysterious disappearing act on Christmas Eve, she'd tried not to think too much about what it might mean, and concentrated instead on being happy, vowing to talk to him about it in the new year. But then the new year had come and gone, and the snow fell, covering New York in a thick blanket of white, and AJ had asked her to move in with him.

'I hate having to traipse backwards and forwards between our flats in this weather,' he'd said.

'I'd love nothing more,' she'd said, and chose to say nothing about the things that were bothering her because surely now things would change. They agreed she would wait until Easter, to give Maggie time to find someone else to move in.

But then, just before Easter, on a cold bright day at the beginning of March as the snow was beginning to melt and Central Park was showing the first signs of spring, everything changed.

She'd been feeling happy that day. AJ hadn't disappeared for a weekend since before Christmas and Bea was beginning to believe that, at last, whatever had been occupying his mind and time until now might finally be over and done with. And if that was the case then she didn't need to know what it was. They could put it behind them and never talk about it again.

Then she'd seen him with another woman.

At first she hadn't been sure it was him. Thought perhaps she'd seen someone who looked like him, the way she often did when she spotted the back of a dark head, the flash of a white-toothed smile, and her stomach flipped with desire. He'd been heading towards a café on the other side of Seventh Avenue when she was on her lunchbreak, and when she realised it was him she nearly called his name. But something had stopped her and instead she simply watched as he disappeared inside the café, then headed towards a table in the front corner. She watched in rising horror as a dark-haired woman looked up and smiled at him, and AJ pulled out the chair and sat down, leaning his elbows on the table and smiling back. She stood, frozen, her hands turning numb in the brisk March breeze as she tried to work out what this could mean.

Bea stayed there another five minutes, watching AJ and the woman talking, trying to work out what to do. Should she go and speak to him, demand to know what was happening? But what if it was just a colleague, or an old friend? AJ had lived in New York for years before he'd met Bea and she still didn't really know any of his friends so it was a possibility.

But then the woman leaned over and pressed her hand on top of AJ's and Bea had snapped out of her daze and done the only thing she could do. She ran away.

Her heart still ached when she thought about the events that unfolded after that. She'd waited until later that evening, when AJ was due to come and help her start moving her things to his apartment. Maggie was out, on another date that was destined to fail, and Bea had sat, motionless, on the sofa until she heard the scrabble of AJ's key in her lock.

'Bea?' he called, but she didn't reply.

AJ came into the room and sat beside her on the sofa, the springs squeaking in protest, and when he placed his hand on her arm she tugged it away, remembering the way the woman's hand had held his just hours earlier.

'What's happened Bea? Are you all right?'

She stared straight ahead at the worn rug and tried to muster the energy to ask him who that woman was, even though she didn't really want to hear the answer.

'I saw you,' she croaked. She clamped her hands between her thighs.

'Saw me? What do you mean, where?'

She turned to look at him. She couldn't make out the blue of his eyes in the gloom but she could see the question in them.

'With a woman. In a café on Seventh Avenue.'

A moment's silence followed where neither of them took a breath. Then:

'It's not what you think.'

A cliché, then. Disappointment flooded her. She searched his face, looking for a clue. Was he sorry? Or just sorry he'd been caught?

She rolled over in bed now, not sure she could bear to go over what happened next one more time because it hurt too much. And yet she also knew she would, knew that she would bring it out again, study it from all angles, try to work out whether she'd done the right thing, reacted in the right way – or whether she'd made the biggest mistake of her life.

She pulled herself up to sitting and hugged her knees to her chest, then let her mind drift back again, back to that moment in her apartment in New York, where everything had hung, suspended.

AJ had tried to take her hands but she'd snatched them away, not wanting him to touch her until he'd said what he needed to say.

'She was a journalist,' he said, letting out a huge breath.

Bea snapped her head round to look at him. 'What?'

'The woman you saw me with was a journalist. I'm not having an affair with her, if that's what you think.'

For a moment Bea felt nothing but relief. AJ wasn't having an affair!

But then: 'Why? Was it to do with work?'

She hoped it was something that simple, that he would explain and she would realise how stupid she'd been to jump to conclusions, and they could move on and forget about it.

But something in his tone told her it was more than that.

'She wanted to interview me. About my wife.'

All the air left Bea's lungs. 'Your...' She swallowed. 'Your *wife*?'

A silence filled the air. Then AJ nodded, his head lowered. She watched as he moved his lips, trying to form the words, and she could see this was almost as hard for him as it was for her.

'Bea, I don't know how to tell you this.' His voice was like broken glass. 'I'm married.' He breathed in deeply, but Bea said nothing. She felt like an empty shell.

'Cassie and I married in 1998. She's the reason I moved here. She – we – loved New York and I was more than happy to leave Ireland behind and start a new life. It felt exciting, working in advertising in the Big Apple.' He stopped, his hands clenched in his lap. His knuckles were white. 'Cassie grew up here. New York born and bred, wealthy parents who live out near Long Island. Her father bought us an apartment, the apartment I live in now, and we were so happy. Her parents were far enough away not to bother us too often, I had my job, and she was a successful lawyer.' His voice cracked. 'She was fierce. Clever.' He glanced at Bea, his eyes dark. 'You would have loved her.'

It took a moment for Bea to notice the past tense. 'Would have?' she said.

AJ looked back down at his hands, his jaw tight. 'She's not dead. More's the pity.' He gave a bitter laugh and Bea's heart thumped as she waited for his next words.

'Cassandra was badly injured during the 9/11 attack. She'd been at work that morning and...' He stopped, rubbed his face. 'She was running away when a piece of debris hit her in the head and she was knocked unconscious. It was utter chaos, you have no idea, and she was lying in the road for ages before an ambulance came for her. By the time she got to hospital she was in a coma.'

Bea didn't speak for a moment. This was all too much to take in. She couldn't process it, it wasn't possible.

'So...' She hesitated. 'Is she still in a coma?'

AJ shook his head. 'She came out of the coma three months later but she...' he choked. 'She never recovered.'

'So... what does that mean?' Bea's voice was a whisper.

'She's in what doctors call a permanent vegetative state. Sometimes she opens her eyes, sometimes she smiles. Sometimes she even cries, or laughs. But she...' He stopped, tripping up on his next words. 'She doesn't have a life, Bea. She lies in her bed day after day, she can't feed herself, she doesn't know where or who she is. She... she...' He put his head in his hands. 'She'd rather she was dead, and so would I.'

The room felt as though all the air had been sucked out of it. Bea didn't move, didn't know what to say. After a beat, AJ lifted his head. He looked grey, as though the pressure of the secrets he was carrying had leached him of life. 'I've tried to be there, Bea. I tried so hard for the first few months. But after six months doctors told us there was almost zero chance of Cassie ever getting better and suggested we might want to start thinking about letting her go.'

'Letting her go? Do you mean switching off machines?'

AJ shook his head. 'No, she can breathe by herself.' He gave another bitter laugh. 'That's about all she can do. When someone has been in this state for six months, or a year, doctors usually know whether things are ever likely to change. At six months they categorically told us that Cassie would never get better. That this would be her life forever.' He steepled his hands in front of his face. Bea longed to reach out and touch him, comfort him, but something told her it wasn't the right moment. He carried on. 'They said in order to peacefully end her life, we would need to agree to withdraw nutrition. Basically, to stop feeding her, under the guidance of doctors. They explained it all, and how it was for the best.

'I told them I thought it was what we should do. But her parents had other ideas. Her mum, Sandra, in particular, couldn't let go.' He shook his head. 'Of course she couldn't, how could anyone? I tried to explain how this was the kindest thing to do. That it's what Cassie would want. And then we agreed that, if there was no change by September, a year after her accident, then we would let her go.'

'But she changed her mind?' Bea asked gently.

AJ gave a curt nod. 'She did. She refused to let us end Cassie's life. Cassie's dad, Anthony, even he thought it was for the best by then but Sandra she just... she couldn't do it.'

A silence hummed in the room, filling all the spaces.

'So do you...' She stopped, unsure what to ask. 'Do you help look after her?'

'No. Not any more. I did at first, I was there every day. But now... I can't. I can't be complicit in letting this continue.' He shook his head. 'I visit once a week. Sometimes less. But that's all I can give.' He smacked his hand against the arm of the sofa, making Bea jump. 'Cassie would *hate* this. I know she would. I've told Sandra this over and over again, but she just can't see it.'

He turned his head to look at her, searched her eyes. Bea looked away.

'So when you met me...' Bea started, hoping AJ would fill in the blanks.

'The first time we ever met, on the plane, I was on my way back from a work trip to London to spend Christmas with them. I didn't want to. By then it was three months on from the anniversary of Cassie's accident, which was when we'd all agreed that would be that. But I didn't want to let everyone down. I wasn't in a good place.'

'And after that? The following year?' The words felt like shards of glass in Bea's throat.

AJ started to reach for Bea's hands but seemed to change his mind halfway there and settled his hands in his lap. 'By then I'd told Cassie's parents I couldn't do it any more. I told them I needed to move on with my life, that Cassie was no longer the woman I fell in love with that I'd promised to love for the rest of our lives. Cassie was gone, and all that was left was a shell. I'd grieved for her already.

'It was the hardest thing I've ever done, but they seemed to understand. They *agreed* with me. And yet Sandra still couldn't agree to pulling the plug.'

As his words settled, the missing pieces of the jigsaw slowly began to slot into place for Bea. AJ's disappearances. His expensive apartment in the West Village that he'd never explained how he could afford. His reluctance to let her stay there very often.

Then something else occurred to her.

'That's who came to the apartment that time, when you were out, wasn't it? Cassie's mother.'

He nodded sadly. 'I think so. She never said anything, but it must have been her. She's the only person apart from my own mother who calls me Alvin.' His eyes glistened. 'I know this is a huge shock, Bea. But I hope you can understand why I've never told you before.'

Bea wanted to say of course she understood. That it didn't matter to her, and that they could carry on as they had been. But her chest felt tight and she was struggling to breathe and she didn't know if she would ever be able to process everything AJ had told her in the last twenty minutes. She couldn't begin to imagine how awful it must have been for Cassie's parents. For AJ.

Yet she couldn't shake the persistent thought that, even though she had been with AJ for just over a year, he had been married all this time. And he'd kept it from her.

She stood. Her legs felt wobbly.

'I need you to go,' she said, trying to keep her voice strong.

'But Bea.' He stood beside her, moved towards her, but she shook her head and took a step away. 'I need time to think.' He dropped his hands by his sides, picked up his jacket and walked towards the door, his head low. He looked like a lamb to the slaughter and everything in Bea's body had screamed at her to tell him to stay.

Letting him leave was the hardest thing she'd ever done, and when the door shut behind him she buckled, collapsing onto the sofa and sobbing until she had no more tears left to cry.

That had been eight months ago. After much soul-searching she'd told AJ it was over. She couldn't do it to herself and she couldn't do it to Cassie's parents – although she regretted it the instant the words left her mouth. She felt utterly broken and over the next few months she'd tried to mend herself by going on terrible dates with unsuitable men, or double dates with Maggie and her new boyfriend Todd, all the while wishing she could be anywhere but New York, where everything reminded her of what she'd lost. Mia had flown out to be by her side but finally Bea had known where she needed to be: back in London with the people who really knew her best. And so she'd given up her apartment, quit her job, and flown home.

That was in November, and now it was Christmas again, and she was back in her childhood home, in what had once been her childhood room but was now a spare room and office space with a back-breaking sofa-bed.

And she was alone.

* * *

She must have dropped off again because she was woken by a hammering on the bedroom door, then, before she'd even properly opened her eyes, the door swung open and Mia jumped on the end of her bed.

'Wakey wakey sleepy head!' she said, bouncing up and down like an excitable puppy.

Bea groaned and pulled the pillow over her head. 'Go away,' she mumbled.

But Mia was having none of it and yanked the pillow away. 'Come on, you can't stay in bed all day. We've got plans.'

Bea opened her eyes and cocked her eyebrow at her friend. 'What plans?'

'We, Bea Preston, are having a girls' day out, just you and me. We're going to get our nails done and drink champagne.'

'Uh-uh.' Bea shook her head and finally pulled herself up to sitting. 'You seem to have forgotten that I don't actually have a job and therefore no money whatsoever.'

'No, I haven't forgotten. But this is my treat.'

'But—'

But Mia cut her off. 'No arguments. Your mum's already told me you're not doing anything today, and if I can't treat my best friend who I've barely seen over the last three years to a day out four days before Christmas, then when can I? So come on, get out of your pit and get dressed.'

'Thank you Mee,' Bea said, her throat thick with tears.

Twenty minutes later Bea was ready. She'd even applied a bit of make-up for the first time in at least a month.

'Oh you look lovely,' her mum said, clapping her hands together in delight as Bea walked into the kitchen where Ange was, as usual, preparing enough food to feed half the street.

'I've only washed my hair,' Bea said, grimacing.

'Well, you look better than you have in ages,' Ange said. 'Thank you Mia, for getting her out of her dressing gown.'

'You're welcome Mrs P.'

'Right you two, get out of here, make the most of your day.' She kissed Bea gently on the forehead and smoothed her hair back from her face. 'It really is good to see you up and about properly sweetheart,' she said. 'Have fun.'

It was a grey, murky day, the clouds hanging low over the city, threatening rain. As Bea and Mia walked arm in arm towards Manor House tube station, Bea felt a sense of calm settle over her, the like of which she hadn't felt for months.

'I love this city,' she said.

'Even more than New York?'

Bea thought about it. Did she love London more than New York, the place she'd always dreamed of escaping to? New York had the glamour, the excitement. But London was her heart and, she realised now she was finally here, it would always, always be her home.

'Definitely,' she said, and Mia squeezed her arm tightly.

By the time they ascended the escalators at Oxford Circus, the rain was coming down in sheets, and they hurried, hoods up, elbowing their way through the crowds along Oxford Street.

'Remind me why I thought Oxford Street four days before Christmas would be a good idea?' Mia said, shaking rainwater from herself like a dog as they finally stepped into the Christmas fairy-tale of Selfridges.

'Because you're a nutter?' Bea said, and Mia slapped her arm.

'Right, come on, third floor,' Mia said, grabbing hold of Bea's hand and almost dragging her towards the lifts.

The beauty department was as busy as ever, with throngs of people queuing, and women at every stool having their make-up done.

'Do we have a plan?' Bea said, hovering uncertainly.

'We do. We're having a manicure, then we're having our make-up done, then we're heading to the champagne bar downstairs. I was worried it was a bit lame staying in Selfridges for everything, but I'm glad I did now it's pissing it down.'

'But that's going to cost you a fortune,' Bea said. 'I can't let you pay for all that.' She hated having no money.

Mia took Bea's arms and held her face right in hers. 'Beatrice Preston, you're my best friend and I've missed you. The new job I got that meant I couldn't visit you as much in New York at least means I can afford to spend some money on you as and when I choose. Now stop worrying, and just relax.'

Bea brushed a tear from her cheek. 'I don't know what I'd do without you.'

'Just as well you'll never have to find out, isn't it?'

An afternoon laughing and gossiping with her dearest friend was, as it turned out, exactly what Bea needed. She loved her New York friends – she missed Maggie in particular – but nothing could ever beat the feeling of having a friend that you knew had your back no matter what and asked nothing in return, and Mia was and always had been that friend.

'So, have you heard from him?' Mia said as they collapsed into seats in Pitcher and Piano later that afternoon.

'AJ?'

Mia nodded, her lips in a thin line. 'I wasn't going to say his name.'

Bea smiled. 'I love that you're protecting me but it's really fine.'

'Is it?'

Bea felt the burning sensation at the back of her throat that told her she was about to cry and shook her head. 'Not really. But I hope it will be eventually.' She took a huge gulp of her Chardonnay and wiped her mouth with the back of her hand. 'But no, I haven't heard from him. Not since I've been back in London.'

'Bastard.'

Bea shook her head. 'Not really. I made it very clear that I didn't want him to be in touch. I thought it would be the easiest way. I thought...' What had she thought? That it would help her forget him? That if she didn't hear from him she might not feel the physical pain in her chest every time she thought about him?

'He's still a bastard. A lying, cheating one at that.' Mia topped their glasses up as Bea shook her head. The pub was packed with festive drinkers: shoppers, tourists and office workers who had finished work for Christmas were all squeezed into the compact space which meant they struggled to hear each other over the cacophony of voices.

'I did hear from Dom again though.'

Mia froze with her glass halfway to her lips. *'What? When?'*

Bea shrugged, instantly regretting mentioning it. 'Yesterday. And a few days before that.' She squirmed. 'He's sent me a few messages since I've been back.'

'What the *fuck?*'

'It's fine Mee, honestly. I've got it all under control. He asked if we could meet up, said he'd missed me. But I told him no and he seems to have got the message.'

'Not if he contacted you again last night.'

'Maybe. But you don't have to worry. I *really* don't need any more complications in my life.'

'Well good. But the bloody cheek of him.'

'To be fair, he didn't actually do anything wrong. When I left, I mean.'

Mia peered at her over the rim of her glass, her eyes narrowed. 'He must have done something, otherwise you wouldn't have left in the first place.' She took a gulp of wine and put her glass down on the table so hard it almost smashed. 'But actually, that's a good point. What *did* make you up and leave? I mean, you never actually told me, and you were always so upset when we spoke long-distance I didn't like to pry. But now – well, you owe me, Preston.'

Bea's heart sank. So much time had passed since she'd walked out on her life that it was hard to put into words the way she'd felt back then. But Mia was right, she *did* need to tell her the truth. At last.

'I was assaulted. At work.'

Mia went so still she looked as though she'd frozen. Bea

wondered whether she should say something else, fill in the gaps, but before she had the chance, Mia exploded.

'What the *fuck*? By who? And more to the point why the *hell* didn't you tell me before?'

Bea reached for her wine glass and drained it. The warmth spread through her body and she felt suddenly braver. She told Mia all about it. About her boss Jonathon making a pass at her, how he'd made her feel like it was her fault, and how he'd promised to give her a promotion if she agreed to keep it quiet.

'Then when I refused, he threatened to sack me.'

'The absolute bastard.' Mia's voice was ice cold, her hands clenched. She reached over and covered Bea's hands with hers. 'Why didn't you tell me this at the time? We could have sorted it out together. You could have stayed and everything could have been so different.'

'I know. But I was so ashamed. I just wanted to pretend it had never happened and then – well, then there were the problems I was having with Dom anyway. You know, the way he was...' She trailed off. 'I just knew he'd make me feel like I was overreacting or something. I just – I couldn't do it any more.'

Mia stared at the table for a moment, lost in thought. Then she shook her head.

'I can't believe you think Dom would have down-played it.'

'But it's true, you know what he's like. He hates drama, it makes him anxious. He would have tried to convince me to carry on and pretend it had never happened. And the sad thing was, I probably would have done.' Bea shook her head, remembering the way she'd felt all those years ago. 'I just needed to leave. Get away from everything, start again.'

'But you'd been with Dom for *years*. It was... it was pretty tough for him.'

'I know. And that was what made it so hard to go. But I'll never regret it. Not for me at least, even after everything that's happened. I'm a stronger person now, Mia. I've grown up.'

Mia studied Bea for a moment, as though trying to work out whether she believed her. Then, finally, she smiled.

'You're right. You are stronger. But fuck, Bea, it was a pretty drastic way to go about finding yourself.'

Bea grinned. 'I know. But it worked. I think.'

Mia held her glass up and it sparkled in the lights from the Christmas tree. 'To friendship, and it being more important than anything else.'

'Cheers to that.'

* * *

The living room looked like Santa's grotto, with tinsel draped over every picture, paper chains and foil swags stretched from the central light fitting into every available corner; fairy lights were strung round the fireplace, and all the furniture had been pushed to one side to make space for the ridiculously over-sized Christmas tree Ange insisted on putting up every year. You could barely see the branches for the tinsel and lights weighing it down. Maggie would have a fit if she could see it, and Bea smiled at the memory of watching her friend lining all the baubles and lights up perfectly on their own tasteful, table-top Christmas tree last year.

The room was also packed to the rafters – in fact, the whole house was. The TV was turned down low because Ange had insisted on playing Christmas tunes through the CD player. 'We've got speakers in here *and* in the kitchen,' she'd told Bea proudly, as though she was a technical genius for having something most other people had had for years. Her dad was in the corner quietly reading the paper, and upstairs Bea could hear her nieces arguing about something, accompanied by the occasional bang.

'Lara, Ava, what have I told you?' Alice yelled as she stomped up the stairs to sort out her children and Bea felt relieved she didn't have to get involved. She was in the middle of sending a text to Maggie telling her all about her chaotic day when her mum poked her head round the living room door.

'Bea, can you set the table for me love?'

'Sure.' Bea quickly pressed *send* then hauled herself up with a sigh and dragged herself through to the dining room. Doing nothing always made her feel lethargic and she wished her mum would let her help out in the kitchen more, but she seemed to revel in running herself ragged.

In the dining room Ange had already laid the folded tablecloth, plates and piles of cutlery on the sideboard ready, so Bea shook the tablecloth out and spread it across the extended dining table. There was a motley selection of chairs, and Bea mentally calculated how many places she needed to set: there was her, her mum, dad, gran, Alice and her husband Andrew and children Lara and Ava, as well her brother Charlie who was on his way with his wife Annabel and their three children Josh, Martha and Molly.

Thirteen. Good grief. And it was going to be even more of a squeeze on Christmas Day when Charlie's twin, Rob, and his glamorous partner Coralie arrived. They'd be out in the garden.

She set about laying the places carefully, working out who would be most comfortable in each seat and next to whom, and folding napkins as neatly as she could. It was good to have a task to take her mind off her worries and she got lost in it for a few contented minutes.

She stood back to admire her handiwork, a spare set of knives, forks and spoons clutched in her hand, and rolled her eyes. Her mum had miscounted again. She pulled the extra chair away from the table, folded it and left it in the corner of the room, then went to return the cutlery to the drawer.

The kitchen was like a sauna, and her mum had her head half in the oven.

'Things aren't that bad are they?' Bea said, and Ange closed the door and turned round, her face rosy.

'Flippin' chicken doesn't want to cook,' she said, smoothing her hair down. It stuck up again in wild tendrils.

'Don't worry, nobody minds waiting.'

'I know love, but it's all about timing, isn't it? Everything else will be ready when the chicken's still half raw.'

'Honestly Mum, it'll be fine.' Bea stepped towards the drawer and went to return the spare cutlery.

'We need them,' Ange said, and Bea paused.

'No, you put out one set too many,' she said. 'Must be all the numbers in your head with the timings making you forget how to count.'

'Ah.'

Bea froze, her hand halfway to the drawer again. She knew that tone, and it usually meant her mum had something to confess.

'Come on, out with it. What's going on?'

Ange's eyes darted from Bea to the door and back again, her hands clasped round an oven glove. She opened her mouth, then closed it again.

'Dom's coming,' said a voice behind Bea, and she spun round to find Alice in the doorway, looking defiant.

'What?'

Ange stepped forward, 'I'm sorry I didn't tell you love, I was going to but your sister...' She stopped, obviously realising she was about to say something she shouldn't.

'Mum's right.' Alice stepped into the room and prised the cutlery from Bea's grip. 'It was my idea not to tell you because I knew you'd get angry.'

Bea finally found her voice. 'But *why*? Why would you invite him if you thought it might upset me? What's the point?'

'Because you two need to talk.'

'Why?' she repeated, like a stuck record.

Alice looked surprised by Bea's question, but quickly recovered herself. 'Because, baby sister, Dom is a lovely man, and he still hasn't got over what you did to him.' She sighed dramatically, as though Bea were the most infuriating person she'd ever met. 'And because he's struggling, and he asked if he could see you, I said yes. I think it would be good for him. For both of you.' She stuck her chin out defiantly.

'And you know all this how?'

Ange wiped non-existent stains from her hands with the tea towel. 'We still see him sometimes.' Her voice was a whisper.

'*Still?*' Bea exploded. 'But you told me you'd stopped! You promised!' Bea could hear the petulance in her voice, but she didn't care.

'Don't blame Mum. This was my idea,' Alice said.

'I blame you both.' Furious, Bea pushed past her sister and into the hall. She was about to run up the stairs when the doorbell rang and she stopped, hand hovering over the banister. Would that be Charlie and her nephews, who she'd been really looking forward to seeing for the first time in three years – or Dom?

Before she could decide whether to answer or ignore it, her dad appeared.

'Why are you just standing there like a lemon?' he said. Then he strode towards the door and opened it and Bea's heart stopped.

There was Dom: the man she'd loved, but whose heart she'd broken. The man she hadn't seen for three years.

'Hello Pete,' he said, his voice so familiar to Bea.

'Come in,' Pete said, stepping aside. And that was when Dom noticed Bea, and his face reddened.

'Oh. Hello Bea.'

'Dom.' His name came out crackly, like she was trying it out for the first time.

'I – I hope it's okay that I'm here. Alice said it would be.'

Seeing Dom here, in her parents' house, for the first time since she'd left him, was giving her feelings she was struggling to identify. On the one hand, she was angry. She *knew* she was angry, and rightly so. But not with Dom. Because he clearly felt as awkward as she did. And that made her feel unexpectedly sorry for him too. Protective, even.

There was something else there too, bubbling under the surface, something she was trying to ignore. Was that... did she still feel attracted to Dom, even after all this time? She tried not to notice his dark eyes and the sprinkle of stubble across his chin that made him seem older, wiser than he used to.

'Well you're here now,' she said, and instantly felt bad when she saw his face fall. 'Mum's in the kitchen, I'm just going upstairs.' Then she ran up the stairs and into her room and fell onto her bed, pressing her face into her pillow and letting out a muffled scream.

Oh God, oh God, oh God, why did Dom have to turn up, and why did everyone always have to try and control her life? Missing AJ had been hard enough; she didn't need this added complication.

She sat up and pulled her phone from her pocket. She had an overwhelming urge to ring AJ. Just to hear the sound of his voice, to remind herself that it was him she really wanted to be with, him she loved.

But she'd deliberately cut AJ out of her life and it had finally, *finally,* started to feel a little less painful over the last two months. Ringing him now would set her right back again.

And yet...

Her thumb hovered over the number for a few seconds. She

was going to do it. Just to wish him Merry Christmas. It would be fine.

Suddenly her phone buzzed in her hand and a message appeared on the screen.

Sounds great – wish I was there! Miss you loads, come back and see us soon. Love Mags x

Maggie's message snapped her out of it. What was she doing? Of course she shouldn't ring AJ. She needed to stop wallowing, get downstairs and grow a pair.

She tucked her phone back in her pocket, stood and straightened her hair in the mirror, slicked some lipstick on, and headed down to face the music.

* * *

Dinner was as awkward as Bea had feared – at least at first. Someone had returned the missing chair to the table, and Bea was squeezed between Alice's husband Andrew on one side, and Dom on the other.

'So, have you started looking for a job yet?' Andrew said, spearing a piece of carrot with his fork and popping it in his mouth.

'Not yet,' Bea said.

'Ah well. You've only been back three weeks. There's plenty of time in the new year. The offer's still there if you want to come and work for me, you know that.'

Bea would rather gouge her eyes out with a teaspoon than work for Andrew's accountancy firm, but he was only trying to be kind so she pasted a smile on her face.

'Thanks Andrew. I'll bear it in mind,' she said, trying to ignore Alice's pointed look from across the table. She shoved a piece of chicken in her mouth and chewed slowly. Beside her, Dom was talking to her gran. Over the general chatter and the kids' yelled arguments she couldn't hear what they were saying so she kept her head down and hoped nobody would speak to her. So far she'd managed to avoid all conversations about AJ and she had no intention of telling any of them what had really happened – at least not yet. In fact, her friends were the only people who knew the truth because honestly, she couldn't face Alice's *I told you so*, or her mum's over-protective anger. It was easier just to keep quiet.

'Bea, tell Dom that story about the man in Central Park.' Bea looked up at her mum who was watching her expectantly from the end of the table.

'What?' Bea snapped. Beside her, Dom's head turned in her direction.

'Remember? That man in Central Park who was running in his underwear.'

'Oh, right. Yeah.' She turned to Dom. 'There was this man in Central Park running in his underwear.' She turned away and took a mouthful of potato.

'Bea!' Her mum sounded frustrated. 'Tell him more.'

Bea chewed slowly, and swallowed. She looked at Dom and shrugged. 'Sorry, there's not much more to tell than that.'

'It's fine Bea,' Dom said quietly. 'You don't need to talk to me.'

A spear of guilt pierced Bea's heart and she looked down at her plate then back up into Dom's familiar face. 'Sorry. I don't mean to be a bitch.'

'You could never be a bitch,' Dom said, so softly that she had to lean a little closer to hear him.

'Apart from when I walked out on you, right?'

He shook his head. 'No. I never thought you were a bitch. Never.'

Bea felt her heart soften, and the tension seep from her shoulders. She put her fork down and picked up her wine glass. 'Well, then you're a nicer person than me,' she said, taking a sip of the cold wine. 'But then I guess you always were.'

Dom didn't say anything else, but took a sip of his own wine and resumed eating. Bea could see her mum watching them from across the table, and she was certain Alice would be too, but she refused to look at either of them.

For the rest of the meal, conversation was easier, and there was even some laughter about the days before Bea had turned everything upside down. Charlie regaled them with funny stories about the kids, and Bea finally got a chance to chat to her gran, who was utterly thrilled to have Bea back.

'You'd better not go buggering off again,' she said, stabbing a piece of carrot and popping it in her mouth. 'I'll be dead by the time you come home again.'

'Don't say that Gran!' Bea said, but the older Beatrice just shrugged and scooped up a pile of peas.

As the day went on and the wine flowed, for the first time since she'd got back to London, Bea felt herself begin to relax. The ache in her chest from missing AJ hadn't dimmed, but there were other feelings diluting it now, including a warm feeling which she put down to being back with her family. To being home.

Just before dessert there was a lull, a moment of quiet where nobody seemed to be talking. And into that quiet Pete suddenly piped up: 'You two lovebirds doing anything nice after this?'

Bea looked up to see who he was talking to and realised, to her horror, that he was talking to her and Dom.

'Um... we...' She glanced at Dom who looked just as confused as she felt. 'We hadn't planned to do anything Dad,' she said.

Pete frowned. 'But haven't you got plans? You know, it is nearly

Christmas, and when you're newly in love you don't want to be hanging out with us old crusties.'

A strange silence hung in the air. Then, to Bea's relief, Alice spoke. 'Don't be daft Dad, you know Bea's staying here. I'm sure Dom will have plans of his own though.'

For one awful minute Bea thought Pete was going to say something further. But then he seemed to decide it wasn't worth it, and pushed his plate away, throwing his napkin on top of it so that the gravy soaked into the red cloth.

'Right, I'm just going to clear these plates,' Ange said, standing quickly.

'I'll help,' Bea said.

'Me too,' Alice said.

The second they were in the kitchen, Alice kicked the door shut.

'Mum, is there something wrong with Dad?'

Ange was facing the sink, rinsing the plates one by one under the hot tap, and she shook her head but didn't turn around. Bea glanced at Alice and saw the worry she felt reflected in her sister's face. Carefully, they placed their armfuls of plates down on the worktop and stepped closer to Ange. Alice touched her on the shoulder and when she eventually turned around her eyes were brimming with tears.

'Mum, what's going on?' Bea said quietly.

Ange shrugged and looked at the floor and Alice took her hands. 'Talk to us. Please.'

Ange's face was pale in the harsh overhead light, and she took a long shuddery breath. 'Your dad keeps forgetting things.' Her voice wobbled. Ange was always so strong, so capable, and neither of her daughters knew what to do.

'How long has this been going on?' Alice said.

Ange shook her head. 'On and off for a while.' She took her hands away from Alice's and wrapped her arms round herself protectively. 'But most of the time he's completely fine, so I'm sure it's nothing to worry about.'

Bea was about to ask something else when the kitchen door burst open and Charlie came in. He stood looking at them for a moment.

'What's going on? Has something happened?'

Alice shook her head as Charlie closed the gap between them. 'Mum? Is this about what Dad just said?'

Alice put her hand on her brother's arm. 'Mum was just telling us that Dad is getting a bit... forgetful. Isn't that right Mum?'

Ange nodded miserably.

'But... but that's just because he's getting older, isn't it? I mean, that's what happens, right?' He looked from each woman to the other, desperate for them to reassure him.

'I'm not sure.' Ange's voice was quiet. 'I've told him to go to the doctor's but you know what your dad's like, he's a stubborn old fool and won't be having any of it. But... but...' She burst into tears and all three of her children moved to comfort her. When her tears finally subsided, Alice was the first to speak.

'I'll talk to him. If he's starting to forget things we need to know if there's something more serious going on. And if there is, at least it means we can help him.'

'Thank you love,' Ange said, sniffing. 'I'm sorry this had to happen today. I was hoping to talk to you about it in the new year.'

'Mum, we're grown-ups now. You don't need to protect us from everything bad in the world any more,' Bea said.

'Well, me and Bea are grown up, I'm not so sure about Charlie,' Alice said.

'Hey!' Charlie said, giving her a playful shove.

'Stop it you lot!' Ange said, and for a moment it felt as though normality was restored again.

'I'll talk to him, okay?' Alice said. 'Now, let's get this dishwasher loaded and get some dessert out to the hoards.'

As they stacked the dishwasher in companionable silence, Bea realised she'd even forgotten to be cross about her mum and sister inviting Dom to dinner behind her back. It just didn't seem important any more.

* * *

Dinner finished, Dom stood to go.

'Thanks Ange, that was amazing, as always,' he said, patting his belly.

'You're always welcome, you know that.'

'Right. Well, thank you. I'd best be off.' He hovered for a moment. 'Um, Bea, do you – er, fancy a quick drink?'

Bea looked up from the TV where she'd been mindlessly watching some game show. 'Huh?'

Dom cleared his throat and shifted his weight from foot to foot. 'I was just wondering if you fancied a quick drink. With me.'

'Oh!' Bea felt her face redden. God, what was wrong with her, behaving like some schoolgirl? This man used to be her fiancé, for God's sake.

'Go on, we're all cleared up here. Go and have some fun,' Ange said.

'I...' Bea hesitated. She'd been about to say no. Going for a drink with Dom didn't feel like the best idea in the world given her mind was still in turmoil over AJ. But then again, that ship had well and truly sailed – she'd made sure of that – and she wasn't doing herself any favours by sitting around moping all day. Plus, she'd enjoyed Dom's company more than she'd expected today.

She hauled herself off the sofa and smiled. 'Sure, why not?'

Which was how she found herself, just fifteen minutes later, sitting in a crowded pub, 'All I Want For Christmas Is You' just audible above the roar of the drunk Christmas crowd, having a drink with her ex-fiancé.

No one was more surprised than her by this turn of events.

She'd texted Mia as she got ready to come out, hoping for some words of wisdom – or at least some words of warning to stop her doing something she might regret, but so far, nothing.

She poured them both large glasses of red wine and took a gulp.

'Thanks for coming out,' Dom said.

'Anything's better than sitting there listening to the kids screaming the house down.' Dom's face fell and she felt mean. 'Sorry, it wasn't just that. It's really nice to see you.'

'Is it?'

Bea looked up at him sharply. 'Yes. Why wouldn't it be?'

Dom shrugged, his fingers fiddling with a cardboard beer mat as he spoke. 'I didn't think you'd be too pleased about me coming today. I told Ange and Alice as much but they both insisted you wanted me there. It was the only reason I agreed.'

Bea rolled her eyes. 'Trust them.' She twirled her glass around. 'As you could probably tell from my reaction, I didn't know you were coming. But I'm glad you did.'

Dom looked up, his dark eyes watching her. 'I'm glad I did too.'

The air between them hummed. Was it simply familiarity, or was there something more here than Bea was prepared to admit?

Something about Dom definitely seemed different. Where he used to be so sure of himself, so convinced his way was the right way, now he seemed uncertain, as though doubting his every move. Bea felt a wave of affection wash over her as he fiddled with his wine glass, his shoulders hunched.

'Mum said you'd been struggling.' It seemed best to get it over and done with, like ripping off a plaster. Dom looked up at her, surprised.

'Oh, right. She told you.' He nodded sadly. 'Yes, I – well, I stopped taking my medication for a while.'

'Oh Dom.'

He shrugged. 'I know. Self-destructive, given that I know how much I need them, eh? But I didn't see the point once you'd gone...' He trailed off.

She reached out and wrapped her hands round his and was surprised how good it felt to have that physical connection. Her skin burned against his.

'I'm so sorry for hurting you,' she said. 'You know I never meant to.'

He looked up at her, his eyes filled with hope. 'Why *did* you leave, Bea?'

'I...' She stopped. She still didn't know how he'd react if she told him about her boss's assault. It felt like another lifetime ago, and the rage and anger she'd felt had now cooled to nothing more than a simmer. What if she brought it all up again and Dom played it down, the way she'd feared he would at the time; made her feel as if she'd somehow misread the situation? And after all this time, she was scared she'd probably believe him.

She took a deep breath. 'I—'

'Well, well, well, if it isn't Dominic Sutton,' a familiar voice cut across her, and Bea and Dom both looked up to see Mia almost upon them. Behind her was a grinning Ashton, and a more serious-looking Michael, with Harry trailing behind looking concerned. Bea snatched her hands away from Dom's and stood, almost tipping her chair over. She was overwhelmingly grateful to see them all. She'd missed them so much when she was in New York, and having them back in her life made her feel warm, and safe.

'What are you lot doing here?' she said.

'I rounded up the troops to help me save you from yourself,' Mia whispered in her ear.

'You didn't need to,' Bea said, as she hugged her friends one by one and they sat down. Harry hovered behind Michael. 'I'll get a round in,' he said, and dutifully took their orders.

'I'll give you a hand,' Dom said, standing and following Harry to the bar. Ashton disappeared too, clearly glad to get away.

'Is everything all right between you and Harry?' Bea said as Michael shrugged off his coat.

'Oh Harry's just in a mood because he doesn't agree with me about you.'

'About me?'

Michael slid a glance towards Dom at the bar. 'He thinks it's a good thing Dom seems to be back in your life, but I think it's a total shitstorm.'

As always, Michael didn't mince his words, and Bea couldn't help but laugh. 'A shitstorm? That's a bit harsh.' She flicked a glance at Mia, who shrugged and ran her finger through some spilled wine on the table.

'It's true though.'

'Maybe. But he's hardly back in my life.' She put air quotes round the words. 'Today is the first time I've seen him for three years.'

Michael sighed heavily. 'I know dear heart, but it was inevitable. But more importantly, I know you're still madly in love with your delicious Irish heartthrob, and that anything that might happen with Dull Dominic can only be a rebound thing. You deserve better than that.'

Bea knew Michael had adored AJ when he and Harry had finally made it over for a visit to New York last year, but she still felt defensive of Dom in the face of Michael's harsh words. He didn't deserve them.

'Dom's not dull. He's kind and loyal. And I'm not on the rebound, as you call it.'

'So kind and loyal that you buggered off and left him and didn't look back?'

Bea had no response to that. She sighed. 'I'm not planning to get back together with Dom.'

Michael flicked his gaze over to where Dom was paying for the drinks, then back to her. 'You might not think so, but he does. Just be careful, promise me?'

'You have my word.'

Harry, Dom and Ashton reappeared and set a tray of drinks down, some of them splashing messily onto the table.

'You're an angel,' Mia said, reaching for her gin and tonic. She turned to Bea. 'So, how was your day with the family?'

'Oh the usual. Mum ran around trying to please everyone, Alice had her holier-than-thou face on and Charlie let the kids run wild.' She shrugged.

'And your dad? How's he?'

Bea frowned. Mia rarely asked after her dad. She knew she still saw her parents from time to time, and she wondered whether Mia had noticed something awry with him.

'He's fine,' she said, vowing to speak to her friend about it later.

'We're so glad to have you home, aren't we everyone?' Harry said, holding up his glass of wine for everyone to toast.

'Too bloody right,' Mia said, holding her own glass up.

They clinked glasses and as the conversation flowed easily, Bea let herself relax. These were her people, and she was utterly content to sit here and just be with them all, laughing and listening and taking the piss after so long away. She studied Dom too, as everyone talked. Lovely, kind, funny Dom, who was taking this unexpected intrusion from his former friends in his stride; who deserved to be treated so much better than she had treated him. She studied the curve of his chin, the dark flash of his eyes, the long tapering fingers that curled round his glass and felt a stirring deep inside her. From the wine? Maybe. But then again, maybe it was more.

'Didn't you Bea?'

'What?' She looked up to find Ashton looking at her expectantly.

'Ignore him, he's being a pain as usual,' Harry said.

'I was only saying that you left New York just to spite me so I couldn't hook up with your hot friend Maggie,' Ashton continued, oblivious.

'Ashton, you could have been the very last man with a pulse in the whole of New York State and Maggie still wouldn't have gone anywhere near you,' Mia said, tipping her head back and laughing.

'Ah come on, you're only jealous because you wish we could get back together,' Ashton said, nudging Mia's elbow and sending more gin and tonic splashing across the table.

'You're kidding me!' Mia replied and, while they bickered, Bea met Dom's eyes across the table.

'All right?' he mouthed, and she nodded, a wave of affection spreading through her.

By the time last orders were called, Bea felt the world swimming, and the blast of cold air as they finally piled out of the door was like a slap in the face. It sobered her up though, and as everyone said their goodbyes and headed off towards home through the bitter night air, Bea wondered what was going to happen next.

'I'll walk you home,' Dom said quietly, slipping in beside her as Mia hurried after Ashton, demanding he be a gentleman and walk her home safely.

'You don't have to,' Bea said.

'I know.' Dom held his elbow out and Bea tucked her arm through his. She felt as though she had never been away.

* * *

It was only a ten-minute walk, and soon they were back at Bea's parents'. The doorstep was dark, the only light from the glass panel above the door from the hall. Bea couldn't make out Dom's features in this light, so she couldn't tell what was going through his mind.

'I...' She began, but her words were cut short by the gentle press of Dom's lips on hers. It took her by surprise, and by the time she thought to respond, he'd pulled away again.

'I'm sorry,' he said. 'I didn't mean to do that.'

The space between them felt cold now and Bea reached for his hands. His fingers were freezing, and she wrapped hers round them and brought them to her lips. 'I'm glad you did.'

Dom moved closer to her and this time when he kissed her she kissed him back. She'd thought it would simply feel comforting, familiar, like an old blanket, so she was surprised to feel a fizz of desire spark in the pit of her belly. His lips were warm, and tasted of wine and she didn't want to stop whatever it was that was happening here, so when he snaked his arms around her and pressed his hands into her spine she arched her back and moved against him, her heart thumping against her chest.

Finally, Dom pulled his face away. His breath was warm against her lips.

'I've loved seeing you today,' he said, his voice rough.

'Me too,' she said.

She meant it. She knew Dom almost as well as she knew herself, and after the last few months, she needed to feel loved and wanted by someone she could trust. The seconds ticked by and Bea could feel Dom's pulse beneath his coat, beating in time with her own. It would be easy to love this man again. She just needed to let herself.

A light flickered on in the living room behind Bea and broke the moment. Dom stepped away.

'I'll see you soon then,' she said, a half-question.

'I hope so,' Dom said.

She hesitated a moment longer, caught between wanting to say something more, to let him know this was good – that this was more than good – and wanting to say goodnight and take a moment to arrange her thoughts.

'Bye Dom,' she whispered, then she let herself in and closed the door. She stood for a moment, breathing slowly, eyes closed, wondering whether Dom was still out there doing the same.

Her mind was all over the place but she knew that, no matter what happened between her and Dom after this, being with him tonight had been exactly what she'd needed to help her begin to piece her broken heart back together.

She opened her eyes, took a deep breath and poked her head round the living room door. Her dad was in his armchair next to the Christmas tree, staring at the blank TV screen.

'Hey Dad.'

He snapped his head round at her voice. 'Hello Bea.' He smiled.

'Everything okay?'

'Yes love. Just couldn't sleep.'

She watched him for a moment longer, then nodded. 'Okay, night Dad. Love you.'

'Love you too.'

She hung her coat on the hook, then ran upstairs to bed, her mind whirring with thoughts of her dad, and of Dom, and of that kiss. She pressed her fingers against her lips, which still tingled.

She brushed her teeth, scrubbed her face clean and was just

climbing into bed when her phone beeped. She smiled, expecting to see a goodnight message from Dom. The words took their time to swim into focus beneath her wine-fuelled gaze.

And when they did, her heart stopped.

Merry Christmas Princess Beatrice. Love AJ x

She stared at the message, frozen. Then, before she could change her mind, she deleted it.

8

STAY

December 2005

'Merry Christmas!' Mia held her glass in the air and everyone leaned towards her and clinked theirs against it. Behind her, the lights of the city sparkled through the floor-to-ceiling windows, and even though she'd lived here for so long now, Bea still couldn't get used to the incredible view.

Bea didn't think she'd ever seen her best friend look as happy as she did right now, and her heart felt full as she watched her leaning towards Frank, her boyfriend of four months, for a kiss.

'Can I have a kiss too?' a voice murmured in her ear and she turned her head and pressed her lips against the ones right beside hers.

'Merry Christmas baby,' she murmured.

'Merry Christmas, Princess Beatrice.'

Bea settled back into AJ's chest and felt his arms snake round her waist. This was shaping up to be the best Christmas she'd ever had, and it was only just getting started.

'To AJ, and to him letting us stay in his amazing apartment!' Mia said, holding her glass up again.

'Ah, it's good to have you,' AJ said, waving his glass in her direction.

'So, tonight we thought we'd have a quiet one here,' Bea said, leaning away from the speakers so she could be heard over Mariah Carey. 'But tomorrow, do you mind if I steal Mia for a few hours, Frank, so we can do some proper girly shopping?'

'Be my guest,' Frank said. 'I'm sure I can find something to keep me busy.'

Bea smiled. She was so thrilled for Mia that she'd finally found her Mr Right – even if he did live three thousand miles away from home.

'We've got AJ to thank for bringing us together,' Mia told her.

'Really?' Bea said.

'Yep. If AJ hadn't pestered you, you would never have come to live here, and I would never have met Frank.' She beamed at Frank and he beamed back.

'Sure, you guys would have met somehow. You were destined to be together,' AJ said.

Bea murmured her agreement. But her mind was already elsewhere, and as her friends chatted she let it wander further.

The truth was, as happy as she was right now, she always had an underlying feeling of guilt about what she'd done to Dom.

After she'd interviewed AJ last December, she spent a lovely Christmas at home with Dom and her family. They'd squeezed everyone into their flat, somehow, and cooked dinner for fifteen people. Over Christmas they'd rested and recharged their batteries, and Bea had been looking forward to the new year.

Then, on New Year's Eve, as Bea stood at the top of the hill by Alexandra Palace with Dom, Mia, Ashton, Michael and Harry, watching fireworks going off all over London as the clock turned to midnight, her phone had buzzed. After she'd hugged everyone, and kissed Dom, she'd pulled it from her pocket with gloved hands and read the message. And her heart had stopped for just a moment.

> Happy New Year Princess Beatrice. I hope you're having a wonderful one. AJ. x

A single kiss. She'd stared at it for so long her fingers began to turn numb. Although she and AJ had exchanged numbers, she hadn't really expected to hear from him again unless it was to do with the article. But this was a message just for her, and she felt a smile creep across her face.

'What you doing?' Mia stumbled into her back, almost sending her flying into the mud. 'Oops, sorry.' Mia swung the bottle round her head and giggled.

'Nothing,' Bea said, shoving her phone back in her pocket and swiping the bottle from Mia's hand. But even though she carried on celebrating as though nothing had happened, she couldn't stop thinking about that text all night.

She couldn't stop thinking about it the following morning either as she and Dom huddled on their sofa nursing a hangover. She couldn't stop thinking about it when she got back to the office and her editor sent the feature back with a note saying, 'This is wonderful Bea. Just a couple of questions and then it's good to go. Good work.' And she hadn't stopped thinking about it when AJ sent another text a few days into January.

> I hope you didn't think my message was inappropriate. I was just thinking about you, in that moment. AJ.

This time, she replied immediately.

It wasn't inappropriate. It was lovely to hear from you. Happy New Year to you too.

She hadn't signed it with a kiss, despite wanting to, and had left it at that.

But over the next few weeks, they'd begun to chat regularly via text. Often, a message would arrive just as Bea was leaving work, AJ telling her about his morning, or wondering what she was up to that evening. The messages were friendly, not flirty, and yet she made the decision not to tell Dom about them. Because she knew how it looked, and she knew how she'd feel if the situation were reversed.

It didn't mean she didn't feel guilty though.

Then at Easter, Dom took a day off work. By the time Bea got home he was still in bed, and her heart sank. She knew from bitter experience that when Dom spent the whole day in bed, it was usually the beginning of a downward spiral.

'I'm so sorry Bea,' he said, when she lowered herself onto the end of the bed.

'You don't have to be sorry.'

He shook his head, and looked over at the bedside table. She followed his gaze. A blister pack sat beside a glass of water. It was still full.

'You stopped taking your medication.'

Dom nodded.

'But you promised me,' she said. 'You said you wouldn't do that again.'

'I know.' He hadn't said anything more and she could see the light in his eyes was already half extinguished.

'Why, Dom?'

He stared at his fingers, threaded together on top of the duvet. Goosebumps covered his bare arms. She felt a flare of frustration.

Why did he keep doing this – thinking he was better, stopping his medication, getting ill? It was a vicious circle that Dom seemed to stubbornly believe he could break simply by the sheer will of wanting to. She wanted to bash his head against a wall, make him realise that the medication was given to him for a reason. She wanted to scream and shout and cry about the injustice of it all. It wasn't *fair* that she had to keep putting up with this, year after year, regular as clockwork.

And then she felt like a petulant child, making it all about her, when the only person it was really about was Dom.

Dom, who she'd loved since she was a girl.

Dom, who kept promising her he'd stay on his medication, stay on an even keel.

Dom, who kept breaking that promise, thinking he knew better.

Dom who, she realised now, was making her feel helpless, and utterly miserable.

She stood, the sudden movement causing Dom's body to roll to the side. She needed to get out of there. Out of that room, out of the flat, out of London.

Out of Dom's life?

The thought shocked her and she stalked from the room, almost slamming the bedroom door behind her, and went into the kitchen. She didn't bother turning the light on but stood, in the darkness, taking deep gulps of air, trying to get her heartrate under control.

With shaking hands she pulled her phone out of her bag and rang Mia.

'I'm going to leave Dom.' Just saying the words out loud to her best friend felt like releasing a plug, and she felt herself deflate.

'Wait, what?' Shouts in the background, pounding music, then a rustling sound. Seconds later, Mia's voice came back on the line.

'Sorry Bea, I'm in the pub near work. What did you say about Dom?'

Could she say the words again? Did she really mean them or was she just letting off steam?

'I said I'm leaving him.'

A silence followed and Bea wasn't sure what it meant. Then Mia said, 'Oh.'

'You don't sound very surprised.'

'I'm not.'

'Why?'

Another silence and Bea's heart thumped. 'Come on, I've seen how you look when you talk about AJ.'

Bea's stomach dropped to the ground. 'What? How do I look?'

'Just – you know. Loved up.'

Bea waited a moment. Was there any point in lying to Mia, who always saw right through her? 'Do you think Dom knows?' Her voice was small.

'Probably.'

'Fuck.'

'Yeah.'

'This isn't really about AJ though. I mean, it's not like we're ever going to be together. He's literally married to someone else and he lives in New York. But...' She stopped.

'But you've realised that if you can't stop thinking about him then you shouldn't stay with Dom?' Mia finished saying what Bea couldn't.

'Pretty much.' She swallowed. 'He stopped taking his medication again.'

'Oh Dom.'

'I know.'

'Come and meet me.'

'Aren't you out with colleagues?'

'Yeah, but fuck 'em. This is more important. Come to Soho and we'll talk some more.'

Bea did, and by the end of the night, she knew it was over with Dom. She just couldn't do it any longer, knowing she had feelings for someone else.

'Are you going to tell AJ how you feel?'

'God no.'

'You should.' Mia was drunk, her words slurring into each other. 'Why don't you ring him now.'

'Absolutely no way. He's *married*, Mee.'

Mia waved her arm in the air in an alarming way, her wine sloshing over the glass and spraying anyone unlucky enough to be within a two-metre radius. 'Sorry,' she mumbled over her shoulder. 'He's not really married though, is he? Didn't he tell you he said goodbye to her a long time ago?'

'Yeah.' Bea nodded sadly. 'But he is still married and while Cassandra is still alive, he always will be.'

'Send him a text then.' Mia swiped Bea's phone from the table and started scrolling through her contacts.

'Mia! No!' Bea leapt up and tried to grab the phone from her friend, but Mia was taller than her and when she stood too and held it out of reach, Bea had no chance.

'Mia, please don't.'

Mia brought the phone back down to the table and dropped it. 'Fine. But I still think you should tell him how you feel.'

'Maybe,' Bea said, mainly to placate Mia, not because she had any intention of doing any such thing. 'But let me handle things with Dom first.'

It was one of the hardest things Bea had ever done, in the end. Ending a relationship was painful at the best of times. When your partner was in the depths of depression, it was almost impossible. Which was why it took over a month after

Dom re-started his medication before Bea could even broach the subject.

But when she did, Dom accepted it with a weariness she hadn't expected.

'Will you promise me you won't stop taking your medication though,' she said.

He nodded miserably. 'I only think I can do without it when I'm happy,' he said, and Bea wanted to throw her arms around him and tell him she'd stay.

But she also knew it wouldn't be fair to him, or to her, so instead she brushed his hair away from his face, then stood and left. Her heart felt like it was breaking in two.

She moved out the following week and into her parents' house and they made plans to sell the flat. After a few weeks of living with her parents again, Bea knew she needed to make a change. That's when Michael's words from two years before drifted into her mind when they'd spoken about her aborted escape to New York. *For what it's worth I think you should have gone.*

Back then, she'd chosen to stay for so many reasons – Dom being one of them. But now she was on her own. She'd loved New York when she'd visited at Christmas, and still dreamed of living there. *Could* she really do it, this time?

I'm thinking of coming to spend some time in New York, she tentatively typed to AJ one evening. He didn't reply for ages, and she began to wonder whether she'd scared him off. A long-distance friendship was one thing. But what was she really hoping for, by telling him she was thinking of going over there? After all, nothing had changed for him. He was still married. Cassandra was still his wife.

He didn't reply until the following morning, by which time Bea had decided she would probably have to delete his number and never contact him again. But when her phone buzzed and she saw it was him, her stomach flipped over.

> Sorry it's taken me so long to reply. I was with Cassie last night. This is brilliant news. I'd love to spend some more time with you, in person. Can I ring you later? AJ x

Bea read the message over and over, trying to read between the lines. What did he mean by wanting to spend more time with her? As a friend? Did he think there might be more? Although still firmly in the 'friendship' zone, their texts had definitely become more flirty, more intimate over the last few weeks, and she'd told him things she rarely talked about with anyone else, including what had happened at work with her old boss and how worried she was about her dad. She felt as though she knew AJ almost as well as she knew Mia, or Michael.

And yet, she was also very aware that there could never be anything more between them, at least not while Cassandra was still alive.

> Yes, I'll be here from 6 p.m. Ring you then? B x

Two weeks later, Bea was on a flight to New York. As she sat on the plane watching films and eating her dinner, trying and failing to read a book, she couldn't quite believe she was actually doing this.

'Oh not this again, I thought you'd got over this fantasy,' her mum had said when she'd broken the news to them. 'How long are you going for?'

'I don't know.'

'What do you mean you don't know? How can you not know?'

'I'm going to play it by ear.'

'Well that's responsible,' Alice said from the sofa beside their mum, while her youngest, Ava, climbed all over her. 'Leaving your job, your home, your friends, your *family*. For what? A fairy-tale?'

Alice's words felt like bullets, because Bea knew she was right. She *was* being irresponsible. Plus she knew she was twisting the knife in Dom's back.

But this was something she'd wanted to do her whole life, and she'd already changed her mind once. Even if she only ended up staying a couple of weeks, she needed to do this. For her.

Luckily, Bea's boss had been more pragmatic. 'You'll be brilliant, Bea. Have an absolute ball.' At least someone believed in her.

As Bea dragged her suitcase behind her on the long walk from passport control to the arrivals hall at JFK airport, she thought her legs might give way. She might have chatted with AJ via text, but Bea had only ever met him in the flesh once and had no idea how he saw their friendship. Yet he had insisted on meeting her at the airport.

Her nerves dissipated the instant she walked through the automatic doors. AJ was holding up a sign that read: 'Welcome to NYC Princess Beatrice', and grinning at her like a loon, and as she approached, he pulled her in for a hug that lasted far longer than a friendly hug should. The press of his body against hers in the middle of an airport full of people felt – well, it felt incredible.

'Let's go,' he said, releasing her and taking hold of her suitcase in one hand, then tucking his sign under the other arm and taking her hand. She followed, her heart skittering in her chest. She was here, she was doing this – and AJ seemed pleased to see her.

Whatever happened next, right now she felt happy.

AJ had insisted she stay with him for the first few nights, even though she was adamant she was going to book a hotel. 'I've made up the spare bedroom for you,' he said, opening the apartment door with a flourish.

'Thank you,' she said, smiling.

That first night they sat up late, talking into the night. Although Bea had told AJ plenty about Dom, she had never felt it completely fair to tell him everything. How bad Dom's depression sometimes got, how she blamed him every time it returned because it felt as if he believed he knew better than the doctors.

And while Bea already knew about Cassandra – Cassie, as AJ always called her – thanks to the interview she'd done, there was so much more to find out about him. The small details – did he like coffee, or tea; was there a film he'd seen over and over; a book he loved; what was his favourite song; what did he like to eat? Was he tidy or messy, an early riser or a night owl? She felt as though she would never find out enough about him, never satiate her appetite to get inside this man's head and get to know him from the inside out.

Was she falling in love? She didn't know, and it wasn't something she wanted to give too much thought to either. But it sure as hell felt different to anything she'd ever felt before. With Dom, there had always been certainty, a kind of comfort that came with having known each other for a long time. And although she did remember feeling butterflies back when they'd first met, the way AJ was currently making her feel was something else entirely. Forget butterflies, she felt as though her entire body was being buffeted by waves until she didn't know which way was up.

Except she couldn't tell him any of that.

During Bea's first few days in New York, she was happy to spend time soaking up the sights she hadn't had time to see on her previous flying visit; strolling through Central Park, winding up the spiral slope of the Guggenheim, zipping to the top of the Empire State building. It was summer so the air was humid, thick with traffic fumes as taxis idled and the traffic crawled along almost at a standstill. She queued for pastrami on rye sandwiches at Katz's diner and took a walk over the Brooklyn Bridge, strolling along the waterside promenade in Brooklyn Heights with its peaceful gardens and amazing views of the Manhattan skyline. She wondered whether she'd ever shake the feeling of living in a fairy-tale, or a film set. Whether she would ever become immune to the thrill of being here. She doubted it.

But she knew she also had to find somewhere else to stay. She couldn't sleep in AJ's spare room for weeks on end, and as the days wore on she became increasingly worried that Cassie's parents might drop by – AJ said they did from time to time and it would have felt wrong. So while AJ was at work, Bea began to look for somewhere to live. She wasn't really sure where to start. She didn't know anyone, and the people AJ put her in touch with couldn't help either, plus finding something temporary was harder than she'd imagined. Then one day she was queuing for a coffee on Seventh Avenue when a voice behind her said, 'Excuse me, I think you've spilt something on your skirt.'

She turned to find a tall, leggy, dark-haired woman smiling at her and pointing at a smudge on the back of her dress.

'Oh arse,' Bea said, rubbing it ineffectually with her finger. 'That looks like it's going to stain.'

'That's a pain in the ass,' the woman said. Bea was about to turn back round when the woman stuck out her hand. 'Hi, I'm Maggie, nice to meet you.'

'Oh, hi. Bea. Beatrice,' Bea said.

'Like the princess?' Maggie said, and that was when Bea knew this woman was going to be her friend.

'Exactly like the princess,' she said, shaking Maggie's hand.

They stood with their coffees outside on the street chatting, until Maggie suddenly realised the time.

'Oh shoot, I'm gonna be late for work,' she said, pushing her bag up onto her shoulder. She rummaged inside and pulled out her phone. 'This might sound weird but do you want to give me your number? I could show you round the city some?'

'I'd love that,' Bea said, giving Maggie her UK phone number.

She wasn't sure whether she'd ever hear from Maggie again, so was thrilled when she rang the next day to ask if she fancied going to the theatre with her because she had tickets for *The Color Purple* and her friend Nancy had cancelled on her.

Maggie, it turned out, was the answer to all of Bea's problems. Not only had Bea found a brand-new friend, but Maggie was about to start looking for a roommate.

'Mine moved out a couple months ago and I can't afford the rent by myself,' she said. 'It's only small, but it's a great apartment, and you'd be doing me a favour if you took the other room, even if it's only for a short while.'

A week later, Bea moved in. The apartment *was* small, but Bea didn't care. She was living in New York.

Now she just needed a job because her savings weren't going to last forever.

'I know it's not what you really want to do, but there's an admin job going at my place,' AJ told her one evening when he came round to see the flat and meet Maggie.

'I'll take anything at the moment,' Bea said. 'Do you think they'd interview me?'

'Well, we'll need to sort you out a proper visa, but I'm sure they'll help.'

As the searing heat of the summer finally began to wane, Bea started working at AJ's company, which meant that they were spending most days and evenings together – Bea, AJ, and Maggie, when she wasn't out on another disastrous date.

'Haven't you got any other friends to hang out with?' Bea teased AJ.

'Yeah, but they're all much busier and more important than you,' he said.

Bea wasn't complaining. She loved her new life and, even though she only knew two people, they were two very special people indeed. She felt blessed.

'I still can't believe you've abandoned me so easily,' Mia said only half-jokingly on one of their regular calls.

'Come and stay for a bit,' Bea said.

'I think I'd better. Sounds like you need reminding how much you love me.'

Two weeks later Mia arrived – and met Frank on their very first night out.

'I'm going to marry that man,' Mia said, as they lay on Bea's bed later that night.

'What?' Bea laughed, but stopped dead when she saw the look on Mia's face. 'You're serious?'

'When do I ever joke about matters of the heart?' she said.

'But he lives in New York and you... don't.'

Mia shrugged. 'Doesn't matter. He's The One. And maybe if you and AJ ever bloody get it together, we can go on double dates when I come over next time.'

Bea didn't respond to that. She and AJ were very much still in the friend zone, and, as thrilled as she was for her friend, she wished things were as straightforward for her as they seemed to be for Mia.

One evening shortly after Mia reluctantly returned to London – 'I'll be back as soon as I can though,' she promised, as she kissed Frank urgently at the departure gate – Bea and AJ were watching TV, the sounds of the city drifting through the cranked-open window, when Maggie texted to say she was caught up at work and wouldn't be home in time for the takeaway they had planned.

AJ sprung up from the sofa. 'Let's go for dinner.'

'Dinner?'

'Yeah, you know. A restaurant, nice food, a glass of wine.'

'But...' Bea trailed off. She was bored of pleading poverty, but her rent and bills were sucking most of her pay-packet dry.

'My treat,' AJ said, before she'd even got that far.

'Oh no, that's not what—'

'Come on Bea, I fancy some pasta and I don't want to eat alone.' He cocked his head to one side. 'Pretty please?'

Bea hauled herself off the sofa. 'Okay fine. But only because I can't stand the thought of you being lonely,' she said.

'You're so selfless.'

As they walked along the slowly darkening street side by side, Bea tried not to imagine how they might appear to outsiders. Did they look like a regular couple, out on a date? She would take a bet that no one would ever guess how complicated their friendship really was.

Because that's all it was. Friendship. And those times when she caught AJ watching her, or when something he said or did made her stomach flip over with desire? They were nothing, They didn't matter.

AJ was still married, and there was nothing she could do about that.

Over dinner they chatted about colleagues, and laughed about something they'd watched on TV the night before. The candle flickered between them and Bea tried very hard to focus on what AJ was saying.

'Do you think I hang out with you too much?'

'What?' Bea looked up from her plate to find AJ looking at her seriously.

He leaned forward so his face was in the light. 'I worry I might be cramping your style. You know...' His eyes flicked down to the table. 'That I might be stopping you finding other people to hang out with. Other men.'

'Oh!' That was the last thing Bea had been expecting him to say and it knocked her off balance. 'No, I...' She stopped. She couldn't say what she really meant, which was that she literally couldn't think of anyone else in the whole world she would rather be hanging out with. So instead she just said, 'Don't be daft. It's... I've loved having you and Maggie in my life these last few months. I feel very lucky.'

'Good.' His eyes studied her closely. She shifted in her seat. Did she have something in her hair? On her cheek? 'I just...' He swallowed. 'Bea, I really love spending time with you and I don't want to stop, but I've deliberately kept you and my other friends apart because...'

'Because of Cassie?'

He nodded. 'Yeah.' He twiddled with a piece of skin on his thumb. 'Most of them were our friends, mine and Cassie's. And they – not everyone understands that at some point I'm going to want to move on. Find someone else.'

Bea's heart thumped loudly. Her hands gripped her wine glass tightly. 'I see,' she said. She watched him, grappling with something. Then finally, he looked at her again and she felt the intensity of his gaze. 'The thing is, Bea, I—'

'AJ, you don't have to—'

They both stopped.

'You don't have to explain anything,' Bea said.

AJ shook his head. 'No, I want to. Because I...' He swallowed. 'I like you. A lot.' He smiled. 'Well, I think you know that. But I...' He sighed. 'I'd like there to be something. Between us.'

The world around them seemed to press pause for a moment,

to fade away and leave just the two of them sitting at this white-clothed restaurant table.

'I would too.' Bea's words came out as a whisper.

They sat motionless for a few moments, until the waiter came over to take their plates, then they sprang apart like guilty children who'd been caught doing something they shouldn't. AJ paid the bill without looking at her, but as they left the restaurant he slipped his hand in hers and they walked back through the empty streets. When they reached Bea's apartment, AJ turned to look at her and her legs felt weak. Then he filled her vision and she could see the sprinkle of stubble on his chin, the glow of his eyes, the soft curl of his lip. And then those lips were on hers and it was as though she was made of air.

Seconds passed, or years, and when AJ pulled away she could still feel his breath on her mouth.

'Are you coming up?' she asked, her voice hoarse.

'Do you want me to?'

'More than anything.'

Neither of them needed asking twice.

* * *

Their first night together was everything Bea had dreamed of. When they woke in the morning, she lay and watched AJ sleeping for a few minutes, drinking in his smooth skin, the tattoos that snaked down his arms, the gentle in-out of his chest. He was so beautiful, and she couldn't quite believe he was in her bed.

She laid her hand on his chest and he opened his eyes and looked at her, a warm smile spreading across his face like butter.

'You're here,' he said.

'I'm here.'

It felt like a miracle.

They couldn't hide what had happened from Maggie, and when she saw AJ emerging from Bea's room that morning looking sheepish, Bea was certain the whole of Manhattan would have heard the scream of excitement.

'It's about bloody time you guys,' she said, bursting into Bea's room seconds later.

But they both knew they couldn't ignore the elephant in the room forever, and after what felt like endless discussions that were going nowhere, AJ made a suggestion.

'I think you should come and meet Cassie.'

Bea stared at him, momentarily speechless. 'What?'

'I know it sounds crazy, but Cassie would have loved you, and I know she'd be pleased I've found someone to be happy with. And I think it might help you to understand why this isn't wrong, Bea. To see that Cassie is never coming home.'

Eventually, Bea agreed, and a few days later they drove out east to the care home where Cassie was being looked after.

'Will her parents be there?'

'No, not today. I told them I'm coming, so they usually take the day off when I'm there.'

'Do they know about me?'

A pause, then: 'Not yet. But I will tell them, when the time is right. I promise.'

Bea didn't dare say any more. Her chest was tight with anticipation, and by the time they pulled up outside the care home she thought she might be sick. As they approached the door, AJ took her hands. 'Don't be scared. You'll be fine.'

The nurses were kind and when they entered Cassandra's room, the first thing that struck Bea was the warmth, the homeliness. She'd expected a stark grey hospital room, with tubes and beeping machines. But this room was painted a soft buttercup yellow, with a vase of tulips on a small side table, a soft, spongy carpet underfoot and an armchair tucked on either side of Cassandra's bed.

This must be what money can buy you, Bea thought, as her attention finally turned to the bed and, more importantly, the figure lying in it.

They approached Cassie, and AJ threaded his fingers through Bea's. Her pulse thumped in her temple, her breath shallow.

'Cassie, I've brought someone to see you,' AJ said, his voice soft. He reached his other hand out and laid it on top of Cassie's, which was resting on the cover. 'This is Bea.'

Cassie was propped up on pillows. AJ had shown Bea a photo of Cassie, so she knew she had been stunning: long, glossy dark hair, tall and willowy with sharp features and a wide smile. Bea could still see the ghost of the woman she had been beneath Cassie's lopsided smile, her matted hair and empty eyes, and her heart broke for her.

AJ perched on the edge of Cassie's bed and indicated for Bea to take the chair by Cassie's head. It was hard to tell whether Cassie knew who AJ was, but AJ had told her the doctors said it was extremely unlikely. What did AJ see when he looked at Cassie? Did he see the strong, beautiful woman she'd been before, the one he'd fallen in love with? Or did he see this empty shell, whose mind had long given up?

She let him talk to Cassie, his gentle voice washing over her in this over-warm room. The murmur of voices from other rooms, and nurses walking past, their soles shushing quietly against the padded tiles were the only sounds Bea could hear apart from AJ's voice and she wondered what happened to you if you didn't have rich parents, or excellent medical insurance. Would Cassandra even have been given the chance to be kept alive?

'Bea?' She looked up at the sound of AJ's voice. 'Shall we go?'

Bea nodded, then followed him out of the room, back along the corridor, and out of the main entrance into the fresh air. Relief washed over her like warm water – relief at being out of that stuffy room, but more, relief about leaving behind Cassandra and all the sadness that hung in the air.

'Thank you for coming,' AJ said, as they made their way back to the car. 'I know it was hard, but it was really important to me for you to meet her. And her to meet you.'

Bea nodded. 'Of course. I know.'

She felt AJ looking at her and she tried to keep a neutral look on her face. 'Bea, look at me.'

She turned to face him, his handsome face, full of life. He pressed his palm against her cheek. 'What's the matter?'

'Nothing.'

He stopped dead and she was forced to stop too. 'Tell me Bea.'

She hung her head, ashamed. 'I just... I can't stop thinking about how beautiful she was and whether... whether you still love her.'

A beat, long enough for Bea to fill it with her own, unwanted answers. 'I'll always love Cassie, in some way,' AJ said gently. He lifted her chin with his finger. 'But I'm in love with you. Cassie is part of my past now and while I'll never abandon her while she's still alive, you're my future. At least, if you'll have me?'

Bea felt her heart leap from her chest, her breath leave her body. 'I'll have you,' she said.

* * *

Now she was here, in New York, with a whole new life and a whole new future spread out in front of her. When she'd made the decision to stay in London all those Christmases ago, she'd assumed that was it; she'd lost her chance. It just went to show it was impossible to predict the future.

She stood and grabbed another bottle from the side. Although she felt at home in AJ's apartment these days, she was glad she still had her own flat. Even though they'd agreed they wanted to be together, Bea had made it clear she couldn't go all-in while Cassie was still alive.

'But what if she keeps going for years? Decades?' AJ had said.

'Let's just take it one year at a time, shall we?' she said.

Bea wasn't sure whether she had ever been happier in her life than she was right now.

'Top ups?' she said, popping the cork from the bottle.

'Does a bear shit in the woods?' Mia said, and Frank chuckled.

'I don't think I'll ever get tired of hearing your English expressions.'

'You ain't heard nothing yet,' Mia said, giving him an exaggerated wink.

'And wait 'til you hear some of AJ's Irish ones,' Bea said.

'She's right, there are some right corkers,' AJ said, tipping his head back and draining his glass.

Bea was about to sit back down next to AJ when she felt her phone vibrating in her pocket. She checked the screen and her heart sank. Alice. Her sister was still cross at Bea for leaving Dom, and she mentioned it every single time they spoke – as well as the fact their mum had invited Dom for Christmas dinner so he wasn't on his own. Bea put off returning her calls or pretended she was busy every time Alice rang her. Guilt pricked her this time, and she headed into the bedroom to answer it.

'Hey,' she said, aware suddenly that she was a bit drunk.

'Oh, you are still alive then?' Alice was in a mood, and Bea was already regretting not sending her through to voicemail.

'Very much so,' she said, trying to keep her tone light.

'Hmm. Well, sounds like you're having a nice time.'

'Mia's here with Frank,' Bea said.

'Right.' Alice hadn't been over to visit Bea yet, and Bea wasn't sure if it was because she genuinely couldn't get away from the kids or because she couldn't bear to see Bea and AJ happy together. She suspected the latter. 'Well, it doesn't sound like a good time to call, but it is fairly important, so can you ring me tomorrow?'

'It's fine. You can talk to me now,' Bea said, resigning herself to another lecture from Alice about why she should come home and face her responsibilities. She sat on the bed and leaned against the cushions.

'It's Dad.'

'Dad?' That was the last thing Bea had expected Alice to say and she felt instantly sober. 'What about him?' Alice hesitated for a moment and Bea held her breath. 'Alice? Has something happened?'

'I don't know.' Alice's voice had lost all its usual bluster, and instead she just sounded sad. Bea waited. 'He's... he's been getting confused a lot.'

'Right?' Bea felt her pulse thump in her temple.

'He asked me what time you were coming round last night. And when I told him you were in New York he said of course he knew that and he'd only been joking. But it's not the first time. He struggles to follow conversations, and he's forgotten how to get to places a few times – he even forgot how to get home from the football the other day and he's been doing that every weekend for most of his life.' She stopped and Bea heard a sob burst from her. 'Sorry. It's just – I don't know what to do.'

'Oh Alice. What does Mum think?'

Alice gave a mirthless laugh. 'Mum's in complete denial. Andy thinks I should make Dad a doctor's appointment but how can I? Mum would just refuse to take him.'

Bea didn't know what to say, and for a moment she stared at the phone resting on her knees. She hated being so far away at times like this. All she wanted was to go round and see for herself how her dad was, whether there really was anything to be worried about. And if there was, she would help Alice, they would be able to help him, together.

'Sorry Bea. I don't know why I rang you. It's not as if you can do anything about it.' She sounded like she was crying.

'No! You must ring me, always. I'm just... I'm so sorry I'm not there.'

'It's okay. I'm sorry for giving you a hard time about it. I'm proud of you really.'

'Are you?' This was news to Bea.

'Yeah. I just – I suppose I'm a bit jealous. That you got to fulfil your dream.'

'But you've got your dream, Ali.' All Alice had ever wanted was to get married and have children.

'I know. But it doesn't seem like very much, does it?'

Alice was four years older than Bea, and had always been the sensible one, the reliable one. Bea, on the other hand, had been allowed to get away with being flighty, indecisive, away with the fairies. It had never once occurred to her that Alice might want to be a bit more like her, sometimes.

'You've got a lovely life, Ali. Never assume the grass is greener. I live in a tiny flat, and can't afford to breathe let alone go on swanky holidays. I have an admin job I don't love and...' She didn't say anything about the amazing city, or the fact she had the man of her dreams. It wasn't what Alice needed to hear right now.

A sniffle, then: 'I know. Sorry. It's just all this stuff with Dad has got me thinking about things. You know. About how short life is.'

'But Dad's going to be okay, isn't he?'

'I hope so. I really do.'

'Will you ring me when you've decided what to do?'

'Course. Now go and enjoy the rest of your evening with your glamorous American friends.'

'I will.'

'And Bea?'

'Yes?'

'I love you.' Then she was gone, leaving Bea staring at the phone in shock. She couldn't remember the last time her sister had told her she loved her.

9

GO

December 2006

Bea stood at the door of the bedroom she shared with Dom. The room was silent, the only sign there was anyone in there was the crumpled heap of blankets on the bed, beneath which she knew Dom was probably asleep, or at least pretending to be.

She walked in and picked up the packet of pills beside his bed and counted them. He hadn't taken them. Again.

She threw them back down and walked out of the room, closing the door quietly but firmly behind her. She really didn't want to wake Dom right now because things were easier when he was asleep.

What an awful thing to admit.

Bea made herself a cup of coffee and sat on the sofa, staring at the forlorn-looking Christmas tree in the corner, two wrapped presents beneath it that she'd put there herself a couple of days before in the hope that Dom might notice. A piece of tinsel dropped from the bottom branch, catching the insipid sunlight trickling through the window and creating sparkles on the wall. She was meant to be at work in an hour, but it was the last day before the office closed for the holidays and she knew nobody would actually be doing anything today apart from nursing hang-overs and clock-watching until 5 p.m. She just needed a few minutes to get going.

The steam from the coffee swirled round her face and she closed her eyes. Just another five minutes...

She let her mind drift back over the last few months. Every Christmas since she'd run away to New York seemed to have been a turning point for her – starting a new life, meeting AJ, moving in with AJ, coming back home to London. But this year Bea felt as though her life had become stuck in a rut, trundling along the same old path without any idea how she got here – or how to get out of it.

After Bea and Dom's kiss last Christmas, Bea's family had been thrilled when, early in January, they had announced they were back together. Dom had wanted to get engaged again, but Bea had said no way. One step at a time. She moved back into the flat she'd left four years before, and within days it felt as though nothing had ever changed, as though the last four years had been nothing but a hiccup, a lucid dream. A 'phase', as her mum had always put it whenever she or her brothers and sister had expressed an interest in anything as children.

The main difference for Bea was that she had a much better job now. Her two and a half years as feature writer for a top magazine in New York had made it much easier to find similar work back in London, and now she was features editor for a weekly magazine based in Camden, just a few tube rides from their flat in Tufnell Park.

New York was a distant dream. Back in London, Bea and Dom

enjoyed nights out with friends in Soho and Camden, falling out of The Astoria on a Saturday night and stumbling along Oxford Street for a Big Mac. She went for dinner with Dom at their favourite Italian round the corner from their flat, and drinks at the Good Mixer after work with her colleagues – two for one every night before 7 p.m., meaning she was fuzzy-headed before dinner time. Every Sunday Bea and Dom were a regular fixture at her mum and dad's house where her mum would cook a Sunday roast. Life was good.

Good. Talk about damning with faint praise.

Bea knew she ought to feel more grateful for what she had. But the truth was, almost as soon as she'd moved back in with Dom, she'd been worried she'd made a mistake. Had she been too much of a pushover, too eager to please everyone else rather than considering what she actually wanted? Had she only got back with Dom because it was better than being alone?

She hoped not.

But the sad truth was, no matter how happy she felt with Dom – and much of the time he *did* make her happy – no matter how much she tried to tell herself he was the one she was meant to be with, she still struggled to get AJ out of her mind. She'd deleted his number from her phone, but it didn't mean she didn't think about him any more, and it definitely didn't mean she didn't feel anything for him either. She missed him, and she was scared that a part of her would always feel empty without him in her life.

Then, just as she'd been getting her life back on track, just as she'd begun to think that maybe she could stop thinking about him forever, there was *that* phone call, six months ago on a boiling hot summer day.

Bea had been in Alexandra Park drinking prosecco and eating crisps with Mia and Ashton – who had snogged a few times but still insisted they weren't together – Michael, Harry and Dom when her mobile had rung. She'd ignored it at first. But then it had rung again, and again, and when it rang the fourth time she reluctantly pulled it from her bag and checked the screen.

It was a New York number.

She still spoke to Maggie regularly, and Lori and Nancy from time to time, but it was none of their numbers. Perhaps they were ringing from work? She moved away from the group slightly, her thumb hovering over the answer button uncertainly. Then she pressed it.

'Bea?'

Her heart stopped, her legs felt weak. She turned away from her friends, her boyfriend, and walked across the park, her phone burning into the side of her head.

'Bea, are you there?' The voice was tinny and hollow.

'I'm here.'

'Oh thank God.'

'What do you want AJ?'

A moment's hesitation, and Bea's imagination filled it with all kinds of wild imaginings.

'It's about Cassie.'

She said nothing, her breath stuck in her chest. Her hand shook.

He cleared his throat. 'She died.'

Two words. Thunder roared in Bea's ears.

'AJ, I'm so sorry,' she said.

'I know it's weird, me ringing you to tell you this but I just – I needed to hear your voice.'

'It's fine. What happened?'

Silence hummed and Bea wondered whether he'd heard her. Then: 'It was just time.'

'Sandra didn't change her mind then?'

'No. I think Cassie did.'

Neither spoke for a moment. Bea could hear a clanking, and the roar of cars in the background of wherever AJ was and she pictured him outside his office on Broadway, or in the car park at the care home, the sun beating down on his head, his skin tanned. She wanted so desperately to wrap her arms around him and hold him, tell him she was there, that she would never leave him.

But the distance between them now was uncrossable. A canyon.

'Listen AJ, I have to go, I—'

'Can I come and see you?'

They both spoke at the same time but Bea heard what AJ said.

'What?'

'I'm sorry. I know you said you don't want to see me ever again, but I – I need to see you. I feel like I can't breathe I miss you so much and I—'

'Don't. Please don't AJ.' She felt like the ground had opened up beneath her and she was freefalling away from reality. 'I can't. I'm...'

'You're back with Dom, aren't you?' His voice was so quiet she had to press her phone right against her ear to hear him over the hum of a lawnmower and the cars on the nearby road.

'I...' she started. 'Yes.'

'So I guess that really is it then?'

'It has to be. I can't hurt Dom again. And nothing has changed between us.'

'But I thought...'

'What, AJ? You thought that now your wife had died I'd take you back?'

'Well, I guess...'

All the months of pain she'd gone through to get over him – all the bad dates, the terrible kisses, the hours of crying and feeling wretched – surged up and erupted. 'Nothing has changed AJ. You still lied to me and made me love you when you knew I could never have you.' Her voice broke. 'I'm sorry about Cassie but please don't ring me again. Ever.'

She'd ended the call, and stood, her whole body shaking. She didn't know how long she'd been there, but when she turned round her friends were quite far away, and she could see Dom watching her, a strange look on his face. She walked slowly back towards them, trying to arrange her face into a neutral look.

Dom stood as she arrived and slipped his arm round her waist. 'Everything okay?' he murmured, pressing his lips into her hair.

'Yes, fine.'

He pulled away and looked down at her with a frown. 'You look like you've seen a ghost. Are you sure you're all right?'

'Yes, sorry. Just an old friend with some bad news about a family member. No one you know.' She pecked him on the nose and sat back down on the rug. Mia was giving her a weird look and she knew she was going to have to explain herself later – but she also knew she would never be able to tell Dom about this. They pretended those three years in New York had never happened, and they certainly never mentioned AJ. Dom's depression seemed to have lifted for now, and he was back to being his loving, funny self. But she was always aware of it hovering, just out of sight, waiting to engulf him again at any moment, and something like this was bound to trigger it. No, this was something she would need to process by herself.

She almost jumped off the sofa now as hot coffee tipped all over her belly. She leapt up and ran to the bathroom and whipped her top off, her skin burning in the cold air.

'Shit, shit, shit,' she said, splashing cold water on her skin. Somehow she must have nodded off and she was now dangerously close to being late for work. She threw on a clean top, gave her teeth a perfunctory clean, checked on Dom – still asleep – and ran out of the door.

It was cold enough to see your breath, and she fumbled with her coat buttons as she marched towards Archway tube station. She felt flustered and grumpy and her hands were cold. She reached the station and flew down the escalator and straight onto the train just as the doors slid closed. At least something was going her way today.

As it was so close to Christmas, most workers had left London in a mass exodus a couple of days before, so the tube was quiet and she threw herself into a spare seat with relief. Her ghostly reflection watched her, hair curled in ringlets around her face, her scarf wrapped too tightly round her neck. She shook it loose and sat back, trying not to catch the eyes of any fellow passengers.

By the time she emerged at Camden, she had two missed calls. She was already five minutes late but, seeing it was Dom, she called him back.

'You left without saying goodbye,' he said. His voice was an empty monotone.

'Sorry love, I didn't want to wake you.' She kept her voice steady, appeasing. He didn't say anything else and after a few seconds she realised he was crying. She knew he wasn't doing it on purpose but she shifted from foot to foot impatiently.

'Dom love, what's the matter?'

He sniffed and she heard his breath squeeze tightly through his throat before he spoke again. 'I'm just so scared,' he said. 'I need you.'

'I'll be back in a few hours,' she said. 'Why don't you put the TV on and watch a nice Christmas film until I get home?'

'Yeah.'

She waited a beat, then: 'Will you be all right? I'll ring you again in a bit, okay?'

'Okay.' Then he hung up and Bea was left standing in the middle of the pavement wondering whether he really meant it, or whether she should make an excuse and go home and check up on him.

After a few seconds' hesitation she shoved her phone back in her bag and marched towards the lifts and up to her floor, where the only people still in the office were her editor (who seemed to live there) and a couple of her feature writers.

She loved this job – it wasn't as glamorous as the feature writer job she'd bagged in New York, but her job as features editor of a weekly women's magazine was something she knew she was good at. She loved the pace of a weekly – you had long enough to spend time crafting a feature rather than rushing it like you often had to on dailies, while also being fast-paced enough to give her a thrill, especially as deadline day approached. She loved her team too and she got on well with her editor, Fiona. For Bea, it was also a welcome escape from Dom's increasingly all-consuming depression.

'Where's your Santa hat?' Fiona called from her desk a couple of rows behind her as she sat down.

Bea grinned and put her hands to her head as she turned round. 'Oops, it must have blown off in the wind.'

'Likely story,' Fiona said, stalking over to Bea's desk. She handed her a sheaf of A3 papers. 'Flatplan's looking great for the next issue, I think everything's pretty much there. Thank Christ.' She wiped her arm across her brow dramatically. 'Ten whole days off, can't fucking wait. What are you doing for Christmas?'

'Oh, I'm... just at home. With Dom.'

'Not seeing your mum and dad?'

'Yeah, on Christmas Day. But...' She trailed off. She hadn't told her boss – or any of other colleagues – about her dad since his diagnosis had been confirmed three months before, as if by not saying it out loud would help to make it less real. 'Dad's not very well so I'm kind of dreading it.'

'Oh no, what's wrong?' Fiona laid her hand on Bea's shoulder and Bea felt tears well in her eyes, the way they always did when she thought about the news that had rocked her world.

'He's been diagnosed with dementia.'

'Oh darling, I'm so sorry. I know how much you adore him.' To Bea's surprise Fiona pulled her into an awkward sideways hug. When she moved away Bea wiped the tears from her face and looked away.

'Thanks Fiona.'

'Listen, we're more or less done here. Why don't you go home, put your feet up?'

Bea shook her head. 'No, it's fine. Honestly.'

Fiona sat down beside her and pulled her chair right next to Bea's. 'Are you sure?'

Bea nodded miserably. 'Honestly, things are so shit at home I'd rather be here.'

She couldn't quite believe she'd just said that, but it was out there now – and it wasn't a lie. As well as coping with Dom being in the house all day – he'd been signed off work for the foreseeable future after his depression had begun to spiral out of control again after the summer – Pete's dementia diagnosis had been made official in September.

Early in the year Bea and Alice had made their mum face up to the fact that something wasn't quite right with Pete.

'He got confused on the way back from the Arsenal match the other day Mum,' Alice had said.

'He was fine, I think he just wanted to sneak out for a drink,' Ange had said.

But as much as Ange had wanted to pretend it wasn't happening, over the next few weeks it became increasingly clear that Pete's memory was deteriorating. In the end, even Ange had to admit he probably needed to see the doctor.

'I know you're scared Mum, but me and Alice are here,' Bea had said.

So Pete had been packed off to see his GP. After tests and scans, the result had been conclusive. Pete had the early signs of Alzheimer's.

If the official diagnosis had come as a shock, the speed at which he'd gone downhill since had been even more of one. Now, just a year on from the first signs of anything being awry, Pete had good days and bad days – but on the bad days he seemed completely lost, unsure where he was or who they were. It broke Bea's heart to see not only what it was doing to her always stoic dad, but how much it had broken her mum.

'I just don't know what to do for him,' Ange had confessed a couple of nights ago after she'd stopped Pete from going to the shops in his pyjamas. 'He gets so angry if I tell him not to do something, but he's going to end up doing himself a mischief if he keeps on like this.'

Bea and Alice had both promised to spend as much time at the house as they could, and even Charlie and Rob had vowed to help out when they could. But then Alice had fallen pregnant again – 'It was a bit of a shock,' she'd told Bea primly, when she announced it, and Bea couldn't help smirking at the fact that Alice, who liked to plan everything, had been sent such a curveball after believing her family to be complete – and Bea knew it wouldn't be long until they had to make a decision about what to do next. And she couldn't bear it.

'Come on, let's get everything sorted here, then I'm going to take you for a drink, how does that sound?'

'That sounds like a plan I can get on board with,' Bea said, smiling through her tears.

By just after lunchtime they were finished, and as promised, Fiona took them to the Edinboro Castle where they polished off a bottle of wine in just over an hour. By the time they left, the world seemed a little fuzzier round the edges and Bea allowed herself to relax.

'You take it easy, okay, Bea?' Fiona said, her huge padded coat pressing into Bea's face as she cuddled her. 'And be good to yourself. Merry Christmas.'

'Merry Christmas Fiona.'

As Fiona walked away towards Chalk Farm, Bea stood for a few moments, taking in the icy London air. Camden was packed now, people ready for nights out, all Christmas-tree deeley-boppers and scarves of tinsel. Most of the time Bea loved Christmas but this year she felt a sense of dread in the pit of her stomach as she stood alone in a sea of Christmas cheer.

Merry Bloody Christmas, Bea Preston.

* * *

Although she'd promised Dom she'd be home as soon as she could, Bea decided to take a detour to check on her dad. She tapped out a text to let Dom know and shoved her phone back in her bag. As she marched along the path on the familiar route past Finsbury Park to her parents' house, she took deep breaths, the air around her turning to steam. Lights sparkled in windows and lit up hedges and fences all along the route, and even though usually it lifted her spirits, today she struggled to find that spark of excitement.

She wondered whether Dom was out of bed yet.

She wondered whether her dad would be having a good day or a bad day.

She was completely lost in thought as she rounded the corner into her parents' street, which meant she was nearly at their front door by the time she noticed the figure hovering by their gate.

There was still some light left in the day, and the weak winter sun glowered behind the figure, throwing them into silhouette. She slowed down, watching them. They had a hood up and seemed to be staking out her parents' house. Were they planning to break in? Her heart thumped in fear, and she was about to call out when they seemed to notice her, and stepped into the light, pushing their hood down at the same time.

'Princess Beatrice.' The Irish twang was so familiar it made Bea's heart somersault. Her breath seemed to have deserted her and she couldn't get any words out.

AJ was right in front of her now, blocking her way. Finally, she found her words.

'What the hell are you doing here?'

'I'm in London for work and I just needed to see you.'

'I—'

'I know you said you never wanted to see me again and I respect that but... fuck Bea. I miss you so much it hurts. Right here.' He punched his chest with his fist. 'I just wanted to know if you'd missed me too.'

Bea still hadn't looked him in the eye, but now she raised her gaze. As she looked into his bright blue eyes, all resolve seemed to evaporate, dissolve into the air and get carried away on the breeze.

'I've missed you so much.' The words came out of their own volition, but Bea wouldn't take them back even if she could. Because they were completely and utterly true.

They stood for a moment, unmoving. Bea wondered what she'd do if AJ made a move to touch her. But before she could think about it, AJ said, 'Can we go for a drink? Just one. Just to talk.'

Bea thought about Dom, waiting for her at home. About the fact that he could barely get himself out of bed these days, but still kept resisting taking his anti-depressants. She thought about the promises she had made to him, that she would never leave him, that she loved him. That she would never hurt him again. None of this was his fault, she knew, and she was doing her best to be there for him.

But now, faced with AJ, she knew that there was no comparison. That there never would be. He made her heart sing.

'One drink. But I'm not making any promises.'

10

STAY

December 2006

As a child Bea had always drawn Christmas cards for her siblings, snowy scenes with pine trees and snow inches-deep, people yomping through the drifts wrapped up against the cold. She'd spent hours on these drawings, her imagination running wild.

Today, Bea felt as though one of her drawings had come to life as she and AJ hiked through the thick, powdery snow in warm boots, hats, gloves and scarves, surrounded by the white-tipped Catskill mountains. Pine trees heavy with settled snow and the occasional wooden cabin dotted the road.

As idyllic as it was to look at though, Bea's fingers were starting to turn numb, and she was glad when their cabin finally came into view. She couldn't wait to settle in front of the fire and feel the warmth tingle back through her fingertips, her toes.

'You're like a five-year-old,' AJ said, laughing as Bea kicked snow flurries, and picked sprigs of mistletoe and ivy, squashing them down in her pockets.

'But look at it!' she said, spinning round, arms held out.

Suddenly, she lost her footing and was on her back in the snow, the cold seeping through her coat. As she tried to pull herself up, AJ threw himself on top of her, holding himself just far enough away so he wasn't squashing her, and kissed her. His lips were warm against her frozen ones and she kissed him back greedily, despite the fact her back and legs were turning numb.

'Are you all right?' he said, concern in his eyes.

'I'm absolutely fine. It was a soft landing. But if you don't get off me and let me get up in a minute, I'm going to have frostbite,' she said, laughing as she pushed him away and clambered to her feet. Once she'd got her balance again, his arms were round her waist and she stumbled into him. 'Goodness' sake man, what's wrong with you today?' she said, not really meaning a word of it.

'There's nothing wrong with wanting to give my wife a kiss is there?' AJ said, pressing his nose against Bea's.

'I suppose not,' she said. 'But can we at least wait until we're back indoors and I can feel my toes again?'

'Spoilsport,' he said, grabbing hold of her gloved hand and pulling her along. They fell through the door of the cabin and slammed it shut behind them. The residual warmth from the fire they'd started earlier made the air inside feel soft, and the heat enveloped Bea like a hug. She tugged off her boots, leaving behind a trail of rapidly melting snow, and began to peel off her layers one by one. Beside her, AJ did the same.

'Right, you put your feet up and I'll get the fire going again,' he said, gesturing to the couch in front of the open fireplace.

'I'll make drinks, shall I?' Bea said, padding over to the kitchen area instead.

'Okay. But then you need to sit down and rest, okay?'

Bea rolled her eyes. 'I'm not an invalid AJ,' she said, but she kept her tone teasing so he knew she was only joking.

'I know,' he said, turning from where he was crouched in front of the fireplace, piling logs on top of the smouldering embers. 'But I just want to make sure both of you are okay after your little fall. There's nothing wrong with that, is there?'

'No, course not. But I promise we're fine, okay?'

'Okay.' He turned back to the fire while Bea made hot chocolates for them both. By the time she sat down, the fire was roaring again, and she snuggled into the crook of AJ's arm and let her eyes droop. She suddenly felt exhausted. It must be all the fresh air.

When AJ had suggested they take this trip two and a half hours north into the Catskill mountains just before Christmas, Bea had been unsure. There was always so much to do in the run-up to Christmas, especially since they had AJ's parents coming over from Ireland to spend it with them this year.

'They won't care whether we've spent days preparing for their arrival or not,' AJ said. 'And I want to spend some time just me and you before everyone descends – and while this baby is still our secret.'

In the end she'd agreed, and now they were here she was so glad she had. It had been a tumultuous year, and one she wouldn't want to repeat. But at least the outcome was a good one.

Around Easter, Cassie's parents had called one Sunday morning.

'Is everything okay?' Bea heard AJ say into the phone.

Cassie had been having fits and they thought he might want to go and say goodbye 'just in case'. He'd gone, of course. And while it hadn't been the end that day, over the next few weeks Cassie's fits became more frequent. AJ was on constant high alert, waiting for the call that told him she was approaching the end.

Finally, that call had come late one June evening. They were at Bea's flat watching TV with Maggie, the apartment windows thrown open to the muggy city air when AJ's phone rang. The moment she saw AJ's face Bea knew it had happened.

Cassie had died.

AJ was all over the place, grieving for the woman he'd once loved, but who he'd also said goodbye to a long time ago, and worrying about how Bea was feeling.

'You know I'm really only saying goodbye to her body, not her mind,' he assured Bea.

'It's fine,' she told him. 'Of course you need to say goodbye to her.'

The funeral took place in early July.

In August, Mia moved to New York to be with Frank, and Bea was over the moon to have her best friend so close by.

'But what about Deacon?' she'd said. 'You love the bones of that cat.'

Mia shrugged. 'I love Frank more, so Deacon's gone to live with my aunt.' Bea shook her head.

'I never thought I'd see the day,' she said, smiling.

Then AJ asked Bea to move in with him. She was unsure; it felt too soon. Besides, how could they start planning their future when his past was all around them?

'Let's stay as we are for now and think about getting our own place together soon,' Bea said. AJ reluctantly agreed. The reality, of course, was that they spent most of their time in AJ's apartment anyway, where there was more space. More privacy.

Then at the end of September, Bea had some news to which she wasn't sure how AJ was going to react.

'I'm pregnant,' she told him, holding her breath as she waited.

There was barely a second's hesitation before AJ grabbed her and whirled her round. She laughed as he put her back on the ground, relieved. But then she saw there were tears shining in his eyes.

'Hey, what's wrong?' she said.

He swiped the back of his hand across his face and looked away.

'I just... I didn't realise how much I wanted this after... you know, after everything.'

She did know, and she felt the same.

'Let's get married,' AJ said, two days later.

'What? When?' It was so out of the blue that Bea didn't even have time to notice that this proposal was hardly the height of romance.

'I don't know. I don't care. But let's just do it. I love you Bea and I just want to be with you, and our baby.'

'I will marry you, but there's no need to rush it is there?'

He shrugged. 'I know I'm not religious or anything, but I'm still Irish and – well. I've always assumed I would be married before I had a baby. Call me old-fashioned.'

How could she say no? Three weeks later they flew to Vegas and tied the knot in a small ceremony just off the Strip in The Little Church of the West. At the last minute, Mia and Frank decided to join them and, as Bea and Mia clutched their small posies of roses and said their vows to the men they loved, Bea didn't think she had ever been happier.

Now Bea and AJ were in the Catskills for a few days, just the two of them. When they got home, Bea was finally going to meet AJ's parents. She was nervous, but AJ assured her they'd love her.

There was one cloud on the horizon, however, and Bea was reminded of it now as her phone buzzed. She glanced down to see a text from her mum.

Can you talk?

Reception was patchy up here and non-existent inside the house. She hauled herself off the sofa and AJ looked up at her.

'Where you going?'

'I need to ring Mum.'

AJ glanced at the window. It had begun to snow again, the flakes falling thickly. 'You can't go out there, you'll freeze.'

'I'll be quick,' she promised. 'It might be important.'

AJ didn't argue and minutes later Bea was bundled up and heading back into the snow again. She shivered as a blast of wind slammed the door shut behind her. The sun had gone in now and a band of cloud hung low. She quickly pressed 'redial' then pulled her gloves on. Her mum answered almost straight away.

'Hey, is everything all right?' Bea pressed the phone to her ear to hear her response above the wind.

'...dad... asked... you... dinner... told him... another... what...'

'Hang on Mum, I can't hear you properly, I need to move further outside.' Bea stepped out from under the shelter of the porch into the snow which was now falling diagonally. She blinked the flakes from her eyes and headed for the shelter of a nearby pine tree.

'Sorry Mum, what did you say?'

'Oh it's nothing love, I shouldn't really be bothering you.'

Bea's heart sank. Her mum never rang her out of the blue so she knew it must be something, and she was so cold she didn't feel like spending ages trying to coax it out of her.

'Mum, has something happened with Dad? Please tell me, I'm worried.'

There was a moment's hesitation, then her mum said, 'I just don't know what to do for him. He tried to walk to the corner shop in his pyjamas last night. I keep trying to tell myself everything's okay, that he'll be okay, but he's not, is he? He wouldn't be doing things like this and thinking there's nothing wrong with it otherwise.'

'Oh Mum,' Bea said. Her dad had been getting worse for a while, the official dementia diagnosis coming only a few months ago – and that had been the first time Ange had been willing to admit her beloved Pete was getting worse. It sounded as though things had gone downhill again.

'I'm sorry love,' Ange said. 'I shouldn't be bothering you. Only with Alice being pregnant again I don't like to stress her out, she already does so much...' She trailed off, and the familiar cloak of guilt wrapped itself round Bea. Not only had Alice taken on the brunt of helping their mum care for their dad – Charlie and Rob made the odd appearance but Alice was the closest – but Bea hadn't told her mum about her own pregnancy yet either. She almost blurted it out there and then, but decided against it. She wanted to tell her properly, when she could see her reaction – not when her voice was crackly and indistinct and she was feeling so scared and alone.

'Is there anything I can do?' Bea said.

'No love. It's fine. I just worry about him so much. But we'll be fine. You've done enough.'

Bea had been over a couple of times this year, but she was well aware it was nowhere near enough.

'Okay Mum. I'll ring you when I'm back in the city, all right?'

'All right. Love you.'

'Love you too.'

Then Ange was gone. Bea stood beneath the tree for a moment longer, thinking about her parents. She wished she could be there to help, to spend time with her dad before he disappeared inside his dementia forever.

She looked up at the sound of AJ's voice. He was standing at the door of the cabin, a look of concern on his face. She traipsed through the snow towards him, stamping the snow from her boots once she reached the porch. Her whole body felt numb with cold.

'You were just standing there,' AJ said as she stepped inside and they closed the door. 'Is everything okay?'

'Yeah. It's Dad,' she said, explaining about her dad's attempted shopping expedition. 'I just feel so guilty, leaving Mum and Alice to do everything.'

'I know my love,' AJ said, kissing her frozen nose. 'And that's what I love about you so much. But you know there's nothing much you can do, don't you?'

Bea nodded. 'I just hate being so far away.'

'We'll go and see them in the new year, promise. Okay?'

Bea nodded, sadly.

* * *

The next couple of days passed in pretty much the same way – late mornings, hot chocolate by the fire, walks in the snow. But the snow continued to fall, and the night before they were due to head back to the city, AJ peered out of the window in concern.

'Do you think we should head back tonight? I'm worried the main roads will be un-driveable if we leave it much longer.'

Bea looked outside too. Their car, which they hadn't used since they'd arrived, had a thick layer of snow on the roof and bonnet, and the tyres were half-buried in drifts.

'Maybe. But it's already getting dark, won't that be even worse?'

In the end, with dusk already upon them, they agreed to stay until morning. But when they got up at first light the next day, conditions looked even worse.

'My parents are landing in a few hours so we have to get back. I'll just drive super-slow,' AJ said, loading the last bag into the back of the car. He'd already spent half an hour clearing snow from the roof and the few metres surrounding the car, but they both hoped the chains on the tyres would be enough to get them to the main road, which, AJ assured her, was regularly ploughed. 'Not like London where the slightest hint of snow throws everyone into a panic,' he said. 'They have to be prepared here.'

They inched out of the driveway and onto the small side road. The thick, fresh snow crunched beneath the tyres, and Bea tried not to think about the towering piles falling on top of them. It took three times longer than it should have, but finally, they were out on the main road which, as AJ had predicted, had been cleared overnight. There were hardly any other cars on the roads, most people already, sensibly, where they needed to be just two days before Christmas, but a mist had begun to descend so AJ still kept his speed down and as the road slipped by beneath them, they listened to Christmas songs blasting from the radio. She'd had a lovely relaxing break, but now couldn't wait to get back to New York – to Maggie, to Mia, to her job.

A sudden shout from AJ made her stiffen, and when she whipped her head round to see what had happened, the look on his face – of pure terror – made her heart leap into her throat.

Then she looked at the road, and in that split-second she could see what was going to happen, but was utterly helpless to stop it...

The deer stood, stock still in the middle of the road.

AJ yanked the steering wheel to the right.

The tyres skidded on the icy road.

The deer fled.

But it was too late.

They were careering towards a tree.

Then everything went black.

11

GO

December 2007

'Silent Night' was playing in the background, so quietly Bea could only really hear it if she held her breath. The lights twinkling on the Christmas tree in the corner and the fire dwindling to nothing in the grate were the only sources of light in the room, and Bea felt her eyes drooping, her breath slowing. She was so tired she could have fallen asleep right here, and if she just let go she...

A snuffling sound, the sensation of a small body wriggling, and she snapped her eyes open again. On her chest, baby Jack was swaddled in a pale blue blanket, his mop of blond curls matted against his head. Bea watched as he shuffled, holding her breath to see if he was about to wake up then, when she was sure he'd settled again, she let out a long, slow breath.

'Everything all right love?' Bea looked up and smiled at Dom hovering in the doorway.

'Yeah, just trapped under a sleeping baby,' she whispered.

'Want me to take him for a bit?'

She shook her head. 'No, I'm good. I wouldn't mind a cup of tea though.'

'And a biscuit?'

'You're an angel.'

Dom disappeared again and she heard clattering, the kettle humming, the schwup of the fridge door opening and closing again. She carefully reached for her mobile which lay next to her on the sofa. There was a message from Mia.

> Can you escape tonight or shall I come over with a
> bottle of gin? xx

Bea smiled and tapped out a reply with one hand to tell her that, as much as she'd love to see her, she was absolutely exhausted and was planning on doing nothing more exciting than having some sleep. She clicked on BBC News, and Facebook, and was mindlessly reading a story about how to wrap weird-shaped Christmas presents when Dom sat beside her, balancing tea and a plate of biscuits carefully on the side table.

'Chocolate Hobnobs, I'm honoured,' Bea said.

'Nothing but the best for my princess.' As Dom planted a gentle kiss first on her head then on Jack's, Bea tried not to think about the last person who had called her Princess.

Princess Beatrice.

'Shall I put the telly on?'

'Sure, but keep it quiet.' Bea reached for her tea and took an awkward sideways sip so she didn't have to bring the hot liquid above Jack's head. The TV sprang to life and Dom settled back, propping his feet up on the coffee table.

Just as he got settled, the doorbell pealed.

'Who the hell is that at this time of the evening?' Dom said, even though it was only just after 5 p.m. The weird forever-twilight of a sleeping baby. He hauled himself off the sofa and disappeared to answer the door.

Bea heard the front door opening, a murmur of low voices, then the door closing. Two sets of footsteps came along the hallway, then—

'Baby Jack-Jack!' came a voice from the doorway, as a blast of cold air entered the room at the same time.

'Shhhhh!' hissed Bea and Dom simultaneously.

'He's asleep,' Bea explained, pointing her chin at her sleeping baby.

'Oh right, sorry.'

AJ flung himself down onto the sofa beside Bea as Dom disappeared in the direction of the kitchen, then leaned over and kissed Jack on the head. 'How is he?'

'He's good. What are you doing here, I thought you weren't coming 'til tomorrow?'

AJ rubbed his face. He looked exhausted, dark circles under his eyes. 'Yeah, sorry. I was just passing and I thought I'd pop in and see if the little man was awake. I thought I might take him out for a walk or something.'

'You could have messaged first.'

Beside her, she felt AJ bristle. 'I don't need to ask permission to see my own son, Bea.'

She rubbed her hand across her face. 'No I know you don't. But you know how hard this is for Dom, and it just makes it worse when you drop in unannounced like this.'

AJ sighed heavily, then lifted his hand and gently rubbed his son's head. Bea had to look away. They might both be trying to make this arrangement work, but it didn't mean Bea found it easy to be around AJ these days.

After AJ had come to find her outside her parents' house last year, they'd gone for a drink. They'd talked for hours, and AJ had tried to explain how sorry he was that he'd lied to her about Cassie. He told her he still loved her and didn't want to live without her.

It would have been the easiest thing in the world for her to have thrown herself into his arms and told him she wanted to be with him too. Every part of her body told her to do exactly that. But as she sat in the warmth of the pub texting Dom that she'd be home soon, the guilt became too much. She'd made a promise to Dom that she would never hurt him again, and she couldn't let him down. He deserved better.

This time, as AJ walked away from her, it was almost harder than before – because this time she knew it had to be forever.

The next month was hell. She didn't mean to, but she began to blame Dom for everything that went wrong. As he started taking his medication again and slowly working his way out of his pit of depression and back to his old self, she pulled herself further and further away from him until she felt as though the thread connecting them would snap at any moment. She felt angry with him, resentful.

And then AJ came back.

He was waiting for her one evening as she left the office and the moment she saw him her whole body roared.

'Hello AJ,' she said.

'Hello Princess Beatrice.'

His hair had grown longer and he pushed back a lock that had fallen across his forehead. She wanted to run her fingers through it, her body ached with the need to touch him. She clenched her fists by her sides and held her breath.

Then he held out his hand and she took it, fire sparking through her palm where they touched.

'Come for dinner with me? Please?' His voice was hoarse and she shivered with desire.

This time, as the evening drew to an end, she knew she wasn't going home to Dom. And as she let AJ touch her and she lost herself in him, she knew her life was never going to be the same again.

'Fuck, Bea,' Mia said, when she told her about it the next day.

'I know.' Bea burned with shame and guilt.

'So is this it? Are you leaving Dom?'

'I don't know.' Bea shook her head. 'I can't. I promised him. I...' She stopped. 'It's like an addiction, this thing with AJ. Having him in my life is just... it just makes me want him more. What am I going to do, Mee?'

In the end, she did what she knew was the right thing to do.

'I can't see you again,' she told AJ.

'But you love me,' he said. He sounded wounded, his voice raspy.

She looked down at her hands, swallowed. 'I can't. I just can't.'

She threw herself back into trying to be happy with Dom again. And for a while, it worked. Dom was getting better all the time. He was fun and sweet and attentive, and was trying so hard to make it up to her. As she lay in bed with him at night, his arm slung across her, his breathing slow and gentle, she watched him; the crease of his eyelids, the tip of his jaw, the slope of his chin, and she still felt drawn to him, could still see the boy she had fallen in love with.

And yet. He wasn't AJ and she wasn't sure how she was ever going to reconcile herself with that.

'I think I should tell Dom what happened with AJ,' Bea said to Mia one day.

'Why on *earth* would you want to do that?'

'I promised him we'd be honest, that I wouldn't keep anything from him again. The guilt is eating me up.'

Mia shook her head emphatically. 'Uh-uh. Absolutely no way. It will finish him off.'

Bea sighed. She knew Mia was right, deep down. So she'd

agreed, and instead worked hard to earn back the trust Dom didn't even know he should have lost in her.

Then she found out she was pregnant.

'And there's no way it can be Dom's?' Mia said when Bea had turned up at her house, frantic, and shoved the pregnancy test in her face back in April.

Bea shook her head. 'His depression... we haven't for months...' Her breath hitched in her chest and she struggled to breathe. 'Fuck, how can this be happening?' She buried her face in her hands as Mia's cat Deacon curled up on her lap, his paws peddling gently against her thighs.

'Drink this,' Mia instructed, pouring her a large shot of whisky. Bea hated whisky but she tipped it down her throat and almost gagged. Then her eyes widened. 'Oh God, I shouldn't be drinking either, should I? I'm already the worst mother ever and I can't do this, I just can't...'

Mia held her as she sobbed, and when she finally calmed down she felt numb.

'Feel better?' Mia said.

'Not really.' She pulled in a shuddery breath. 'I don't even know if I *want* a baby. And now I'm going to hurt Dom all over again, for nothing.' She shook her head. 'This is a nightmare.'

'It doesn't have to be.'

Bea looked up sharply. 'What do you mean?'

'I mean, this could be fate trying to tell you something.'

'You don't believe in fate.'

'Maybe I do now.' Mia smiled a sad half-smile and took hold of Bea's hand. 'All I'm saying is that maybe this is life's way of telling you that you're with the wrong man.'

'Is that what you really think?' she said, her voice small.

'You know I love Dom but,' Mia sighed, 'you're closing in on yourself, Bea. You're not happy, Dom's not happy and AJ... well, I know how you still feel about him. I can see it in you every time you mention his name. When you're with him you're more...' She paused. 'More *you*.' She shrugged. 'So maybe you need to consider that being with him really *is* the only way you're going to be truly happy.'

Bea shook her head. 'Maybe you're right. But none of that matters now anyway because I've royally fucked things up.'

There was one thing Bea was certain of though. She was going to keep this baby, even if she had to do it on her own. It might not have been planned and it might not have been conceived under ideal circumstances, but as Bea got used to the idea, she realised something. Perhaps this was nature's way of telling her it was time.

She just had to tell everyone else.

AJ was first, in a phone call.

At first he didn't say anything at all, and she listened to the static hum on the line.

'Are you serious?' he said, eventually.

'Would I joke about something like this?'

'No, course not. Fuck.'

'Good fuck or bad fuck?'

A hesitation. 'Good fuck. Definitely good. I just – I don't...' He'd stopped. He sounded breathless.

'It's a lot, right?'

'Yeah. Yeah it's a lot. I mean it's not exactly what I'd expected when...' He broke off, laughed. 'Call me old-fashioned but I always imagined I'd be married before I had a baby. Must be the Irish upbringing.'

She heard the sadness in his voice and she softened, suddenly desperate to see him.

'Can I come over? Sort things out?' he said, as if he could read her mind.

'I'd like that.'

But she also had to tell Dom – and that hadn't gone as well.

At first, he'd been silent. Stony-faced, so that she wasn't entirely sure that he'd heard her. But then he simply stood and left the room. She waited a few moments, wondering whether he was planning to come back and talk to her about it; ask her anything. But when she heard the slam of the front door it became clear he wasn't. She sat there for two hours, waiting, hoping he'd come home, praying he hadn't done anything stupid. When she heard the slide of his key in the lock, relief flooded through her and she ran to the door. They stood facing one another in silence until Bea eventually said, 'Are we going to talk about it?'

'There's not really much to say.' Dom's voice sounded flat and she recognised it as the tone he spoke in during his worst bouts of depression.

'You don't think there's anything we need to talk about?'

He shrugged. 'I assume you're keeping it.'

She nodded and reached for his hands but he flinched away. 'I want to, yes,' she said, her voice scratchy.

'Then that's decided.'

She couldn't blame him for being cold. She'd betrayed him in the worst possible way. But she also knew they couldn't avoid it forever.

They talked in the end, of course. Endlessly, it felt to Bea, round and round in never-ending circles. She promised Dom she wasn't going back to AJ, no matter what. Even saying the words felt like tiny needles jabbing into her heart, but this was about her and the baby now. Nothing and no one else.

'Let me support you,' Dom said.

'What do you...'

'Stay with me and we can bring the baby up together.'

'But – what about AJ?'

Dom shrugged. 'I couldn't care less what he does but of course he can spend time with him – or her – if he wants. If you want to stay with me, of course.' His voice sounded like broken glass and Bea thought she might cry.

She thought about Dom's offer. She still cared deeply about him. She didn't want to be a single parent either. So, in the end, she said yes.

But then AJ announced he was moving to London.

'I know you don't want to be with me, but I can't be thousands of miles away from my child,' he said. 'Family is too important, however unconventional ours is.'

So that's where they were now – a baby with a mother and, effectively, two fathers, who tolerated each other but in reality could barely stand to be in the same room. It wasn't ideal, but it was better than any alternative Bea could think of, because in every other scenario someone else ended up getting hurt.

Her leg had gone to sleep so she stretched it out, pointing and flexing her toe to inject some life back into it. The fire had almost gone out and the room was getting chilly. On her chest baby Jack was beginning to stir.

'Here, he's waking up,' she whispered to AJ. 'If you give me a minute to feed him and change his nappy, you could take him out for a walk if you like.'

AJ's face lit up. She loved the way he couldn't get enough of his son. You never knew how someone was going to parent, but AJ had shown himself in the best light possible – devoted, loving, kind. Dom had too, although she could always detect a slight reserve in his response to Jack, as though he was permanently aware that this little boy had someone else's blood. But he was warm and attentive and she knew how lucky she was. How lucky Jack was.

'Great, thanks.' AJ hauled himself off the sofa. 'I'll go and make you a cuppa then, this one's gone cold,' he said, as Bea unhooked her bra and baby Jack pressed his lips to her nipple and began to feed. Relief spread through her that she'd caught him before he started screaming, and she tipped her head back and closed her eyes, the gentle rhythm of her son's sucking helping her to relax. She'd never expected to take to being a mum as well as she had. It hadn't really been something she'd ever thought about, even as she approached her thirties. None of her friends in London had settled down and had kids, and neither had her New York friends, and it occurred to her that perhaps she'd been trying to stay young by surrounding herself with people who weren't tied down.

But now baby Jack was here and she couldn't imagine her life any other way. Even the sleepless nights and the long days that sometimes stretched out endlessly weren't as bad as she'd imagined. Perhaps it was because she had so much support with Dom and AJ as well as her mum, who adored spending time with her youngest grandson, and Alice, who she was seeing more of these days now they both had babies.

'Is he done?' Bea opened her eyes to find AJ hovering over her. She quickly covered up her boob, which baby Jack had left exposed when he'd fallen back to sleep, and sat up. He might have seen everything before, but this was very different. There were only two men who were allowed to see her boobs these days – Dom and Jack.

'Sure, I just need to change him.'

'I'll do it.' He held out his arms and gently cradled Jack to his chest, a look of complete and utter adoration in his eyes. Bea remembered when he used to look at her like that and had to look away.

Ten minutes later AJ had Jack all bundled up and in his pram, and Dom helped him carry it down the stairs and out of the front door. Bea sipped her still-warm tea and tried to enjoy the feeling of a few minutes of freedom.

Was it weird to miss someone who you'd only known for a couple of months so desperately?

'Hey.'

Bea smiled as Dom came back into the room and sat beside her. He snuggled into her and she pecked him on the lips. It felt good to have Dom back again. After everything that had happened over the last few months, he'd religiously taken his medication and his mental health was back on an even keel. In fact he was better than he had been in years, since even before Bea had left to go to New York. He seemed to have matured and no longer dismissed her ideas as silly, or crazy, but really listened to her, took her seriously. Maybe it was becoming a parent that did that to you. Whatever it was, she liked it.

'He said he'll be gone for a while, if you fancy a bit of...' Dom waggled his eyebrows and tipped his head towards the bedroom. The truth was the only thing Bea felt like doing in bed right now was sleeping. But she knew how important it was to Dom to keep the physical side of their relationship going, given all the months that he hadn't wanted to be near her. Those months when she'd ended up in bed with AJ.

'Sure,' she said, taking his hand and letting him lead her into the bedroom. Even though her whole body ached with exhaustion, and she had half an ear open to the doorbell going at any time to announce the return of AJ and her son, she let herself open up to him. She needed to be reminded of how much they loved each other just as much as he did.

* * *

'What time are you coming round tomorrow?' AJ said, as he got ready to leave later that evening. He'd been out for a good couple of hours with baby Jack in the end and Bea had been close to dropping with tiredness by the time they returned. Now all she wanted to do was to curl up in bed and close her eyes.

'What time are your parents arriving?'

'About eleven. I said I'd pick them up from Heathrow.'

'Well let me know when you're home and I'll get Jack ready and come round.'

'Okay.' He turned to leave, then, just as Bea was about to close the door, he turned back. 'Thanks Bea.'

'What for?'

He shrugged. 'For everything. For letting me see my son, letting me be part of his life. For meeting my parents.'

She shook her head. 'Of course I want to. They're my son's grandparents.'

AJ nodded and held her gaze. God, those eyes. She looked away. 'Anyway, well thanks for bringing him back. I'll see you tomorrow. Night AJ.'

His eyes were still on her as she closed the door, and she heard him whisper, 'Night Princess Beatrice.' She stood on the other side of the closed door for a few seconds and took a deep breath, trying to compose herself. She hated when she let herself get like this. Most of the time it was fine – transactional dealings with AJ to hand Jack over before she rushed off to go to the supermarket or do some other chore un-hindered by a crying baby. But from time to time, like tonight, she let her feelings overwhelm her and she just needed a minute to decompress.

She climbed the stairs and checked in the bathroom. Jack was lying on the floor in just his nappy, kicking his legs happily, while Dom tested the temperature of the bath water with his elbow and her heart surged with love for them both. For this man who had not only forgiven her infidelity, but had welcomed her son with open arms. And for the tiny little man who had upended her life in so many ways but was still the best thing that had ever happened to her.

She left them to it and went and poured herself a glass of wine. She might be breast-feeding but that didn't mean she couldn't have the odd drink. She savoured the first mouthful. Her phone vibrated in her pocket. She pulled it out and squinted at the screen, her tired eyes grainy.

> Please tell us you're still coming for dinner tomorrow night – it feels like centuries since we last saw you. Also we have exciting news. Love M and H xx

Bugger. She'd completely forgotten she and Dom were meant to be going to Michael and Harry's for dinner tomorrow night along with Ashton, his new girlfriend Charmaine, and Mia. Right now she couldn't imagine having the energy to leave the house let alone get dressed and spend the evening socialising. But she also desperately missed her very best friends, and she didn't want to let them down.

This, she realised, as she tapped out a message asking AJ if he could have Jack overnight tomorrow night, was one of the advantages of her situation – of co-parenting with someone you weren't actually with. Easy childcare.

> I'd love to have him. I'll stock up on nappies. AJ x

> Thank you. You're the best xx

* * *

'Fuuuuuuuck, it's good to see you,' Mia said, the instant Bea walked into the room, Dom trailing behind her. Her best friend opened her arms up wide and threw them round her. She clung on for longer than normal and when Bea peeled herself away she saw Mia's eyes shining with tears.

'Hey, what's wrong?' she said in a whisper.

Mia shook her head and wiped her face with the sleeve of her Christmas jumper. 'Oh nothing, ignore me, I'm just a bit pissed.'

Bea peered at her friend more closely. 'Come on, out with it. What's happened?'

Mia shook her head again. 'Nothing. I'm just sick of being the only tragic singleton in the whole bloody world.' She smiled sadly. 'Even Ashton's got his new girlfriend with him tonight so it's just little old me sitting in the corner all green and prickly.'

'You, Mia Hancock, are the least tragic singleton I've ever met. Anyway, it's not as if Dom and I are going to be slobbering over each other all night is it?'

Mia glanced behind Bea to where Dom was still hovering, and he grinned at her. 'She wouldn't let me even if I tried.'

'Ah sorry Dom. I'm being maudlin. It's just I realised as you arrived that I should be out trying to find the love of my life rather than sitting here with you bunch of saddos—'

'Hey!'

'Kidding,' she smirked. 'But it's true though, innit? I'm never gonna find love sitting around getting pissed with you lot.'

'Yeah, but you love us,' Bea said, planting a kiss on her friend's cheek. Mia gave her a look. 'All right then, I do.' She grabbed Bea's hand. 'Come on you two, you've got some catching up to do.'

That was an understatement, Bea realised as she walked into the living room where Michael was holding court, telling a story about something that had happened earlier that day, arms wind-milling wildly in the air to make his point.

'And that was when – oh hello you two, thank God someone sensible is here at last. This lot don't give two shiny shits about bad service but I know you'll appreciate it.' Michael beckoned them in, giving Bea and Dom hugs.

'Beatrice, Dominic!' Harry was in the kitchen doorway holding a bottle of champagne, his cheeks redder and shinier than usual. His blond hair stuck up in tufts all round his head and that was how Bea knew the usually well-turned-out Harry had already had a skinful.

'God you lot, how long have you been at it?'

'Oh Michael and I have been drinking since before lunch,' Harry said, his words slightly less well-enunciated than usual. 'Mia got here just after lunch and Ashton and Charmaine have been here a couple of hours.'

Bea turned to where Ashton and Charmaine were snuggled up on the sofa, giggling like school children. Bea could see why Mia was feeling so out of sorts about being a gooseberry with them all over each other like this.

'Oi you two, get your tongues out of each other's mouth for one minute and come and say hello,' Bea said.

'They can't, I think they're surgically attached,' Michael said, handing them both a glass of champagne that was almost overflowing. Bea took a sip from the top and savoured the taste. She needed that.

'Well anyway, sorry we're so much later than planned. It was hard to get away.'

'From the little one?' Charmaine said.

'Well, yes. Sort of.' Bea shuffled uncomfortably.

'It's all right Bea, you *can* talk about it,' Dom said, and Bea felt her face redden.

'Yes, sorry. I've just had dinner with AJ and his parents. They wanted to meet Jack.'

Dom couldn't have missed the looks of sympathy thrown his way but to his credit he said nothing and just shrugged his coat off and sat down on one of Michael and Harry's stylish dining chairs.

'Wow, is this the first time they've met him?' Harry said, walking round and topping up everyone's glasses.

'It's the first time they've met *me*, let alone Jack,' she said. 'When' – she glanced at Dom but he was studying his feet very intently – 'when I was with AJ we didn't get round to visiting them and they didn't come over before... well before everything.'

'So how was it?'

Bea shrugged. 'It was fine. They were lovely. They adored Jack. Of course.'

'And is Jack with his dad tonight?' Michael said.

Bea saw Dom flinch at the word 'dad' – she knew he hoped Jack would call him that too one day, but they'd cross that bridge when they came to it – and nodded. 'Yeah. Which means we can get pissed. I've even pumped some milk, so we have zero responsibilities for a change – at least not until tomorrow afternoon.'

'Well in that case drink the fuck up,' Michael said, and Bea and Dom both did as they were told, Bea draining her glass and letting out an almighty belch.

'Sorry.'

She might not have wanted to come this evening but now she was here she couldn't have been more grateful for this amazing bunch of people she was lucky enough to call her friends. She threw herself down beside Ashton and slapped him on the back of the head.

'Budge up loser.'

Ashton looked at the space she was trying to squeeze into and smirked. 'Oh dear, have you been eating too many mince pies Bea?'

Bea elbowed him in the side and he yelped, but moved. Bea knew he was only joking, but she still felt conscious of the extra baby weight and didn't want Ashton to know he'd hit a sensitive spot.

'Anyway, we wanted to quiz you two,' Harry said, gesturing at Bea and Dom.

'Did you? What about?'

'About parenthood.'

'Oh?' Dom said, intrigued.

Harry threw Michael a coy look and Michael gave a tiny nod. Harry turned back to them and said, theatrically, 'We're going to be dads!'

Mia gasped. 'Oh my God! This is amazing!' she said, leaping up from her seat on the sofa where she was squeezed in awkwardly on the other side of Charmaine and throwing her arms round Michael and then Harry.

When the exclamations of congratulations and delight were done, Bea sat forward. 'How come this is the first time we're hearing about this?'

'We wanted – well, we didn't...' Michael seemed lost for words, unusually for him, which was how Bea could tell how important this news was to them both. 'We just wanted to be sure it was all going ahead before we told anyone,' he said. 'We just didn't think they'd let people like us adopt...'

'I'm so, so thrilled for you,' Bea said.

'Yeah guys, it's the best thing in the world,' Dom said. His voice was soft.

'I'm not sure we're the best people to ask though, are we love?' Bea said. 'We're just making things up as we go along.'

Dom nodded. 'She's right. We're utterly clueless. But it is amazing, and you just work it out somehow.'

The look in Dom's eyes as he spoke about being a dad made Bea's heart clench with love for him, and she smiled as he caught her eye.

'But we'll tell you whatever you need to know – the good, the bad and the ugly.'

'And there's plenty of ugly when nappies are involved,' Dom said, laughing.

* * *

Later, when Bea felt as though she had probably caught up with everyone on the drunk stakes, she was sitting on the floor beside Mia, their heads tipped back against the sofa. The ceiling was spinning and Bea was wishing she'd eaten more of the delicious dinner Harry had cooked to soak up the alcohol.

'It's funny, isn't it?' Mia said, her words slurred.

'What's funny?' Bea slid her eyes across to look at her friend.

'Just – you know. Life.'

'Woah, deep Mee.'

'Fuck off.' She laughed. 'You know what I mean though. Who would have thought this time last year that you'd be a mum, Harry and Michael would be dads-to-be... that Ashton would have found a woman to put up with him—'

'Oi, I'm right here!' he said, sticking his foot in Mia's back.

'Love ya really, shit-head,' she said. She let out a sigh. 'I'm still eternally single though.' She turned to look at Bea. 'Maybe I'll never find anyone to love.'

Bea shifted round to look at her friend. 'Of course you'll find someone. You're amazing.'

'Men don't seem to think so.'

'Oh darling.' She took Mia's hands and gave them a gentle kiss. 'Then they don't know what they're missing. You're the kind, funniest, intelligent-est—'

'That's not even a word.'

'Don't care. You are it.'

'Yeah maybe. It just feels... I dunno.' She let out a long breath of air, her cheeks puffing out. 'I can't see it happening.'

'You just said yourself you hadn't seen this happening, right now. So who knows where we'll all be this time next year.'

'Do you think you'll still be with Dom?'

'What?' Bea felt her heart thump. She looked round. Dom was deep in conversation with Michael and hadn't heard Mia's question. Bea lowered her voice. 'Why did you ask that?'

'You know why.'

'I...' Bea stopped. Of course she knew why. Mia had made it clear she thought Bea was with Dom for all the wrong reasons – 'You can't be with someone out of duty, because you feel responsible for them,' she'd told Bea on more than one occasion, and, 'You can't make yourself love someone.' Now, Bea simply said, 'I don't know.'

'And AJ?'

She shook her head. 'No!'

'Even though he's Jack's dad?'

Bea whipped her head round to face Mia. 'Honestly, no. That ship has sailed.' She hoped Mia would let it drop, but Mia clearly didn't get the message.

'But you still love him.'

Bea held her gaze for a moment and thought about all the ways she could respond to that. But then she simply shook her head and looked back at the ceiling, her heart thumping.

They both stayed like that a few more minutes before Mia said, 'How's your dad?'

'Not great.'

'Poor Pete,' Mia said, sadly.

'I know. I can't bear to see him like this. It's worse than ever. It's not just forgetting to drink his tea or getting lost on the way back from the football. He's started getting angry now, and I think it's because he knows what's happening to him.' She felt a tear trace down her cheek and she brushed it away.

'And how's your mum coping?'

Bea shrugged. 'You know Mum. In denial, won't let anyone else help. Not as much as she should. I mean, she's almost seventy, she needs to slow down.'

'She never will though.'

'I know.'

'I always hope for a love like your mum and dad's. I just can't imagine them ever having any doubts about each other. It all just seems so straightforward.'

'You're right.' She turned to look at Mia again. 'We just like to make our lives complicated.'

'Ain't that the truth.'

As they sat there, the Christmas lights twinkling, the drunken chatter of their closest friends swirling around them, Bea tried not to think about how different her life could have been if she'd been able to forgive AJ for lying to her.

A different city.

A different man.

A different life.

12

STAY

December 2007

'Come on Dad, let's get you to bed.' Bea tucked her arm through her dad's and led him slowly up the stairs to the room that used to be the one her twin brothers shared. It had been hard to convince Ange to let him sleep in his own room.

'What if he gets up in the night and tries to get out of the house?' Ange had worried. 'At least when he's with me I can hear him.'

'Keep the doors locked and it'll be fine,' Alice had said. Eventually, lack of sleep forced Ange to reluctantly agree.

'Bea, what are you doing?' Bea and Pete had just reached the bottom of the stairs when her mum's voice made her jump. Ange shooed Bea out of the way and took Pete's arm herself.

'Go and sit down, you shouldn't be doing this, not with your leg,' Ange said, making her slow way up the stairs with her husband.

'I keep telling you, I'm fine,' Bea said, but she might as well have been shouting into an abyss for all the notice her mum took of her.

Giving up, she went back through to the living room and lowered herself carefully onto the sofa. She grimaced as a pain shot through her knee and tipped her head back on the sofa. Her mum seemed to have toned down the Christmas decorations slightly this year, although the room still felt like a grotto. Bea shook her head. Would Ange ever slow down?

Bea felt guilty all the time. Not only did Ange have Pete and his worsening Alzheimer's to look after, but now she had Bea as well. Bea tried not to give her mum anything else to do, but Ange often insisted, telling Bea to rest, that she needed to heal.

It had been almost exactly a year since the accident, since her life was thrown upside down, and Bea still tried not to think about it too often.

Sometimes, in bed at night, she replayed that moment in her mind: the moment the deer stared at her through the car windscreen, and she knew it was hopeless as AJ battled fruitlessly with the car on the icy road.

Everything after that was a blur. She remembered waking up in hospital, AJ on one side of the room, his left arm in a sling, the other arm scrolling through his phone; Mia and Maggie were on the other side, Mia flicking through a magazine. Before she could work out where she was, Mia leapt to her side.

'You're awake!'

AJ winced as he stood, and the side of his face that had been hidden was bruised and swollen. Bea tried to push herself into a seated position but a pain shot down her leg and she stopped.

'Hang on,' AJ said, fumbling with something beneath her bed. She began to move up, her body gently folding until she was sitting upright. She reached out her hand to touch AJ's face.

'What happened?' she said. Her voice was rough, unused, and she coughed.

'I had a bit of a run-in with a tree,' he said, but his voice sounded sad. 'How are you feeling?'

Bea did a mental inventory from top to toe. There was some level of pain in most of her body, but worse than that was the sense of dread about something she couldn't quite remember. 'I'm not sure,' she said.

'Do you want some water?' Mia said, holding a cup to her lips. Bea sipped it gratefully as it soothed her dry throat.

A look passed between AJ and Mia above Bea's head. 'What?' she said.

Neither of them replied. 'Come on, what's happening? Tell me.'

AJ took her hand and Mia took the other one, while Maggie placed her hands gently beside Bea's legs. Bea held her breath as she waited for one of them to speak.

'We lost the baby,' AJ said. His voice broke on the last word.

The baby.

Of course.

She had been pregnant.

And now, she wasn't.

Instinctively she pulled her hands away and placed them on her belly. 'Oh.' Her body felt heavy, her mind empty.

She looked at AJ. 'Are you okay?'

He smiled sadly. 'I'll get there. I just need to look after you,' he said. Tears shone in his eyes. Bea looked across at Mia.

'I'm so sorry Bea,' she said. 'I wish there was something I could say to make this better.'

Bea looked down at the bed, the shape of her legs beneath the blanket. And then she noticed. One leg looked huge compared to the other. She tugged the blanket free and stared at them, trying to work out what was going on.

'You shattered your kneecap,' AJ said gently. 'When we crashed.'

Bea felt strangely detached, probably as a result of the strong painkillers she was taking.

'Will I—'

'The doctor says you'll be out of action for a good few weeks, maybe even months. But you will get back to normal eventually.' AJ answered the question before she'd even had a chance to ask it.

'And the good news is you're going to have me and Maggie as your nurses,' Mia said.

'But how? What about work?'

Mia shrugged. 'I'm only freelancing, and I can still do that from home,' she said. 'But AJ and I have agreed I'm going to come and look after you during the day.'

'And I'll come early evening for a couple of hours,' Maggie finished. 'We're not taking no for an answer.'

Bea didn't want to argue. She wanted to cry with gratitude. There was still so much to process, but at least she would have her best friends by her side while she was doing it.

That all seemed so long ago now. So much had happened since then, she could barely believe it had only been a year.

She pulled herself up from the sofa just as her mum came into the room.

'Dad's asleep at last,' Ange said.

'Good. Why don't you sit down and I'll make you a cup of tea,' Bea said.

'You sit love, I can do it.'

'Mum!' She hadn't meant to be so sharp, and her mum looked at her strangely. 'Sorry. I just wish you'd stop treating me like an invalid. I'm fine.'

'Well, you might think so, but I can see you're in pain with that leg of yours.'

'It's getting better,' Bea said. She didn't want her mum to know that she was worried, a year on from the accident, that it might never get better than this, that she might always have a limp. She didn't want her to know, either, that her leg was the least of her worries.

'Hmmm,' Ange said, unconvinced.

'Go on. You're exhausted,' Bea said. 'Please just let me make you a cup of tea.'

'Fine, if it stops you nagging,' Ange said, flopping onto the sofa. 'But be careful!'

'Yes Mum!' Bea said as she left the room and headed towards the kitchen. She closed the door behind her and switched on the radio, volume low. 'Merry Christmas Everyone' by Shakin' Stevens was playing, and Bea hummed along as she busied herself making tea – in the pot, the way her mum preferred it – and dug a couple of mince pies from the cupboard. The kettle was reaching boiling point when her phone buzzed.

> Just at work and missing you so much. I love you, Princess Beatrice xx

She smiled and tapped out a reply.

> I miss you too. B x

She sighed and poured the water into the teapot. She wasn't sure how she was going to get through this Christmas without AJ. She felt lost without him – and yet she wasn't going to see him until the new year.

After the accident, Bea had finally gone to live at AJ's apartment, despite her protestations that she wanted to stay in her own place with Maggie.

'But mine is much bigger so it's easier for you to get around, especially while you're in a wheelchair,' AJ had argued. 'Plus, we *are* married. I thought you would be moving in anyway.'

She had given in to keep him happy, but he'd been right of course. Getting round had been harder and more painful than she'd imagined once the painkillers wore off, and having room to manoeuvre a wheelchair made life much easier. She just had to try and ignore the echoes of Cassie.

As promised, Mia and Maggie took it in turns to stay with her every single day. Sometimes, when he wasn't too busy, Frank popped round too, and Bea loved seeing how happy he made Mia.

On the flipside, though, Bea felt increasingly unhappy.

She loved AJ. That was never in question. But losing the baby had affected them both more than they realised, and it began to drive a wedge between them. Especially when, a couple of months after the accident Bea had realised that what she wanted more than anything else was to have a baby. It might have been unplanned the first time, but now she was single-minded in her determination.

Unfortunately, AJ didn't agree.

'It's too soon,' he said, when she mentioned it at the beginning of March.

'Why?' she said, petulant.

'We're both still grieving. I just think we need a little more time before we throw ourselves into parenthood. Make sure we're certain.'

But Bea *was* certain, and the more certain she became, the more uncertain AJ became until finally, by the beginning of the summer, things came to a head.

'But I'm almost completely better now,' Bea yelled, when AJ told her she was still too frail to think about having a baby.

'I don't mean physically,' he said.

'For God's sake,' she said. 'How long would you like me to wait then? A year? Two years? A fucking *decade*, and then realise I'm too old and my ovaries have dried up like an old prune?'

He'd winced at her words, but refused to give in. There seemed to be no way through it, no way to compromise, and in the end Bea made a decision.

'I'm going home for a while,' she said.

'Home? As in London?' AJ said, bewildered.

'Yes.'

'But your home is here, with me.' He wrapped his arms around her and she stiffened, determined not to give in.

'But this is tearing us apart, AJ,' she said, in a whisper. 'I need time to heal.'

'Can I come with you?'

There was nothing she wanted more than for him to come with her back to London. For them to make a fresh start somewhere else, away from the reminders of what might have been. But instead she said, 'It's up to you.'

In July, they had moved back to the UK. Bea had tried not to think too far ahead, to wonder whether this could be a permanent move or if it was just for a short while, because if she realised she didn't ever want to go back to New York, what would that mean for her and AJ? Would he be prepared to leave behind the life he'd made for himself to be in north London with her? She didn't feel strong enough to ask him directly. So she didn't.

They found a flat to rent just round the corner from Bea's parents and close to Alice, and for that summer, it finally seemed as though things might just work. That they might be able to get through this and come out stronger.

AJ flew back and forth to New York every couple of weeks for work, but other than that he seemed to love London – slow strolls round the parks, drinks by the Thames, weekends shopping in Soho.

But as the weather began to cool and autumn set in in full force, Bea could see he was becoming restless. Finally, in the middle of

October, just before he flew to New York for the week, she confronted him.

'You're not happy, are you?' she said.

AJ stood in the middle of the living room, his carry-on bag packed and ready at his feet. He was still so handsome it made her belly somersault when she caught sight of him unexpectedly, and she tried not to let it influence what she wanted – needed – to say.

'I'm fine, Bea. We've been fine. Haven't we?' he said, looking bewildered.

'Is fine what you want though?'

'You know what I mean.' He stepped towards her, crouched down to her level, where she had her aching leg propped up on some pillows. 'I'm happy, Bea. Aren't you?'

She looked into his eyes, his beautiful, deep blue eyes, and wanted to say, 'Yes, I'm totally happy,' and pretend everything was perfect. But she knew it would come to a head sooner or later, and she couldn't just sit around and wait for it.

'Not totally. I – I still think we want different things.' She swallowed. 'I mean, I still want a baby. Do you?'

The seconds ticked by, and Bea knew with a sinking, sick feeling, that she'd hit the nail on the head. That this was the thing driving the wedge between them and preventing AJ from being completely content. He looked down at the floor, then back at her, his eyes heavy.

'I don't know,' he said.

There wasn't anything else that could be said. AJ flew out that afternoon and by the time he came back, Bea had made a decision.

'I think you should go back to New York,' she said.

'With you?' AJ sounded so hopeful it broke her heart.

'Not yet.'

'But – why? Why would I want to live there without you?'

She pressed her palms against his cheeks, her heart breaking. 'I know you don't want to be in London. Your heart is in New York.'

'My heart is wherever you are,' AJ said, but Bea shook her head. 'No, not completely. I think you should go back and wait. I'll come back when I feel ready.'

'So you will come back?'

She hesitated, then gave a small nod. 'Soon.'

'And if I don't change my mind about wanting a baby?'

'Then we'll talk some more.'

AJ flew back to New York two weeks later, and Bea had never regretted anything so much in her life. If she'd thought AJ not being around might help her get her thoughts in order she couldn't have been more wrong. She only felt bereft.

He was, at least, coming over for Christmas in a couple of days' time. Although with the weather worsening over there and flights being cancelled due to high winds, she was worried he might not make it at all. The odds felt stacked against them.

She finished making the tea, then picked up the mugs and the plate of mince pies and carried them through to the living room. Her mum was staring out of the window, and looked round in surprise when Bea walked in.

'Sorry I was so long,' Bea said, setting everything down on the coffee table. The Christmas tree lights flashed, illuminating Ange's face in staccato bursts, like a broken street lamp.

'It's all right, I was just thinking.'

'Oh?' Bea picked up a mince pie and sat in the chair opposite her mum. Ange didn't answer right away. 'What about?'

Ange let out a long, shuddery sigh. 'Nothing really.' She looked exhausted.

'Mum, you know you don't have to do everything yourself don't you?' Bea said.

'But I don't, love. You and Alice have been such a help these last few months since...' She trailed off. She might have accepted Pete's diagnosis, but it didn't mean she was willing to admit he was deteriorating in front of their eyes.

'You don't let us help as much as you could. You don't always have to take on the weight of the world on your own.'

Ange shook her head and looked down at the mug of tea cradled in her hands. 'You've been through so much, Bea. I've been so worried about you, you don't need the extra worry. And with Alice with the new baby...' She waved her hand dismissively. Bea could see she was trying hard to keep the tears at bay. She stood and went to sit beside her mum and pulled her into a hug. Ange had always been small, but now she felt tiny, as though her frail frame might snap at any moment. How did people grow old right in front of you, without you even noticing?

'Sorry Bea, I—' Ange began, but whatever she was about to say was cut short by an almighty bang. They both leapt off the sofa and hurried into the hall to find a chair at the bottom of the stairs. Pete was standing at the top in his pyjamas, swaying precariously. He looked scared.

'Pete love?' Ange said, stepping over the chair and walking carefully towards her husband.

'Dad?' Bea followed as Ange gently led him away from the top of the stairs. Bea hadn't realised she'd been holding her breath, but now her heart was racing as they led Pete back into his bedroom. He perched on the end of the bed, looking lost.

'What happened Dad?' Bea said, sitting beside him and holding his hand in her lap as Ange fussed around plumping pillows and straightening the duvet.

'I...' he started, but then stopped as though his mouth couldn't remember how to form words.

'Why is there a chair at the bottom of the stairs?' Bea said gently.

He looked at her blankly, then smiled. 'It was broken,' he said.

Bea felt as though her heart was shattered. Her dad, who had always been so strong – an Arsenal-loving, beer-drinking, hard-working, family-loving man's man – was reduced to this confused shadow of himself.

She wanted to cry.

'Come on, let's get you back to bed and I'll make you a cup of tea, okay?' Bea said, and Pete let himself be led to bed and tucked under his duvet. Bea left Ange sitting with him, but as the kettle boiled she knew she'd have to speak to Alice and her brothers soon. This couldn't go on. They needed to convince their mum to get some proper help, before Pete hurt someone – or himself.

* * *

The last thing Bea felt like doing tonight was going out. But she'd promised Harry and Michael she'd go round for dinner, and she knew how much effort they put into it, so she had a shower and got dressed and curled her hair. By the time she arrived at their flat she was glad she'd come – and in desperate need of a drink.

'Hey, what's wrong baby girl?' Michael said as he let her in.

'Is it that obvious?' she said.

'I can read you like a book, Bea Preston. Sorry, Flynn,' he corrected. Bea smiled sadly.

'AJ just rang,' she said, trying not to let her voice wobble.

'Oh?'

'He said... he's not going to make it for Christmas.' She felt a tear trace down the side of her face.

'Oh Bea-Bea,' Michael said, enveloping her in a bear hug, and Bea snuggled in, grateful for the easy affection from one of her oldest friends. When Michael pulled away he looked down at her. 'Is it the flights?'

Bea nodded. 'I've been worried about it all week and they've finally cancelled most international flights out of New York,' she said. 'Strong winds apparently, it's too dangerous.'

'And he can't get another one, presumably?'

She shook her head. 'Not until the twenty-seventh.'

'Well then, we'll just have to make sure we celebrate when he gets here, won't we?' He tucked his arm into Bea's, kissed the top of her head, and led her into the living room. 'Everyone, Bea needs to get ridiculously drunk!' he announced as they walked in. Harry was in the kitchen doorway holding a full bottle of champagne, and Ashton was on the sofa with his new girlfriend, Charmaine, who Bea had only met a couple of times but seemed lovely. They all looked at her and she attempted a smile.

'Maybe not *that* drunk,' she said.

'We'll be the judge of that,' Harry said, swooping towards her with a glass of fizz. She took it gratefully. 'How bad is it?'

'Her *husband* is going to miss Christmas,' Michael said.

'What?' Harry was outraged.

'Oh no!' Charmaine said.

'It's the weather,' Bea explained, drinking some more from her glass and lowering herself down beside Ashton. 'Loads of flights are cancelled and he can't get another one. I'd been dreading this happening for days.'

'Oh darling, and after last year's disastrous Christmas too. I'm so sorry,' Harry said.

'Me too.' Bea tried not to think about last Christmas.

'Sorry Bea,' Ashton said. 'That really sucks.'

'Thanks Ash.' He liked to pretend he was all jokes and laughs, but she knew Ashton felt things deeper than he let on.

'Let's not dwell on sad things,' Harry said, bringing in a plate of what looked like home-made canapés and handing them round. 'Let's just try and have fun tonight.'

'Hear hear,' said Michael. 'Although I do just want to say how bloody weird it is to be here without Mia.'

Bea nodded in agreement. There was a huge Mia-shaped hole in her life, and tonight only emphasised it.

'Shall we Skype her?' Ashton said.

Bea checked her watch. 'It's only three in the afternoon there.'

'But she'll have finished work for Christmas. Shall we give it a go, before we all get too tipsy?'

Michael found his laptop and, after a few minutes of swearing, he turned the screen round. Seconds later Mia's face filled the screen. 'Fuuuuuuck, it's so good to see you!' she cried.

'You too!' everyone chorused back.

For the next few minutes everyone exchanged news. Mia had indeed finished work, and she and Frank were in a bar near Frank's apartment enjoying a cosy cocktail together. 'You're lucky I brought my laptop with me just in case work needed me,' she said. 'Anyway, I'm trying to convince Frank that we always drink booze at this goddamn early hour at Christmas.' She laughed as Frank pulled a face behind her.

'Whether it's true or not I don't really give a damn,' he said, holding up his glass and they all screeched with laughter to see it was a tequila sunrise with an umbrella.

'Listen, we're annoying everyone here, so we'd better go, but it's so good to see your faces,' Mia said, wiping away a tear.

'Hey, don't cry, we still love you,' Harry said.

'I know.' Mia sniffed. 'I just wish I was there with you all.'

'Hey!' Frank said behind her. She turned and blew him a kiss.

'With you as well of course,' she said. 'Honestly, I feel so sad I won't be seeing you. But you all promise you'll come and visit soon?'

'We promise!' they said, then said their goodbyes. As they hung up, Bea's phone beeped and she glanced at the screen.

> I love you, my Bea. I promise to look after AJ until
> he can get home. M xx

Good old Mia, always looking out for her. God, she missed her with a ferocity she hadn't expected.

She tuned back into the conversation and tried not to think about her best friend and her husband being in New York for Christmas while she was here, helping her mum look after her dementia-ridden father.

'Hey everyone, Harry and I have news,' Michael said, glancing at his husband and then at Bea. She frowned, suddenly nervous.

'We don't want to make a massive fuss about this,' Harry took over. 'But, well... we're going to be dads.'

Charmaine gasped and Ashton said, 'Bloody hell that's awesome,' but Bea was aware she hadn't said a word, so she painted a smile on her face and said, 'That's brilliant news you two.' Harry glanced at Michael again, then turned to Bea. 'I'm sorry to spring it on you out of the blue,' he said gently.

Bea blinked back tears, then stood and walked across the room.

'You daft buggers, I can't believe you were worried about telling me,' she said, throwing her arms around them. 'I'm totally thrilled for you, truly.' And she was surprised to find she really meant it. Maybe this was progress.

'So, what happens next?'

'We're not sure. We – we kept putting it off because we didn't think they'd let... people like us adopt,' Harry said. 'But it turns out they do.'

'Well it's brilliant news,' Bea said, sitting back down next to Ashton. 'And I hope you'll let the baby's aunty Bea help out.'

'Always,' Michael said, holding his glass up and blowing her a kiss.

* * *

By the end of the night Bea was more drunk than she'd intended, and as she tumbled into the back of the cab, the world spun. Ugh, she was going to pay for this tomorrow.

The taxi rumbled along the quiet London streets, stop-starting at traffic lights along the way. Bea stared out the window. It had begun to frost over and she thought about the snow at the cabin last year, about how magical it had been, and how lucky she'd felt. How things could change in a heartbeat.

She pressed her nose against the glass and let it steam up, distorting the outside world. It had just cleared when she felt her phone buzz in her pocket. Bollocks, had she left something at Harry and Michael's? She squinted at the screen, the words swimming as she tried to focus. And then, she did.

> Hello Bea. I kept telling myself not to contact you, but your mum said it would be okay. I just wondered how you were, and if you fancied a drink one day over the holidays? No worries if not.
> Dom x

13

GO

December 2008

Bea held Pete's elbow and steered him back to his chair by the window. He loved to sit and watch people passing by, the buses come and go, the chug and hiss of the hydraulic brakes every time they stopped at the bus stop. This morning it had started snowing and Pete's face lit up like a child's as he gazed out of the window in wonderment at the flakes drifting lazily from the sky.

'Can we build a snowman?' he said.

'Maybe later Dad,' Bea said, tucking his blanket around his knees. The electric fire had been on for most of the morning and the room was boiling, but Pete still got cold when he sat still for too long.

'Where's Ange?' He glanced round the empty room, his look turning to panic.

'She's just popped to the hairdresser's. She'll be back soon.' Bea had learned not to tell her dad he'd already been told something because it distressed him so much, so she just pretended he'd never known in the first place.

Bea was working from the kitchen table at her parents' house this morning so she could keep an eye on her dad. Over the last few months Pete had been getting slowly worse until, one morning in early September, Ange had finally broken down and admitted she couldn't cope.

'I can't bear for him to go into a home though,' she said. 'We haven't been apart a day in our whole marriage and I don't want to start now.'

Bea, Alice and her brothers Charlie and Rob had held an emergency meeting to work out how they could best help their parents. Of course it had fallen to Bea and Alice to do the majority of the care because they both lived in London, while Charlie was in Brighton and Rob in Manchester.

Over the next few weeks they had put a plan in place which meant that every Monday and Wednesday Alice helped her mum out, while on Tuesdays and Thursdays, Bea worked from her parents' house to give her mum a break. Her boss Fiona had been brilliant about it and she was so grateful. Today was her last day before she finished for Christmas, and she couldn't wait – she missed baby Jack when he was at nursery three days a week, or with AJ on Fridays, or Dom on Mondays, and she was excited about spending the next week and a half with him. At just over a year old he was hilarious now, desperately trying to talk and running rings round her.

She couldn't help feeling sad though about how much had changed – again – since last Christmas. And not necessarily for the better.

She had never expected to be a single mum, but that was what she seemed to have become. Although she was aware that, as single mums went, she was luckier than most – because she had two very hands-on dads to help out with Jack in AJ and Dom.

She had tried to make it work with Dom. She really had. And

she'd been happy, most of the time. But Mia's words had never really left her head – *you can't make yourself love someone* – and finally, by the time the summer rolled around, Bea had realised Mia was right. She was with Dom for the wrong reasons – to keep him happy, to stop him slipping back into depression; to keep her mum happy because she didn't want to give her anything else to worry about; because she didn't want to be on her own. Not because she couldn't live without him.

There was also that other pesky problem: that you couldn't make yourself *not* love someone either. And she knew that, truly, she'd never stopped loving AJ, no matter what she told herself.

So she'd finally told Dom it was over. That she needed to be on her own, to work out what she really wanted.

He'd been distraught at first, of course. Refused to speak to her and went to stay with his dad in Hampshire, which at least meant she and Jack could stay in the flat. She'd been terrified Dom would stop taking his anti-depressants again, and every time the phone rang she was on edge, waiting for terrible news. But finally, a few weeks later, he rang and asked if he could still be part of Jack's life, and she'd known then that Dom was going to be all right. His love for Jack had pulled him through.

Now Bea and Jack were living in the flat and Dom was renting round the corner while they tried to sell it. It was unconventional, but it was working. For now.

At least as long as she could ignore her feelings for AJ.

Mia couldn't understand why she didn't just get back together with him.

'I can't,' Bea said. What she really wanted to say was 'because I'm scared he won't want me' and 'I'm scared of getting hurt again'. She could still remember how she'd felt when she found out about Cassie; when she'd realised the man she loved had a whole other side to his life that she'd known nothing about: like she'd been kicked in the stomach.

She wasn't willing to risk feeling like that again. So, for now at least, this was the best of both worlds. Jack got to know his father, and she got to see AJ.

The trouble now was that AJ had a girlfriend, and she didn't know how to deal with that. So she did what she always did and buried her head in the sand, and got on with worrying about everything else.

Like her father, for one.

She stood, stretched her arms in the air, heard the sound of her shoulders crunching, and filled the kettle before she went to check on her dad. When she got to the living room her heart stopped. He wasn't in his chair at the window. She looked round the room in panic – despite everything the ceiling still heaved with decorations, while the over-sized tree in the corner sagged beneath the weight of baubles and tinsel – but her dad was nowhere to be seen. Heart hammering, she stepped back out into the hall. The door to the downstairs loo was half-open and she popped her head inside but he wasn't there either. Her legs felt weak with worry. What if he'd gone wandering off, got himself lost or, worse, walked out in front of a car? She was meant to be looking after him. In a blind panic she raced to the bottom of the stairs, swung round the newel post and took the stairs two at a time.

'Dad?' she called as she ran. Silence.

She looked in the first room, but it was empty, dust motes lying undisturbed in the chilly air. She peered in the bathroom, she opened the airing cupboard door as she passed. What was she *doing?* Her parents' bedroom door was ajar and she pushed it open carefully, heart hammering. There he was, perched on the end of the bed, hands on his knees, staring at a spot on the floor.

'Dad?' she said gently. He looked up but there was a frightened look in his eyes as though he'd seen a ghost. She lowered herself next to him. 'What are you doing up here?' she said, and he stared at her with wide eyes.

'I was looking for something.' His voice trembled.

'Were you? What?'

He looked back at the floor and then back at her. 'I... I don't know.'

Tears prickled behind her eyes but she didn't want to frighten him by getting upset so she pulled him into her arms. He sat perfectly still, not responding and she felt her heart break for the silent but strong and loving man her dad had always been. That man was long gone now, and in his place was this quiet, frightened unsure-of-himself person who couldn't remember why he'd come upstairs or couldn't be entirely sure who she was. He *looked* like her dad – albeit a thinner, paler version – but it was only the shell of him. Inside, she'd already lost him.

She pulled away then stood and held her hand out to him. 'Shall we go and get you some lunch?'

He looked up at her. 'Haven't I already had lunch?'

'No Dad,' she said gently. 'Not today. We've got soup, does that sound okay?'

He nodded and stood, shuffling towards the bedroom door. 'I like soup.'

Bea followed him, her heart breaking a little bit more.

* * *

'How's he been?' Ange said, bustling in and bringing a blast of freezing air in with her. She pulled her hat from her head and unwound her scarf, hanging it on the hook by the front door. When she realised Bea hadn't answered she looked up, worried. 'Oh no, has something happened? Has he fallen?' She ran into the living room and Bea pulled herself together and followed her. By the time she'd caught up, Ange was already kissing the top of Pete's head affectionately.

'Sorry Mum, no. He's fine. He's just been particularly forgetful today, that's all.'

Ange turned to face her. 'What do you mean? He seems fine.'

Bea's heart sank. Her mum still refused to admit her dad was getting worse – and Bea understood why, of course. But they seemed to have this same conversation, or at least a version of it, almost every day, and she hated the part where she had to explain to her mum that Pete wasn't getting better, that he wasn't safe to be here on his own and that, eventually, they were going to have to get him more help.

'He is fine now,' she said, appeasing. 'We've had lunch and he's got a cup of tea, but he didn't want to watch *Homes Under the Hammer* today.'

Ange smiled, reassured for now. 'He's gone off that bloke, Martin, who presents it,' she said. 'Told me he was bloody irritating the other day. So you see, he hasn't forgotten that.'

'No Mum, you're right.' Bea stepped forward and wrapped her mum in her arms, feeling the tiny proportions of her. 'Anyway, your hair looks lovely.'

Ange's hand fluttered to her head. 'Oh, is it not ruined now? I had to put my stupid hat on because it started to snow and I thought it would be all flat.' She squinted into the mirror above the electric fire.

'No, it looks gorgeous,' Bea said.

'Thank you love.' Ange glanced at Pete who was watching passengers get off the bus across the road. The look of love in her eyes made Bea's heart swell. She hoped when she was her parents' age she'd have someone she loved as much as they obviously loved each other. The way things were going though, it didn't seem likely.

'Anyway, you get on, I know you've got work to do,' Ange said, adjusting a piece of tinsel that had slipped from its branch.

'It's all right, I'm nearly done for Christmas now. Let me get you a cup of tea. Or some soup? There's some more in the fridge.'

'No love, don't fuss, I'm fine.'

Bea sighed. She wished her mum would let her help more. It was all well and good being a martyr, but when you were pushing seventy and looking after your husband almost full-time it was good to have a break from time to time. But she knew it made her mum happy, to feel useful.

'Well if you're sure you're okay now then I will get off. I've still got a couple more presents to buy for Jack and AJ.'

'You are getting something for Dom, aren't you?' Ange said.

'Yes Mum, of course I am.' She put her hand on her mum's arm. 'But you do understand that me and Dom are not getting back together, don't you?'

Ange looked at Bea for a moment, her eyes filled with something Bea couldn't read. She clasped her hands together. 'I know, but you can't blame your old mum for asking.'

Bea kissed her mum on the cheek, then leaned in and did the same to her dad. He looked up in confusion and smiled vacantly. 'Bye Dad,' she whispered, her throat raw with emotion. 'I love you.'

She left then, and as she walked the familiar route away from the house she grew up in her heart felt heavy with grief. It was clear that Pete was getting worse and she felt scared every time she thought about the possibility that this might be their last Christmas together.

She felt her phone ringing in her bag.

'Hey Alice,' she said, pressing it against her ear to hear her properly.

'What's wrong?' Her sister was never one to beat about the bush. 'Your voice sounds funny.'

'I've just left Dad.'

'Oh.' A beat of silence. 'How was he today?'

She sighed. 'He wasn't great. I lost him at one point.'

'What?'

'It's fine. He hadn't actually gone anywhere. I found him upstairs sitting on his bed staring at the floor and he had—' Her voice caught in her throat. 'He had no idea what he was doing there.'

Alice didn't answer.

'Alice?'

'I'm here. I... I was just working out what to say.'

'Yeah. Me too.'

'He's definitely got worse, hasn't he?'

'Much worse.'

Bea heard a sniff and realised her big sister was crying. 'Let's get through Christmas Day, then we have to talk to Mum.'

'About the care home?'

'We have to, Bea.'

'Yeah, I know.'

'Okay. What are you doing now?'

'Going for some last-minute things in town.'

'For Dom?'

Bea sighed. Not Alice too. 'No, Alice. For my son.'

'Oh right. Course.'

She couldn't face having the same conversation with Alice as she'd just had with her mum, so she said nothing more. She knew they both loved Dom, but she wished they'd stop talking about him, making her feel guilty about not being with him any more. She'd speak to them in the new year as well, once everything with her dad was sorted.

She quickly finished the call and by the time she said goodbye she'd reached the tube station. As she went to put her phone away it buzzed again and she glanced at the screen. Clicking it open, her heart melted. It was a picture of Jack, dressed as a Christmas pudding, smiling at the camera with his two front teeth on display.

Hurry home Mummy, we miss you xx

The message was from AJ, who had already finished work and was looking after Jack today. A surge of longing overwhelmed her as she stood on the freezing street in the slush, her heart swollen with love. She knew it was love for her son. But was it for his father as well, and the life they had once shared? The future they had both dreamed about?

She flipped her phone closed and headed down into the depths of the underground, and tried not to think about another year, another Christmas, another city.

14

STAY

December 2008

Bea heaved herself off the sofa and picked her way carefully to the door.

'You all right love?' her mum said, leaping up to help her.

'I'm only going to the loo, Mum, I think I'll be all right.' She smiled to show Ange she wasn't annoyed, and Ange dropped her hands to her side. 'Ah sorry, I don't mean to fuss.' She sat back down on the stiff wooden chair by the door, ready for action in case anyone needed an emergency mince pie, or glass of wine, cup of tea. God forbid anyone got it themselves.

Bea stepped out into the hallway and closed the door behind her. She could hear Alice's husband Andrew telling everyone about something that had happened at work, and the kids were running around the garden even though it was only a couple of degrees above freezing. Bea lumbered up the stairs to the bathroom, her injured knee twinging with every step, locked the door behind her and lowered herself onto the loo with relief. She *had* been desperate for a wee – that's what happened when you were almost seven months pregnant – but she had also been desperate for a few minutes' peace – an almost impossible task in this house at Christmas. She took a couple of deep breaths and let the tension seep from her shoulders. The bathroom was freezing, the small window above the bath propped open, the way it always was no matter the weather. *It's good to let some fresh air in the house,* Ange said.

Maybe so, thought Bea, but not when it was freezing outside. She stood, closed the window and sat back down on the loo.

She didn't have long. If she was any longer than about five minutes someone would come looking for her, convinced she'd fallen and hurt herself, or, worse, gone into labour on the bathroom floor. She closed her eyes and rested her head in her hands, elbows on her knees, baby bump tucked between her legs like she'd stuffed a giant beachball up her jumper.

She ran her hands over it, the skin taut and smooth beneath her palms. The baby must be asleep now, but every now and then she felt her shifting – she knew it was a girl, as they'd found out at the twenty-week scan – legs and arms flailing as she moved position in her tiny, safe and warm home. It was almost impossible to imagine there was a baby in there, a fully formed human who, if she were to be born right this minute, would be able to breathe and cry and feed all by herself. How was that even a thing?

She sat there a couple of minutes longer, trying to imagine how much her life was about to change. Then she heard footsteps up the carpeted stairs, and a gentle knock on the bathroom door.

'Bea?'

'I'm fine,' she said. 'Just having a wee.'

'Okay but let me in.'

Bea stood, flicked the lock open and Mia marched in, locking the door behind her. She perched on the edge of the bath. 'How are you two doing?'

'Really good.' Bea felt a smile spread across her face. 'Just needed a break.'

'I don't blame you.' She grinned. 'I wouldn't have it any other way though, you know that.'

'Me neither.' Bea flushed the loo and stood to wash her hands. 'How's Frank coping with my family?' Mia had come home for Christmas this year, and brought Frank with her 'to have a proper British Christmas' she'd told him, even though Bea was fairly certain it wasn't much different to an American Christmas.

'He's quieter than I've ever seen him,' Mia said.

'Poor Frank.'

'Poor Frank nothing. He's loving all the fuss everyone's making of him, although I'm not sure he's ever experienced anything quite like a Preston family Christmas.'

'I don't suppose he has.'

Mia's face suddenly dropped. 'Your dad has got so much worse,' she said, her voice quiet.

Bea shook her head. 'I know. I don't think he has any idea what's going on.'

'He seems happy enough though.'

'For now. I just hope he doesn't get upset, the way he sometimes does. It's hard to watch.'

Mia looked at the floor. 'Why do things have to change? Why can't life be like it always was when we were thirteen?'

'I'm not sure Mum and Dad would be too impressed if I'd been in this state at thirteen,' Bea said.

Mia reached her hand out and laid it on Bea's bump. 'I can't believe you're going to be a mum in two months' time,' she said, her eyes wide in wonder.

'I know. I still feel like a child myself.'

'Ah but at least this baby will have a grown-up for a father.'

Bea smiled. 'That's true.' Dom couldn't wait to be a dad, and he was the happiest Bea had ever seen him. It was as though he'd been waiting for this his whole life, as though it was the answer to a question he hadn't even known needed answering. 'He's going to be a great dad,' Bea agreed.

'And you're going to be a great mother. The best,' Mia said.

'I hope so.'

'I know so.' Mia stood. 'Right, are you coming back down or do I have to report you missing?'

'Give me five minutes and I'll be there, okay?'

'Okay. But if Ange wants to check up on you, don't expect me to get in her way.'

Mia let herself out and Bea locked the door behind her again.

She thought about what Mia had just said. She hoped she would be a good mum, although she wasn't sure how anyone ever had any idea what they were doing. But she *was* completely certain that Dom was going to be an amazing father.

She thought back to how they had got here.

After Dom's text last year, Bea had drunkenly agreed to meet him for a drink. She already regretted it the following morning, but felt too guilty to cancel.

They met the next night. She hadn't seen Dom for more than two years and was surprised how quickly any awkwardness disappeared and they slipped back into their old ways, chatting easily. It was like putting on an old glove. He was the same old Dom – except, Bea quickly realised, he seemed more content than he had for years and something in him seemed to have softened, mellowed. It suited him.

'I've been having counselling,' he admitted, four gins into the evening. Bea's head was swimming, and she let her fingers graze against his on the tabletop. 'I'm glad you're happy,' she said, and their eyes locked for a moment.

By the time they were another couple of gins down, their tongues had loosened more.

'I've never got over you,' Dom blurted.

'What?' Bea was sure she'd misheard.

The silence was filled with unsaid words and Dom looked as though he was about to change the subject. But then he said, 'I never stopped loving you.'

Bea couldn't speak, her tongue thick with gin and shock.

'It's okay, you don't have to say anything.' Dom's voice was gentle. 'I shouldn't have said it, I'm sorry, I know you're still married. It's just, well...' He shrugged. 'My therapist told me to be honest.' He drew circles with his finger in a puddle of condensation, then looked up at her, his dark eyes blazing. 'So that's what I'm doing.'

She looked at him, this man she had once loved, and was surprised to feel a stirring of something. What was it? Not love. At least, not the kind of love she felt for AJ. Sympathy then? Or was it just the memory of what they'd once had, tricking her drunk mind into thinking it was something else?

They hadn't talked about what he'd said again for the rest of the evening but later, as they walked home through the frigid night air, Dom said, 'So what happened, with you and AJ?'

She stopped in her tracks, the question unexpected. Except had it really been? They'd been skirting round it all night, and it was only with the lubrication of alcohol that Dom had been brave enough to ask her.

'It's complicated,' she said, her breath an ineffectual puff of smoke.

'It usually is.'

She didn't say anything else as they carried on along Green Lanes. Bea listened to the uneven clip of her footsteps and the muffled flump of Dom's on the frosty pavements, the roar of the occasional car racing between traffic lights.

'I lost a baby.'

The words rang out, taking on their own shape in the air, and Dom slowed beside her. She didn't stop though, because if she looked at him she would freeze up, stop talking. So she kept walking, her gaze fixed on the pavement in front of her, her knee screaming at her to slow down, and when he caught up again she found it all coming out: the accident, the baby, the fact that losing something she hadn't even known she wanted had formed a fissure in their marriage; a tiny crack that had slowly widened until they were at opposite sides of it with no idea how to cross it.

'He thinks we should wait until I'm healed emotionally before we try for another baby,' Bea said, putting invisible speech marks round the words.

'But you think having a baby will help you heal.'

Bea finally turned to look at Dom. 'Yes,' she whispered. 'That's exactly it.'

They walked in silence for two more streets, then rounded the corner to Bea's flat, where they stopped and turned to face each other. Their breath clouded in the air between them. Dom took her gloved hands and she didn't pull them away.

'I'd have a baby with you,' he said, softly.

Then he left her standing there watching him walk away.

* * *

Bea had barely slept, the alcohol combining with Dom's parting words to create a knot of feelings she had no idea how to untangle.

AJ had arrived the following afternoon, which meant she had hardly any time to think about what Dom had said, but it was never far from her mind. She thought about it while she and AJ had dinner with her parents; she thought about it while they strolled through the park; shamefully, she even thought about it as they made love, the thought that they could be making a baby right now foremost in her mind.

For the first time since she met him, Bea felt as though she was walking on eggshells around AJ, as if one misstep could ruin everything. The worst thing was that she knew it was entirely her own fault. But as she lay in bed beside him she felt wired, sleep an impossible dream as guilt battled for attention alongside her longing to be a mum; with her love for AJ; with her life in New York.

Three days into the New Year it was time for AJ to fly back.

'Are you coming with me?' he said, as they kissed goodbye.

She wanted to say *yes*. But something – some*one*? – was holding her back.

'Soon,' she promised, and tried to ignore the hurt in AJ's eyes. He held his palms to her cheeks and planted a gentle kiss on her nose.

'I know you're hurting, Bea. But all I want to do is be with you. I think we can heal together.'

As she watched him leave in a taxi, her brain felt like a scribble of Christmas lights packed away in a box.

But what worried her most was that she also felt relief that he'd gone.

* * *

'I need to talk to you.' Bea rang Mia the moment AJ had left. Mia was due to head back to New York a few days later and Frank had already gone ahead because he needed to work.

'Hey, what's wrong?'

'I can't stop thinking about Dom,' she blurted.

A silence on the other end, then, 'I'm coming round.'

Mia was at Bea's flat within half an hour, and they sat on the sofa cross-legged, huge mugs of coffee in their hands. A family-sized packet of crisps sat ripped open between them, but neither of them were eating.

'Tell me everything,' Mia said.

Bea stared at the swirls of froth on the surface of her coffee, then let out a huge lungful of air and raised her eyes.

'Remember I told you I went out with Dom just before Christmas and we got really drunk?'

'Yes, and I also remember telling you it was a bad idea.' Mia was only teasing but a tear slid down Bea's cheek nonetheless. 'Fuck, Bea, I didn't mean to upset you.' Mia shuffled over and pulled Bea into a hug. 'Did something happen that night?'

Bea shook her head. 'Not like you think.'

Mia waited.

'He told me he still loved me.'

'What?'

Bea swallowed. 'It wasn't just that, though.' Bea swallowed, her hands twisting in her laps. 'He told me he'd have a baby with me if I wanted one.'

'What the...?'

'Oh, no! I don't think he meant it like that, he didn't mean *now*, in these circumstances. I think he meant that if he was AJ he would never refuse me a baby. And I – I can't stop thinking about it.'

'Is this why you've been so quiet?'

Bea shrugged. 'Yeah.' She rubbed her face. 'I just felt so guilty the whole time AJ was here and now he's gone I can't stop thinking about Dom again. About what he said.'

'But you love AJ.'

Bea nodded. 'Of course I do. But also, I really, really want a baby. The accident, it – it made me realise how much I want to be a mum. And AJ just...' Her voice broke, and Mia put her coffee on the floor and pulled Bea right in for a hug. Bea's breath was shuddery as she fought back tears. Mia rubbed her back.

Eventually, she sat back up again.

'You're not thinking about it are you?'

'About having a baby with Dom?'

'About going back to him.'

Bea didn't answer. *Was* she thinking about it? It had definitely crossed her mind, but she didn't know how seriously she meant it.

'Bea!' Mia said. 'What about AJ?'

Bea shook her head. 'No, I'm not thinking about it. I just – it's made me think, that's all.'

Mia smiled. 'You're just confused. It's understandable when you're living so far away from your husband.' She lowered her voice a little. 'Bea, won't you come back with me next week?'

'To New York?'

'To your life. To your husband.'

Bea looked her friend in the eye. 'I'll think about it.'

* * *

She didn't go in the end. She still wasn't ready to be back in the city where everything had gone wrong. Plus her mum needed help with her dad, who was getting worse by the week.

And slowly, without Bea even realising it was happening, Dom became part of her life again. At first it was just the occasional text to check in on her. Then it was popping round to see her at her parents' house, or seeing if she fancied a walk in the freezing winter evenings. By the time spring arrived Bea still hadn't gone back to New York, and she was enjoying spending time with Dom more than she should.

She hadn't told AJ about it, of course, because she knew how it looked.

Then, one night, after a row with AJ that had left her feeling wretched, she did something stupid.

She slept with Dom.

They were both drunk after going for a couple of drinks for Dom's birthday. Bea had convinced herself she was just helping a friend to celebrate, that it was nothing to feel guilty about. But at the end of the night when Dom walked her home, this time he didn't move away and as they said goodnight, Bea asked if he fancied a drink. He accepted, and after a glass of whisky they were sitting too close to each other on the sofa, and Dom's arm was touching Bea's and when he turned his head to look at her, she could feel his breath on her lips. The air between them seemed to crackle. And then...

And then his lips were on hers and their limbs were tangled and even though she knew she should stop it, should tell him she didn't want to do this, enough of her *did* want to do this, did want to see how it was with the man she used to love, and who still loved her and who wanted a baby with her and...

Oh God.

As they lay in Bea and AJ's bed afterwards Bea tried to work out how she felt. Guilty, of course.

But a small kernel of happiness nestled among the guilt too, and when Dom turned to her and told her he loved her she realised that perhaps she still loved him too.

'But I'm married,' she whispered into the darkness. 'I can't do this. I can't. I'm sorry.'

For a few weeks she kept away from him, telling herself it was the right thing to do. She still spoke to AJ every day and the guilt gnawed away at her as she told him about work and about her dad's health, and he told her he missed her, and that Mia missed her too.

How he was ready now, if she wanted to come home and start trying for a baby. He was ready.

'I'll come home,' she said, and relief flooded through her that she'd made the decision at last.

Then she'd found out she was pregnant.

Six weeks pregnant.

She hadn't seen her husband for five months.

* * *

Telling everyone wasn't easy, but Bea knew beyond a shadow of a doubt that she was keeping this baby, no matter how much of an implosion it caused in her life.

First she told Dom, and as his eyes lit up she felt like the worst person in the world.

'I'm bringing this baby up on my own,' she said.

'But Bea, we love each other,' Dom said. 'We can do this together, can't we?'

She looked at him, at his handsome face and his kind eyes and she knew she definitely *could* do this, with him. And yet she also knew that what she felt for Dom wasn't the kind of love she wanted. She loved him deeply, yet it was more affection than passion, the way you love an old friend. Not wildly, like a lover, a husband.

AJ was the only person she loved in that way but she had betrayed him in the worst way possible. She wouldn't make Dom feel like second best, no matter how much he believed he'd be happy with that.

'I'm sorry,' she told Dom. 'I do want this baby, and I want you to be part of its life. But not us, not together.'

Dom looked so miserable, as though his insides had been scooped out, that she nearly changed her mind. But she knew it would be unfair, on all of them.

Then the worst part of all. She couldn't tell AJ over the phone, so she booked a flight and went to see her husband. She didn't tell him she was coming because she knew he'd meet her at the airport and she couldn't let that happen. She didn't feel she could just let herself into their apartment either, so she rang the buzzer and when she heard his electronic voice crackle over the speaker, she almost lost her resolve.

'It's me. Bea.'

'Fuck, Bea. Come in, come in.'

He buzzed her up and she got into the lift, her knuckles white as she gripped her small case, her pulse thumping in her throat. She thought she might throw up.

The doors slid open and there he was, waiting for her. He looked so uncertain that her heart lurched for him, for what she was about to do. He opened his arms and she fell into them and let him hold her, felt her body meld to his the way it always had, felt their breath syncopate. She could have stayed like that forever; never moving on to the next moment, the moment she was dreading. Eventually he pulled away and looked down at her, his face a question. He pushed her hair back from her face and held his hand there.

'What's going on Bea?'

'I...' She stopped. Not here, not in the hallway. 'Can we go inside?'

'Sure.' AJ stepped away from her and her body felt suddenly frozen, like she was freefalling into disaster. She followed him, her feet heavy, and let the door close behind her. The apartment was alien to her. Everything still looked the same but she felt so different from the last time she was here, it was as though someone had come in and moved everything slightly out of position.

AJ was facing her from the other side of the sofa, as though he knew he needed some sort of protection from what she was about to say.

'Not that it's not amazing to see you, but I get the impression you're not here to tell me you're moving home?' AJ held her gaze and it burned into her. She looked away, down at the rug beneath her feet, and shook her head.

'Do I need to sit down?'

She looked back up at him. 'I'm pregnant, AJ.' Her voice felt like sandpaper in her throat, and the words hung in the air. She saw the moment they landed, because AJ's face dropped, his shoulders slumped. He looked as if the light had gone from his eyes.

'Dom, I assume?'

She nodded. 'I can't... I don't know how to tell you how sorry I am. It wasn't planned. And we're not back together. It was just one stupid night and I wish it had never happened, except...'

'Except you're glad it did because now you've got exactly what you've wanted for the last year?'

Bea shook her head. 'Not exactly, no. I wanted *your* baby, AJ. But you wouldn't... you didn't...' She thought her legs were about to buckle beneath her and she hurried over to the sofa before she fell down. AJ moved away from her, as though touching her might burn him.

'People don't usually sleep with other people just to get their own way.' AJ's words were like darts and she flinched. She deserved every single thing he could throw at her. And yet she could hardly bear the thought of him hating her.

'I know. It was a mistake. The whole thing. But... but I have to keep this baby. I have to.' She was desperate for him to understand, and she watched his face as he tried to work out how he felt, what to say to her.

'But I told you I wanted a baby,' he said, his voice like nails. 'I just wanted it to be the best time for us.'

'I don't know what to say,' she said. 'I'm so sorry.'

'I think you should go.'

'What?'

He said nothing else, his face stony.

'But we need to talk.'

'Please go.'

Bea stood on shaking legs, took hold of her suitcase and opened the door. Before she closed the door she turned to look at AJ but he had his back to her. His shoulders were shaking gently.

'Ring me if you want to talk.'

Then she closed the door and left behind the tatters of her marriage.

* * *

'I've ruined everything.' Sobs wracked Bea's body as she curled into Mia's arms. She thought she would never stop crying.

When she finally did feel the tidal wave of emotion ebb, she sat up and looked at her friend. Mia was studying her with a look Bea couldn't read.

After leaving AJ behind she'd walked aimlessly for a while, along familiar streets and through Central Park, but not taking any of it in; not the blossom on the trees, nor the ice blue of the spring sky, nor the smell of hotdogs on street corners. It all washed over her. Finally, when she felt able to speak, she'd rung Mia, her voice a tremble, and said she needed to see her.

'You're in New York?' Mia said, incredulous.

She'd been here for an hour now and had already told her friend everything. She felt like a wrung-out dishcloth.

'What a fucking mess,' Mia said, her voice low.

'I know.' Bea's voice cracked. 'And it's all my fault.'

Mia didn't respond straight away, but finally, she shook her head. 'No. It's not.' She took hold of Bea's hands. 'Yes you fucked up. Sleeping with Dom was a bloody stupid thing to do, but you don't need me to tell you that.'

'I hope there's a *but* coming,' Bea said, weakly.

'There is,' Mia replied. '*But...* AJ was being a dick. No excuse for sleeping with someone else, we both know that, but he was. You were vulnerable, after everything that happened with the accident, and losing your baby. And then what? He just fucks off back to New York and leaves you in London on your own?'

'We both agreed it was for the best,' Bea said.

'Sure. But you practically *begged* him to have a baby. And it's not as though it was out of the blue, he'd been thrilled about it before.' She shook her head. 'No, he's got to take some of the blame for this. *Dom,* though...' She trailed off.

'This isn't Dom's fault.'

Mia shook her head. 'You're not serious? He knew you were vulnerable, he knew you were married, and he knew just what to say to get you into bed.' She sighed loudly. 'I bet he thought you might get back together with him, didn't he?'

Bea shrugged. 'I think... yes, maybe.' She didn't say that she'd thought she would, too. That Dom's love and attention had been just what she'd needed, that he'd made her feel happy again.

'Oh Bea, come here,' Mia said, pulling her in for a hug again. 'This isn't the end of the world. It's massive bloody curveball, but you've coped before, you'll cope again.' She stopped, looked at Bea. 'You're coming back to New York to have this baby though, right?'

'I...' Bea stopped. *Was* she? The truth was she'd been focusing so much on what she had to do right now that she hadn't given much thought to the reality of bringing up a baby on her own, or even what happened next. 'I don't think so,' she said, realising as she said the words that they were true. 'New York feels like a different part of my life. Plus I've promised Dom he can be a part of the baby's life, even if we're not together. And then, with AJ here, I... I need to be at home.'

'Oh Bea,' Mia said again. 'I hate being so far away from you.'

'Me too.'

'Just promise me you'll come over and stay with me and Frank as soon as the baby is old enough?'

'Try and stop me,' Bea said, smiling. 'And in the meantime you'll just have to be Aunty Mia via Skype.'

'Okay,' Mia said, and then her eyes widened.

'Does Maggie know you're here?'

Bea shook her head.

'Oh God, she'll go mental if she finds out you're here and no one told her.' She paused, thumb hovering over her mobile. 'Okay if I ring her? She can come over and get pissed on tequila with us.'

Bea shook her head. 'I'll have to leave the drinking to you two, but I'd love to see her.'

Mia slapped her forehead. 'God, course you can't drink, what a div.' Then she dialled Maggie's number.

* * *

'Bea!' A hammering on the bathroom door brought Bea back to the here and now, and she stood and smoothed her dress over her enormous bump. She was sure it had grown even more since she'd come upstairs.

'Coming!' she said, and opened the door to find Dom standing outside looking concerned.

'I thought you'd fallen down the toilet or something,' he said.

'No, sorry. I was just having a moment away from the chaos.' She smiled and nodded her head towards the stairs, where the sound of Alice shouting at one of her kids floated through the living room door.

'I don't blame you.' He took hold of her elbow but she shook him off.

'I don't need a chaperone,' she snapped. He looked wounded and she felt a flash of guilt – the way she always seemed to when she was around Dom. Things were much better between them now – good, even – but it didn't mean she'd forgotten what she'd done to him, and how much he was still hurting. It didn't help that he still made it perfectly clear he would take her back in a heartbeat if she'd have him.

'Sorry,' she said.

They headed back downstairs and into the living room. Bea squeezed onto the sofa beside Alice. Baby Ernie was asleep on her shoulder.

'Everything all right?' she whispered, as Bea sat. Dom was on the other side of the room pretending not to watch her.

'Yeah, all good.' Bea and Alice's previously fractious relationship had mellowed significantly in recent months, Alice taking her role of big sister very seriously and not wanting Bea to lift a finger when it came to helping Ange.

She glanced over to her mum, who was talking to her dad. Pete was staring at a fixed spot just over Ange's shoulder as though he hadn't even noticed she was there.

'Poor Mum.'

'I wish she'd admit things are getting too hard. Dad has no idea what's going on but she thinks being somewhere familiar will be good for him.'

'Any news from AJ?'

Bea shook her head. She was ashamed to admit that, even though they hadn't spoken for six months, she still held out a glimmer of hope that he might at least send her a text today – the anniversary of the day they met. She'd composed a dozen texts to him but deleted them all because the words sounded too trite or the sentiment too desperate.

Alice laid her hand on Bea's. 'I'm sorry Bea. I know you still love him.'

Bea blinked back tears. 'Thanks,' she said, simply. Because how could she deny it? The trouble was he didn't love her any more. He didn't even want to speak to her.

And she couldn't blame him at all.

15

GO

December 2009

There was no snow yet, but the sky was gun metal grey and it looked like it might start at any moment. Bea shivered as the wind whipped through her coat, and she heaved Jack further up on to her hip.

'Cold Mama,' Jack said.

'I know sweetie, you can go inside in a minute,' she said, planting a gentle kiss on the end of his nose.

'Here, I'll take him in.' AJ appeared at her side and scooped Jack from her arms. 'No point you both freezing out here.'

He leaned in and kissed her, a comforting peck rather than the long, passionate ones he usually offered, and she was grateful for it.

She watched as he led their son indoors, Jack toddling in his smart shoes, his hand stretching up to hold his dad's. Something about the back of his head, the way his hair curled at the nape of his chubby little neck, made her heart squeeze with love and she watched until they were out of sight.

Her two favourite men in the whole world – at least now her dad had gone.

Bea had been in two minds as to whether Jack should be here today.

'A funeral is no place for a two-year-old,' she'd told AJ.

'But he'll want to say goodbye to his grandad just as much as you want to say goodbye to your dad,' AJ said. 'Besides, it might be good for you to have him there.'

He was right, in the end. As the officiant spoke about Pete; as Alice gave a eulogy, and as the curtain drew slowly round her dad's coffin, the press of Jack's body in her arms and the reassuring presence of AJ beside her had kept Bea grounded, calm.

She turned away and saw that people were beginning to emerge from the crematorium, pulling coats and hats and gloves on to protect them from the frigid December air. Five days before Christmas and here they were, saying goodbye to the first man Bea had ever loved.

She stretched her hands out as her brother Charlie approached, and he clasped them, then wrapped her in a hug. It had been a long time since either of her big brothers had hugged her, and she clung on in the hope it might make her feel like her dad was still here, somehow. Finally, Charlie pulled away, but kept his hands on her upper arms.

'You okay Be-Be?' he said, his voice low.

She gave a small nod, not trusting her voice.

'Have you seen Mum?'

'She's over there,' she said, pointing to where her mum was being comforted by her sisters and a couple of friends. She was glad to see she wasn't alone.

Charlie stood next to her as they greeted mourners, accepting hugs and condolences from red-eyed friends, family and colleagues. Soon Rob took his place on Bea's other side, his partner

Coralie a little away from the group. Alice stood the other side of Rob, and Bea realised this was the first time she had been with all of her siblings in more than a year. She couldn't help wishing it was under different, happier circumstances.

Later, at the Tollington Arms near Pete's beloved Arsenal football ground, they gathered round the sausage rolls and sandwiches, making small talk with distant cousins, aunts and uncles they hadn't seen for years, and old friends. Jack was off playing with his cousins, who delighted in looking after him, and AJ kept Bea's hand clasped tightly in his own. She was grateful for the comfort.

AJ always found it so easy to talk to anyone. 'Total gobshite that's why,' he always said. But she was glad of it today, glad of his ability to deflect attention away from her, from her grief, and keep the conversation light, entertaining. Even funny. Who'd ever have thought they would be laughing on a day like today?

Across the pub she spied Dom chatting to a couple of people she didn't know. Every now and then he glanced over.

'Back in a minute,' she said, removing her hand from AJ's grip. She weaved her way towards Dom and tapped him on the shoulder. When he turned round his face lit up. 'Hey you,' he said, and leaned in for a perfunctory hug. She breathed in his smell which was so familiar, so comforting.

'So sorry I haven't had a chance to speak to you before,' she said.

'Don't be daft. You've got a lot going on. Anyway, it's not as if I never see you.'

'True.'

'So how are you doing?'

She was about to say her standard 'okay' but stopped. How was she really? She thought about it. She had expected to spend the day crying, to feel the weight of grief sit heavily on her shoulders. But the truth was she actually felt as though a load had been lifted. Not only because today was over and done with after weeks of planning, but because she had finally been able to say goodbye to the father she'd lost years ago. She'd grieved for him while he was still alive, and now she felt at peace.

'Relieved,' she said, and Dom nodded, seeming to understand.

'I'll miss Pete though. He was good to me.'

Bea smiled. 'He always loved you. He always wished we'd stayed together.'

'He's not the only one.' Dom smiled. 'But sometimes things just aren't meant to be, are they?'

Bea cocked her head. 'Do you really mean that?'

Dom frowned, as though he hadn't really thought about it much himself. 'Do you know what, I think I do. I mean, things have been much easier since we split up than when we were together. We get on so much better, don't we?'

Bea nodded. 'We do. But I didn't realise... I didn't know...'

'That I was okay with that?'

She nodded again.

'It's taken me a while but I really am now. I've realised that life's too short to be miserable.' He put his hand on her arm. 'I'm just glad you and Jack are still a part of my life.'

Bea blinked rapidly, not wanting to let the tears slip out. There had been too much of that today, and she knew her dad would have wanted them to be happy.

'I'm glad too,' she said, her throat a rasp.

Dom nodded his head towards where AJ was deep in conversation with Mia and Michael. 'Everything all right with...'

'Yes. It's good now. It's...' She trailed off, aware she didn't want to sound too loved up talking to Dom. 'We're good.'

Dom nodded solemnly, then shrugged. 'At least he's still happy for me to see Jack.'

'God of course he is,' she said. 'You're a huge part of Jack's life. He adores you.'

'I adore him too. I just never thought...'

'I know.' He didn't need to say it. Neither of them could ever have imagined being here, in this situation. But finally, after years of heartache, here they were, making it work.

'So, who are you chatting to?' She painted a smile on her face and turned to the man and woman Dom had been speaking to before she came over.

'Oh, this is David, and this is Tiff.'

They turned to smile at Bea and shook her hand. 'We both used to work with Pete,' Tiff said. 'He was a really lovely man, I'm so sorry for your loss.'

'Thank you,' Bea said, already slightly distracted. She turned back to Dom as soon as it seemed polite to do so. 'Listen, sorry, I need to go and find Mum.'

'Course.' He touched her arm lightly. 'I'll see you later, okay?'

Bea scanned the room, trying to pick out the tiny frame of her mother among the crowds of dark clothing. Finally, she spotted her across the other side of the room by the pool table. For the first time today she was alone, and Bea headed over quickly before anyone else accosted her.

'Hey,' she said, sitting in the chair beside her.

'Hey sweetheart,' Ange said, taking hold of the hand Bea offered her.

'How're you holding up?'

Ange shrugged. 'You know.' Her voice was husky and there was a tell-tale redness around her eyes. She dabbed a scrunched-up tissue under her eye and gave a watery smile. 'Sad.'

'Yeah.'

They sat in silence for a moment. 'Have you had some sandwiches?'

'Not yet Mum.'

'You must. They'll go dry.'

Bea smiled. Even today her mum fussed, always the carer. She lifted her mum's hand to her lips and kissed it.

'What was that for?'

'I just love you. You know that right?'

'Course I do. I love you too.' She looked up at Bea, her eyes shimmering with tears. 'I've never been without your dad, you know. Not even for a day, not since I left home.' Her voice was small. 'I don't know how to be on my own.'

'Oh Mum.' Bea threw her arms around her. She felt so fragile. 'You're not on your own. You've got me and AJ and Jack, and Alice and her lot, and that's just within a couple of miles. You've got so many people who love you.'

Ange smiled sadly. 'I know. I'm lucky really.' She let out a long, shaky breath. 'It just won't be the same without my Pete. He might not have been the most outwardly affectionate man in the world but he loved me. And he loved his family. It was all that mattered to him.'

Bea felt her heart tighten and swallowed down tears. 'I know,' she whispered. 'I know.'

Before they had a chance to wallow, the moment was broken by a tiny body launching itself at Ange's legs. 'Mee-ma!' Jack said, and Ange lifted him onto her lap and pulled him to her. He was clutching a half-eaten sandwich in one hand.

'Hello Jack-Jack, what have you got there?' Ange said.

'Sammidge!' he cried, showing it to her, the bread squashed into his tight fist.

'Yum,' Ange said, pretending to eat some.

'No Meema, Jack's!' he cried, wriggling in delight.

'Hey Baby J,' said a voice, and they turned to see AJ approaching. 'Don't use Grandma as a climbing frame,' he said, leaning to rescue Ange from Jack's clutches. But she pulled him away. 'Oh no you don't,' she said. 'Jack's cheering me up, aren't you sweetheart?'

'Yep,' he said, taking a bite of his sandwich and looking up with big eyes as he chewed solemnly.

'Well then I'd better leave him to do his job then hadn't I?' AJ said, ruffling Jack's mop of dark curls. 'Shall I make myself useful and get us all a drink?'

'Please,' Bea said, and AJ disappeared again to fetch glasses of white wine and a cup of blackcurrant for Jack.

'He's a good man that one,' Ange said.

'He is,' Bea agreed.

'You've got two good men there,' Ange added and Bea felt her shoulders drop.

'You mean Dom?'

'Of course Dom.' She glanced at Bea. 'I saw you talking to him earlier. Everything all right with you two?'

Bea nodded. 'Do you know what Mum, for the first time since we split up, it really is.'

'I worry about him you know.'

'Honestly, there's no need. He's doing better than I've seen him in years. He seems... content.'

'Well. Good. I always thought you two would end up back together you know.' Ange pressed her lips against the top of Jack's head. He rested his head against her chest.

'I know.' Bea didn't know what else to say so she stood. 'Mind if I go and find Mia for a minute?'

'No, you go. Me and Jack are all right here, aren't we?'

Jack's eyes were beginning to droop and he gave a small nod.

'Bea, you're here,' Mia said, seeing her approach. She wrapped her in a tight hug and when she pulled away she was looking at Bea with a concerned expression. She hooked a stray hair behind Bea's ear and rested her palm against her cheek. 'You okay?'

'I'm okay.'

Mia pulled her hand away and tucked her arm into Bea's. 'Me and Michael were just talking about Tam,' she said, referring to Michael and Harry's adopted son.

'Oh, everything all right?' Bea said.

'Yes, he's fine,' Michael said, his smile revealing the extent of his love for his boy. 'I was just wondering where he was and then Harry said all the big kids are looking after the little ones and not to worry.'

'Ah yes, my nieces seem to be running some sort of crèche through there. Jack was there too until they wore him out.'

'Well it's good to have someone helping out. I wasn't sure whether I should even bring him at all but...'

'It's all fine. Dad would have wanted the kids here. He loved having them around.'

Michael snaked his arm round her shoulders and pressed his lips against her temple.

'You're right, he would.' He pulled away. 'Now, do you want a drink?'

'Oh, AJ was getting me one, he...' She craned her neck to look round but couldn't see him anywhere. 'Go on then. A large glass of white please.'

As she waited for her drink, Bea stood with her arm linked through Mia's, letting the warm hum of voices flow round her, and took some deep breaths. This wasn't the happiest of days, of course. She would do almost anything to have her dad here with them, for this to be a birthday party, or a wedding, rather than his funeral. But despite all that, for the first time in a long time, she was beginning to feel like herself again. After much discussion, she and AJ had managed to sort things out between them at the end of the summer, and agreed to give things another go, with promises that Dom would still be a part of Jack's life. At around the same time

Bea had been promoted to assistant editor at work and, with Jack getting older, she felt as though she'd found her perfect little family at last – no matter how rocky the road to get here had been.

In fact, there was only one dark cloud on the horizon, and that was the one concerning Mia right now.

'Has AJ said anything else about New York?'

Bea sighed, the breath leaving her body in one go. She shook her head. 'Not for a few days. But I think that's only because of Dad. I don't think he's changed his mind.'

'So, what are you going to do?'

Bea took her glass of wine from Michael and gave him a smile of thanks. 'I...' She stopped. She really had no idea what she was going to say to AJ about his suggestion that they move back to New York. He'd been desperate to get back for the last few months, determined they could rebuild a life for themselves out there, the three of them.

'But what about Mum?' she'd said when he first mentioned it, when her dad was still alive. She wanted to ask what about Dom too, but it hadn't felt right. 'I can't leave her to cope alone.'

'But she's not alone Bea. She's got so many people to look out for her. You always wanted to be in New York, and it's the place I love the most too. Please promise you'll at least think about it?'

Bea had said she would, although shortly after that her dad had gone rapidly downhill, and now her mum really was alone. How could she even contemplate it?

She took a big gulp of her wine and swallowed. 'I really don't know. I can't imagine it, not at the minute.'

'But?'

Bea looked up at Michael. 'But what?'

'Come on Bea. AJ's right, you know. New York was always your dream. You went there intending to stay, and you fell in love and built a life there. So did he.' He shrugged. 'Much as we love you, I think you should be over there too. You've got to live the life you want, not what someone else wants you to do.' He grinned, 'Besides, it would give us somewhere to come on holiday.'

'Hey,' Mia said, slapping his arm. 'Don't encourage her. I can't cope with her being so far away again.'

'Don't worry, I won't be going anywhere any time soon,' Bea said.

'Well don't make any rash decisions without me, all right?' Mia said, bumping her hip against Bea's.

'Promise,' Bea said.

16

STAY

December 2009

The sky hung grey and heavy over the city like a blanket. It was bitterly cold and it looked as though it might snow soon. Bea shivered as a wind whipped through her and she tugged her coat tighter.

'You okay?' a voice whispered beside her. She gave a tight nod and forced a smile. 'I'm going to get Amelie in the car before she gets too cold, okay?'

Bea bent down to the pushchair Dom was rocking back and forth where their daughter was bundled up, hat pulled down tightly over her head, eyelashes splayed across her cheeks as she slept. She truly was the most beautiful thing Bea had ever seen. She planted a gentle kiss on the top of her head and stood. 'Good plan.'

Dom leaned over and kissed Bea, then began to walk slowly towards the car park. They hadn't hesitated in bringing Amelie to Pete's funeral with them today. She was only ten months old, but she had brought such joy to her grandad in his last few months, and the memory of the two of them together would stay with Bea for the rest of her life.

She turned back towards the crematorium where people were beginning to emerge, pulling on hats and gloves and scarves against the bitter December air. Five days before Christmas and here they were saying goodbye to the first man Bea had ever loved.

'Hey you,' her brother Charlie said as he approached, and she gave him a brief hug. 'You okay Be-Be?' he said, pulling away.

'Yeah,' she said, her voice wobbly. 'I thought I was going to pass out when the curtain went round the coffin.'

'Me too,' he said, and Bea felt unexpectedly grateful to have her big brother here. She slipped her hand into his as they turned to accept hugs and condolences from all the people who had loved Pete. Soon, Rob arrived to stand on Bea's other side, his partner Coralie a little apart from the group, and Alice took her place on the other side of Rob.

Once everyone had dispersed, they drove to the wake, which they'd chosen to hold in the Tollington Arms, Pete's favourite pub just round the corner from his beloved Arsenal football ground.

As they stood eating sandwiches and sausage rolls, drinking tea and making small talk, Bea spotted Dom across the other side of the room, holding baby Amelie and talking to a woman she didn't recognise. She wondered who she was and whether she should feel jealous. She wasn't sure what it meant that she didn't.

After last Christmas, it had become perfectly clear that AJ wanted nothing more to do with her. Texts and phone messages remained unanswered (or unread), emails were ignored, and when she tried to ring the landline at the apartment, she got a 'this number is no longer working' message.

'It's like he's deleted me from his life,' Bea sobbed to Mia.

'You can't blame him,' Mia said. 'He loves you, but he can't cope with you having another man's baby.'

Bea started the year determined to try and put that part of her life behind her. She remained married to AJ, for now, but it hurt too much to think about everything she'd lost, so she made the decision to focus on what she had instead.

When Amelie was born in February, Dom was there to hold her hand. He was there when she needed sleep, and when she felt like she was going mad from being stuck in the house all day he came to give her a break. He was adept at changing nappies and feeding – better than her, in fact – and seemed to take to fatherhood like a duck to water. And when Ange needed help with Pete as his health deteriorated, he was there to step in.

In fact, the more time they spent together, bonding over their little girl, the more Bea began to wonder if she was making a mistake, shutting him out. She'd pushed him away before because she'd wanted to be with AJ. But that was no longer an option. Dom was.

By the time Amelie was three months old, in May, Bea made a decision.

'Do you still want us to be together?' she said, as Dom was in the middle of changing a particularly ripe nappy. His body stilled, but his hands continued their work as if he was so used to doing the task by now that they did it on auto-pilot. He didn't reply and Bea began to wonder if she'd made a terrible mistake. Why did she do things like this? Everything had been working perfectly well as it was, and now she'd ruined it.

Dom did the poppers of Amelie's sleepsuit back up, wiped his hands on a baby wipe, then picked her up and held her against his shoulder. She stared at him lovingly, and he kissed her tiny fist softly. Bea watched all this with her breath held, wondering what he was about to say.

'Do you mean it?' He wasn't looking at her, but at Amelie, so Bea couldn't read his face.

'Of course I do,' she said.

Finally, he turned his head to face her. 'I don't want to be hurt again, Bea.'

She stepped towards him, so that only Amelie was between them, and put her hand on his waist. His eyes were warm, and as she studied the face that she'd known for so long close-up, she felt a surge of love that she'd never expected to feel with Dom again. She felt, dared she say it, content.

'I won't hurt you,' she said, her voice a whisper.

'Then yes. I do want us to be together.' He turned to Amelie, who was wriggling in his arms now, and pressed her little button nose. 'And I'm fairly sure this one would agree with me, if she could speak.'

'I think so too,' Bea said.

So that was that. Bea handed in her notice on the flat she and AJ had rented and moved back in with Dom. Ange was thrilled when they told her the news of course. But not everyone thought she'd done the right thing.

'But what about AJ? You're still married,' Mia said when she rang her a couple of nights later.

'He's made it perfectly clear he doesn't want to know me.'

'He'll come round.' Bea knew Mia saw AJ from time to time because he was still friends with Frank, but she'd asked her friend not to tell her anything about his life. She couldn't cope with hearing about him meeting someone else, moving on. Now, though, it sounded as though Mia was trying to tell her that he hadn't, that he was still hoping they could be together one day, and she didn't know what to do with that information.

She chose, in the end, to try and forget it. She'd made her choice, and she was with Dom now. She wasn't ever going to hurt him again.

Now, she turned to the people chatting around her. 'Excuse me a moment,' she said, and made her way over to where Dom was still talking to the mystery woman.

'Hey,' Dom said, smiling at her as she approached and reaching for her hand with his spare one. 'How are you doing?'

'I'm okay,' Bea said, turning to the woman with a smile. 'Hi, I don't think we've met,' she said. 'I'm Bea, Pete's daughter.'

'Tiffany,' she said, holding out her hand. Bea shook it firmly. 'I used to work with your dad, he was such a lovely man. I'm so sorry.'

'Thank you,' Bea said.

'Tiff and I have just been talking about this one,' Dom said, turning to Amelie, who was sound asleep in his arms.

Tiff. Bea noticed the familiarity but didn't comment on it.

'I was just saying how lovely they are at this age,' Tiffany said.

'Sometimes,' Bea said. 'Have you got children then?'

'No, sadly not yet,' Tiffany said, shaking her head. 'But I would love them.'

Bea nodded, unsure what else to say. She removed her hand from Dom's and glanced over his shoulder.

'Do you mind if I take Amelie to find Mum?'

'Course,' Dom said, handing their daughter over. She felt boiling hot against Bea's body and she peered up at her blearily. 'Sorry sweetie,' she said, pressing her lips to her sleepy daughter's blonde hair. 'Excuse me won't you,' she said to Tiffany, then turned and scanned the room, trying to pick out the tiny frame of her mother among the crowds in dark clothing. Finally, she spotted her sitting alone on an uncomfortable-looking wooden chair. Bea headed over.

'Hey,' she said, lowering herself carefully into the chair beside her.

'Hey sweetheart,' her mum said.

'How are you holding up?'

Ange shrugged. 'You know.' Her voice was husky and there was a tell-tale redness around her eyes. She dabbed a scrunched-up tissue under her eyes and gave her a watery smile. 'Sad.'

'Yeah.'

Ange leaned in to kiss her granddaughter's cheek. Amelie looked up at her and smiled. 'Ah, she's always got a smile for her nanny, haven't you darling?' Ange said. 'Mind you, it was her grandad she really loved wasn't it?'

'She did love Dad but she loves you just as much,' Bea said.

'Can I have a cuddle?'

Bea handed Amelie over. She was wide awake now and Ange bounced her gently on her knee as she took in the room with saucer eyes.

'Have you had some sandwiches love?'

'Not yet.'

'You must. They'll go dry.'

Bea smiled. Even today her mum fussed, always the carer. She lifted her mum's hand to her lips and kissed it.

'What was that for?'

'I just love you. You know that right?'

'Course I do. I love you too.' She looked up at Bea, her eyes shimmering with tears. 'I've never been without your dad you know. Not even for a day, not since I left home.' Her voice was small. 'I don't know how to be on my own.'

'Oh Mum,' Bea said, throwing her arms around her. She felt so fragile. 'You're not on your own. You've got me and Dom and Amelie, and Alice and her lot, and that's just within a couple of miles. You've got so many people who love you.'

Ange smiled sadly. 'I know. I'm lucky really.' She let out a long, shaky breath. 'It just won't be the same without my Pete. He might not have been the most outwardly affectionate man in the world but he loved me. And he loved his family. It was all that mattered to him.'

Bea felt her heart tighten and swallowed down tears. 'I know Mum,' she whispered. 'I know.'

'Hey Ange, how are you holding up?' They both looked up to find Dom beside them.

'Hello Dominic,' she said, her eyes lighting up. 'I'm okay. Baby Amelie is cheering me up.' Amelie giggled and held her hands up to her daddy.

'I'm glad. Can I get you a drink?'

'Please,' Bea said, and Dom disappeared to the bar.

'He's a good man that one,' Ange said.

'He is,' Bea agreed.

'Have you thought any more about your divorce?'

Bea flinched at the word. She tried not to think about it in the hope that it would go away. But she knew she needed to deal with it sooner or later and make some sort of commitment to Dom.

'Not yet. It's hard when your husband won't speak to you. But I know I'll have to get on it in the new year.'

'He'll marry you in a heartbeat you know,' Ange said, nodding her head towards where Dom was standing at the bar. He was talking to Tiffany again, Bea noticed.

'I know. One thing at a time though, hey?'

They sat in silence for a moment, then Bea said, 'Do you mind if I leave you with Amelie for a minute while I go and speak to Harry and Michael?'

'No, you go. Me and Amelie are all right here.'

'Thanks Mum.' As Bea walked away she passed Dom and Tiffany at the bar. She couldn't quite put her finger on what was bothering her, but she didn't have time to think about it before Michael spotted her and enveloped her in a huge bear hug.

'My darling,' he said, finally pulling away and gripping her by the shoulders. 'How are you feeling?'

'I'm okay,' she said.

Michael kissed her on the forehead then tucked his arm through Bea's. 'Me and Harry were just talking about Tam,' he said, referring to his and Harry's adopted son.

'Oh, everything all right?' Bea said.

'Yes, he's fine,' Michael said, his smile revealing the extent of his love for his boy. 'I was just wondering where he was and then Harry said all the big kids are looking after the little ones and not to worry.'

'Ah yes, my nieces seem to be running some sort of crèche through there.'

'Well, it's good to have someone helping out. I wasn't sure whether I should even bring him at all but...'

'It's all fine. Dad would have wanted the kids here. He loved having them around.'

Michael pressed his lips against her temple.

'You're right, he would.' He pulled away. 'Now, do you want a drink?'

'Oh, Dom was getting me one, he...' She craned her neck to look round but couldn't see him anywhere. 'Go on then. A large glass of white please.'

As she waited for her drink, Bea stood, the warm hum of voices flowing round her, and took some deep breaths. This wasn't the happiest of days, of course. She would do almost anything to have her dad here with them, for this to be a birthday party, or a wedding, rather than his funeral. But despite all that, for the first time in a long time, she was beginning to feel like herself again. She was back together with Dom and they finally felt like a proper little family. Even Dom's mental health had been stable for ages now.

In fact there was only one dark cloud on the horizon, and Harry was the one to voice it.

'It's not the same without Mia here is it?' he said, taking his husband's place and slipping his arm through Bea's. She rested her head on his shoulder and sighed.

'No, it's really not. She's devastated not to be here.'

'I bet.'

Mia had been mortified when Bea had told her when the funeral was.

'Oh God, my parents are flying over that day to spend Christmas with me and Frank's parents,' she said. Her voice shook and Bea knew she was trying not to cry. 'I'm so, so sorry Bea. I loved your dad.'

'I know you did,' Bea said. 'And he loved you too. But you can't abandon your parents.'

'Will you tell your mum how sorry I am?' she said.

'Of course. But please don't be sad.'

'I am sad. I wanted to be there for you as much as me.'

Mia being several thousand miles away felt like something Bea would never get used to. As happy as she was for Mia that she'd met the man of her dreams in Frank, she was heartbroken that her best friend had upped sticks and moved to New York. But there was no way Bea would ever get back there now. Not only did she have Dom and Amelie to think about, but her mum needed her too.

'Do you never think about moving back?' Michael said, handing her a glass of wine, as though he'd read her mind.

'To New York? No!' Bea said, accepting her drink gratefully.

'Really, really?' Michael studied her so closely Bea had to look away. She felt her face flush.

'Of course not. My home is here now.'

Michael nodded but didn't say anything, just sipped his whisky.

'What?' Bea said. Michael glanced at Harry.

'Nothing. We just – sometimes it seems like you think you made a mistake.'

'A mistake?' Bea felt her heart hammering and her indignation rising.

'Moving here, getting back together with Dom.'

'Of course I don't think that. I love Dom.'

'So you don't love AJ at all any more?'

'I...' Bea stopped, flustered. Michael always seemed able to do this to her – throw her off course with his eerily accurate observations. 'It wouldn't make any difference even if I did,' she said quietly, so no one else could hear. 'It's all too late now.'

Michael studied her for a moment, and she felt as though he could see right into her mind, to her deepest darkest thoughts, even the ones she wouldn't admit to herself. Then he shrugged. 'It's only too late if you want it to be.'

'But—'

Michael held his hands up. 'Don't listen to me. If you're happy then we're happy for you, aren't we H?'

'Yes, we are,' Harry said pointedly. 'And you,' he said, digging his husband in the chest with his finger, 'have got to stop being such a bloody stirrer.'

'Moi?' Michael said, mock-innocently.

Bea took a gulp of her wine so she didn't have to say anything else and tried not to think about what Michael had just said, or about how different her life might be right now if she hadn't slept with Dom and had ended up going back to AJ.

Because how could she ever regret that, when it would mean she wouldn't have Amelie, the most precious thing in the world to her?

No, she'd made the right decision. Her life was in London now, with Dom, their daughter, and her friends. This was the way things were always meant to be; this was her future.

17

GO

December 2010

The lights glittered as far as the eye could see. It looked like a life-sized Christmas grotto, like the house in *Home Alone,* and Bea felt a warm glow fill her from head to toe. She'd always imagined a Christmas like this, but she'd never actually thought it would happen. And yet here she was.

Fingers slipped through her gloved ones and she turned to face their owner. His face was lit up by flashing Santas and colourful fairy lights, and she kissed him firmly on the lips.

'What was that for?' he said. 'Not that I'm complaining.'

Bea shrugged. 'I just love you.'

He studied her for a moment, a frown creasing his forehead, then shook his head. 'I love you too, even if you are a nutter sometimes, Princess Beatrice.'

Bea stuck out her tongue and turned back to admire the street again. Behind her, she knew their display was meagre compared to most of their neighbours. But they were beginners, mere amateurs in the Christmas decoration business. By next year, they'd have upped their game. Next year they'd really go to town.

'It's so beautiful isn't it?'

'It's not too bad from where I'm standing,' AJ said, laughter in his voice, and when Bea looked at him he wasn't looking at the lights, he was staring at her, and she felt herself flush.

'Mummy!' Bea whipped her head round to see Jack barrelling across the dark lawn towards her, arms windmilling, his whole face shining with happiness. She bent down and scooped him up and swung him into her arms.

'Hey baby boy, what's up?' she said, smothering his face in kisses. She couldn't believe how much she loved the bones of this boy.

'My friend Sam said it's only three sleeps 'til Santa comes, is it true?' Jack was almost breathless with excitement.

'Well yes baby, Sam is right. Santa will be flying over there' – she pointed at a spot in the sky where a star shone particularly brightly – 'in three days' time!'

Jack gazed up, his eyes wide, his chubby cheeks red beneath his knitted bobble hat, and breathed, 'Wow!', the word long and full of wonder.

'Let me take him, you shouldn't be carrying such a big lump like him around,' AJ said, reaching out for Jack and lifting him from Bea's arms.

'Heeeey!' Jack objected, legs kicking in mid-air seconds before he landed in his daddy's arms.

'Only teasing buddy. But we've got to look after Mummy and the baby haven't we, so we can't have your great big feet kicking against her tummy.'

Jack reached down to try and touch the swell of Bea's belly through her coat. 'Will Santa bring the baby presents too?'

'Not this year darling. But next year, when he or she is finally here, they'll get just as many presents as you.'

'Kiss!' Jack said, and AJ bent his knees and guided his son's face so he could kiss Bea's tummy. 'I go play now!' he announced, wriggling until AJ put him down, and he immediately raced off to join the other neighbourhood children running round the garden screaming in the way that only sugared-up kids could.

Bea wrapped her arms round AJ's waist and pressed her face into his shoulder. 'Did you ever think we'd get here?' she said, her words drifting out into the cold night air. For a moment she wondered if AJ hadn't heard her and she tipped her head up to look at him. He was gazing ahead, the lights reflected back in his dark pupils.

'I never doubted it,' he said, smiling.

Bea grinned back and huddled back into the warmth of her new husband's arms.

It had been a long and winding road, but finally, eight years after getting on a plane bound for New York three days before Christmas and with no idea what she was going to do once she got there, Bea had the life she'd always dreamed of.

Last Christmas had been bittersweet. Bea, AJ and Jack had enjoyed their first Christmas together as a family. But the gap left by Pete had been impossible to ignore, and all of them – Ange, Alice, Rob, Charlie – had felt a sadness settle deep inside them. As the turkey was carved by Rob instead of Pete, as Pete's favourite Christmas song 'White Christmas' came on the playlist, as the armchair in the corner where he always sat remained empty all evening, the shadows of his presence had been everywhere.

But then the new year had come, and the fog of grief slowly began to lift.

At the same time, AJ had started ramping up his campaign for the three of them to move back to New York. Every time Bea had an objection, he had a counter-argument.

'It's your dream,' he said, when Bea had said she needed to stay in London.

'But what about Mum? I can't just up and leave her all on her own,' she argued.

'She's got Alice.'

'I can't take Jack away from Dom. He's important to him.'

'He can visit as much as he wants.'

When Bea tried to argue that she loved London, he reminded her how happy she'd been in New York. Her friends? They could visit, and she'd make new friends too.

'Why are you so desperate to go back there?' she'd asked eventually.

AJ went quiet. 'It's always felt like home,' he said. 'I never fitted in in Ireland, was always the rogue son, the one who let people down. But when I came to New York with Cassie it felt like it was the place I was meant to be. It felt like the city understood me.'

'You've never told me any of this before,' Bea said.

AJ shook his head. 'I guess I'd never realised how much it was a part of me until I left.'

'And you couldn't learn to feel the same way about London, given time?' To Bea, London was an amazing city, full of promise, full of love. Right now, New York felt like light years away, and she struggled to remember how much she had loved it.

'I could try,' AJ promised. 'For you.'

But Bea had known AJ's heart wasn't in it and as the months had passed, she began to think about it more and more. Could she really move all the way across the Atlantic away from all the people she loved again? Could she really take Jack away from Dom who had been prepared to bring him up as his own?

If she didn't, would she lose AJ – and Jack lose his dad?

It felt like an impossible situation.

Then one day Ange had asked to speak to them both. Worried, Bea had arrived at her mum's house with AJ and Jack in tow one evening. As they sat dutifully on the sofa in the living room, the spring sunshine slanting through the window and Jack's sleepy little body pressed against her, Bea's heart had thumped wildly. What news did her mum have to tell her? Was Bea about to lose her too, so soon after losing her dad?

Ange brought in cups of tea and slices of cake on tiny plates, plumped cushions and straightened ornaments.

'Mum, will you stop fussing and tell us what's wrong?' Bea said.

Ange stopped what she was doing and stood, her hands clasped in front of her. Bea's heart stopped beating as she waited to hear the terrible news her mum had to impart.

'I want to move to New York.'

'*What?*' Bea stared at Ange as dust motes swirled in the strip of sunlight between them, and Ange opened and closed her mouth like a goldfish. Seconds ticked by. Then suddenly Ange sat down and leaned forward, her eyes bright.

'I've been thinking about it a lot, over the last few weeks,' Ange began. 'I know you're only staying in London because of me—'

'No that's not—'

Ange held up her hand. 'Let me finish, please.' Bea stopped, chastened. Ange took a deep breath. 'AJ, I know you want Bea to move back to New York. And Bea I know you love it there too. I don't want to be the reason you're staying here, because you think I need looking after.' Ange looked down at her hands in her lap, then back up at them both. 'So if it's all right with you, I'd like to move to New York with you.'

For a few moments nobody spoke, and Ange's words hung in the air. Bea tried to picture Ange living in New York: shopping on

Fifth Avenue, walking through Central Park, having breakfast at the Comfort Diner. She couldn't do it.

'But London is your home,' she said. 'It's your heart.'

Ange shook her head. 'London is my home, but my heart was with your father.' She sniffed. 'But since he went, I've felt so lonely, Bea. So sad. And I don't...' She stopped again as her words caught in her throat. 'I don't want you to be sad too. I want you and AJ and Jack to be together, and if that means being in New York then that's where you should be.' She stuck her chin out defiantly. 'And why shouldn't I have an adventure? Life's too short not to do things while you can. If nothing else, your dad's death taught me that.'

Bea didn't know what to say. Her mum was right – part of the reason she'd been resisting moving was because of her mum, because she couldn't bear to leave her. But this was so unexpected, so out of the blue, she didn't know what to say.

'But what about Alice? What about the house?'

Ange shook her head. 'Alice will be fine. She's got Andrew, her job, the kids. She's busy enough. And this house – well, we can sell it. Or rent it out.' She threw her hands in the air. 'I don't know Bea. But I've given this quite a lot of thought, and if you'll have me, it's what I want to do.'

Ange made it all sound so simple. Except it wasn't really, was it?

'But what about Dom? I can't take Jack away from him after everything he did for us. He loves him.'

'I think you should talk to him about that love. I think you might be surprised.'

Ange refused to say anything else on the subject. But when Bea went to see Dom later that evening, it all became crystal clear.

'I'm happy to move to New York too,' he said.

Bea stared at him. 'What?'

Dom looked at his feet, shuffled them. When he looked back up at her he was smiling. 'I – I've met someone.'

'You have?'

He nodded. 'Do you – do you remember Tiff? From Pete's funeral?'

Bea let her mind rewind to that day, and vaguely remembered the name. 'The woman you were talking to?'

'Yes.'

Bea's eyes widened in sudden realisation. 'You're together.' It was a statement rather than a question, but Dom nodded.

'You don't mind, do you?'

'Why would I mind? I'm thrilled for you!' She frowned. 'But I'm still not clear what this has got to do with New York.'

'Well, Tiff's company have offered her a transfer. I've asked for one too, and if I want it, they've agreed.'

It took a moment for the meaning to sink in, but then – 'Oh my God. You mean you'll move to New York too?'

Dom shrugged. 'Yeah.'

'But this is a huge upheaval.'

'I know. But I've got bugger all to stay here for, and Tiff's excited about it. And it means you're happy, and I get to see Jack still. If you'll let me.'

'Of course I'll bloody let you, you fool,' Bea said, throwing her arms around him. She could hardly believe this was happening. It felt like fate aligning.

After that day, things had moved surprisingly quickly. Bea and AJ looked into houses to rent or buy in New York, AJ arranged to move back to the New York office, and Bea's boss Fiona was thrilled for her, promising her plenty of freelance work. It felt like it was all coming together; like it was meant to be.

Alice had been outraged at first. But she'd come round, especially when Bea and AJ decided to get married before leaving the UK in a small registry office ceremony at Islington Town Hall and asked Alice to be Maid of Honour.

'I suppose I'll forgive you for taking Mum away from me,' Alice said, wiping away a tear as she sank her seventh glass of wine at their reception afterwards. 'As long as you let me come and stay whenever I want.'

'Of course, you have to,' AJ said. 'We want everyone to come.'

So, at the beginning of September, AJ, Bea and Jack had flown to New York to start their brand-new life all over again; this time, together.

Then Bea had found out she was pregnant, and it truly felt like a fresh start.

Now here they were, three days before Christmas in their brand-new house half an hour outside Manhattan in a pretty little town called Hastings-on-Hudson, living the American dream, with her mum living in the granny annexe, and Dom and Tiff living in the next town over.

Bea heard someone call her name and looked round to find Wanda, her next-door neighbour and, she hoped, new friend, waving something in front of her face.

'I've made you a pumpkin pie,' she said, handing the baking tray to Bea. 'I know you've lived in New York before but I bet you've never tasted anything as good at this.' She smiled, shyly. 'It was my grandma's recipe.'

Bea held it to her nose and inhaled deeply. It smelt divine. 'That's so kind, thank you so much,' she said.

'It was nothing.' She turned towards Bea's house. 'Your lights look great.'

Bea followed Wanda's gaze and smiled. 'We're getting there, although it'll be years until they're even a patch on yours.' They both turned to take in Wanda's garden and porch which were taste-fully decorated in enough lights to light up the entire street.

'It's Walter's pride and joy,' she said. 'He started when the kids were little, and even though they're all grown up now, he still loves to do it. He adds to it every year.' She glanced towards Bea's belly. 'By the time you're as ancient as us, yours will be this good too.'

Bea smiled. She loved it here but she still felt like a Londoner at heart, was still adjusting to her life as a New Yorker. She wondered whether she would still be here in twenty years' time, like Wanda and Walter, when their kids had grown up and moved away.

'I'd better get the pie inside,' Bea said. 'Thanks again, it looks amazing.'

'You're so welcome,' Wanda said. 'See you later.'

Bea tramped across the frosty lawn towards the house. She couldn't quite believe she lived here. It looked like something out of a movie: white clapboard with black shutters, a wrap-around porch, a driveway big enough for three or four cars and a garden full of mature trees. She felt her heart swell with gratitude.

She jogged up the steps and went in through the back door into her kitchen. It was a bit dated, the old wooden cupboards in need of a refresh, but she still couldn't quite get over the size of the place. Coming from a small, terraced house in north London, places this size at home were only for the mega-rich. But thanks to the proceeds from AJ's flat and her mum's house – her old family home, which she still couldn't quite believe she was never going to see again – this was what they'd been able to afford, just about.

She placed the pie on the worktop and stood for a minute with her hands on her belly. She could hear the shrieks of the neighbourhood children from the street, and she peered through the window into the back garden – or yard, as she needed to get used to calling it – where the lawn stretched out beyond the light. Her mum's annexe was attached to the house but extended out into the back garden, and she had her own private entrance, which meant they all had their privacy but they could still see each other whenever they wanted. So far, it was working well. Ange had taken to New York immediately, which had surprised Bea.

'I always thought you were a London girl through and through,' Bea said when they'd been there a month and Ange had already enrolled in numerous classes and made several new friends.

'Oh I am,' Ange said. 'But back home I didn't really have many friends. It was always just me and your dad. I loved it but... well, you have to move on, don't you? I'll always love your dad and I'll always miss him, but he'd want me to be happy. And I am. Thanks to you.'

'Here you are!' A familiar voice made Bea turn and she smiled.

'Hey Mee,' she said, folding her friend into her arms.

'What are you doing in here all alone?' Mia said as she pulled away.

'Just putting this down and trying to defrost my fingers.'

Mia glanced at the pumpkin pie and gave a low whistle. 'Woah, you really are settling in, aren't you? Pumpkin pies, Christmas light displays to rival Harrods. You're already a true New Yorker.'

'I'm not sure my neighbours would agree with you, but I'm doing my best,' Bea said, smiling. Her fingers were beginning to come back to life and she rubbed them together. 'Where's Frank?'

A smile spread across Mia's face that lit her up from within. 'He's just gone to the loo,' she said.

'God look at you, all loved up,' Bea said.

'I'm not loved up,' Mia said.

'If you say so.'

Mia laughed. 'Okay I am. But don't tell him, right? I'm trying to play hard to get.'

'Are you now?' said a low, booming voice from behind her and Mia spun round as arms snaked round her waist. Bea waited while Frank kissed her friend then let her go, leaving his arms wrapped tightly round her waist.

'Okay, maybe not so hard to get. But how can I resist you eh?' Mia said, giggling.

'Come on you two, get a room,' Bea said, grinning.

'Sorry Bea.' Mia didn't look sorry at all.

Bea was so thrilled for Mia that she'd met the man she'd been waiting for all these years. Frank Miller was a colleague and friend of AJ's. He and Mia had met on a night out two months ago and it had been love at first sight. Although Mia was only visiting for now, there had already been talk of her moving over to be with Frank permanently.

'So, what are you two lovebirds doing for Christmas Day?'

Mia looked up at Frank and smiled. 'I'm meeting Frank's parents,' Mia said, her voice full of excitement.

'No way! That was quick!'

'I know. But we just...'

'I wanted my folks to meet the woman I've fallen in love with,' Frank said, kissing the top of Mia's head. He shrugged. 'I mean come on, it's taken me long enough to find her.'

'Ah, Mia's worth waiting for though,' Bea said.

'She sure is.'

'Well, I'm really happy for you both. Truly.'

'Thanks Bea. Anyway, it's AJ we have to thank really.'

'AJ?'

'Yep. If he hadn't been so determined to move back to New York, Frank and I would never have met.'

'I'll make sure I tell him.' She frowned. 'Speaking of AJ, does anyone know where he is?'

'I saw him just now out the front with Jack and your friend, the leggy one with the black hair,' Frank said.

'Maggie's here and no one told me?'

'Sorry, she arrived about twenty minutes ago, I thought you knew.'

'No! 'Scuse me a second you two.' Bea ran to the front door. It had been almost three years since she'd last seen Maggie in person, and apart from the fact she'd got rid of her long black hair and had it cropped into a pixie cut that made her cheekbones look amazing, she had hardly changed. Now here she was, holding Jack and looking for all the world like a catwalk model.

'Maggie!' Bea yelled, stepping carefully down the steps onto the lawn. Maggie looked round and her face lit up.

'My Bea!' she said, running towards her, Jack jiggling up and down in her arms. When she reached Bea, she threw her spare arm round her and squeezed her as hard as she could without squashing Jack.

'I get down now?' Jack said.

'All right, but I need a proper hug later, deal?'

'Deal,' Jack said, giving Maggie a high five before she lowered him gently to the ground.

They both watched as he ran over to AJ and Ange, then turned back to each other.

'I can't believe you came,' Bea said, squeezing Maggie's arms.

'I can't believe it's taken me so long,' Maggie said. 'I'm sorry it did.'

'Don't be silly. I'm thrilled you're here now. Shall I show you around? It's a proper grown-up house.'

Maggie looked down at her feet and Bea stopped.

'What's wrong?'

'Can I just... introduce you to someone?'

'What? Of course! Have you brought someone?' Bea looked round but could only see familiar faces.

'Yeah, I hope you don't mind. We – we're kind of together...' She trailed off and Bea wondered why she was looking so coy. It wasn't like her feisty friend at all.

Moments later a glamorous blonde woman came up the path, bags of presents in each arm and stood next to Maggie and it slowly – too slowly – dawned on Bea what was going on.

'Bea, this is Laura. My girlfriend.'

Bea waited while Laura put her bags on the floor and held out her hand, then she shook it warmly. 'It's so lovely to meet you,' Bea said.

'You too. I hope you don't mind me gate-crashing the party, it's just that Maggie has told me all about you and I so wanted to meet you.'

'Oh, of course! The more the merrier,' Bea said. She turned to Maggie. 'So how long have you two...' She waggled her finger between them both.

'About six months.'

'Six months, and you haven't told me?'

'I know. I'm sorry. We kind of wanted to keep it low key for a while. I knew you had a lot going on, and when I found out you were moving back, well, I guess I thought I might as well wait and tell you in person.'

'Well, I'm so happy you've found each other,' Bea said. She turned to Laura. 'Be warned though, if you haven't found out already, she's a total pig to live with.'

'Oh, I've already discovered that,' Laura laughed, over Maggie's objections. 'But I'm a clean freak so it's all good.'

'A match made in heaven then,' Bea said.

She glanced across the lawn to where her perfect match stood, with their son in his arms, both of their faces glowing in the lights from the street, and felt a warmth bloom through her. It might have been a long time coming, and she might have made plenty of mistakes along the way. But all the choices she'd made, all the things she'd done, had led her here, to this time, this place, with these people she loved. And she realised that, even though it didn't always feel like it, she'd made the right choices.

Because she wouldn't want to be anywhere else, but here, in her perfect fairy-tale New York, with the man of her dreams.

18

STAY

December 2010

Bea stood at the huge picture window and drank in the scene before her. Not for the first time she had to pinch herself that she was actually here. The art deco tower of the Chrysler building, the unexpected stretch of green and frosty white that was Central Park, the towering skyscrapers that glittered and winked in the flickering winter sun. She could make out slices of sky between the rooftops and if she pressed her forehead against the glass, the street below was visible, tiny people scurrying and miniature cars beetling.

Behind her she heard a voice and as she turned, an arm slipped round her waist.

'Hello you,' the voice said. His face was lit up by the lights of the Christmas tree and she kissed him firmly on the lips.

'What was that for?' he said. 'Not that I'm complaining.'

Bea shrugged. 'I just love you.'

He studied her for a moment, a frown creasing his forehead, then shook his head. 'I love you too, even if you are a nutter sometimes, Princess Beatrice.'

Bea stuck her tongue out and turned back to admire New York once more. It truly looked like a postcard from up here.

'It's so beautiful, isn't it?'

'It's not too bad from where I'm standing,' AJ said, laughter in his voice, and when Bea looked at him he wasn't looking out of the window, he was staring at her, and she felt herself flush.

'Mummy!' Bea turned to find Amelie toddling towards her. She held her arms out and scooped her daughter up in her arms and twirled her round.

'Hey sweetheart,' she said, smothering her face in kisses. She couldn't believe how much she loved the bones of this girl.

Amelie pressed her sticky fingers into Bea's hair, no doubt rubbing chocolate all through it, but Bea found she didn't care. She pointed at the sky. 'Santa will be flying over there in three days' time,' she said. Amelie looked up to where she was pointing but clearly had no idea what Bea was talking about.

'Let me take her, you shouldn't be carrying her around,' AJ said, reaching out for Amelie and lifting her from Bea's arms. Bea felt a warm glow to see Amelie snuggling into AJ, her fingers in her mouth as she rested her head against his chest.

Bea wrapped her arms round AJ's waist and leaned on his shoulder. 'Did you ever think we'd get here?' she said. AJ didn't answer straight away and she tipped her head back to look at him. He was gazing out of the window at a spot in the distance, the lights reflected back in his dark pupils.

'I never doubted it,' he said, smiling.

Bea grinned and huddled back into the warmth of her husband's arms. It had been a long and winding road but finally, Bea had the life she'd always dreamed of.

Last Christmas had been hard. Saying goodbye to her dad had been one of the most difficult, heart-breaking things she'd ever done; afterwards, the gap left by Pete had been impossible to ignore, and all of them – Ange, Alice, Rob, Charlie, Dom – had felt a sadness settle deep inside them. As the turkey was carved by Rob instead of Pete; as Pete's favourite Christmas song 'White Christmas', came on the playlist; as the armchair in the corner where he always used to sit remained empty all evening, the shadows of his presence had been everywhere.

But then the new year had come, and the fog of grief slowly started to lift. And even though Bea still felt a deep, visceral sadness about the fact she would likely never speak to AJ again unless they were arranging their divorce, she knew it was time to look to the future; a future that involved her, Dom and Amelie.

Then, a couple of months into the new year, Dom had dropped a bombshell that no one had seen coming, least of all her.

'I've been seeing someone.' They were watching TV; Amelie was asleep upstairs. Bea stilled for a moment, unsure whether she'd heard him correctly. Surely Dom hadn't just told her he'd cheated on her?

One look at his face in the dim light from the TV told her she had heard perfectly well. She shifted her feet from where they'd been tucked under Dom's thighs.

'Who?'

She watched and waited, her breath tight in her throat. Dom slowly turned to face her, one side of his face blue from the TV screen, the other in semi-darkness. His hands were clasped in his lap and he looked down at them before he spoke.

'It's...' He stopped, cleared his throat, then looked her in the eye. 'Tiffany.'

It took Bea a moment to work out who he was talking about. She didn't think she knew anyone called Tiffany. Then realisation dawned.

'From Dad's funeral.' It wasn't a question. She'd known on the day there had been a strange chemistry between Dom and the woman who had worked with her dad, but grief had smothered her instincts.

'I'm really sorry Bea, I didn't mean for this to happen.'

'Right.'

Shock had almost rendered her mute. This had come seemingly from nowhere but when she thought about it now it was obvious really, wasn't it? She'd never fully committed to Dom and he knew it. Perhaps now he'd met someone who would give him what he really needed.

'So, is it serious?'

Dom's silence told her everything she needed to know. She nodded, and stood. Dom looked up at her in surprise. 'Where are you going?'

'To bed.'

'But we need to talk about this.'

'Do we? Or do you?'

'Bea, I...' Dom's words died as she walked out of the room. She didn't want to talk about this woman with Dom. Not now, not later, not ever. And even though she knew she'd have to, eventually, for now all she wanted to do was give her daughter a kiss and go to sleep.

She didn't hear Dom come to bed that night and when she got up to check on Amelie in the early hours she found him asleep on the sofa, wrapped in a couple of blankets he must have found in the airing cupboard. She studied him for a moment, trying to untangle her feelings. She'd told herself she loved this man, that he was the man she wanted to spend the rest of her life with, and she thought she'd believed it. But if she had, surely she would be feeling wretched right now – when all she actually felt was calm. Surprised, but calm.

She dug out her phone and in the dark of her bedroom, she did what she always promised herself she wouldn't do: she started looking at old photos of her and AJ together. Her heart ached as she scrolled, memories of the life she'd left behind – *thrown away?* – and tears fell down her cheeks uncontrollably.

It was still only three-thirty in the morning, which meant it was only ten-thirty in New York. She called a number and listened to the buzz on the other end.

'Bea?' The voice when it answered sounded confused, concerned.

'Hey Mee,' she said. 'Can you talk?'

'Sure, hang on.' The sound of shuffling, then the background noise subsided. 'Sorry, I was watching TV with Frank. What's happened?'

Bea told her everything.

'Fucking hell Bea,' Mia said. 'This is the last thing I ever expected.'

'I know.'

'What are you going to do?'

'I have no idea.'

'Come over here.'

'What? I can't just up and leave.'

'I don't mean forever. Just for a break. Bring Amelie. Stay with me and Frank for a few weeks, get away from everything.'

'But...' Bea started, but then stopped. She'd been about to say she couldn't do that. That her mum needed her, that Dom needed her, that Amelie was settled here. But the truth was, apart from her mum, there was no real reason to stay in London any more. She hadn't gone back to work since Amelie was born, and she'd only been doing a part-time admin job anyway. Her best friend was in New York, and Dom had just told her he'd cheated on her. And although she hadn't realised it before, now she knew that there was nothing in the world she wanted more than to spend some time with Mia. 'What if I see AJ?'

'This is a city of eight million people. The chances of you randomly bumping into him are miniscule. Anyway, we can warn him you're here and if he chooses to stay away then that's his decision.'

Bea felt a warmth spread through her body, the stirrings of excitement. Could she really be about to agree to this?

'Okay,' she said, and the instant she said it she knew it was the right thing to do.

The next morning when she told Dom, he wasn't so impressed.

'You can't take my daughter away just to punish me,' he said, his voice in shreds.

'I'm not doing it to punish you,' she said. 'I'm doing it for me. Because I need to get away for a while. I need Mia.'

'And you're going back to AJ.'

Anger flared in Bea's chest. 'I'm not going back to AJ as it happens because, as you know, he refuses to speak to me since I chose you over him. But even if I were, I don't think it's anything to do with you any more, is it?'

Dom stepped towards her, imploring. 'But you can't take Amelie. She's my world.'

There were so many things Bea wanted to say – you should have thought about that before you slept with someone else being the main one – but she wasn't an ogre and she could hear the anguish in Dom's voice.

'I'm not taking her away forever. We're just going for a while.'

'How long?'

'A few weeks at most.'

Dom's head dropped. 'But what if you decide to stay? I can't lose her.' His voice broke and she wanted to give him a hug, but she couldn't shake the image of him with Tiffany from her mind, so she waited until he'd composed himself. Finally, he looked up, his eyes heavy.

'I know I can't stop you. But I just want to say I honestly didn't mean to hurt you. Me and Tiff it just – it just happened.' He looked at his feet and back up again. 'She loves me, Bea. More than you ever have.'

Bea didn't know what to say to that. How could she argue when she knew it was probably true? In fact, she hoped, for Dom's sake, that it was.

'I don't need details, Dom. And I don't need explanations. But I promise you I won't keep your daughter away from you. I wouldn't do that to either of you.'

Two weeks later, Bea and Amelie flew to New York. It was a tricky flight with a one-year-old, but the minute they came out of the arrivals gate, Mia came flying towards her, coat flapping, and wrapped her in a hug, and Bea knew it had been worth every second.

'It's so good to see you,' Mia said, wheeling Bea's suitcase towards Frank who was standing looking sheepish a few metres away. 'God I've missed you.'

'Missed you too,' Bea said, the words woefully inadequate to convey just how much.

Bea's first two weeks in New York had been wonderful: visiting places she hadn't seen for ages, spending time with Mia and Frank, and reconnecting with old friends including her old flatmate Maggie. She took Amelie to the park, and on the Staten Island ferry to see the Statue of Liberty even though she knew she was far too young to remember any of it. Then a couple of weeks into her visit, when Bea was trying to work out how much longer to stay, Mia arranged for Frank to babysit Amelie while they went for lunch.

'I want to treat you before you go home,' Mia said.

Bea arrived at Raoul's on Prince Street as arranged by Mia. But when she got there, Mia was nowhere to be seen.

'Can you tell me which table Mia Hancock has booked please?' she asked the maître d'.

He looked it up and pointed. 'The other person has already arrived,' he said, gathering a menu. 'Follow me.'

Bea followed him, threading through the tables of diners, until he came to a stop. Then her legs turned to jelly. She saw the exact moment her 'date' noticed her too, because he turned pale.

'Bea?'

Bea couldn't speak.

The maître d' made a subtle retreat, and Bea sat. She felt breathless.

'I think we might have been set up,' AJ said, a wisp of a smile on his face.

'Mia.'

AJ nodded.

'I can go if you like,' she said, even though now she was here that was the last thing she wanted to do.

'Of course not,' he said. She took a moment to properly look at him. He was still so handsome it took her breath away. His dark hair was longer now, his piercing eyes bluer than ever, even in the dim light of the restaurant. The tattoo on his left arm peeked out from beneath his rolled-up shirt sleeve, and her heart hammered with unexpected desire.

'It's really good to see you Bea,' AJ said, and hearing her name on his tongue made her stomach flip over.

'It's good to see you too. I – I honestly didn't know about this,' Bea said. She felt hot in her coat and slipped it off. She couldn't believe how nervous she felt around her own husband.

'I know you didn't. Me neither, although I've had my suspicions Mia and Frank were going to do something like this. They've been trying to get me to meet you for feckin' ages.'

Bea nodded, mute.

AJ leaned forward suddenly, elbows resting on the table. 'I've missed you.'

Bea's heart stopped. 'Have you?' Her voice was a whisper and she cleared her throat. 'I thought you hated me.'

AJ shook his head. 'I've never hated you.'

'But you changed your number, your email address. I...' She stopped, her voice a sob.

'I know. And I'm sorry. I was so angry with you. Then when I stopped being angry I was just sad, and angry with myself for being so stupid and reactionary.' He looked at his hands on the table. 'I shouldn't have shut you out. I should have let you explain, talked to you, then maybe none of this would have happened.'

'It's always been you, you know.' Bea hadn't known those words were going to come out, but once they were she wasn't sorry.

'I do know. I just – I didn't handle it very well, after the accident. I drove you away.'

Bea shook her head. 'I was an idiot, thinking Dom was the answer.'

'We were both idiots.'

AJ's hands slid across the table towards hers and when their fingers touched a jolt of electricity shot through her. A tear slid down her cheek, plopped onto the tablecloth.

'I love you, Princess Beatrice. Always have, always will,' he said. She looked up at him.

'I love you,' she said.

The rest of the restaurant may as well not have existed as they talked and talked about their past, their present and – perhaps? – their future. Later, they strolled hand in hand up Sullivan Street to Washington Square Park, then stopped for a drink, where AJ had a question for her.

'Would you consider staying here?'

'In this bar?'

'Ha ha.' He swallowed. 'In New York. With me.'

Every part of Bea wanted to say yes. Yes, of course I'll stay here, with you, I'll do anything. But she reluctantly shook her head. 'I can't,' she said softly. 'Amelie needs to be with her dad.'

AJ nodded. 'So what you're saying is, if I want us to be together, I have to come and live in London?'

'I think so,' she said. 'I'm sorry.'

He nodded. 'Me too.'

Over the next few days, Bea and AJ met again. When Bea introduced AJ to Amelie she'd been worried how he might react to this evidence of her other life, the life she'd been prepared to build with Dom, away from him. But his eyes lit up the second Amelie smiled at him, and Bea's heart melted.

By the time Bea left to go home, she was no closer to working out what her future might bring. She knew AJ didn't want to move to London and, although she also knew he'd probably do it for her, she didn't want to drag him there against his will. Experience had taught her these things never worked out in the long-run.

She needed to work out a way to make things work.

Back home, New York felt like a million miles away, slipping further from her reach with every day that passed. Dom moved out of their flat and in with Tiffany and Bea found she was more relieved than upset. AJ rang every day and it felt like it used to when they'd first met, heart flutters and butterflies and the excitement of what might still be to come.

Yet neither of them could work out a solution that was right for everyone. It seemed impossible.

Then, one Friday night at the beginning of the summer, Dom came to pick Amelie up for the weekend. But instead of disappearing the moment he'd put the buggy and bag of clothes in the car, he hung around on the doorstep, Amelie in her car seat that hung limply from his arm.

'Everything all right?' Bea said.

Dom shuffled from foot to foot. 'I...' he started.

'Dom? What's happened?' Bea felt herself begin to panic, although she wasn't sure what she was panicking about.

'Can I come in?'

Bea paused. Dom rarely came in the house. Although she felt no anger towards him any more, she preferred to keep their interactions business-like – handing over their daughter, exchanging pleasantries. It was easier. But he clearly had something on his mind so she stepped aside. 'Sure.'

He spoke before she'd even offered him a drink, as though he was so desperate to get the words out they almost fell out of him.

'We can all move to New York.'

Bea stared at him.

'What...?' she started, then stopped.

Dom sat down, placing Amelie carefully at his feet in her car seat. He was almost vibrating with tension and Bea was struck by how far he'd come since the days when even the slightest setback would send him spiralling into depression. He leaned forward, his elbows on his knees, fingertips pressed together. His eyes shone.

'Tiffany and I have been talking and we think we should all move to New York.'

Bea stared at him, as confused as though he were speaking a language she'd never heard before. Unperturbed, Dom ploughed on.

'I know you want to go back and be with AJ, and I know he doesn't want to live here. So Tiff and I have been talking and we think we've come up with a solution.'

Bea still didn't speak.

'Tiff runs her own business these days and can work from anywhere, and I've spoken to my boss and asked about transferring to the New York office and it's all arranged. If you want it to be.' He stopped, suddenly, as though he'd run out of breath, and looked at her, waiting for her to speak.

'Are you serious?' Bea's mouth felt dry, her hands shook.

'Absolutely serious,' Dom said. 'Look, I know it sounds crazy but I've given it a lot of thought. We're both happier with other people, and let's face it, what's keeping us here? You always said New York was amazing, Tiff loves it there, so it's the perfect solution for everyone.' Dom's eyes shone like a little boy on Christmas morning.

'I... I don't know what to say,' Bea said. 'It seems like you've made up your mind.'

'I have, if you'll let us.'

'Let you?'

Dom's face reddened, and he looked down at his hands. 'I don't want you to think I'm trying to take over your life, Bea. I know you don't want to be with me any more, and I understand if you'd prefer me not to be around too much. But' – he looked up at her – 'I can't be parted from Amelie and I'm scared that's what will happen, eventually.' He shrugged. 'So this seemed like a solution I could live with.'

'But you can't just up sticks and leave for me.'

'But that's just it, I'm not. Tiff's excited, and now I've got my head round it, I am too. This could be the best thing I've ever done. I mean, you adore the city, so there's got to be something pretty special about it, right? And if we're all there, then all the other problems go away.' He took a breath. 'At least think about it, all right?'

'I will,' she said, too stunned to say anything else.

Dom stood and picked up Amelie, who had fallen asleep while they were talking. 'I'd better get this one home, but promise you'll give it some proper thought? I need to let my boss know for sure.'

Bea nodded dumbly and followed him to the door. As he

stepped outside, she touched his arm. 'Thank you, Dom. You don't know what this means to me.'

He smiled and she saw the man she used to love. 'It's for all of us,' he said. Then he was gone.

Two months later, Bea and Amelie flew to New York, and a month after that Dom and Tiffany came too. They were now living in an apartment a few blocks away in Greenwich Village. Their flat was smaller – most flats were – but Dom's pay rise had meant they could afford something half-decent so now Amelie spent her time between Dom and Tiff's apartment and AJ and Bea's. Bea had been unsure about living in the apartment that had belonged to AJ's former wife, but in the end they'd both agreed they would never be able to afford something better, and that being together was all that mattered.

Now here they were, about to spend Christmas together. It was about as unlikely a scenario as she would have been able to picture a year ago, and even thinking about it made her laugh with the absurdity of it all. But it seemed to work.

Even AJ and Dom got on just fine, and Bea found she liked Tiffany more than she'd expected.

Reluctantly, she pulled away from AJ's embrace, and turned towards the kitchen.

'I need to get dinner ready.'

AJ shook his head. 'I'm cooking tonight, remember. What time are they arriving?'

Bea checked her watch. 'In about an hour.'

'Right, you go and relax and I'll get started. You should be resting.'

Bea smiled gratefully. 'Thank you.'

He leaned forward and pressed his hand against the slight swell in her belly. 'I've got to look after my girls.'

Bea laughed. 'You have no idea whether this baby is a girl!' she said.

'I can feel it in my bones,' AJ said, leaning in to give her a kiss. 'But I don't care either way, you know that.'

Bea padded to the sofa and stretched out gratefully. She was only three months pregnant but it seemed to have knocked her for six this time around and she was grateful for the rest before everyone descended. As well as Dom and Tiff, Mia and Frank were coming, and Maggie was bringing her new partner who Bea hadn't met yet.

Ange was coming too, and as Bea closed her eyes and listened to 'Walking in a Winter Wonderland' playing gently on the radio, to AJ clattering about in the kitchen, she allowed herself a smile. Her mum had been the biggest surprise in all of this. Leaving her behind had been Bea's biggest reason for resisting this move. Then one day, while Bea and AJ were still trying to work out what to do, Ange had asked to speak to her urgently, and, worried, Bea had arrived at her mum's house with Amelie in tow. As they sat on the sofa in the living room, the evening summer sun slanting through the window onto Amelie's sleepy little body, Bea's heart had thumped wildly, terrified about what her mum was about to tell her. She didn't think she could take any more bad news.

Ange brought in cups of tea and slices of cake on tiny plates, plumped cushions, and straightened ornaments.

'Mum, will you stop fussing around and tell me what's wrong?' Bea said.

Ange stopped what she was doing and stood, her hands clasped in front of her. Bea's heart stopped beating as she waited to hear the terrible news her mum had to impart.

'I want to move to New York.'

'*What?*' Bea stared at Ange as dust motes swirled in the strip of sunlight between them, and Ange opened and closed her mouth like a goldfish. Seconds ticked by. Then suddenly Ange sat down and leaned forward, her eyes bright.

'I've been thinking about it a lot,' Ange started. 'I know you're only staying here because of me—'

'No that's not—'

Ange held up her hand. 'Let me finish Bea, please.' Bea stopped, chastened. Ange took a deep breath. 'I know Dom has offered to move to New York. He told me,' she added, before Bea could ask how she knew. 'We're both worried you're only not agreeing to this because of me.' Ange looked down at her hands in her lap, then back up at her. 'So if it's all right with you, I'd like to move to New York too.'

For a few moments, Bea said nothing, and Ange's words hung in the air. Bea tried to picture Ange living in New York: shopping on Fifth Avenue, walking through Central Park, having breakfast at the Comfort Diner, but she couldn't do it.

'But London is your home,' she said. 'It's your heart.'

Ange shook her head. 'London is my home, but my heart was with your father.' She sniffed, and held her head up. 'But since he went, I've been feeling so lonely, Bea. So sad. And I don't...' She stopped again as her words caught in her throat. 'I don't want you to be sad too. I want you and AJ and Amelie to stay together, and if that means being in New York then that's where you should be.' She stuck her chin out defiantly. 'And why shouldn't I have an adventure? Life's too short not to do things while you can. If nothing else, your dad's death taught me that.'

Bea didn't know what to say. Her mum was right – part of the reason she'd been resisting moving was because she couldn't bear to leave her. But this was so unexpected, so out of the blue, she didn't know what to say.

'But what about Alice? What about the house?'

Ange shook her head. 'Alice will be fine. She's got Andrew, her job, the kids. She's busy enough. And this house – well, we can sell it. Or rent it out.' She threw her hands in the air. 'I don't know Bea. But I've given this quite a lot of thought, and if you'll have me, it's what I want to do.'

So she'd put her house up for rent – for now, at least, they agreed it was a good idea to hold onto it in case she changed her mind – and followed them to New York just a few weeks after they left. It felt like a miracle to Bea, to have everyone here with her.

Alice had been outraged at first. But she'd come round, especially when Bea and AJ had told her she could come and visit whenever she wanted.

'Escape from the kids for a while? You won't be able to get rid of me,' she said, grinning.

Now, Ange lived in small apartment nearby, with enough room for herself and Amelie when she visited. She had taken to New York immediately, which had surprised Bea.

'I always thought you were a London girl through and through,' Bea said when they'd been there for a month and Ange had already enrolled in numerous classes and made several new friends.

'Oh I am,' Ange said. 'But back home I didn't really have many friends. It was always just me and your dad. I loved it but... well, you have to move on, don't you? I'll always love your dad and I'll always miss him, but he'd want me to be happy. And I am. Thanks to you.'

The buzzer pulled Bea out of her thoughts, and she heaved herself off the sofa and pressed the intercom button.

'Hurry up Bea I'm freezing my tits off out here!' Bea grinned as she buzzed Mia and Frank into the building, and when the lift doors opened a few minutes later she was thrilled to find Maggie had arrived at the same time.

'We bumped into each other outside,' Mia said, hugging Bea briefly and moving aside to let her greet Frank and Maggie.

'It's so good to see you all,' Bea said.

'You too.' Maggie looked sheepish and Bea looked round, confused.

'Are you not bringing your new boyfriend?' she said.

'Um, not exactly.' Maggie looked even more awkward and Bea wondered if she was missing something. Then it all became clear.

'Bea, this is Laura. My new girlfriend.'

Realisation dawned as a glamorous blonde woman stepped forward and Bea clapped her hands together in delight. 'Wow, you're a dark horse,' she said to her friend, who was watching Laura with love in her eyes.

'I know. I'm sorry. I...'

'I can't believe you didn't tell me.'

'That Laura was a girl and not a boy?' Maggie looked suddenly shy. 'Yeah, sorry about that. I wanted – we kind of wanted to keep it low key, for a while. And I knew you had a lot going on. Then I guess I thought I might as well wait and introduce you in person.'

'Well, I'm so happy for you,' Bea said. She turned to Laura. 'Be warned though, if you haven't found out already, she's a total pig to live with.'

'Oh, I've already discovered that,' Laura laughed, over Maggie's objections. 'But I'm a clean freak so it's all good.'

'Well, a match made in heaven then,' Bea said. 'Right, come in,' and she ushered everyone inside to find AJ racing round the kitchen like a headless chicken.

'Something smells amazing,' Mia said.

'It's just a couple of curries,' AJ said, greeting each of them, and being introduced to Laura. 'Although I hope you're hungry because I've cooked enough to feed most of Manhattan.'

'Always,' Frank said, rubbing his belly, and everyone laughed.

Ange arrived a few minutes later, and Dom and Tiffany a while after that. Amelie ran wild between everyone, loving being the centre of attention and, as Bea watched the room full of people that she loved, she felt a warm glow spread through her. It might have been a long time coming, and a bumpy ride along the way, but all the choices she'd made had led her here, to this moment, with these people. And finally she realised, even though it didn't always feel that way at the time, perhaps she had made the right choices after all.

Because she wouldn't want to be anywhere else but here, in her perfect, fairy-tale New York, with the man of her dreams.

ACKNOWLEDGEMENTS

I feel as though I thank the same people every time I get to the end of another book – and as this is my ninth – NINTH! – book, I feel a bit like a stuck record. But that's because there are always people who support and help me with the writing of each book, and without whom I wouldn't be able to do this job that I love so much.

First and foremost is, of course, my husband Tom who, although not a reader himself, always listens to me talking through the beginnings of a new novel idea, and is happy to help me to brainstorm ideas when I get stuck (I don't always take any notice but it's STILL helpful!). He also supports me and holds me up whenever I start to doubt myself. Mum and Dad and my brother Mark and his lovely wife Sophie are also very supportive, so thank you all.

My editor Sarah is wonderful. She always trusts me to do my own thing, which is priceless, but always with a caution – 'don't go too dark' being one I've heard more than once! This book, though, she loved from the minute I presented her with my first draft, and she is very excited about it – so I really hope my readers feel the same excitement as you do Sarah!

As always I'm surrounded by some wonderful friends. I always mention Serena because she lifts me up and is my biggest champion, so I'm not going to make an exception this time. Every time I've sent her something to read she says: 'I think this is your best one yet', and I'm choosing to believe her. Also thank you to many other supportive friends including, but not limited to, Nuria, Zoe, Jilly and Nicki.

A special mention also has to go to Tami Brown Lucker for her help with the details of living in Manhattan during the early 2000s. Although I have been to New York a number of times and love the city, she helped me to understand where people lived and drank and ate and partied back then, and it was super helpful, so thank you! Anything that isn't quite right in terms of the New York geography is either my fault, or deliberate because, at the end of the day, this is fiction and it needs to work for my story!

I also have some lovely, lovely author friends to thank. Laura Pearson deserves a special mention for not only championing me, but she has also recently become a very useful ear to bend when I need some brain-storming/working through of ideas. Not only is she excellent, but she's very kind and generous with her time too. I repay her in homemade cinnamon buns so it's worth her while. Lisa Timoney is also a relatively new author friend who has given me more than one pep talk over recent months, and I've also been really grateful to have her in my life.

A huge thank you must also go to the wonderful book bloggers and avid readers who run some of the brilliant reader groups on social media. By far the most supportive ones for me have been The Friendly Book Community, Chick Lit and Prosecco and The Fiction Café Book Club – all lovely spaces for book chat and book love. Go and check them out if you're not already members.

And finally, thank you to each and every one of my readers. Without you, I really wouldn't be able to do this, and I'm so honoured you choose to spend your precious time reading the stories I've written. And to all those who have asked me to hurry up and write more, I promise I'm writing as fast as I can!

ABOUT THE AUTHOR

Clare Swatman is the author of seven women's fiction novels, which have been translated into over 20 languages. She has been a journalist for over twenty years, writing for Bella and Woman & Home amongst many other magazines. She lives in Hertfordshire.

Sign up to Clare Swatman's mailing list here for news, competitions and updates on future books.

Visit Clare's website: www.clareswatmanauthor.com

Follow Clare on social media:

 facebook.com/clareswatmanauthor

 x.com/clareswatman

 instagram.com/clareswatmanauthor

ALSO BY CLARE SWATMAN

Before We Grow Old

The Night We First Met

The Mother's Secret

Before You Go

A Love to Last a Lifetime

The World Outside My Window

The Lost Letters of Evelyn Wright

Last Christmas

LOVE NOTES

LOVE IN EVERY CHAPTER

WHERE ALL YOUR ROMANCE
DREAMS COME TRUE!

THE HOME OF BESTSELLING
ROMANCE AND WOMEN'S
FICTION

 WARNING:
MAY CONTAIN SPICE

SIGN UP TO OUR
NEWSLETTER

https://bit.ly/Lovenotesnews

Boldwood

Boldwood Books is an award-winning fiction publishing company seeking out the best stories from around the world.

Find out more at www.boldwoodbooks.com

Join our reader community for brilliant books, competitions and offers!

Follow us
@BoldwoodBooks
@TheBoldBookClub

Sign up to our weekly deals newsletter

https://bit.ly/BoldwoodBNewsletter

9 781785 130722

Milton Keynes UK
Ingram Content Group UK Ltd.
UKHW041822250924
448792UK00001B/7